The Bonehead Gate

Narelle King

BLACK COCKIE PRESS

The Bonehead Gate

Published by Black Cockie Press

Copyright © Narelle King 2024

The moral right of the author has been asserted

Cover design © Natalie Muller 2024

Distributed by IngramSpark

Printed by IngramSpark

ISBN: 978-0-6454896-5-1

About The Author

Narelle King is the author of the thrilling contemporary Australian fantasy novel the Bonehead Resistance.

Narelle has a background in environmental science, which has led to her stalking giant pandas through bamboo thickets in China, wandering around the Australian bush at night with an unreliable spotlight and living for six months in the middle of a zoo. On one occasion, she caused the evacuation of a university chemistry lab, which is why she now works with words rather than dangerous chemicals.

Whenever possible, Narelle escapes the real world by reading, writing or daydreaming about magic and monsters.

Narelle lives on Gundungurra land in the Blue Mountains, Australia, with her son and ninja cat. You can connect with her at instagram.com/narellekingauthor.

Dedication

For Marion and Max, who introduced me to the magical worlds inside books.

One

Bec squatted on an eroded dirt road near the top of Mount Stromlo. A mountain bike hurtled up a track towards her, its wheels kicking up clouds of dust. The rider pedalled as though the forces of hell were after him.

She stood. The rider skidded to a stop in front of her. He was short, with weathered skin, his head hidden by a helmet. His thick leg muscles suggested he was a regular mountain biker. He was squeezing the handlebars so tight that the veins on his hands had popped out. Above his hands, his arms were rigid.

'Are you -'

'Bec.'

'Viking Mountainbiker,' he gasped, using the handle he'd used on the private messaging app when they arranged to meet. He had a strong German accent. He looked back the way he'd come, a wild look in his eyes.

Bec followed his gaze. A mix of pine and eucalypt trees grew further down the slope. Between the trees, she could see Canberra spread out below them. To her left, the mountain bike track crossed the road and continued its winding way on the other side. A mob of kangaroos lay in the long, yellow grass next to it, their ears sticking up over the grass. She couldn't see any reason for Viking Mountainbiker's fear. 'What -'

The kangaroos rose and bounded away.

'Wombats incoming!' Luke yelled, appearing from behind a patch of casuarinas on the other side of the road and sprinting towards them. Viking Mountainbiker flinched.

'It's okay – he's with me,' Bec said.

Two of the strange, carnivorous marsupials that looked like

giant wombats loped up the mountain bike track. For animals with large bodies and short legs, they could run fast.

'Damn, I hate those things.' Bec felt a twinge in her left shoulder, where a giant wombat had bitten her a little under three months ago. 'Get behind us,' she ordered Viking Mountainbiker.

Viking Mountainbiker dumped his bike and scuttled behind them, gasping as though he was hyperventilating. Bec raised her rifle. 'I've got the one on the left.'

She fired, hearing a crack next to her as Luke shot at the wombat on the right. The bullets stopped an inch from the wombats and fell to the ground. The wombats didn't stop.

'Shit,' Bec said. 'They've got THONGs.'

'The hard way, then.' Luke swung the rifle over his shoulder and unsheathed a hunting knife with a double-edged blade and wooden handle. He planted his feet, an intense look in his pale blue eyes.

Bec drew a long, thin sword. It was similar in design to the ones carried by the Boneheads, but the hilt was wrapped in brown leather, not black – a sign that it had been made by the Resistance.

The first wombat leapt through the air towards Luke. Luke squeezed the knife in his right hand. A moment before the wombat landed on top of him, he ducked to the left and struck upwards, stabbing hard and fast into the wombat's heart. He levered the knife back and forth and yanked it out. Blood spurted. The wombat crashed into his left side. Its weight knocked him to the ground.

The second wombat snarled and raced towards Luke, its teeth bared to rip his throat open. Bec stepped in front of Luke, holding her sword at chest height, and slashed downwards onto the wombat's neck. The wombat made a screeching sound and turned towards her. She sliced the sword back across its throat.

It collapsed.

Gunfire rang out down the hill, and a stream of bullets hit the shield around Bec, created by the THONG she was carrying. The bullets fell to the ground. Viking Mountainbiker helped Luke push the wombat away. Luke scrambled to his feet, covered in blood.

'Go!'

Luke and Viking Mountainbiker ran up the dirt road, towards the layby where Luke's sister Ash was waiting with their battered, tan sedan. Bec felt for the collars on each wombat and yanked the THONGs free, then pounded after the men. Ash had started the car engine. Luke and Viking Mountainbiker fell into the back. Bec tumbled after them and slammed the door shut.

Bullets hit the side and back of the car. Ash rammed her foot on the accelerator and careened onto Mt Stromlo Road, in front of a dark blue four-wheel drive. The driver slammed her hand on the horn. The sedan flew down the mountain, leaving the four-wheel drive behind. Close to the bottom, Ash braked hard and stopped. Several cars waited in a line, most of them with bike racks attached to tow bars or roof racks. The four-wheel drive pulled up behind them.

Soldiers appeared on the road and swarmed around the vehicles in front, pointing rifles in the windows of each car.

'Fuck!' Luke swore.

Ash flung the car into reverse, swinging its rear end around and within an inch of the four-wheel drive. The driver pummelled the horn. Ash put the car into drive and swerved onto the wrong side of the road. She flew past the line of cars. Bec could hear the soldiers shouting. More bullets hit the vehicle.

'Look out!' Bec shrieked.

A large army truck appeared in front of them, blocking the road. Ash slammed on the brakes and tried to swing the car around to avoid hitting the truck. There wasn't enough room. The car clipped the shrubs on the edge of the road. Ash struggled to control it. It slid off the side of the road and stopped in a shallow ditch.

Bec's body was thrown forward and back in her seatbelt. There was a sharp pain in her chest. She gasped for air. Before she could catch her breath or pick up her sword, soldiers flung the car door open and wrenched her from the car. She landed on her knees in the dirt, and curled over her stomach. One of the soldiers dragged her to her feet and patted her down, removing two concealed knives, her phone, her THONG and the two THONGs she'd taken from the wombats.

Ash and Luke had been disarmed, too. They met Bec's gaze, their eyes wide. A soldier pushed Viking Mountainbiker towards them, his head still encased in his bike helmet. He stumbled and landed on his knees in front of Bec. He stayed there, sobbing. Civilians stared at them from their car windows.

The soldiers between her and the cars moved aside to allow two new soldiers to approach. Bec recognised the tanned face and dark curly hair of the younger soldier – Private Jerome. He muttered to the older soldier. The older soldier eyed Bec with interest. He had a thin face with deep wrinkles, a long thin nose and ears that stuck out.

'I was hoping we'd catch some Resistance fish,' he said, his voice crisp, 'But I never thought we'd net Rebecca Williams.' He stepped forward and pointed his rifle at Viking Mountainbiker's face. 'Vincent Werner. Give me what you stole.'

He had a solid grip on his rifle, his shoulders relaxed, his chin firm. He struck Bec as someone who would kill, but only if he thought it necessary.

Viking Mountainbiker continued to sob. He seemed to be verging on hysteria. It wouldn't benefit Bec if the soldier killed him – either way, she wasn't getting the information.

She nudged him with her foot. 'Give him the files.' He looked at her. His eyes were red and tears dribbled from his nose. She decided the name Vincent suited him better than Viking Mountainbiker.

He wiped his eyes on his sleeve, then dug in his pocket and pulled out a USB drive. The soldier lowered his rifle and held out his hand. Vincent dropped the USB drive into it, and he slid it into a pocket on his chest.

There was a crackle from his hand-held radio. The soldier frowned. 'What?' he snapped.

'It's some Boneys, Captain,' a voice replied.

The soldier's brows lowered. 'Tell them we've got it under control.'

'Too late.'

Bec sucked in a breath. A Bonehead strode along the bitumen towards them. The civilians in the row of vehicles ducked their heads below the windows. One couple got out and ran into the trees, abandoning their car. Bec couldn't blame them. The Bonehead was smaller than some of the Boneheads she'd run into before, but no less terrifying. The bony plate that covered its forehead, starting from its nose and ending in a half-circle over the back of its head, with six horns evenly spaced around the half-circle, was grey. It matched its grey, wrinkled skin. A small mercy was that it was wearing sunglasses, hiding its all-black eyes and lack of eyebrows.

The older soldier stared at the Bonehead. 'What are you doing here?'

'Making sure you don't mess this up,' the Bonehead snapped. It had the same clipped accent as other Boneheads Bec had heard speak. It pointed at Bec. 'Do you know who she is?'

'Rebecca Williams.'

'Correct. My bosses are very interested in speaking with her.' It turned its face to Jerome. 'And they are well aware that this one has let her slip through his fingers more than once.'

Jerome's face and neck turned red.

'I'm here to retrieve her.' It waved a hand at Vincent. 'And the traitor.'

The older soldier drew himself up. 'Lieutenant Colonel Nichols -'

'The Lieutenant Colonel answers to my bosses. Are you going to stand in my way, or are you going to take the prisoners to my vehicle?'

The soldier's eyes narrowed. 'I haven't had any orders -'

'I have,' the Bonehead said. 'You can escort them, if you like, but I am taking them. Now.'

The soldier considered for a long moment, then nodded and jerked his head at the other soldiers. 'We'll escort.'

The Bonehead strode back the way it came, past the line of cars. The soldiers prodded Bec, Ash, Luke and Vincent to follow. Several army vehicles surrounded a roadblock at the end of the road. The Bonehead walked past to a black four-wheel drive parked on the main road. Its engine was running. A second Bonehead was at the wheel, also wearing sunglasses.

The four-wheel drive was extra large, with eight seats. The soldiers pushed Ash and Luke into the back row, and Vincent and Bec into the middle row. The Bonehead sat in the front passenger seat. The older soldier sat behind it, next to Bec. He held his rifle firm in his weathered hands – pointed at Bec.

The Bonehead driver roared down the road, ignoring the speed limit and safe driving practices. It seemed to expect the other drivers to get out of the way. Two army trucks followed behind. The streets rushed past in a blur.

Bec didn't like the way the Bonehead in the passenger seat stared at her from behind its sunglasses. She squeezed her hands into fists, her nails cutting into her palms.

The driver slowed as a line of cars appeared on the road in front of them. Another roadblock. Bec squinted through the windscreen, surprised to see two Boneheads manning the roadblock. That kind of work was usually left to human soldiers. The driver twisted the steering wheel and swerved onto the wrong side of the road to pass the cars. The Boneheads manning the roadblock opened the gate and waved them through, but closed it on the two army vehicles following. The driver pushed the accelerator down hard and left the roadblock behind.

'Wait!' The soldier leant forward. 'We've lost our escort.'

The Bonehead in the passenger seat turned and, without a word, stabbed a knife straight into the side of the soldier's neck. It wrenched the knife sideways. Blood spurted across the car. Bec ducked and leant against Vincent, raising her arm to protect herself from the blood spray. When she lifted her head and lowered her arm, the soldier was dead.

Bec's breath came out in gasps. She felt dizzy. She'd watched people and Boneheads killed in front of her before – she'd even been instrumental in killing dozens of people when her first resistance group had blown up Governor Macquarie Tower – but she'd never seen such a quick, clinical killing.

Vincent was shaking. In the back seat, Ash drew in a sharp breath. Bec's eyes flicked to her. Her face and shirt were splattered with blood.

Bec closed her eyes and took several deep breaths to slow her breathing. When she could speak without her voice trembling, she opened her eyes again.

'What do you want with us?'

The Bonehead removed its sunglasses. Bec jerked back. Her shoulders hit the leather behind her. She gripped the edge of the seat to stop her hands from shaking. Instead of black eyes, this Bonehead had a dark red ring around the edge of the sclera on each eye. It was even more terrifying than the black pits she was expecting.

'You're in the Resistance.' It was a statement, not a question. 'My family sent me – to negotiate.'

Bec blinked. 'You want to negotiate with the Resistance?'

'Not the Resistance – Amber Yu.'

Bec's eyes widened. 'You want to negotiate with Amber?'

'She has the lechiko.'

'The – ley-chee-ko?'

The Bonehead nodded. 'The curse.'

Bec stared at the Bonehead. 'Do you mean the power? That lets her move fast? Why would you call it a curse?'

'What would you call it? It's an illusion – it makes you think that you are stronger, faster, that you feel no pain, and then delivers all the pain that you should have felt in one hit when you let it go.'

Bec rubbed her forehead. Sweat mixed with blood. She grasped at what she could understand. 'What do you want from her? What are you offering?'

The Bonehead shook its head. 'Not yet. We will discuss our offer later – when the Resistance is ready for it.'

'Why not now?'

'You don't know that you need it yet.'

Bec felt a sense of disquiet. What didn't they know they needed – and why was the Bonehead confident that they would find out?

'In the meantime,' the Bonehead said, 'I have a gift for you.'

'A gift?'

The Bonehead tossed her a mobile phone. Bec caught it in two hands. 'The location of your friend, Mr Zhou Hui. It's saved in the contacts.'

Bec stared at the phone. 'How do you know about Zhou?'

The Bonehead's lips curved. 'My family knows many things about you, Rebecca Williams. Don't worry – our interests align. Or they will, soon.'

'Are you some kind of Bonehead resistance?' Luke asked.

The driver snorted. The Bonehead glanced at the driver, and shook its head at Luke. 'We have no need for such things. We don't allow any individual as much power as you give your Prime Minister.'

'We don't give our Prime Minister that much power, either,' Bec muttered. 'He just took it.'

The Bonehead turned back to the front and spoke to the driver in a guttural language. Bec opened the contacts on the phone. There was only one – an address. She memorised it, then let the phone slide onto the floor and kicked it under the driver's seat.

She watched the Boneheads. They were looking at the road. Bec took another deep breath in, and reached across the seat to the soldier's chest. Her fingers touched wet, sticky blood. She gritted her teeth and slid the button of his pocket out of the buttonhole. She slipped her fingers into the pocket and gripped the USB drive. She pulled it out and whipped her hand back as the Bonehead turned.

The Bonehead stared at her with its strange red eyes. Bec felt sweat form on her face.

'We'll drop you off now, and get rid of this vehicle.'

Bec wrinkled her brow. 'Won't you get in trouble for letting us go?'

The Bonehead put its sunglasses back on. 'Humans think we all look the same. The only thing those soldiers will be able to report is that two Grey Bones took you away. If that creates anxiety among the Red Bones,' the Bonehead's lips turned up in a cold smile, 'It won't hurt my family's interests.'

The driver swung the car right. Bec glanced out the window, and her whole body went cold. She'd been so focused on extracting the USB drive, she hadn't noticed where the driver was taking them – a street of modern townhouses, with a single, small maple or eucalypt planted on the nature strip in front of every third house. Several blocks held blackened shells where the

Boneheads and soldiers had destroyed a townhouse or apartment building in retribution for some unknown crime. Most of the houses on the street had boards over one or more windows – not damaged by soldiers, but by a group of looters in their late teens and early twenties who had rampaged through the street a few weeks earlier.

The driver stopped the car in the middle of the road, in front of a white, two-storey townhouse with a grey fence, glass balcony and bright blue feature wall on the top storey. It was one of the few with no signs of damage.

'I believe this is your stop,' the Bonehead said.

Bec's heart was racing. 'How did you know?'

The Bonehead sniffed. 'Next time, don't be so fast to scare the looters away with rifles. There's always some spies among the brainless ones.' It turned to face the windscreen, and leant back in its seat. 'We'll be in touch.'

Bec gave the Bonehead a wide-eyed look, unsettled by its confidence that it would be able to contact her. She pressed her elbows into her side.

Ash and Luke swung open the back door and jumped out. Vincent fumbled with the door handle and joined them. Bec slid across to the door and paused. 'Apparently you know everything about me. Can I at least know your name?'

'You may call me Yorilla.'

Bec slid to the ground. As soon as she pushed the door closed, the Bonehead driver pressed its foot on the accelerator. The four-wheel drive roared around the corner.

Two

Dan flew out of the front door, an open laptop clutched in one hand. He was wearing a worn pair of cotton shorts and a T-shirt with a picture of Australia's first female prime minister on it. A chunk of grey hair had escaped its man bun and fell into his eyes.

'Please tell me that's not your own blood you're covered in.'

'It's not,' Bec said.

Dan rubbed his free hand over his face. 'Fucking hell. Nath said the place was crawling with soldiers. We thought you were dead.'

'Where's Nath now?'

'On his way back.'

A man with thinning hair and thongs came out of the townhouse opposite, carrying a full garbage bag. He froze on the step, his mouth dropping open.

Bec winced. 'Let's get inside – we look like chainsaw massacrists.'

Dan pushed open the front door, revealing an open-plan lounge, kitchen and dining room with white walls, grey stone features, wood floors and floating wooden stairs leading to the bedrooms. Bec bundled Vincent inside.

'You probably don't need the helmet.'

He removed his helmet and let it fall on the floorboards. His blonde hair was cropped close to his head. It was wet with sweat. His eyes were haunted. 'I shouldn't have agreed to meet you.'

Luke put a hand on his shoulder and directed him towards the stairs. 'Let's get cleaned up.'

Dan locked the door.

'We're going to have to get out,' Bec said. 'Those Boneheads know where we are.'

'Yeah – I got that.'

'Can you contact Ren or Sam – ask them if they've got anywhere safe for us to go?'

Dan nodded and headed to the dining table, which was covered in computer equipment: three laptops; two large screens; a tower server; and cords running everywhere. Dan perched the laptop in his hand on top of another laptop and pulled on a headset.

'I'll wash and start packing,' Ash said. She trotted up the stairs after Luke and Vincent.

Bec took a deep breath and leant against the couch. She closed her eyes. They felt itchy and sore. An image of Yorilla stabbing the soldier filled her mind. She blinked her eyes open and focused on the room. It was the nicest place she'd ever lived. She was going to miss it.

Dan pulled the headset down around his neck. 'Sam said he'll get back to us. He asked if we can upload Vincent's info before we leave.'

Bec dug in her pocket and held out the USB drive. He screwed up his nose at her bloody fingers and took it from her with one finger and thumb. She watched him plug it into the laptop and transfer the files.

Ash appeared at the top of the stairs, in fresh clothes, her hair wet. 'The bathroom's free.'

Bec pushed herself away from the couch and jogged up the stairs. Two bedrooms, a bathroom and separate toilet opened into a short hallway at the top. Vincent was sitting on the bed in the main bedroom, drying his wet hair. He was wearing a pair of Luke's jeans and an old T-shirt of Dan's with the words 'Make Lying Wrong Again' emblazoned across the chest. Two air mattresses and sleeping bags were laid out on either side of the unmade bed. Backpacks overflowing with clothes, computer equipment, THONGs and weapons lay on the floor. The en suite door was closed, and Bec could hear the shower running.

In the smaller bedroom that Bec was sharing with Ash, more clothes and weapons were strewn on the floor surrounding two single beds. Bec grabbed some crumpled clothes from the floor and ducked into the bathroom. She leant against the tiled shower wall. The warm water ran over her and carried the blood down the drain. Her head felt light. Her hands shook.

'I need some food.'

When she was dressed, Bec returned downstairs. The dining room table was clear; all the computer equipment was now in boxes on the floor. She rummaged in the fridge. There were three slices of leftover pizza from two days before. She devoured them cold, and finished off with three chocolate biscuits.

Ash padded down the stairs, a backpack bundled in her arms, trailing clothes. Vincent followed. He held a large cardboard box in front, and leant past it to see where to place his feet on the steps.

Bec shoved another biscuit into her mouth and ran up the stairs, dropping biscuit crumbs. She put one of the air mattresses on top of the other, leaving the sleeping bags on them, and scooped them into her arms.

She passed Ash and Vincent on their way back up the stairs. In the garage, Dan leant against the boot of his silver hybrid car, talking on his phone. It was the same car that he'd had in Newcastle, but they'd changed the number plates a few times since then. He hung up as Bec threw the bedding into the boot.

'Sam says he's called in a favour and found us somewhere to stay, but you'll have to do some negotiating. He said to tell you to be nice, unless you want to be homeless.'

Bec snorted. 'I'm nicer than he is.'

Nathan drove into the garage in their white ute. He parked next to Dan's car and leapt out.

He wrapped an arm around Bec's shoulders and squeezed. 'I thought you were a goner.'

'I kind of thought so, too,' Bec said. Except they'd been saved by a Bonehead. She pushed the thought to the back of her mind. She didn't have time to think through the implications of that.

It wasn't long before the house was cleared of their belongings. Bec tied up the rubbish bags and threw them into the tray of the ute. She didn't want to risk leaving anything behind for the Boneheads or soldiers to find. Yorilla had known everything about her. She pushed that thought to the back of her mind, too.

'Need anything else from us?' Luke asked.

Bec shook her head. 'We'll see you there.'

Ash, Nathan and Luke climbed into the cab of the ute and drove away with a wave. She nudged Vincent towards the passenger seat of Dan's car. Dan came down with the last laptop cradled in his arms.

'All done?' Bec asked.

Dan nodded. 'Let's get out of here.'

Dan drove for an hour through the Canberra suburbs – taking side streets, avoiding CCTV cameras, doubling back, entering shopping centre car parks from one entrance and exiting from another with a different set of number plates. Bec hoped it was enough to lose anyone trying to follow them. She leant her head against the headrest. The late morning sun poured through the window and made her head ache. The pizza and chocolate biscuits sat like a ball in her stomach. The smell of stale cigarette smoke in Dan's car didn't help, either.

She sat up as Dan pulled into the grounds of a primary school to the north of the city. Several low, red brick buildings with white eaves and metal roofs clustered around a car park full of sedans and four-wheel drives. White-trunked spotted gums and other eucalypts shaded the grounds. A plastic and metal playground, painted in bright, primary colours, stood next to a large oval. Rounded hills, covered in trees, rose up behind the school.

A woman with shoulder-length grey hair, large earrings and a floral peasant top approached the car. Dan lowered his window. 'Sam sent us,' he said.

The woman ran her eyes over Dan and Vincent. She stopped at Bec, her eyes widening in recognition. 'I'm Karen, one of the teachers here. You can park out here, or in the gym, if you need to hide the vehicle.'

'It might be safer,' Dan said.

'Sam said there's six of you?'

'The other three should be here soon.'

Karen directed them to the school gym, which was twice the height of the other buildings. She opened two large, double doors. It took Bec's eyes a moment to adjust to the dim light. Several vehicles were parked in a row on the vinyl floor. Dan parked next to the car closest to the doors.

They climbed out and joined Karen.

'Should we bring our gear?' Bec asked.

Karen looked at her sideways. 'Later. First you need to convince Monique to let you stay.'

'Sam said -' Dan started.

She drew her brows in. 'We're not part of the Resistance, and we don't take orders from Sam. Knowing him got you entry – that's all. Monique will make her own decision.' She gave Bec another sidelong glance.

Bec quirked her lip up to the side. It was clear that Karen didn't think Monique would let them stay.

Karen closed the doors and led them past the playground to a long building with several classrooms in a row. She opened a door with a window set into it. Bec's ears were assaulted by noise – people talking over the top of one another, and children yelling and crying. The classrooms were separated by concertina doors, which had been pushed open to create a single, very long room. All the windows were open, but the room felt stuffy and smelt of sweat.

The vinyl floor was covered in gym mats, air mattresses, blankets, sleeping bags, pillows and cushions. People of all ages sat or lay on the bedding, or on chairs dotted around the walls. Children ran around the room. Bec noticed a woman in pyjamas lying on a mattress near the windows, staring at the ceiling. Several children jumped over her in a game of Tip. She didn't seem to notice. A man sat on a child's chair near the door they'd come in. He was wearing an old, worn and dirty brown suit. A black face mask covered most of his face, and he wore a grey beanie low over his head, despite the warmth of the room. Dark eyes glittered beneath the beanie.

The school furniture had been piled out of the way at the far end of the room. A gang of children had turned the area into a cubby with blankets and pillows, and were climbing under and over it.

'Mon?' Karen called, pitching her voice to carry without shrieking.

A woman in her early thirties stood from where she'd been kneeling on the floor, talking to one of the families. She had tucked her dark brown hair behind one ear. It cascaded down her back, so sleek that Bec was sure it must be chemically straightened. Bec patted her own hair. It was even wilder than usual, because she hadn't brushed it after her shower.

'I'll go and wait for your friends.' Karen bobbed her head at them, her earrings bouncing, and left the room.

Monique strode over, her eyes on Bec. She was dressed in a black shirt with three-quarter length sleeves, a black leather pencil skirt and black heels with pointed toes. It struck Bec as an odd choice for the setting.

'Rebecca Williams,' she said, her voice clipped. 'Sam was not very candid about who he was sending us.'

Bec screwed up her nose. 'Candid isn't really his style.'

'This is an evacuation centre, not a Resistance group. We take in people whose houses have been burnt down after a mild run in with the soldiers. Not people like you. We can't afford any trouble. The soldiers will shut us down if we give them the slightest excuse.'

'I'm not here to cause trouble.'

Monique snorted. 'You are trouble.' She waved a hand at a large television hanging on the wall to their left, past the man in the beanie. A picture of Bec, her hair wild and a sullen expression on her face, filled the screen.

Bec frowned and moved closer to the television, flanked by Dan and Vincent. Monique followed, her heels tapping on the floor.

The picture of Bec disappeared and the reporter Mike Davies took its place. Mike's bleached hair was tousled just enough to make him look young and carefree. Bec knew that he had wrinkles, because she and Amber had seen him in person once, but they had been smoothed away by a combination of makeup and lighting. He had a serious look on his face.

'We return to our breaking news. Canberra is on high alert tonight, after wanted terrorist Rebecca Williams brutally murdered army captain and family man, Aaron Waters.' The screen switched to a picture of the soldier that Yorilla had killed, wearing casual clothes and patting a golden retriever, with three teenagers sitting around him. 'Waters was last seen alive just after nine thirty this morning, in Stromlo. His body was found at eleven am in a vehicle near the suburb of Crace, where it is understood that Williams was in hiding until recently.'

Dan raised his eyebrows at Bec. 'Been busy?'

'That wasn't me!' Bec's voice rose up into a squawk. 'The Bonehead killed him.'

Mike Davies continued. 'Kevin Moore, a neighbour of Williams, is believed to be the last person to see her.' The camera showed the grey-haired man who had been putting out his rubbish when the Boneheads dropped them off.

'I saw Williams and several accomplices at about ten this morning. They were covered in blood. I was shocked,' Kevin said. 'This is a quiet neighbourhood. We've never had problems before.'

Bec let out a bark of laughter. 'Apart from the soldiers burning down houses. And the looters.'

'Byron Hogan had a close run-in with Williams at the same location only a few weeks ago,' Mike Davies said, as the screen switched to a young man with his dark hair combed into a faux hawk.

'Hang on,' Dan said, 'Isn't that one of the looters?'

Bec frowned. 'Yeah, I think it is.'

'I knocked on the door of the house where Williams was hiding,' Byron said, 'And I was met by Williams and two of her associates with guns. I just fled.' He shook his head. 'I was lucky to escape with my life.'

The screen returned to Mike Davies. 'Sadly, Captain Waters was not so lucky. He leaves behind his wife and three children.'

Bec wrinkled her brow. 'I notice Mike Davies has given up using the word 'allegedly' when he accuses people of murder.'

Dan laughed. 'He's probably not too worried that you're going to sue.'

Monique muted the screen and gave Bec a suspicious look. 'That wasn't you?'

'No. A Bonehead killed him.'

'She's telling the truth,' Vincent said. 'I was there. It was a Bonehead.'

Monique squeezed her lips together. 'Well, if that wasn't you, they've really done a job on you.'

'I'll say.' Bec ran a hand through her hair, leaving it even more frizzy than it had been before.

Monique glanced at the man seated near the door. Following her gaze, Bec caught the man gesturing with his hand. She raised her eyebrows. So the man who looked like he was living on the streets was the decision-maker here, not the woman dressed like a high-powered lawyer.

Monique gave a slight nod in the man's direction. 'That doesn't change anything. We can't risk terrorists staying here.'

'Oh come on, who isn't a terrorist these days, according to the government? They said the ACT Chief Minister was a terrorist the other day. I doubt he's even seen a bomb.'

Monique arched a groomed eyebrow.

Karen returned with Luke, Nathan and Ash. Luke strode over to them. 'How's it going?'

Bec shrugged. 'Mike Davies is framing me for murder. Otherwise, all good. You guys?'

'No problems.' He looked around. 'We're staying here?'

Bec looked at Monique. Her eyes flicked towards the man near the door. She frowned and lowered her voice. 'We have some – friends – being held by the Boneheads. We know where they are, but we don't have the resources to get them out. Sam suggested you might help.'

Bec frowned. 'Where are they being held?'

Monique's eyes flicked toward the door again. The man stood, pushed back his beanie and removed his mask. Dan let out a squeak.

The man pulled a phone from his pocket, and showed Bec an address on a mapping app. Bec felt her body tense. She forced her muscles to relax before Monique or the man noticed. It was the same address as had been saved in the phone Yorilla gave her – where she'd said Zhou was being held.

'We could check it out,' Bec said. 'I can't promise anything else.'

The man nodded. 'That's all I'm asking.' He looked at Monique. 'Let them stay.'

Monique pressed her lips together. 'We need to disguise you. The soldiers inspect us, sometimes. You're too recognisable – especially with that hair.'

Bec shrugged. 'If you like.'

'Do we have to dress like him?' Luke said, looking at the man.

He quirked his lips. 'It's a great disguise. Nobody ever looks too closely at the homeless man. And, for the record, I have seen a bomb.' He pulled his mask back on and walked away.

'That's Gordon Cohen – the Chief Minister,' Dan said.

Bec rolled her eyes at him. 'Yeah, I got that, thanks.' She looked at Monique. 'Who are you, then?'

'I was his Chief of Staff. Now -' She looked at the people on the floor and the children chasing each other around the room, and shook her head. 'I don't know. I guess I'm just dealing with what's in front of me.'

'I can relate to that,' Bec said.

A woman appeared in the doorway holding a large, plastic box. 'Mon?' she called. 'Craig said you need a first aid kit?'

Monique frowned at them. 'Settle yourselves in,' she said. 'Any spare spot on the floor is fine. We'll talk about disguises later.' She took a step towards the woman with the box, then turned back. 'Any trouble, and you can find somewhere else to stay, understand?' She strode away without waiting for an answer, her heels tapping on the floor.

Three

Amber dreamt that she was trying to find Adam, but he was lost in a crowd. After a while, she realised that the crowd was all Boneheads, dripping with blood and walking like zombies, their eyes blank. She tried to escape, but her legs wouldn't work. The crowd parted, and she saw a pile of bodies. Somehow she knew the bodies were the members of the Resistance. Four zombies, covered in blood, stepped between her and the pile. They turned into the two Boneheads she'd killed at the university, one she'd killed in Brooklyn and the human soldier – Johnno - she'd killed in Newcastle.

She blinked open her eyes. Her heart pounded in her chest. She could hear Adam breathing in and out next to her. A tawny frogmouth called in the trees above the tent, its repetitive thrumming sounding more like something mechanical than a bird. Her heart slowed.

She stared at the roof of the tent. Her head ached with tiredness, but she didn't want to go back to sleep, to more nightmares.

It was so dark that she couldn't see anything, but she could hear a large insect flapping against the wall of the tent. Probably a moth, caught between the tent wall and the fly.

Oliver wriggled next to her, and let out a low whimper. She sat up and put her hand on his chest, hoping he'd go back to sleep. Instead, his whimpers turned into a loud wail. She picked him up and rocked him against her chest. His cries lessened but didn't stop.

Jaws, the young giant wombat that she'd adopted, stirred at her feet.

Adam rolled over. 'Do you want me to take him for a walk?' he whispered, his voice drowsy with sleep.

'Nah, I'll take him. I'm awake anyway.'

'You're sure?' Adam murmured, burrowing down into his sleeping bag.

'Yeah.'

Oliver wailed louder. Amber yanked at the tent zip and threw the flap open. She shoved her feet into her boots, clipped the front carrier together and settled Oliver in it. Jaws scrambled up and lumbered out of the tent after her.

She hurried away from the tent, before Oliver could wake too many of the people in the neighbouring tents. He stopped crying, and she felt her shoulders relax. The deep piles of damp leaves, bark and mud muffled the sounds of her steps, making her feel like a ghost in the night.

Jaws insisted on staying within touching distance, getting under her feet and almost making her trip several times. Her foot caught on a tree root, and she fell forwards on the damp leaves. She flung her hands out to stop her body from landing on Oliver. Her right wrist landed next to Jaws, who turned and sank his teeth into it. She cursed and pulled him off, wrapping her left hand around her wrist. She could feel blood seeping through her fingers.

She stood. Her body felt heavy. She dug in the carrier for some tissues, and wrapped them around the lacerations left by Jaws' teeth. Her mouth twisted. Most days it was difficult to remember why she'd adopted the strange animal.

She picked her way through the sleeping tents that were dotted around the southern, downstream side of the camp and climbed the steep hill on the western edge. She waved at the two Resistance fighters standing guard a couple of hundred metres away. They raised their hands in reply. They were used to seeing her and Adam taking it in turns to walk around the camp at night, trying to settle Oliver. She rubbed a hand over Oliver's black, tangled hair. 'You need to learn to sleep in bed.'

Jaws leant his large head against her legs. She caught her breath and shivered in the cool air. Millions of stars shone in a wide swathe across the sky. She drank them in. It had been raining on and off all week, and this was the first time the clouds had lifted enough to see the stars. The camp, which Bec insisted on calling Resistance Headquarters, but everyone else just called Base, was hidden in a tree-covered valley in Barrington Tops National Park. The dense Barrington rainforest covered more than seventy-five thousand hectares, much of it inaccessible to vehicles. Ren said the camp's inaccessibility was its best defence, but Amber thought its best defence was the endless rain and swarms of mosquitoes. No Boneheads would want to come here.

She looked at the dark camp below. She could just make out the outlines of the tallest trees. There was no sign of the dozens of tents that made up the camp. The Resistance fighters were obsessive about keeping the camp hidden. Each tent was positioned so that it was hidden by the tree canopy, and covered in multi-spectral camouflage netting. Lights were banned after dusk, although they were allowed to use dim, red-light torches if necessary. Most people went to bed early.

Oliver shifted in the carrier, and she sighed. Most people. Those whose dreams weren't full of slaughter and death, and who didn't have a child who'd gotten used to sleeping in a carrier and refused to sleep anywhere else. She could have breastfed Oliver back to sleep, but she was determined to wean him. She had loved breastfeeding, once. She had felt so connected to Oliver when he fed. But her pleasure had been tainted, by the soldiers ripping Oliver from her arms and taking him away – not once, but twice. Now all she could think about was expressing milk into a toilet, while picturing him crying for it.

Oliver shifted again. She adjusted the weight of the carrier on her shoulders, gave the soldiers another wave and plodded back down the hill.

Oliver was asleep by the time she reached the bottom. She picked her way past the dark, silent tents to her own, and winced. She'd forgotten to zip the flap, probably letting in hordes of mosquitoes. She kicked her boots off and eased Oliver out of the carrier and onto the sleeping mat, trying not to wake him. Jaws trundled around the tent, sniffing and making quiet hissing noises. She zipped the tent closed, lay down and put her arm out towards Adam.

'All good?' he murmured.

'Yeah.'

Her eyes closed. She prayed that she'd be spared further nightmares. She fell asleep while she was still praying.

She woke to a light patter of rain on the tent roof. The overnight lifting of the clouds had been short-lived.

'We now return to your regular scheduled programming,' she muttered. She rolled over and scrambled among her dirty clothes for a child's watch that Lucy had given her.

'Shit.'

She gave Jaws his bottle of marsupial milk, holding it in one hand and trying to dress with the other.

Adam sat up and took the bottle from her. 'Everything okay?'

'Just late, as usual.' She fumbled with the buttons on a long-sleeved shirt.

'I don't see why they make you train so early, anyway.'

Amber shrugged. 'I guess Kim is a morning person. What are you up to today?'

Adam put the empty bottle down. 'Same as usual. The tests on the new THONG went well, so now Sam wants us to produce a stack of them. I'll have to program them all.'

'That's great the tests were successful.' Amber pulled on thick pants and a heavy leather jacket. Oliver woke, screaming. She glanced at him, torn.

Adam waved her away. 'I've got him. I'll take him to Sarah.'

'Thanks.' Amber gave them both a quick kiss and scrambled out of the tent, pulling on her boots at the entrance.

She trotted to the south-western edge of the camp. Jaws kept pace with her. Several deep holes had been dug in the ground, and canvas strung around them, to create toilets. They were far enough from the camp that the smells didn't reach the sleeping area and far enough from the creek to avoid polluting it. Somebody had left a plastic jerrycan full of water on the ground nearby, with a handheld mirror propped behind it. Amber used the toilet, washed her hands and splashed some water on her face. She ran her hands through her cropped, black hair, pulling a face at the mirror. There was a time when she'd never left the house without full makeup; now she didn't know where her hairbrush was.

She ran past the sleeping tents and the office and storage tents that took up most of the centre section of the camp, towards a clear, flat area on the western side of the office tents. The other sword fighters were finishing a warm-up run up the hill, around the saddle at the top and back to the cleared area. They lined up in two rows facing each other. Kim waved at Amber to join them.

'You're with Reuben.' She saw Amber's lacerated wrist, and frowned. 'Do I need to worry about you?'

Amber pulled a face. 'Jaws bit me.' She slopped some cat food into a bowl for Jaws, hoping it would keep him occupied and out from under her feet while she was training.

Reuben frowned when she joined him. He was one of several sword fighters the Resistance had recruited through a martial arts school in Sydney. A thin, wiry man, with thinning brown hair and no obvious muscles, he was one of the best fighters in the group. She wondered if Kim had paired her with him as punishment for being late. Kim was well aware that Amber and Reuben weren't friends.

They started with drills, taking it in turns to attack and defend. Amber felt tension leaving her body as she settled into the repetitive movements. After almost three months of training, she thought she could do every move in her sleep. She kept her guard up, because Reuben liked to switch things up to prove he was better than her, but he was behaving himself.

Kim skirted around the group, correcting the fighters' stances and showing them how to increase the power behind the moves. She had a slight limp, courtesy of a Bonehead who had slashed her right leg in Dubbo, but it didn't slow her down.

The rain started in earnest, dripping down their faces. Reuben increased the power of his thrusts, trying to push Amber back. She caught the blows on the side of her sword and pivoted away, but he followed, increasing his speed and giving up all pretence of sticking to the drills. Amber was forced backwards, away from the group. Her feet slipped in the mud, putting her off balance.

The ringing of swords around her lessened and disappeared. The rest of the group were enjoying the spectacle.

Reuben swung his sword upwards, surprising her. She managed to block the blow at the last second. She kept her eyes on his torso, trying to predict which way he was going to strike next.

He swung his sword overhead and down towards her head. She lifted her sword to meet it. The blow rang through her sword and pushed her towards the ground.

Reuben swung his sword high again. Her feet were in the wrong position. She wouldn't be able to withstand the blow.

'Damn it.' In the second before the blow landed, she took a deep breath in, and reached out with her mind.

A sense of timelessness and strength filled her senses, and power rushed into her body.

Time slowed. She ducked under Reuben's blow, and jumped into her fighting stance. Reuben, expecting his blow to land on her sword, was pulled off balance by his sword's weight. She struck. She caught his sword from underneath and twisted her sword like a lever. His sword slipped from his hands and landed on the ground. He fell back into the mud with her sword at his throat.

'Enough,' Kim said.

Amber moved back and let her arms drop.

Reuben rolled to the side and stood, brushing the mud from his clothes. He scowled.

Amber let the power go. She felt a wave of nausea, and staggered to the edge of the training ground to vomit in the bushes. Her body was ice cold.

'This is why I hate leaning,' she told the bushes. At least she'd only leant on the power for a few minutes. It was much worse when she held it for a long time.

'Alright, back to it, everyone,' Kim bellowed. 'Switch partners – Amber, when you've recovered, pair up with Megan; Pete, with Reuben.'

Amber wiped her mouth with tissues, and took a gulp from her water bottle.

Kim squatted next to Amber, pulling a face as her right leg complained. 'You're getting better at leaning on the power. You didn't seem to have any trouble today.'

'Easy for you to say,' Amber said. 'You're not the one vomiting in the bushes.'

Kim quirked her lips.

Amber shrugged. 'The more I do it, the easier it seems to get.'

She'd felt like the power had been waiting for her to reach for it, ready to rush into her body. Some of the Resistance members, including Tev, one of the drivers, had accused Amber of being possessed by the power. She insisted that she was just leaning on it for strength. After a while, everyone in the Resistance described what she did as 'leaning', which seemed to give them comfort that it was safe. The power of language, Amber thought, biting her lip. But what if she was wrong? They didn't know anything about the power. Would it stop waiting for her, one day? Would it take over?

She dismissed the thought. She had enough to worry about.

Megan, a short, energetic South African in her early twenties, grinned at Amber as she rejoined the group. 'I love it when you beat up Reuben. Wish I could do what you do.'

Amber sheathed her sword and wiped her shaking hands on her clothes. 'I wish you could, too.'

She looked at the group of sword fighters, drilling in unison. They'd all watched the recordings of the Boneheads fighting. The Boneheads were so strong, and fast, that she didn't know how anyone in the group would defeat one without leaning on the power. The pile of dead bodies from her dream flashed into her mind. She felt a desperate need to teach all of them – even Reuben – to lean. 'We just have to keep trying,' she said. 'There must be a way.'

Her tone must have betrayed some of her desperation, because the smile left Megan's face, and she tilted her head to the side. 'I'm sure you'll think of something. Or Kim will.' She looked at Kim, her eyes bright. Amber followed her gaze. It was an open secret that Megan and Kim were sleeping together. Seeing them in the new, joyful stage of love, Amber felt a bit envious. She and Adam had been like that once.

'I think I've recovered enough,' she said, drawing her sword.

'Great,' Megan said. She lifted her own sword and attacked.

Amber waited as the sword fighters took it in turns to collect sandwiches in the kitchen tent, which was at the northern, most upstream edge of the camp. It wasn't a real tent, but an enormous navy-blue gazebo, open to the elements on three sides, with a canvas wall on the fourth side. Against this wall, the catering team prepared food on a series of trestle tables with gas stoves. The floor was covered in tarps. Logs and tree stumps were dotted around inside, particularly around the edges, along with the odd folding chair. More logs and tree stumps were spread outside the tent. Several small robins hopped around the ground picking at crumbs.

A few of the sword fighters looked at her sideways, with a mix of admiring or fearful glances. Reuben saw the looks, and thinned his lips. Amber ducked her head. She hated it when they treated her as though she was different. She hadn't beaten Reuben – the power had. Reuben would have wiped the floor with her if she hadn't leant on it.

Ben, a member of the Dubbo resistance group and owner of a cafe in Dubbo, was wiping the trestle tables. He looked up and gave her a wide grin. When they'd arrived at Base he'd given up fighting and taken over the catering, pointing out that the place was full of people who could fire a rifle with more accuracy than he could, but nobody else could make a decent cup of coffee.

'Let me guess – coffee?'

'Please,' Amber said. 'A giant bowlful.'

He busied himself with the coffee machine.

Two teenage girls were giggling behind the tray of sandwiches. Claire and Chelsea – Amber couldn't remember which one was which. She selected some sandwiches.

Sarah, a woman in her early thirties with short red hair, was sitting cross-legged on the edge of the tarps, with her back against a log. She kept a close watch on a group of young children, who were playing with an odd mix of worn toys, sticks and some banksia seed pods. One of Sarah's sons had found a caterpillar and was letting it climb over his hands. Oliver was crawling in the dirt next to him. Adam must have dropped him off before going to his 'lab' - the tent where he, Zac, Dom and various other tech experts worked on the THONGs.

Amber took her sandwiches and coffee to one of the tree stumps nearby and sat on a log. Jaws snuffled around her feet. Sarah looked up and gave her a smile. 'Hey.'

'Morning.' Amber sucked in a large sip of coffee with a sigh of pleasure. She took a bite of her sandwich.

Oliver put a stone into his mouth, and Sarah deftly retrieved it.

Kim plonked herself on a log opposite Amber with her own sandwich. Amber eyed her. The blonde highlights in her hair were growing out, but otherwise her hair was as neat as ever, pulled into a tidy ponytail with two bangs on either side. She clearly knew where her hairbrush was.

'You look tired,' Kim said. 'You've got red circles around your eyes.'

'Between Ollie and Jaws, I'm not surprised.'

A girl squealed.

'Ammm-ber!' Ben screeched.

Amber dropped her sandwich and swung around. 'What?'

Claire – or it may have been Chelsea – was standing with her back against the canvas wall. 'Get it away!'

Ben stood in front of her, holding a large ladle over his head, ready to swing. Jaws had his feet planted in the centre of the tent. His mouth was open, revealing his sharp teeth, and he was snarling.

Amber raced over and pulled him into her arms. 'Sorry. He must be ready for some milk.'

Ben shook his head. 'Please keep that thing out of my kitchen.'

Amber dragged Jaws away, which was not easy. He was thirty-five kilograms, which, for a normal wombat, would be large – and he was still growing.

She sank onto her log and gave him a bottle of marsupial milk. At least he was less ugly now that his claws were the right size in proportion to his body. She shoved the last of her sandwich into her mouth with her free hand.

'I had another idea about how to teach you guys to lean on the power.'

Kim sighed. 'Do you ever think about anything else? You might need to accept things the way they are.'

'This is the Resistance. The entire point of this place is not to accept things the way they are.'

Kim rolled her eyes. 'You know why I think you're obsessed about it? You think if everyone else can lean you won't have to fight.'

'That's not it,' Amber said, but she squirmed inside. She had thought that if others were better fighters than her, she could take a step back.

Kim snorted. 'Sure. So what's your new plan?'

'I was thinking – the first few times it worked for me, I was feeling desperate. Thinking the Boneheads were about to kill me, or whatever. Even now, it's easier if I feel under pressure – if Reuben is about to smash my head in, for example.'

'He wouldn't have smashed your head in.'

Amber cast a dark look towards the log that Reuben was sitting on. 'I wouldn't put it past him.'

'So, what, you want to make the rest of us think we're going to die?'

'Nah. But maybe just being under pressure would help. You want to try something this afternoon?'

Kim shrugged. 'Sure.'

The rain was easing when Amber returned to the training

ground. She gave Jaws some more cat food.

Kim and Megan arrived together.

'We thought we'd both give it a shot,' Kim said.

Amber took a breath and reached for the power. She leant on it – just a little. The muscle tiredness from the morning's training faded. 'Remember how I described reaching with my mind? Can you try that while I'm attacking you?'

Kim drew her sword. 'Sure.'

'Let's do this.'

She threw herself forward, her sword carving up the air. Kim matched her strikes. The clang of their swords hitting echoed from the hill. Amber leant more on the power, speeding up, so that Kim had to work hard to keep up. She pushed Kim back, trying to break through her defence. Kim's breath was coming out in gasps. She was avoiding putting weight on her right leg. Amber kept coming, swinging her sword faster and faster. Kim slipped over in the mud, and her sword flew out of her hands.

'I yield!' she yelled, putting an arm over her face. Amber stepped back, dropping her sword.

Kim sat up, shaking her head. 'Sorry, Amber, I tried. I just can't sense any kind of power like what you describe. Why don't you give it a go with Megan?'

'Okay.' Amber glanced at Jaws. He was sniffing the leaf litter under a tall eucalypt. She turned to Megan. 'Ready?'

Megan yielded faster than Kim had. 'Damn it,' she gasped, bent over. 'I'm starting to have some sympathy for Reuben.'

'Did you feel anything?' Amber asked. 'A sense of strength – of something ancient? At the back of your mind?'

Megan shook her head. 'The only thing I sensed was that I'm going to be really sore tomorrow.'

Amber's shoulders slumped. She looked at Kim. 'Want to have one last try?'

'Are you sure?' Kim drew her brows in. 'You've been leaning

for a while. Won't it make you sick?'

'Yeah.' Amber screwed up her nose. 'But I'll be sick anyway. May as well make the most of it.'

'Alright.' Kim hefted her sword.

Amber attacked again. Kim was tiring. Her moves grew sloppier and slower. Amber kept up the pressure, not slowing. All of a sudden, Kim sped up. Her sword danced through the air. Amber had to lean harder on the power to keep up. Megan's mouth fell open. She couldn't see their swords anymore – they were a blur.

'Enough,' Amber called, stepping back. She beamed. 'You did it!'

Kim lowered her sword. She started laughing. 'I did, didn't I? That felt amazing.' She bounced from one foot to the other in a jig. 'My leg isn't even hurting!'

Amber pulled a face. 'It will in a moment. You need to let go of the lean.'

Kim's face was shining. 'How do I do that?'

'Just – release the power. But maybe walk over to the bushes first.'

Kim moved to the patch of scrub on the edge of the training ground, closed her eyes and breathed out. She opened her eyes, the delight gone. 'Oh, shit.' She turned and vomited in the bushes.

'Guess I'd better let it go, too.' Amber walked a bit along from Kim, knelt and released the power. All the muscle pain that she should have felt while fighting Kim and Megan hit her at once. She curled forward, wrapping her arms across her chest. Her stomach churned. She threw up the sandwiches into the bushes, then lay on the ground, spent.

Kim flopped on the ground next to her. 'I'm shattered.'

Megan's face appeared above them. 'Everything okay?'

Amber lifted her hand and held one thumb up.

'Yeah.' Kim let the word out in a gasp. 'All good.'

Megan screwed up her nose. 'I'm not sure I want to do this leaning thing anymore.'

Four

Bec was woken by the sounds of children. A toddler whined, and its mother responded in an exasperated tone. A baby sobbed. She squeezed her eyes shut and tried to go back to sleep, but her mind started racing. What did Yorilla want with Amber? What was her 'offer' that the Resistance didn't know it needed yet?

Dan knelt next to her sleeping bag. His hair was wet and he was wearing clean clothes. 'Sam wants you to call him.'

Bec yawned. 'Now?'

He nodded.

She squirmed out of her sleeping bag. 'How long have you been up?'

He shrugged. 'A while. I couldn't sleep, so I thought I'd have a shower while there's still some hot water.'

Bec used the toilet, then padded outside, still dressed in her pyjamas. The school looked grey in the early morning light. She shivered in the cool air, wishing she'd grabbed a jumper.

Dan led the way to the middle of a basketball court, so that nobody could sneak up and eavesdrop on them. He opened a laptop, connected a headset to it and passed it to Bec.

Sam's trimmed moustache and beard appeared on the screen. He was as attractive as ever – more like a movie star than a Resistance fighter living in a bush camp with no running water. He stepped back and leant against a folding table. A thin, energetic-looking man in an army uniform, with dark hair and olive skin, was seated at the table. Bec hadn't spoken to him before, but she could guess who he was: the unofficial leader of the many small, independent groups that made up the

Australian Resistance. The Resistance fighters called him the MG – short for Major General, although Bec wasn't convinced that he had been a Major General before the war. Most of the Resistance fighters didn't use titles - the rule was to use first names only - but the title probably helped him negotiate with some of the less cooperative groups, or overseas backers.

'Rebecca. Pleased to meet you.' His voice was as brisk and energetic as his appearance. 'Thank you for your help retrieving that information.' He focused dark brown eyes on her. 'Sam tells me you were assisted by a Bonehead. Can you tell us about it?'

Bec shivered. She took a deep breath and launched into the story.

The MG kept his eyes on her as she spoke. When she finished, he was silent for a long moment.

'So the Bonehead – Yorilla – called Amber's power a curse?'

Bec nodded.

'It might be a translation issue,' Sam said. 'Curse might mean something different to them.'

'Maybe,' Bec said. 'I don't think so, though. I don't know how the Boneheads learnt English, but apart from that weird accent and – I dunno, a tendency to speak in short, sharp sentences – they all seem to speak it like natives.'

The MG tapped his fingers against the table that he was sitting at, his eyes unfocused. 'Let us think about it. Don't tell Amber, please.'

Bec nodded. Amber would freak out.

'This address the Bonehead gave you,' Sam said, 'Sounds like a trap.'

'I know,' Bec said. 'But why? It already had us. It could have killed us there and then, like Captain Waters. Or taken us wherever it liked. Why drop us off, only to catch us in a trap later?'

Sam shrugged.

'Anyway, I've committed to checking the address out, in return for a place to stay. Thanks for the heads up about that, by the way.'

Sam raised his eyebrows. 'I assumed you could handle a few refugees.'

Bec snorted. 'Monique is no refugee.'

'Before you check out that address, we'd like you to look into something else,' the MG said. 'Corella Creek Farm.'

'Corella Creek? Sounds like a kids' TV show.'

'It came up in the information that Vincent gave us,' Sam said. 'According to government records, it used to be a small cattle farm, but the owners went bankrupt during the last drought. The new owners are hobby farmers – they've won a few small government grants for work on natural regeneration. But something's a bit off about it – there's far too many deliveries for a small-scale operation. It might be nothing, but since you're in the area anyway -'

'Okay, sure.' Bec shrugged. 'You promised me some gear.'

'It's coming. Two, three hours. I'll text the pickup location to Dan. Bring Vincent with you – he'll be safer at Base. And I'm sure Monique would prefer not to be lumped with him.'

'She'd prefer not to be lumped with me, either.'

A smile flitted across Sam's face. 'I knew she had sense.' He looked at the MG.

The MG gave a brisk nod. 'Let us know how you go.'

Bec ended the call and pulled her headset off. 'Sam's sending us some gear this morning. And he and the MG want us to check out some farm – Corella Creek.'

Dan frowned. 'I thought you were going after Zhou.'

'We are. If we pick up the gear and check out the farm today, we can go tomorrow.' Dan was still frowning. 'What?'

'We've been trying to find Zhou for three months. We finally have a lead, and you're still putting the Resistance first.'

Bec drew her brows in. 'Isn't helping the Resistance free the entire country from the Boneheads a higher priority than rescuing one person?'

Dan slammed the laptop closed and forced it into its bag. He spoke through his teeth. 'He's not just 'one person'. He's our friend. And it's your fault he got captured.' He stood and slung the bag over one shoulder, looking down his nose at her. 'Guess I'm under no delusion about what you'll do if I ever get captured.' He stormed away.

Bec stared after him. What was that about? Shaking her head, she stood and stretched. If Sam was sending their supplies soon, she'd better have breakfast.

Ash drove the ute north of Canberra, over the New South Wales border. The sun poured through the windscreen. Bec tugged the sun visor down, but it didn't do much to block the sun. She put the air conditioner fan on full, and glanced at Vincent in the back. He was staring at the scenery out the window.

Ash glanced at Bec and then back at the road. 'Dan's pissed with you.'

'I don't see why,' Bec grumbled. 'I don't think he and Zhou were that great friends. Half the time he doesn't even pronounce Zhou's name correctly.'

'He's not pissed about Zhou. He's scared.'

'What's he got to be scared about? We're the ones dodging wombats and gunfire.'

'He's scared he'll get arrested for helping you. And you'll prioritise the cause over rescuing him, same as you do with Zhou.'

Bec stared at her. 'How do you know that?'

Ash rolled her eyes. 'Because I actually listen when people talk to me, instead of dismissing their concerns.'

Bec scowled at her, but she was concentrating on the road. She spun the steering wheel and turned onto a dirt road and into a national park. The ute jolted over corrugations. Eucalypts grew right to the edge of the road, their canopy shading the ground, creating a cool place for a riot of tree ferns and bracken. Ash slammed her foot on the brake. A snake dashed across the road, kicking up dirt as it slithered into the ferns.

Ash sped up again. Bec squinted out the windscreen. The forest opened up, revealing the jagged, light yellow rocks of an abandoned quarry. It was like a wound on the landscape, where the ground had been ripped open.

'That'll be the place.'

A station wagon was parked next to the quarry. An Aboriginal woman leant against it, her hair in a messy bun on top of her head.

Ash pulled up behind the station wagon. She leapt out and gave the woman a wide grin.

'Christine!'

Christine smiled back. 'Good to see you.' They clasped hands. She nodded to Bec. 'What happened to your hair? You look almost respectable.'

Bec patted the tight cap of straightened, bleached blonde hair that covered her head. 'Monique. She thought my hair was too recognisable.' She screwed up her nose. 'Nobody ever accused me of being respectable before.'

Vincent climbed out of the ute and looked at Christine with wary eyes.

'And you must be Vincent.' Christine strode over and thrust her hand out, forcing Vincent to shake it. 'Nice to meet you. Sam was very complimentary about the info you gave us.' Vincent frowned, and opened his mouth, but Christine rushed on. 'You can hop in the car, if you like, while I give these guys some supplies.' She lowered her voice. 'Best if you don't look. Plausible deniability is always handy.'

Vincent paled and hurried to the front passenger seat of the station wagon.

Christine opened the boot of the station wagon and lifted the spare tyre out. She leant past Vincent, opened the glove box, and pressed a pen against a magnet hidden inside. The floor of the boot swung upwards, revealing a large secret compartment underneath. Bec looked in. A wide smile appeared on her face. The compartment was full of explosives cases.

'Everything you asked for is here. I think Ren threw in a few specials, too.' Christine grinned. 'After the MG promoted Sam, he gave Sam's job to Ren, but threatened him with demotion if he screws up. Ren's way too proud to let that happen, so now he's being all responsible. But he said someone should have some fun.'

'Awesome,' Bec said.

'Sam sent a message, too. He said,' she put on a fake New Zealand accent, 'Tell her that I expect some results from this lot, or I'll cut her off.'

Bec screwed up her nose. 'I got the info from Vincent, didn't I?'

Christine opened a smaller box. Several round, black balls were nestled among bubble wrap. 'The tech guys sent you these.'

Bec tilted her head. 'THONGs? We already have plenty of those.'

'No, these are new, extra strength THONGs – one of these should provide a shield that covers an entire vehicle.'

'No way.' Bec stared at the box.

'Dom and Zach said that they work off a different – um –' Christine's brow furrowed. 'Ugh, I can't remember, something something technical bullshit – but it means that you should be able to wear your personal THONGs and use these at the same time, without them interfering with each other.'

'That's great.'

Christine fixed her eyes on Bec's. 'Don't rely on them too much.

The basic technology is still the same as what the Boneheads are using, however much Adam tinkers with the security. They might have a way around them.'

'Sure, got it,' Bec said.

Christine gave her a suspicious look, but she closed the box and handed it to Ash, who took it to the ute.

'Help me with the explosives.'

Ash moved the front seats of the ute as far forward as they would go, and flung open a secret compartment under the floor. Josie had told Bec that a drug-dealing motorcycle gang had installed the secret compartments in their vehicles. Bec thought Josie might have been joking, but she supposed that kind of gang would have the expertise.

'How is everyone?' Ash demanded, as they transferred the explosives cases from the station wagon to the ute.

Christine shrugged. 'Same-same. Ben and Michelle said to give you their regards. I haven't seen Mark much, he's pretty busy, they always need drivers. Which is why I got lumped with delivering your supplies. The sword fighting guys are getting pretty good. I heard that Kim has learnt how to do that leaning thing Amber does.'

Bec lifted her head. 'That's great!'

Christine nodded. 'She's found herself a girlfriend, too – one of her sword fighting posse.' They dropped the last box of explosives into the ute with a bang. 'It's all yours. Have fun – don't get yourselves killed.'

'Give our regards to everyone,' Ash said.

Bec bit her lip. 'If you see Amber – tell her I said hi.'

Christine waved a hand, jogged back to the station wagon and drove away. Bec and Ash closed the secret compartment and pushed the seat back.

Bec grinned. 'That was well worth the drive.'

Ash drove back to the school to change the number plates and pick up Nathan and Luke. They drove out of Canberra again – this time heading south-west. After about twenty-five minutes, Ash turned off the highway and took the local roads, which were so narrow that for two cars to pass each other they would both have to put their left wheels in the dirt.

They drove past cleared paddocks dotted with lichen-covered granite boulders. Grey rabbits dashed away as the car approached. Ash pulled over into the long, yellow grass on the side of the road. She fiddled with her phone and nodded at a rounded slope that rose up on the left. 'Corella Creek Farm should be on the other side of that hill.'

Bec slid out into the grass. There were a few wispy clouds on the horizon, but otherwise the sky was clear. She felt too warm in her jacket, and shrugged it off, leaving it on the passenger seat. Luke and Nathan climbed out of the back seat and pulled their packs and rifles out of the ute tray. Nathan slung a large camera case over one shoulder and his rifle over the other.

A rhythmic, metallic sound echoed around the hills.

'Any idea what that sound is?'

Luke shrugged. 'Some kind of farm machinery, maybe?'

He handed her pack and rifle to her. She called Dan and Ash in a group call. 'Any problems from your end?' she asked Dan.

'I haven't heard anything. But you're miles from any CCTV cameras.'

'Alright. We're heading up the hill now.'

She nodded to Ash and followed Luke and Nathan. The grass brushed against their legs, leaving spiky seeds attached to their socks. The metallic sound grew louder.

As they neared the top of the hill, Luke lowered himself into the grass and motioned for them to do the same. They crawled the last metre up the hill. The grass prickled Bec's arms through her shirt and batted against her face. She sneezed into her elbow and slithered over the ridge.

The sun was opposite them. Bec shaded her eyes with her hand. The hill overlooked a long valley. A line of trees twisted along the lowest part of the valley, suggesting that there was a watercourse there. Elsewhere, the vegetation was young trees and shrubs, and more yellow grass. The land was in poor condition – the gullies near the watercourse were eroded and the grass was patchy and short, as though it had been overgrazed in the past.

No livestock grazed the land now. Long, straight lines of Boneheads stretched across the field, drilling with swords.

Bec's stomach churned. She shifted, feeling the grass prickling her skin. There were at least a thousand Boneheads below her. She'd never seen more than a few at a time before – hadn't even imagined there were that many in Australia. The rhythmic clang of swords striking in unison filled the air.

'That's no farm machinery,' Nathan said.

Bec nodded, without taking her eyes off the site. The sound seemed menacing now. She imagined she could feel it in her teeth, and clenched them together. Any one of those Boneheads could kill them without raising a sweat.

Nathan pulled a digital SLR camera out of his camera case, fitted a long lens to it and started filming the site and the Boneheads.

The Boneheads' heavy boots had worn away the short grass, leaving bare dirt. Bec narrowed her eyes. There were a mix of Boneheads with bright mahogany and grey bony plates, but they were clustered in the lines, as though the Red and Grey Bones tended to keep to their own kinds.

She looked beyond the long rows of Boneheads. The hill curved around the valley and sloped down to a wide spur to the north-east, before dropping down to the watercourse. A cluster of buildings sat on the flat spur. Sunlight glinted on metal roofs.

Nathan peered through his camera lens in the direction of the buildings. 'You'll want to take a look at this.'

Luke dug in his pack for a pair of binoculars, and stared in the same direction. 'Who is that guy?'

He pushed the binoculars into Bec's hands and pointed at the buildings. Bec pointed the binoculars in the rough direction he had indicated, and scanned the area. In front of the building, past the lines of Boneheads, a smaller figure was fighting a Red Bone. The man was topless, dressed in light grey tracksuit pants and sneakers. He looked odd next to the Boneheads, who all wore their usual uniform of black combat pants, jackets, gloves and boots. Bec squinted into the binoculars.

'Is that -' She lowered the binoculars and met Luke's eyes, her mouth dropping open. His eyes were wide. 'Keep filming,' she said to Nathan. 'The Resistance needs to know about this.'

'Not a good idea, mammal,' said an icy cold voice behind them, with a clipped accent.

Every muscle in Bec's body tensed. She jerked around and jumped to her feet. Two Grey Bones stood behind them, holding drawn swords and wearing sunglasses. One was taller than the other. The horn on the far left of its bony plate was twisted, giving it an unbalanced look.

Luke and Nathan were on their feet next to her, all three rifles pointed at the Boneheads.

'Rebecca Williams,' the Bonehead with the twisted horn drawled. 'Walker is offering a very large reward for anyone who brings you in. It would be a pity not to claim it.'

Bec's rifle wobbled. Her hands felt slippery with sweat.

'However -' The Bonehead removed its sunglasses. The breath caught in Bec's throat. Like Yorilla, it had a red ring around each eye. 'My family has other plans for you.' It snorted. 'You got lucky. If anyone else had found you, you would be in a world of trouble right now.'

Bec took a deep breath in. The Bonehead, which she named Twisty, was part of Yorilla's family. It wouldn't kill her - she hoped.

The shorter Bonehead eyed Luke and Nathan. 'We could take the other two in. They're Resistance - we'd still get some credit.'

Bec's mind raced. 'You can't,' she said, her voice coming out at a higher pitch than usual. 'Walker might force them to tell him that you let me go.'

Twisty bared its teeth. 'Not if we take them in dead.'

Bec's hands shook. 'No.' She aimed her rifle at Twisty's face and pulled the trigger. The bullet hit Twisty's shield and fell to the ground.

Twisty let out a bark of laughter. 'You'll have to do better than that, mammal.'

Bec flung the rifle at its face and drew her sword in one, swift movement, like Kim had taught her. The shorter Bonehead turned to watch Twisty duck, and Bec leapt forward, swinging her sword around so she stood behind the Bonehead, her sword at its throat. 'Let us go.'

Twisty smiled. 'I'm starting to see why Yorilla likes you.'

The shorter Bonehead growled. 'You think this changes anything, ustiga? I am ready to die, for the honour of my family.'

Twisty stalked around her.

'Freeze, or I'll kill your friend,' Bec spat.

Twisty stopped, and tilted its head. 'I'm not convinced that you will.' Twisty moved closer, its smile widening. 'How are you going, holding that sword up? You seem to be shaking. Arm starting to get a bit tired, perhaps?'

'Freeze!' Bec said.

Twisty looked down its nose at her. 'I think my family may have overestimated your usefulness.' It waved its hand at the ute. 'I suggest you leave - now. You may consider your companions' lives a – favour. We may seek repayment in the future.'

Bec glanced at Luke and Nathan. Nathan was swallowing. Luke nodded at Bec and picked up her pack. She waited until they were halfway down the hill before removing her sword from the Bonehead's throat and trotting down the hill with an odd, sideways gait, to avoid placing her back to the two Boneheads.

Ash had already started the engine. Luke and Nathan threw the packs in the tray and tumbled into the back. Bec dashed the last few metres and dived into the passenger seat. She looked up the hill as Ash accelerated away. Twisty picked up her rifle. The shorter Bonehead watched her, with a scowl on its face.

Luke leant over the centre console. 'Fucking hell, Bec. Our lives are a favour that they want repaid? What do those Boneheads want from you?''

Bec ran her hands through her hair. 'I don't think it's me they want – it's Amber.'

Luke shook his head. 'Whatever. It's not good.'

Bec gave him a shaky smile. 'Hey, if it keeps us alive, it's not all bad.'

She looked at Nathan. His whole body was shaking.

'And at least we got the footage,' she added.

Nathan gave her a glare that made her grateful that looks couldn't kill.

Five

Amber lowered her sword and held out a hand. Grace took it, and allowed Amber to pull her out of the mud.

'Sorry,' Grace said, brushing at the mud in her blonde ponytail. 'I am trying.'

'I know. No need to apologise.' Amber rubbed sweat from her cheeks. 'I'm sorry I can't find a better way to explain it.'

She looked around, meeting Kim's eyes across the training ground. Kim dodged around Pete and Reuben and joined them. 'No luck?'

Amber shook her head.

Kim gave Grace a warm smile. 'Thanks for trying. Why don't you go and spar with Megan?'

Amber watched Grace rejoin the group. 'You managed to lean yesterday; I don't know why it isn't working for anyone else.'

'Maybe they'll take more than one attempt to get it.'

'Yeah,' said Amber. The word came out as a sigh.

Kim squeezed her shoulder. 'You said yourself that we don't know anything about the power. Maybe only certain people can access it?'

Amber nodded with another sigh. She lifted her sword. 'Spar?'

'Thought you'd never ask.'

Kim drew her sword. Her eyes turned blank as she reached for the power. Without warning, she struck, swinging her sword in a backhanded strike towards Amber's chin. Amber leant harder on the power, and time slowed. She caught Kim's sword on hers and forced it downwards. Kim whipped her sword towards Amber's legs. Amber, on her toes, pivoted to her left, out of reach. The sword cut through the air. Amber kicked out with her right leg in a side kick, leaning her body to the left and striking Kim's ribs.

Kim clenched her teeth and leant harder. She attacked Amber again, using a dizzying array of different strikes. She switched the sword between her left hand, to both hands, to her right hand, and back again, so that every strike came from a different angle.

Amber watched each strike as it came and raised her sword to block, or pivoted out of reach. Even leaning on the power, Kim couldn't match Amber's speed.

Kim swung her sword at Amber's head. Amber ducked under it. The momentum of the swing dragged Kim's arms around, and Amber brought the flat of her sword down on Kim's wrists. Kim struggled to regain control of the weight of the sword. Amber didn't give her a chance. Copying the move Kim had tried earlier, she swung her sword in a backhander up and under Kim's chin, stopping an inch from her throat.

Kim raised her hands. Amber dropped her sword and released some of her tight grip on the lean, without letting it go. There were some cheers from the rest of the group, who had paused their sparring to watch. She saw Megan grinning. Next to her, Reuben watched them, his gaze neutral.

She turned back to Kim, who shook her head. 'You're so fast.'

'You'll get there,' Amber said, hoping it was true.

Kim kept shaking her head. 'I'm not sure I will.' She took a deep breath. 'Time to let go of the power. You should too – you've been leaning for a while.'

Amber pulled a face. 'Just once, I'd like to keep my morning coffee in my stomach.'

They moved to the edge of the training ground. Amber let go of the power. She hunched over the bushes, vomiting.

Kim watched Amber, screwing up her nose. She took a deep breath and released the power. Her face flushed and her body shook. She collapsed on the ground.

Amber leapt towards Kim. Her eyes were open, unseeing. Amber put her cheek next to Kim's mouth. She could feel a light breath against her cheek.

Kim blinked her eyes and focused on Amber.

Amber sat back on her heels, relieved. The rest of the group rushed over. Megan threw herself down next to Kim. 'What happened?'

'She fainted.'

Kim struggled to sit up.

'Stay there,' Amber said. 'I'll get someone to check you out.'

'I'll go,' Pete said.

He bolted to the first aid tent and returned a few minutes later with Reena, a middle-aged Indian doctor with short, dark hair and a large shoulder bag. She knelt in the mud next to Kim.

'What happened?'

'I just let go of the power and fainted,' Kim said. 'I'm fine now.'

'Let's check you out.' She shooed everyone apart from Megan away. 'Give her some privacy.'

Some of the group started sparring again. The rest waited, chatting. Amber flopped on the ground and gulped water from her water bottle, trying to remove the vomit taste from her mouth.

After a few minutes, Reena packed up her shoulder bag and allowed Kim to stand.

Kim rejoined them. 'I'm fine,' she said, brushing away their concerns. 'Reena thinks it was just the shock from the pain after I released the power. I just need to be careful. Let's do some stretches and take an early mark.'

She led them in a series of stretches. Seated on the ground, Amber reached forward towards her toes and pulsed, stretching out her hamstrings. She bit her lip. Kim was a far better fighter than her, but even leaning, Kim couldn't keep up with her. And what if Kim kept fainting?

Amber changed the stretch, and reminded herself it was only the second time Kim had leant on the power. She might get faster and stronger with time. Amber hoped so.

Amber returned to the tent. Adam and Oliver were gone. She filled a red plastic bucket with toiletries and Jaws' bowl and food, and slung a towel around her shoulders.

Carrying the bucket in one hand, she followed the creek downstream of the camp. She stopped where the creek wound its way over a large, weathered rock platform, before gushing into a pool a short drop below, forming a small waterfall.

Amber dumped cat food in the bowl. Jaws snuffled at it.

She stripped down to her underwear and waded into the creek, wincing. The thick canopy prevented any sunlight from warming the icy water. Taking a deep breath, she ducked down, immersing her head. The cold sent a sharp shiver through her body. She rinsed the worst of the mud off, then filled the bucket with water. She walked away from the creek to lather herself in soap and rinsed the soap off into the bushes with the bucket of water. She dried herself and pulled on fresh clothes.

It was so humid that by the time she reached the kitchen tent she felt damp again.

'I need a giant bowl of coffee,' she told Ben.

He opened a bag of coffee grinds and spooned some into the filter basket. 'Something wrong?'

She breathed in the coffee scent. 'Nah – just tired.' She scanned the sandwiches until she found one with curried egg and lettuce. Ben handed her a large mug of coffee.

'Josie dropped off some supplies for you. More marsupial milk and cat food.'

'She's back?' Amber was pleased – she hadn't seen Josie for a while.

She carried the coffee and sandwich to her usual tree stump. Since it wasn't raining, Sarah had taken the creche somewhere else. Most of the other sword fighters had finished their lunch and gone elsewhere, but Reuben was deep in a book, and Kim and Megan were having a quiet conversation at another tree stump.

She had taken one bite from her sandwich when a teenage boy ran into the tent and stopped in front of her, placing his hands on his knees and taking deep gulps of air. 'Sam wants you – at the MG's tent.'

Amber frowned. 'What for?'

He looked at her as though she was crazy. 'He didn't tell me that.' He raced away, legs and arms flying everywhere.

Amber stood, taking a large gulp of coffee. She winced as the hot coffee singed her tongue, and put the cup on the tree stump. 'I hope this doesn't take long.'

She jogged to the large tent that the MG used as an office, pushed the flap back and entered with Jaws at her feet. The tent seemed to be full of men, all talking in low voices. The MG was seated at the folding table he used as a desk.

'Amber.' He waved for her to come over. 'I need your opinion.'

Amber wound her way to him. Several people jumped out of the way when they saw Jaws. He had a bad reputation.

Contrary to her first impression, there were a few women in the tent. She recognised many of those present as leaders in the Resistance. Ren was there, and Marissa, a short, reserved woman who was in charge of intelligence.

A large television screen had been set up on another folding table, near the tent wall opposite the MG. A laptop was connected to the screen with a cable.

'Your friend Rebecca sent us this video about half an hour ago. It was taken this morning, on a farm outside Canberra.' The MG waved at Sam. 'Play it, please?'

Sam fiddled with the mouse, then stepped back as a video started playing, with the sound muted. The murmur of voices decreased and then stopped, as the other people in the tent turned to watch the video.

The camera looked down on a yellow field. Lines of Boneheads stretched across the field.

Amber's stomach tightened. 'There's so many of them.'

The Boneheads were drilling with swords. It reminded her of their own sword-fighting group, except that the Boneheads' moved in perfect unison, and didn't expend an ounce more energy than necessary.

The camera zoomed in on a farmhouse, and focused on a topless man and a Bonehead in the foreground. The man's stomach and arms were etched with muscles.

Amber squinted at the screen. 'There's something familiar about him.'

'It appears to be the Prime Minister,' the MG said.

The man and Bonehead prowled around each other, muscles taut, swords drawn. Without warning, the man struck. The Bonehead raised its sword to block, but somehow the man got under its guard before it could complete the move. The man touched his sword to the Bonehead's throat. The Bonehead raised its sword and its empty hand to signal defeat. The man stepped back, and they continued to circle.

Amber frowned.

Next, the Bonehead attacked, its sword weaving furious patterns as it attempted to get through the man's guard. The man met every attack. After a few minutes of this, the man twisted in a sudden movement and sent the Bonehead's sword flying. The Bonehead raised both hands.

Sam paused the video.

Amber swung around to face the MG, her face pale. 'That's the

PM? Walker?'

The MG gave a single nod. 'We believe so.'

'He's leaning.'

There was a sudden loud murmuring of voices from the others in the tent.

The MG leant forward, and the noise dropped away. 'You're sure?'

'Pretty sure. He's way too fast, otherwise.'

Sam and the MG exchanged glances. 'How good is he?' the MG asked. 'Could you beat him?'

Amber frowned. 'I don't know.' She looked at Sam. 'Could you play the video outside?'

Sam shrugged. 'Sure.' He unplugged the laptop from the television. 'Can you bring the table?' he asked Ren.

They set the laptop up outside the tent, on the folding table. The MG joined them.

The crowd of people from inside the tent clustered around the entrance. Amber gave them a sidelong glance. Her face reddened. She didn't want an audience. The MG saw the expression on her face, and waved everyone apart from Sam, Ren and Marissa back inside.

Amber drew her sword, took a deep breath, and leant on the power. She nodded at Sam, and he started the video. As the screen panned to take in the PM, she went deep into the lean. Time slowed. She kept her eyes on the video and tried to match his strokes.

He was very fast. She struggled to keep up. She was expecting his last move, but she couldn't move her sword fast enough to match him.

The video ended. Amber lowered her sword, and let go of the power. Her stomach churned and her head pounded, but she didn't vomit this time. She glanced at the MG and Sam.

Their matching frowns told her they knew.

'He's faster than you,' Sam said.

'I wouldn't be able to beat him.'

'Well,' the MG said, his voice brisk, 'We'll just have to make sure you never face him.' He gave her a nod. 'Thank you for your help. We won't keep you – I understand that we interrupted your lunch.'

Amber nodded back. He and Marissa returned to the tent. Sam picked up the laptop and started to follow.

Amber bit her lip. 'Sam –'

He stopped and raised his eyebrows.

'That stuff – the video – is it a secret? Can I tell people about it?'

'You mean Adam?'

'Actually, I was thinking about Kim.'

Sam nodded. 'Don't splash it around; it'll make some people nervous. But it's not a secret. Just – use your judgement.' He frowned, as though he wasn't convinced that her judgement was any good, and followed the MG inside.

Amber watched him go, her brow wrinkled.

Ren paused. 'Don't worry about it, Amber. It's not all on you.' He jerked his head towards the tent. 'Let that lot in there figure out how to handle this new complication.'

Amber nodded. 'Thanks, Ren.'

She ambled back to the kitchen tent, letting Jaws stop to sniff at things they passed. A light drizzle brushed her face, cooling it. An image of the PM fighting the Bonehead ran through her mind. The PM could lean? And he was faster than her. She chewed on a nail.

The MG said they'd just have to make sure she never faced him, but who else was there? The Resistance had better sword fighters than her – Kim and Reuben, for starters – but if she couldn't match the PM's speed, they wouldn't be able to.

'Well,' she muttered, 'Who says we need to take him out with swords? They could just drop a bomb on top of him.'

'Your coffee got cold, and the birds stole your sandwich,' one of the girls announced when she got back to the kitchen tent. She was pretty sure it was Chelsea.

'I'll make you another coffee,' Ben said. He waved at the table of sandwiches. 'There's plenty more.'

Kim and Megan were still chatting. Amber accepted a mug of coffee from Ben and walked over to them, biting her lip. Kim raised her eyebrows.

'Can I speak to you?' Amber asked.

'Sure.'

'Sit here,' Megan said. 'I need to have a wash, anyway.' She picked up her empty plate and cup and took them to Chelsea.

Amber sat down opposite Kim. She leant forward and spoke in a low voice. 'The MG and Sam showed me a video.'

'Mmm?' Kim took a gulp of coffee.

'It was of the PM. He was leaning.'

Kim choked. She swallowed and coughed. 'Are you telling me Walker knows how to lean?'

Amber nodded. 'He's fast.'

'Faster than you?'

'Yep.'

'Shit.' Kim shook her head, took another sip of coffee, and swallowed. 'So -' she prompted.

'So – what if I have to face him one day? I'm not good enough, Kim.'

Kim frowned. 'It's not all on you, Amber,' she said, unconsciously echoing Ren.

'I'm not saying it is, but -'

'Spit it out.'

'I need to get better at sword fighting.'

Kim narrowed her eyes. 'Are you serious?'

'Yes.'

'Then I'm not the one you should be talking to.' She nodded her head towards Reuben, who hadn't moved from his log.

Amber stiffened. 'No way.'

'His technique is miles ahead of mine. The only reason Sam and Ren want me to train our group, and not him, is they think he's too abrasive. They're worried he'll turn people off.'

Amber snorted. 'No idea why they'd think that.'

Kim glared at her. 'If you're serious about improving, he's the one who can help you.'

'He'll never agree. He hates me.'

'Of course he'll agree,' Kim said, with a wicked smile. 'He'd love nothing better than to tell you what to do.'

Amber filled her cheeks with air and let it out with a pop. 'Okay,' she said, her voice as gloomy as if Kim had asked her to do a hundred push-ups. She stood and turned away from Kim, then turned back. 'What about teaching the others to lean? I can't do that and train with Reuben.'

Kim gave an impatient wave of her hand. 'You can give lessons in leaning in the afternoons, after training, like you did with Megan and me.'

'Right.' Amber took a deep breath and walked over to Reuben.

He looked up from his book. 'You're blocking the sunlight.'

'What sunlight? It's cloudy.'

He sighed. 'What do you want, Amber?'

Amber plonked down on the log opposite him. 'I wanted to ask if you'd train me – in sword fighting.'

He stared at her. 'That's the last thing I expected you to say.'

'I need to get better. Kim says you're the best.'

He shook his head and returned his gaze to his book. 'If you want to improve your sword fighting, try turning up to training on time.'

Amber gritted her teeth. 'If I turn up on time, will you train me?'

He sighed again, put his finger in the book to mark his place, and fixed his eyes on her. 'Every time you're challenged, you reach for that power. You're not working on your technique, you're just using speed to get out of trouble.' He lifted a shoulder in a half-shrug. 'You're never going to improve doing that.'

Amber frowned. She didn't like to admit it, but he made some sense. 'So if I turn up on time, and don't lean, will you train me?'

He gazed at her for a moment. 'Fine. We'll start tomorrow.' He looked down at the book. 'Goodbye.'

Six

A loud screech woke Amber. She leapt upright, her heart hammering in her chest.

Adam moaned and pulled his pillow over his ears.

Amber scrambled around the air mattress for the old mobile phone, without a SIM card, that she'd borrowed from the supply tent. She turned the alarm off and flopped back down, dropping her head onto the pillow and feeling her heart slow. Jaws snuffled at her feet. She looked at Oliver. He was still asleep, his chubby face looking angelic.

She listened to the birds chirping and twittering outside the tent. Her enthusiasm from the day before had faded. Why on earth had she let Kim convince her she should train with Reuben?

Groaning under her breath, she crawled out of the sleeping bag and pulled on her clothes. Adam removed the pillow and looked at her through half-closed eyes. 'I still don't understand why they make you train so early. What have they got against sleep?'

'Beats me.' Amber kissed him and Oliver on their foreheads and slipped out of the tent with Jaws.

She arrived at the kitchen tent in enough time to accept a coffee from Ben and drink the coffee without burning her mouth.

Megan was also getting a coffee before training. 'Wow. It's not like you to be here this early.'

'I set an alarm.' Amber lifted her chin and puffed her chest out as though she was trumpeting a major achievement. Megan laughed.

They walked to the training ground together. A small smile flitted across Kim's face when she saw Amber.

Amber filled Jaws' bowl with cat food.

'I see that Reuben has managed to achieve what I couldn't, and motivate you,' Kim murmured in her ear.

Amber jumped. Not Reuben, she thought, standing. The video of the PM. Goosebumps popped up over her arms. She rubbed her hands up and down her sleeves, wondering if it was the cool morning air, or thinking about the PM, that had brought them on.

They lined up ready for the warm-up run. 'Go!' Kim called.

A few of the more energetic members of the group sprang away, racing each other up the hill. Reuben was with them, of course. Amber stayed in the middle of the pack, enjoying the feel of moving her body, her legs stretching and feet hitting the ground. She disliked the early starts, especially after sleepless nights with Oliver, but she enjoyed running. She allowed her mind to wander into a daydream.

After the run, Kim paired the group members for drills. Reuben drew Amber to the end of the training ground, away from the main group. She wiped sweat from under her eyes. Her shirt was damp with it.

Reuben drew his sword. 'We'll start with the usual drills,' he said. 'Attack.'

Amber drew her own sword and brought it up in an overhead strike.

'Stop,' he barked.

She froze.

'Your grip is wrong.' He moved her left hand further down the hilt. 'You'll have better control if you widen it. Again.'

Amber repeated the move, her sword ringing against Reuben's.

'Do that again, in slow motion,' he ordered.

She did as he said.

'See how you're bringing your elbows wide, your arms over your head? You're leaving yourself wide open for your opponent. You need to keep your elbows in, to protect your face and neck. Do it again – keep it slow until you get it right.'

Training with Reuben was very different to training with Kim. He picked up every error in her technique, and made her repeat the move, in slow motion, until she got it right. Her body cooled. The morning air on her sweaty shirt made her shiver. Her arms ached from holding the sword high. She had to admit, though, that the tweaks to her technique allowed her to ring more power out of each move. By the time the main group finished the last of the drills, Amber and Reuben had only practised three of the moves.

'We'll work on the other moves another time,' Reuben said. 'Let's spar.'

Amber hefted her sword, ignoring the pain in her forearms. Thank goodness. She'd had enough of him picking on everything she did.

Half an hour later, Amber landed on her back on the ground for the fifth time, Reuben's sword at her throat. She flopped her head back, ignoring the mud seeping into her hair.

'Do you yield?' Reuben asked.

'No. I'm just about to leap up and disarm you,' Amber said, not moving.

'Yeah, right.' He removed the sword and held out a hand. Amber sighed. She sat up, took his hand and let him pull her to her feet. 'Kim's about to start stretches,' he said. 'We may as well join in.'

Amber stumbled over to join the group and flopped down next to Megan. She hadn't felt this tired from training since the first days Kim had started teaching her. But at least she'd kept her coffee in her stomach.

'What happened?' Megan asked, as they stretched their hamstrings. 'You were my hero who could beat the crap out of Reuben!'

'I can only beat him if I lean, and I promised him I wouldn't,' Amber said, moving to the next stretch.

Megan froze in the middle of switching stretches. 'Why would you promise such a thing?'

Amber ran her hand through her hair and shook lumps of mud onto the ground. ''Cos I just love landing on my ass in the mud.'

Jaws trundled over and leant his head against her thigh. She closed her eyes, taking deep breaths and enjoying the feel of stretching tired muscles. When she reopened them, she saw Sam approaching.

He beckoned to Amber and Kim. Amber scrambled up, slid her sword into the sword belt and hurried over, with Jaws at her feet. Kim dismissed the group and joined them.

'What's up?'

'The MG wants to speak to you.' Without waiting for a response, Sam swung around and strode towards the office tents, forcing them to jog to catch up. Amber wondered why he hadn't sent a teenager to fetch them this time. He was scowling, but his unhappiness didn't seem to be directed at them. He wove his way to the MG's tent and held the flap back. Amber rubbed her face as she entered, wishing she'd had a chance to clean off the mud and sweat.

The tent held far fewer people than on the previous day. The MG was sitting at the same folding table. Ren was leaning over the desk, looking at a large tablet. The MG gave Amber and Kim a smile as they entered, then returned his attention to the tablet.

'Amber!' Josie hailed her from the back left corner of the tent. Several folding chairs had been arranged in a half-circle. The television that Amber had watched the PM on had been moved, and now stood in front of the chairs. Josie was sitting on one side of the half-circle. Marissa sat on the opposite side, tapping at another tablet. She flicked her light brown eyes in their direction.

Amber smiled and walked over to Josie. 'Welcome back.'

Josie's eyes danced. 'Have you been bathing in mud?'

Amber screwed up her nose. 'Pretty much.'

'It's meant to be good for your skin, isn't it?' Kim said, joining them.

'Yep, glowing skin is my top priority right now.'

The MG joined them, beckoning Ren and Sam to follow. 'Sit, sit,' he said to Amber and Kim. Amber sank onto the chair next to Josie. Jaws settled his body on top of her feet.

The MG waved at Marissa. 'Go ahead.'

Marissa rose and walked over to stand in front of the television, clasping her hands behind her back, as though giving a formal presentation. 'One of my operatives has been in communication with a woman in north-west Sydney. She claims to have vital information about a – tunnel, or possibly gate – her messages have been quite garbled - that the Boneheads were using to, and I quote from her, 'Get into our world.' My operative received the impression that she's willing to share this information in return for us extracting her.'

Josie wrinkled her brow. 'What do you mean, the impression?'

Marissa shrugged. 'When my operative tried to pin her down on this, she became even less coherent. The only thing we could understand was that she said, 'I can't leave. Amber Yu. Send Amber Yu.''

'What?' Amber sat up straight, upsetting Jaws, who snorted his displeasure. 'Who is this woman?'

Marissa moved to the side and looked at Ren, who switched on the television. A photo appeared of an older-style brick apartment building, partly hidden by three tall eucalypt trees, with three levels of apartments. Each apartment had a small brick balcony at the front. Ren clicked a mouse, and the camera zoomed to one of the balconies on the top floor. A woman was standing on the balcony. Ren clicked again, and it zoomed in further, becoming grainy. Amber leant forward.

'Elise. Elise Taylor – Alice and Lucy's mum.' She narrowed her eyes at Marissa. 'You can't trust her. She betrayed us in Dubbo.'

'We're aware of that,' Marissa said, her tone measured.

Josie frowned. 'You said her messages were incoherent? That doesn't sound like Elise.'

'It seemed like she was struggling to get her words out,' Marissa said.

'I guess we don't know what she's been through in the past few months. But why would she want Amber?'

'Maybe it's something to do with leaning?'

'Or it's all an act.' Amber clenched her fists. She hadn't had time to think about Elise for the past couple of months, but now anger rose from her chest into her throat, as though she was back in the compound in Dubbo, realising that Elise had betrayed them. 'It's all garbage, and she's asked for me so she can try to have me captured again.'

'Maybe,' Sam said, 'But it's the only lead we've had on how the PM brought the Boneheads here.' He looked at his tablet. 'The operative has given us an address in north-western Sydney. I want the four of you to check it out.'

Amber could feel her face turning red. 'We can't trust her! Last time she pumped that Quake stuff into me to knock me unconscious! The only reason she didn't succeed was that the power burnt the drug out of me – and even then it left me paralysed for ages. Do you know how scary that was?'

Sam narrowed his eyes. 'Of course we don't trust her,' he said, his voice cold. 'But we need this information.'

The MG raised a hand, silencing him. He leant forward and held Amber's eyes with his. 'We know Elise is just as likely to be taking orders from the enemy as acting on her own initiative. But Sam is right – if there's a chance that she has information that can help us, we need to take it. The Resistance is hamstrung – we don't know where the monsters are coming from, how many there are, what their game is. Ren and Josie will deal with Elise, but I'm asking you to go along in case they need your - particular - skills.'

Amber's heart raced. If only she'd managed to teach the rest of the sword fighters to lean, the MG could have sent someone else. She pressed her lips together and looked at the others. Ren and Sam were frowning at her. Kim and Josie looked relaxed.

'Amber?'

No-one else could fight like her. If she didn't go, and one of the others was killed, she'd feel guilty for the rest of her life.

She twisted her hands together. She was trapped. 'Okay,' she said.

'Does anyone else have concerns?' the MG asked.

Josie, Kim and Ren shook their heads.

'Then please prepare.' The MG looked at Sam.

Sam spoke in a brisk voice. 'We'll meet at nineteen hundred hours on the saddle. Your transport will pick you up just after last light.'

They trooped out of the tent. Amber looked up the hill. The sky was grey with still, heavy clouds, biding their time before dumping more rain on the camp.

She would have to tell Adam she was going. She let out a long sigh. She needed coffee.

Most of their sword fighting group were finishing lunch. Amber accepted a coffee from Ben, helped herself to a sandwich and sat at a tree stump on the edge of the gazebo. She gulped the sandwich in a few bites and sipped her coffee. Elise's face filled her mind. She glared at the trees, the mug squeezed in both hands. She had thought she'd let go of her anger with Elise, but now it rushed back in a roaring flood, as strong as ever. She felt again the moment she'd woken after Elise drugged her with Quake – unable to move, the wooden floor hard under her hips, events that she didn't understand swirling around her. She couldn't think of another time in her life when she'd felt that helpless.

She'd regained control of her body – thanks to the power – but she hadn't been able to stop the Boneheads taking Alice and Lucy.

'You look like you're planning to set fire to the trees,' Ren said, standing over her.

Amber bent her head back to meet his gaze. 'I'm pretty sure they're too wet to burn.'

Ren crossed his arms over his chest. 'I need to know that you'll do what I say on this trip. Not ignore me like you did in Dubbo.'

'Only one time.'

He glared at her.

She tilted her head to the side. 'If I don't agree to do what you say, will you leave me behind?'

'No. I'll get Sam to talk to you.'

'Please, no – anything but that,' she said, in a squealing voice. She rolled her eyes and switched to her normal voice. 'Fine. I'll do what you say.'

'Good.'

Amber watched him stride away. 'Military guys – always bossing people around.'

She took a large swig of coffee and traced a crack in the tree stump with her index finger. Sam said the address he wanted them to check out was in north-western Sydney – where she'd lived most of her life. Where her and Adam's apartment was.

She wondered if the apartment was still the way she'd left it, untouched apart from the door that Lieutenant Colonel Nichols had blown up, or if looters had ransacked it. Her friends Wendy and Helen would try to look after it for her, if they could. She pictured Helen fighting off looters in a bright dressing gown and slippers, and smiled to herself. She'd put her money on Helen over the looters any day.

The smile slipped from her face. It didn't matter if the looters had been there. She couldn't go back. She didn't know if she'd ever be able to. As long as Walker and the Boneheads were in charge, she was a wanted criminal. And how could that ever change? The Resistance seemed so puny compared to what they were up against – their small wins insignificant.

Unless they could figure out where the Boneheads came from, and send them back. She snorted. Keep dreaming, Amber.

She finished the last of her coffee, handed her cup to Chelsea and walked to Adam, Dom and Zac's 'lab'. She took a deep breath and pushed aside the canvas door, wrinkling her nose at the smell of diesel mixed with the damp canvas. The rectangular tent was almost as large as the kitchen tent, but enclosed on all sides. Several large, portable diesel generators were dotted around the walls, running a variety of computers and technical equipment. The tent seemed to be full of people arguing in a foreign language – all technical jargon and acronyms.

'Don't bring that thing in here!' Dom said, as she entered with Jaws at her feet. He made shooing gestures with his hand. 'He left droppings everywhere last time. You need to toilet train him.'

'You try toilet training him. See how much skin you lose in the process,' Amber said, but she backed out of the tent. Adam wound his way through the people and tech to join her outside. They stood under a tree, the rain dripping around them.

Adam frowned, his forehead wrinkling. 'Have you been crying? Your eyes are red.'

'I'm just tired.' She looked down, biting her lip. She drew a line in the mud with her shoe.

'Hey.' Adam took her hands in his, making her lift her head to meet his blue eyes. 'What's wrong?'

'Sam and the MG want me to go to Sydney. With Ren and Josie. And Kim.'

'Oh.' Adam rubbed his fingers over her hands. 'We knew they'd want to send you on an operation eventually. It's what you've been doing all that training for, yeah?'

'I guess.'

'But?'

'They want to rescue Elise. Elise Taylor.'

Adam's eyes widened. 'The woman who drugged you?'

'Yeah.'

Adam dropped her hands. 'Why the fuck do they want to rescue her?' He sounded furious.

Amber felt a rush of gratitude that he felt the same way about Elise that she did. 'They think she's got important information about the Boneheads.'

'Right.' He looked away, into the bush, his eyes unfocused. He turned back to her. 'Are you okay with this?'

'Yes. No. I don't know.' Amber bit her lip. 'She's Alice and Lucy's mum. Maybe she'll be able to tell us where they are.'

'Bec still hasn't found any trace of them?'

Amber shook her head. 'I don't know how much effort she's put into finding them, though. She gets – distracted.'

'Mmm.'

Amber drew more patterns in the mud with her shoe. She took a deep breath. 'I might have to kill again. Boneheads, or soldiers. Are you – will you – be okay with that?'

Adam wrinkled his brow and tilted his head. 'I didn't think you were doing all that sword fighting training just for fitness, you know.'

Amber wriggled her shoulders. 'You just seemed a bit –

uncomfortable – after Dubbo.'

'Oh, well.' He looked away again. 'It was a shock. It hadn't been that long since I'd seen you, and all of a sudden, you had this power, and you were fighting monsters, killing -' His voice trailed away. He met her eyes again. 'I'm okay with it. More than okay. I'm a part of it now, too.' He waved his hand towards his lab.

Amber sighed. 'Yeah, but you're making shields. To protect people, not kill them.'

'Yeah, but why does the Resistance need shields?' He twisted his mouth to the side. 'So that it can kill people. I'm not blind to that.' He wrapped his arms around her. 'I will be fine. Oliver will be fine. You focus on staying safe.'

Amber buried her face in his shoulder, breathing in his familiar scent. 'Okay.'

She left Adam at his lab and collected food, first aid supplies and other essentials from the supply tent, squeezing enough into her hiking pack to last a week. She expected to be back in a couple of days, but things could go wrong. Once her pack was full, she took her sword to the armoury tent. George, a Japanese man in his mid-sixties dressed in a bright red cowboy shirt and white boots, ran his fingers over the sword, making tsk-tsking noises at the nicks and scratches in it. Amber stared at his boots, wondering how he managed to keep them white in the muddy camp.

He removed a whetstone from a bucket of water where it had been soaking, oiled it and started sharpening her sword, keeping up a running commentary on the rain, mosquitoes and deprivations of camp life.

'Every time I have a wash I'm convinced I'm going to have my feet bitten off by a yabby or a piranha or something.'

Amber laughed. 'We don't have piranhas in Australia.'

'Platypuses, then. Or is it platypi?'

Adam approached while George was holding forth on the state of the toilets. He had Oliver on one hip. 'I thought you might want to say goodbye properly.'

'I do!' Amber took Oliver, squeezed him and planted kisses all over his head. What if she didn't come back? Tears filled her eyes, and dribbled down her cheek. She didn't want to leave Oliver motherless.

'Hey.' Adam wiped the tears with his fingers. He met her eyes, his brow furrowed. 'If you don't want to do this, you can say no. I'll support you, either way.'

She sniffed, trying to stop any more tears falling. 'It's okay. I'm okay.'

He nodded. 'As long as you're sure.'

She gave him a long kiss. He took Oliver out of her arms and placed him against his shoulder.

'Stay safe,' he said. 'Come back to us, okay?'

He nodded to George, gave her a last look, and walked away. Amber wrapped her arms around her chest and watched him disappear into the trees. The top of Oliver's head peeked over his shoulder, his black hair tousled. Would she see them again? More tears dribbled down her cheek.

George selected a piece of sandpaper and started polishing the sword, his movements gentle, as though he was caressing the blade. 'You don't seem happy.'

Amber glared at him. 'Why would I be?'

He kept his eyes on the sword. 'Why go, then?'

She slumped down on an upturned crate in the doorway and wiped away the tears with the heels of her hands. 'The Resistance doesn't have anyone else who can fight like I can – yet, anyway. I'm trapped.'

Jaws flopped next to her, putting his large head against her leg. She stared out the tent door at a huge strangler fig that rose into the sky. Its thick roots had fused together into a criss-cross pattern, surrounding a hollow middle where the host tree had once lived, but had long since died and rotted away. A scrub turkey was using its beak to flick leaves away from the roots, its red head and yellow neck bright against the mottled grey roots. For the second time that day Amber thought about her apartment. Scrub turkeys had often roamed her street in Epping, infuriating their gardener by building mounds and scattering leaves and dirt in the garden.

She looked up at George. 'Why did you join the Resistance? If you hate camping so much?'

George ran his fingers down the blade, stopping to use the sandpaper again. 'Same reason you're going on this operation, I guess. The Resistance needs someone who knows swords. There's not that many of us who do.' He held the sword out to her, hilt first.

'Thanks.' She scrambled to her feet, upsetting Jaws, who stood and shook himself. The scrub turkey thrashed its wings and sprung into a low, awkward flight. She slid the sword into its scabbard and pulled the pack onto her shoulders.

'Mind you,' George added, 'If I lose any toes to any damn platypi, I'm heading straight back to Sydney.'

Seven

Amber and Kim climbed the hill to the saddle, dressed in heavy pants and jackets, and carrying helmets. The weight of Amber's pack made her lean forward over her knees. Jaws bumped against her legs.

Ren and Josie were waiting on the edge of the saddle. Sam was speaking with the two soldiers on guard duty. A cold wind blew. Amber turned her face towards it, enjoying the rush of cool air after the walk up the hill.

Josie swung a torch at Amber and Kim's faces. They flung their hands over their eyes.

'You're blinding us!' Kim said.

'Sorry.' Josie pointed the torch at the ground. 'Your eyes are red,' she told Amber.

Amber glared at her, though she couldn't see with the torch pointed away. 'I had to say goodbye to Oliver.'

'Are you really bringing that horrible wombat thing?' Ren asked.

Amber shrugged. 'Nobody else will look after him for me.'

'They've got some sense.'

The thump, thump, thump of helicopter blades interrupted them. They searched the sky. Amber's heart pounded in her chest. For so long, that sound had signalled the enemy. She squeezed the straps of her pack and reminded herself that this helicopter was on their side.

'Where did the Resistance get the chopper from?' Kim asked.

'Same place we get most of our equipment,' Sam said, joining them. 'Private citizens and governments overseas who think the Boneheads might have plans beyond Australia. I believe this one came from an Asian oligarch.'

The thumping increased in volume, but they still couldn't see the helicopter.

'Where is it?' Amber asked, craning her neck.

'It'll be staying low,' Josie said. 'The last thing we need is to bring the enemy straight to the camp.'

It appeared almost on top of them, skimming the tops of the trees – a squat black machine with four blades and a stubby nose. Its tail boom curved up in a sharp angle, so that its rotor was as high as the blades. The pilot lowered it onto the saddle, keeping the blades spinning.

They pulled on their helmets and lowered the visors. Sam raised an arm towards the two crew members. The pilot gave him a thumbs up. Ren, Josie, Amber and Kim ran to a wide doorway on the side, keeping their heads low. Two machine guns were set in mounts on either side of the doorway. Josie climbed in and took their packs from them, storing them in the back.

Amber knelt to pick up Jaws with both hands. She pushed him inside and climbed in. The inside of the helicopter was all black, too. There were twelve seats in rows – more than their small group needed.

Ren slid the door closed. They strapped themselves into the seats. Amber looked out a window next to her. The helicopter rose in the air and sped away from the saddle, over the dark forest, so low that Amber thought they would touch the tops of the trees. They left Barrington behind, flying over agricultural land. Amber looked for lights from farmhouses, but the ground below was dark.

Her stomach churned. She wrapped her arms around it, wishing she was safely on the ground, holding Oliver.

Josie passed around sandwiches. Amber took one and stared at it for a while. She forced down a couple of mouthfuls, and wrapped the remainder and put it in her jacket pocket.

Forty minutes after they'd taken off, the helicopter slowed and started to descend. Amber looked out the window, but there was nothing to see. The ground below was dark. She felt a bump as the helicopter landed.

Ren opened the door and waved for them to disembark, while he spoke to the crew. Amber climbed out first with Jaws. She stared at a long paddock with low grass. Stars lit every inch of the sky, from one horizon to the next, with some small, rounded hills blocking the sky to their west. Kim joined her on the ground. Josie passed the packs out to them, then jumped out herself.

They shouldered their packs and waited for Ren to finish and the pilot to acknowledge them before jogging away from the helicopter. The helicopter lifted off the ground in a flurry of wind and disappeared across the night sky.

Ren and Josie led the way across the paddock. It was harder walking than Amber had expected. The tussocky grass was slippery and uneven. It had been almost three months since she'd worn a pack, and the weight pulled at her shoulders, making her feel unbalanced. Jaws kept getting under her feet.

The paddock seemed to go on and on. Did Ren and Josie know where they were going? Every direction looked the same.

'There he is.' Ren spoke in a low voice.

Amber squinted into the gloom ahead. She could just make out a darker shape against the dark sky. As they approached, she realised that it was a delivery truck, parked on a dirt road. A barbed wire fence separated the paddock from the road. They threw their packs onto the ground on the other side of the fence, and used one of the wooden supports to climb over.

A short, stocky figure appeared at the front of the truck.

'Tev!'

Tevita shook hands with each of them. Jaws made hissing noises. Amber dropped her pack and dug out his bowl and a pouch of cat food.

Tev and Ren tossed the other packs into the back of the truck. They waited, speaking in low voices, until Jaws finished eating and Amber packed the bowl away. Amber dumped her pack in the back and squinted at the truck. It was painted with large logos of one of the major supermarkets.

Tev climbed into the driver's seat. Ren, Josie and Amber squeezed in a row next to him, with Jaws on the floor. Kim sat on Amber's legs and leant forward to press some of her weight onto the dashboard.

Tev drove without lights, peering through the windscreen, his hands squeezing the steering wheel. The windows were heavily tinted. Amber stared out the passenger window, trying to ignore the discomfort of Kim's weight on her legs and Josie's legs and arms pressed against hers. There wasn't much to see – just dark paddocks set against the night sky. Every now and again she picked out a farmhouse, set on a hill, or close to the road, but no lights shone anywhere. It felt difficult to breathe. She pressed her forehead against the cool window and took deep breaths.

Tev turned his headlights on as they passed a dark rest area. He merged onto the M1, heading into Sydney. It was quiet. The truck rumbled over the Hawkesbury River bridge. Amber stared out the window. Hidden in the darkness across the water was the railway bridge that she, Bec, Alice and Lucy had paddled underneath, escaping from Brooklyn. Her chest tightened as she remembered her fear, and the scent of blood from the Bonehead that she had left dead behind them. They'd walked for so many hours to escape Sydney, under the cover of darkness and hunted by helicopters. And now she was going back.

They drove through familiar suburbs – Wahroonga, Normanhurst, Thornleigh. Tev turned off at Pennant Hills and crawled past a small shopping centre. The shops showed signs of damage, though Amber suspected looters rather than soldiers. The ATM near the corner had been ripped out of the wall, and several shop windows were boarded up. Tev turned left into a side street, past the shopping centre's underground car park. A large group of older teenagers in hoodies and face masks were sitting on the edge of the car park, filling empty glass beer bottles with petrol from a large jerrycan and forcing rags into the tops. They leered at the truck. A boy wearing a blue and yellow beanie with a pom pom – the colours of the local rugby league team - stood and mimed throwing one of the homemade petrol bombs at the truck, without letting go.

'What are they going to use those for?' Amber asked.

'Who knows?' Josie shrugged.

Tev continued along suburban streets. Ren spoke into his headset.

'Marissa's people say it's all clear,' he told Tev.

Tev parked on a quiet street of small, brick houses. Ren pointed at the one apartment building on the street, several doors down, on the other side of the road. A streetlight lit the building's facade and garden. Amber recognised it from the photos that Marissa had shown them.

Amber leant over the dashboard, staring at the building. She felt disorientated. The building had few distinguishing features, and could have been a building in any Sydney suburb, but she couldn't drag her gaze away from it. White noise seemed to be emanating from it. Threaded through the white noise, she felt as though someone was calling to her. She rubbed the back of her neck. She had an intense urge to run to the building.

'Can you hear that?'

'Hear what?'

She squeezed her eyes closed and blinked them open. The noise was gone.

'Are you okay?' Josie stared at her with narrowed eyes.

'Yeah. You didn't hear that noise?'

'What noise?'

'Never mind. I'm just feeling a bit dizzy. It's so stuffy in here.'

Ren eyed her. 'Everything okay?'

'Yeah, fine.'

'Josie and I will check the area out before we go in. Marissa's people haven't identified any issues, but we all know there's a good chance it's a trap. Stay here until you hear from us.' His eyes bored into Amber's. 'I mean it. Stay.'

Amber glared at him.

'You can't talk to her like that – she's not a dog,' Josie said. She pushed him in the side. 'Come on.'

Tev opened the driver's door and swung out to let Josie and Ren out. Kim slid off Amber's legs and into the middle of the car. Amber drew a deep breath of the cool night air through the open door. 'Turn on your THONGs, if you haven't already,' Ren added, as Tev climbed back in and pulled the door shut. Ren and Josie hurried away.

Amber dug in her jacket pocket and pulled out two of the round, black THONGs. She ran her fingers over the rotating balls in the surface of the THONGs, watching as they lit up until the lights formed the pattern that Adam had taught her. She pushed one ball back into her pocket and attached the other to Jaws' neck with a light, woven collar.

She glanced at the apartment building again. The world seemed to spin. She dug her hands into the car seat, trying to anchor herself. The white noise filled her brain. Someone was calling her – several someones – not with words, but with a deep, desperate need. It reminded her of how she'd felt when the soldiers had taken Oliver from her.

She needed to go to them. She blinked at the building. Why not, anyway? That was what they were here for. Ren was overcautious.

She closed her eyes and pressed herself into the seat, taking more deep breaths. The urge to run to the building grew stronger. She snapped open her eyes, staring at it. Was she going to let Ren order her to stay?

Her fingers grasped the door handle.

'What are you doing?' Kim asked. Amber looked down. She'd opened the door. Had she meant to do that?

Why not? She should show them that they couldn't boss her around.

She shook her head. She needed help. She reached for the power, but instead of filling her, it skittered away. It stayed within reach, though – not leaving her completely, like when she was angry. She drew her brows in. What was going on?

She swung her legs out of the car.

'What the fuck?' Tev dived across Kim and grabbed Amber's wrist. His fingers bit into her skin.

Amber wrenched her arm free. His grip burnt her skin, but she didn't notice. He swore. Jaws dived out of the car after her.

Her boots pounded on the bitumen. Streetlights created a patchwork of light and dark. The air was cool on her skin.

She reached the building and leapt up the steps to the front door. She pushed the security door, expecting it to be locked, but it swung open onto a stairwell. She raced up the stairs, leaving Jaws behind, and stopped outside a plain, white door with a metal number fifteen stuck on it. Jaws caught up to her. He hissed at her, then rubbed his head against her legs.

The desperate need she'd felt from the car swirled around her brain. She rested her head against the door and gritted her teeth. She turned the door handle. The door swung open, and she stumbled into an open-plan living area.

A woman with red, curly hair was curled on a grey couch, watching the news on a large television. Elise. She sprang to her feet. 'What the -'

Amber ran straight past her to a closed door on the left. Without hesitation, she flung it open.

The room was empty of furniture. Instead, in the middle of the room, a rough arch had been built from bricks, mortared together. The bricks were mismatched – different colours and shapes, some broken. In places, large rocks had been used instead of bricks. No effort had been made to make the arch look attractive.

Amber stared at it, her eyes wide. Her head was full of people calling, with the same desperate need, demanding that she approach the arch. Screwing up her face with the effort, she took a step back, then another. It felt like she was pushing against a strong current.

'Ow!' She'd trodden on someone's foot. Her arms were grasped from behind, and she was yanked from the room.

Elise was standing in the middle of the room, her eyes wide. Ren was near the door, which he'd closed. His face was red. He was glaring at her, his eyes hard and his lips flat. She'd never seen him so furious.

She recognised the smell of the person holding her – Josie.

Ignoring Ren and Josie, she met Elise's eyes. 'What is that thing?'

Elise's gaze darted from her to Ren and back again. 'You must know – how else could you know where it is?'

'I heard – someone – call me.'

Elise clenched and released her hands. She looked at Amber with wary eyes. 'It's the gate.'

Amber wanted to ask more, but her eyes were drawn back to the arch. Josie frowned, and pulled her further into the room. Amber allowed herself to be led, but her eyes didn't leave the arch. Josie kept her fingers wrapped around Amber's arm.

Ren walked to the door of the room and looked in. 'What do you mean, the gate?'

'It used to lead to the Boneheads' world, but it's inactive. Dead.'
Elise looked at Amber and narrowed her eyes. 'Walker shut it
down a few years back. I've never heard it – call – to anyone.'
'Walker built it?' Ren asked.
Elise nodded. 'And opened it. He used to live here.'
'Are there any more?'
Elise opened her mouth to answer, then clutched her head. 'I
can't tell – you need to get these off me!' She held out her wrists
towards Amber, screwing up her face as she did so, as though in
pain. Two flat pieces of metal encircled them, like bracelets.
Amber looked at the pieces of metal and back at Elise's face.
What did Elise want from her? Josie stepped forward and risked
letting go of Amber's arm to touch the pieces of metal. She ran
her fingers around them.
'They seem to be fused, somehow.'
Still screwing up her face, tears now appearing in the corners of
her eyes, Elise pulled at the loose pants she was wearing,
revealing matching pieces of metal on her ankles. Josie dropped
down and looked at them. 'They're quite tight. Maybe if we got
some very thin bolt cutters –'
'No! Amber needs to do it – the power –' Tears poured out of
Elise's eyes. She leant over her legs, her eyes squeezed shut, her
hands wrapped around her head.
Amber blinked at her. What was wrong with her? How was
Amber supposed to do anything about the bits of metal?
Josie stood. She also looked confused. 'I guess you could try
leaning?'
In the truck, it had seemed like the power didn't want her to
lean on it. 'I don't know –'
'Please,' Elise said. Tears dribbled onto her shirt.
Amber glared at her. Was this another trick? An image of Alice
and Lucy flashed in her mind. They would want her to help
Elise.

She gritted her teeth. 'Alright,' she said to Elise. 'For your daughters. Not for you.'

She closed her eyes, took a deep breath, and reached for the power. It skittered away again. Come on, she said. In her mind, she dived at it. The power rushed into her. The white noise filled her mind, louder than before. Dozens of voices called to her. She forgot about Elise's metal bracelets and moved towards the gate. A hand grasped her arm again.

'Amber, snap out of it!'

Amber shook the hand away. Hands grasped both her arms, and shook her. The shaking distracted her from the calling voices, and her eyes met Josie's. She let go of the lean. The call in her mind lessened, but she could still feel it.

She gasped for breath. She felt like she'd been running, but she hadn't moved more than a few steps. 'I can't lean here. The gate – it's too strong. We need to go somewhere else.'

'I can't go anywhere else,' Elise said, clenching her teeth.

Ren interrupted them. He was listening to his headset. 'Kim says there's soldiers approaching – one of them has seen her -'

Amber threw her head up like a startled horse. 'Soldiers?'

Elise's mouth dropped open. 'What?'

Ren moved to the window and looked out at the street, his rifle gripped in his hands. 'I can't see anything. No vehicles.'

'Must be how they got past Marissa's people.' Josie let go of Amber's arms and moved towards the door. She peered out. There were several loud bangs, and pieces of white painted wood from the doorway flew everywhere. None of the bullets reached Josie, protected by her THONG. She returned fire, then turned to meet Ren's eyes.

'Get Amber out of here,' he said. 'I'll cover.'

She nodded, and beckoned Amber over.

'No – wait -' Elise grasped Amber's leg.

Amber looked down at her, noticing for the first time that Elise had large, dark bags under her eyes, which were bloodshot. She'd lost a lot of weight. Her clothes hung off her. Her red curls were oily and matted.

'Come with us,' Amber said.

'I can't – not with these restraints –'

'Amber!' Josie snapped. Gunfire sounded again, and more pieces of the doorway exploded.

Ren grasped Amber's shoulder. 'For once, bloody do what you're told. If you'd stayed in the truck, we wouldn't be in this situation.' He pushed her towards Josie, and flattened himself against the other side of the doorway. He fired into the stairwell, then nodded at Josie. She pulled Amber out the door.

A soldier swung the butt of his rifle into Josie's left temple. She collapsed onto the ground. More soldiers appeared on the stairway, firing at Ren, forcing him back into the apartment. Someone grabbed Amber from behind. Large, gloved hands pressed into her upper arms, pinning her arms against her side. She tried to pull free, but their grip was too strong. A Bonehead. She kicked backwards, but the Bonehead anticipated her move. It dodged the kick, and shook her, hard. Her head pounded.

One of the soldiers snapped a lead onto Jaws' collar. He hissed and snapped at the soldier. The soldier dragged him down the stairs.

'Hurry up,' the Bonehead growled.

A man with short red hair, red beard and ice-cold eyes came into view. Lieutenant Colonel Nichols. His lips curved. 'Amber Yu.' Out of the corner of her eye, Amber saw other soldiers run past and into the apartment. Gunshots rang out, adding to the pounding in her head.

Nichols picked up her left forearm with a cold hand. She tried to wrench it away, but the Bonehead shook her again. When the Bonehead stopped, Nichols snapped a flat metal bracelet around her wrist, identical to the ones on Elise's wrists. He dropped her arm and did the same with her right, then knelt to do the same to her ankles. She kicked towards his face. He ducked out of the way and stood, narrowing his eyes, then punched with his right hand straight into her stomach. She couldn't breathe. She tried to inhale, but the air wouldn't go in. She hunched forward over her stomach, as far as the Bonehead would let her, gasping, desperate for air. Nichols knelt again and snapped the metal bracelets around her ankles.

The Bonehead released her. She stumbled forward and curled on the ground, still gasping for breath. Tears streamed down her face. Through the pain, she could feel something else. It felt like threads, or thin tree roots, were growing inside her brain. She shook her head. A sharp pain streaked through it, bringing more tears to her eyes.

The Bonehead stepped past her and entered the apartment. The gunshots stopped.

Her breathing eased, but now she could feel still more roots, slithering their way through her head. Nichols watched her, the slight smile returning to his face.

She sensed people leaving the apartment, their eyes drifting to her, hunched on the floor. Ren walked out with a soldier pressing a gun into his back. He was wearing handcuffs, but not the metal bracelets that they'd put on her. The Bonehead picked Josie up and draped her across its shoulder, as though she weighed nothing. Amber didn't know if Josie was dead or unconscious. She couldn't concentrate. Her mind skittered away. Several other soldiers left, trailed by Elise.

'Amber -' Elise's eyes were full of tears. 'I didn't betray you - it wasn't me!'

Amber looked at her through bleary eyes. Why did it matter to Elise if Amber thought she betrayed her? The result was the same. She closed her eyes. The roots seemed to have grown throughout her brain. The white noise had vanished. She could no longer sense the voices calling her.

Lean. She needed to lean. The thought came to her through a fog, and even as she thought it, the roots convulsed, sending sharp pains through her head. She clutched her head with both hands. She couldn't think. Couldn't reach for the power.

Lieutenant Colonel Nichols snapped an order to some soldiers. One of them pulled her to her feet. She felt herself stumbling down the stairs and peered through her lashes. Nichols' black pants and shiny black shoes stalked down the stairs ahead of her. Pain shot through her head again. She closed her eyes, and allowed the soldier to drag her the rest of the way down the stairs. The roots burrowed deeper into her head.

Amber felt cool air on her face. Through the fog in her brain, she heard someone call her name. She couldn't respond. The person – a woman – called again, her voice rising as though in a panic. Amber cracked her eyes open.

The soldiers had led her out of the building onto the street, but stopped at the top of the stairs.

Kim was standing on the footpath with her sword drawn. She had blood spatters on her clothes. Behind her, two soldiers lay dead on the ground, their throats cut. It was her voice that Amber had heard.

'Stay where you are,' Lieutenant Colonel Nichols ordered Amber. 'Do not try to help her.'

The Bonehead dropped Josie onto the grass, drew its own sword and strode towards Kim. She backed away. 'Amber!' she shrieked.

Her shrieks pierced the fog in Amber's brain. Amber looked down at her side. Nichols and the Bonehead hadn't bothered to take her sword. The Bonehead would kill Kim. She had to save her. As soon as the thought crossed her mind, a searing pain swept through her head. She fell to her knees, clutching the sides of her head.

'She can't save you,' the Bonehead said to Kim, its tone mocking. 'She can't do anything now.'

Amber sobbed. It felt like an age before the pain lessened, then seemed to seep away through the roots. She loosened her grip on her head, gasping for breath.

Nichols watched her with a smile on his face. 'Thought about it, didn't you? If you don't like the pain, get used to doing what you're told.' He turned his back on her, his gaze on the Bonehead and Kim.

For once, bloody do what you're told, Ren's voice said to her.

Lean. The thought seemed to slip into Amber's mind from somewhere else. She forced her mind away from it, terrified of sparking the pain. The roots dug in, and she drifted away into the fog.

Eight

'I'm just saying that there's something weird about this place,' Nathan said. He removed his fleece jumper, folded it into a cushion shape and sat on it. They'd been sitting on the hard asphalt in the middle of the basketball court since the cool of the early morning. The sun was well up now, warming them. 'If they're using it as a prison, why so little security? And why use it at all, when Canberra has a perfectly good maximum security prison?'

'They do this, though, don't they?' Luke said. 'Use their own facilities, not the prison system.'

'Easier to make people disappear.' Bec squinted at the laptop, which was showing a satellite image of the address that Yorilla had texted her. Until a few months ago, it had been used for playing paintball, and the app still indicated it was a paintball centre. She moved the cursor around to show the site from all different angles. Pine plantations bordered it to the north and south. 'There's probably more security that we can't see.'

Nathan pressed his lips together. 'It's suspicious.'

'You just don't like it because we got the address from Yorilla.'

'Oh, and you trust that Bonehead?' he said, his voice rising. 'The one that sliced Captain Waters' throat open in front of you?'

'Of course not. But Gordon had the same address.'

Nathan looked at Dan, who was standing a few metres away, sucking on a cigarette. 'What do you think?'

Dan dropped the cigarette on the ground and stepped on it. 'I guess it doesn't hurt to check it out,' he said, not meeting Nathan's eyes.

Bec pushed the laptop away. 'We're wasting time.' She looked at Nathan. 'We'll just have a look – see what's what.'

The site was near the New South Wales border, less than five minutes' drive from Queanbeyan. It was a fifteen minute drive from the school, but Ash took an extra half an hour to avoid roadblocks and CCTV cameras. As Ash slowed to drop them off, Bec saw a fence with a sign on it that said Military Target Area. Appropriate, she thought, wrinkling her nose. We're military targets.

Ash dropped Bec, Luke and Nathan at the south-western corner of the pine plantation and accelerated away. A brown, packed-dirt road ran from the road to the site. They avoided it and dived into the trees. The air was several degrees cooler than in the open. Bec settled her pack on her shoulders, enjoying the cooler air on her face. It was easy walking. Pine needles made a soft carpet for the ground. Some grass grew under the pines, but little else. Magpies warbled in the trees. Rabbits raced across the ground as they approached.

A tall fence constructed from green shade cloth separated the paintball firing range from the surrounding bush. Luke drew his knife and sliced a hole in the shade cloth for them to squeeze through. A small bird with a bright red breast landed on one of the fence poles, twittered at them, and darted away.

They passed metal structures, piles of old pallets, rusty cars and metal drums – obstacles and cover for the paintballers. Bec shifted her hands on her rifle, wondering how many people over the years had run around this site carrying guns and dressed in camouflage clothing, the same as her. But those people and their enemies had non-toxic dye in their guns, not lethal bullets, and afterwards they'd have a drink together.

After ten minutes, the pine plantation came to an abrupt end, another green shade cloth fence separating it from a dirt road. Bec ducked low to the ground and peered through the shade cloth. An electricity line ran along the fence. Across the dirt road was a cluster of buildings – an older, rectangular metal shed with a verandah, and several larger aluminium demountable buildings, which looked new. To the left of the buildings was a muddy dam.

A chain-wire fence encircled the buildings. Two utes painted in camouflage colours were parked just outside the fence, in front of the gate. She counted four soldiers moving around the site. Two soldiers patrolled the fence line, rifles clutched in their hands, but they didn't look towards the pine plantation. She frowned. Sloppy. Another two soldiers sat at some long, metal tables under the verandah. One of them flipped through a magazine.

It wasn't just the soldiers that were sloppy. Bec could see a few security cameras attached to the eaves of the buildings, but even from her current position she could see routes around the site that would avoid them.

Bec bit her lip. 'You were right,' she told Nathan. 'The lack of security is weird.'

Nathan took out his camera and took photos of the fence, security cameras and guards.

'I can't think very highly of your friend Zhou, if he can't escape from that,' Luke said.

'He's not the most practical guy,' Bec said. 'He's good at taking photos and videos of himself in attractive poses and writing snappy catchphrases. I don't think he has many actual skills.'

Luke snorted. 'Great. I'm glad we're rescuing him.'

'Gordon's friends haven't escaped, either,' Dan pointed out over the phone loudspeaker.

'Assuming any of them are in there,' Luke said. 'There's no sign of anyone apart from those soldiers.'

'Only one way to find out.' Bec's face lit up with a wide grin.

Nathan groaned and lowered his camera. 'The lack of security –

the Bonehead giving you the address – do they need to paint the word 'trap' in giant red letters on the gate for you to see it?'

'He has a point,' Luke said. 'Maybe we should just watch for a while? See if anything happens?'

They watched the site in silence for the next couple of hours, lying on their stomachs at the edge of the pine plantation and snacking on nuts, dried fruit and muesli bars. The soldiers continued their apathetic patrols of the fence. Bec's eyes glazed over. She yawned.

Out of the corner of her eye she saw Luke's body tense. She focused on the site again. Two men walked out of the metal shed, carrying plates of food. They were wearing green T-shirts and tracksuit pants, like jail inmates. The soldiers moved out of the way so they could put the food on the metal tables. Another two men followed them, carrying plates and cutlery.

'Metal cutlery,' Luke muttered in her ear. 'Even knives.'

Bec frowned. 'Why aren't the soldiers worried about being stabbed?'

One soldier walked to the closest demountable and brought out a group of green-clad people. Bec searched for Zhou, but all of them were women, most of them white. The soldier walked to the second demountable, and brought out a group of men. Bec drew in a quick breath and leant forward on her elbows. Luke raised his eyebrows at her.

'Zhou,' Bec muttered, pointing at a tall, lean Chinese man with messy hair flopping into his eyes.

The prisoners helped themselves to food. They stood or sat on the ground around the verandah. to eat. Nathan snapped photos of each of them.

Bec watched Zhou wait his turn for the food, his shoulders slouching inward, as though he was trying to make himself smaller. That wasn't like him. The Zhou she knew always needed to be the centre of attention.

'Must be killing him to have to wear tracksuit pants and survive without hair gel,' she said, but even as the words left her mouth they felt – wrong. It was because of her that Zhou was here. She rubbed her arms with her hands and pushed the thought away. It wasn't her who had locked Zhou up – it was the Boneheads.

Nathan flicked through his photos. 'I think I've figured out who Monique and Gordon's 'friends' are.'

He held out the camera, showing a woman with intense, brown eyes, wearing a green cap pulled low over short, greying hair.

'That's the Premier!' Nobody had heard from the New South Wales Premier since the protest that Bec had helped organise after Walker cancelled the election. Most of the people Bec had spoken to thought she was dead.

'I count twenty-five prisoners,' Luke said. 'They're not going to fit in the ute.'

'Twenty-five!' Dan said. 'Monique won't want to put them up. She doesn't even want to put us up.'

Bec eyed Zhou. Her throat felt thick. She swallowed. She was sick of planning and negotiating. She wanted to dive down the hill, blow up the fence with the explosives Josie had given them, and take Zhou away.

Luke gave her a sidelong glance. 'What are you thinking?'

Bec squared her shoulders. 'You're right. We don't have enough vehicles, or anywhere to take them. But it won't be just us who are interested in the Premier. Let's collect as much intel as we can, and then -'

'What?' Nathan's voice was wary.

Bec bared her teeth. 'Make rescuing them Sam's problem.'

From the corner of her eye, she saw Luke's shoulders relax. Nathan fell silent. Bec rolled her eyes. They always assumed she'd do something crazy.

She attached the solar charger to her phone, and slid it to the edge of the trees where the sunlight could fall on it.

The prisoners finished eating and cleared away the plates. A few of them brought out boxes and placed them on the metal tables. The other prisoners busied themselves around the boxes.

'What are they doing?' Bec asked.

Nathan squinted through his camera lens. 'I think they're making explosives.'

The day dragged on. Nathan took hundreds of photos. Bec squirmed on the ground, trying to get comfortable. A fly hung around her face, making a droning noise. She swatted it away, but it kept returning.

The prisoners loaded the explosives they'd made into metal boxes. Zhou and three of the other men lifted the boxes and carried them to the gate. One of the soldiers followed, unlocked the gate and watched as they loaded the boxes into the ute.

Bec sat up on her knees, her brows drawn in tight as she watched Zhou lift his box into the ute.

'Come on, dude,' she moaned. 'There's four of you and one of him. Just whack him with that heavy box and you're home free.'

But Zhou put the box down and returned inside the fence. The soldier locked the gate behind them. The prisoners packed away the tools and parts they'd been using, and brought out more food. Once they'd finished eating, the soldiers led them back to the demountables.

Nathan slapped a mosquito on his arm, squashing it and leaving behind a streak of blood. 'You got any insect bite cream?'

'First aid kit, in the top of my pack,' Bec said.

Nathan unclipped the straps and opened the top of her pack. He pulled out the first aid kit, and let out a laugh. 'What's this?' He held up a small blue teddy that had been under the first aid kit. 'Is this yours, from when you were a kid?'

'No.' Bec snatched it out of his hands and smoothed its fur. 'I'm looking after it for someone.'

A smile played around Nathan's lips. 'I never took you for the sentimental type.'

Bec pushed it back into the top of the pack. 'I'm not,' she said, her voice cold. Nathan gave her a sideways glance, but didn't say anything else.

The sun dropped below the trees to their west, taking the heat with it. Goosebumps rose on Bec's arms. She extracted a jumper from her pack and pulled it on.

Just before eight pm, the sound of a car engine echoed across the site. Bec, Luke and Nathan flung themselves flat on the ground as a car roared up, its headlights hitting the edge of the pine plantation where they were hidden. It pulled into a car park and four new soldiers got out. The four soldiers at the site met them at the gate. They had a brief conversation and the first four soldiers left in the ute with the explosives, kicking up yellow dust as they drove out. Two of the new soldiers took over patrols of the fence, while the other two checked the demountables.

'Changing of the guard,' Bec said.

Luke grunted. 'Hope these ones are as slack as the last lot.'

Bec retrieved her phone. 'I'll hang up,' she told Dan. 'Save the battery. We'll call if we need you.'

Dan yawned. 'Have a good night.'

'You too.' She hung up and slid the phone into her pocket.

They agreed to take it in turns to sleep and keep watch over the prison site. Luke took first watch. Bec lay on the pine needle-covered ground, resting her head on her pack. Her eyes ached with tiredness, but she was full of restless energy. Dan thought she was indifferent about Zhou's fate, but it wasn't true. Between them, Amber and Dan had forced her to confront her responsibility for Zhou. She felt her guilt about Zhou as a physical pain – a hard place in her chest. He wasn't the only person she'd hurt – innocent people had died from the bomb she'd left in Governor Macquarie Tower - but in her mind he'd come to represent them all. She needed to rescue him.

She wriggled her head back and forth, trying to make it comfortable on the lumpy pack, and thought of the air mattresses and sleeping bags that they'd left in the school. She couldn't help smiling at herself. Four or five months ago she would have thought sleeping on an air mattress was a great hardship. Amazing how her perspective had changed.

Luke shook her awake to take her turn. 'Anything happen?' she whispered.

He shook his head. 'Boring as bat shit. The soldiers are bored too – they're limiting their patrols of the fence to once an hour.'

Bec had to agree with Luke's assessment that it was 'boring as bat shit'. Apart from the odd patrol by soldiers, nothing happened in the hours she sat, watching the site. Her eyes started to close. She stood and paced to keep herself awake, keeping well within the treeline, though the soldiers never pointed their spotlights towards the plantation. She was relieved when it was time to wake Nathan to take over.

It was hot when she woke. Sweat beaded on her face, and on the skin covered by her warm jumper. She sat up and pulled the jumper off. The sun was well up in the sky. A flock of sulphur-crested cockatoos flew over, filling the air with their harsh cries. A pair of grey fantails fluttered on the ground nearby.

Luke and Nathan had their eyes on the site, where most of the prisoners were sitting around the tables.

'What's happening?'

'Nothing much,' Luke said. 'We thought we'd let you sleep. The prisoners had breakfast, and now they're working on explosives again.'

Bec couldn't see Zhou. She scanned the site. Four of the prisoners were working in a garden near the north-eastern side of the fence. Zhou was among them.

She felt a sudden surge of frustration. She'd go mad if she had to spend another minute sitting on the edge of the pine plantation. 'I'm going down there.'

'I thought we were just collecting intel?' Nathan said.

'Change of plans.'

Luke rolled his eyes. 'I'll come with you.'

Bec swung her rifle over one shoulder and picked her way through the trees to the eastern edge of the plantation. She disturbed a grey kangaroo, which loped away with an easy stride, and passed a red termite mound, almost as tall as her.

She stared at Zhou, who was using a shovel to dig in the hard ground. 'Think we can get over there without being spotted?'

'With the quality of soldiers they've got here?' Luke snorted. 'Definitely. Ask Nath where the soldiers are.'

Bec called Nathan on her phone. 'Can you see where the soldiers are?'

'They're watching the prisoners working on the explosives. Not watching the fence at all.'

'What did I tell you?' Luke said.

'Let's go,' Bec said. They bent over, keeping as low as possible, and dashed across the road to the trees on the other side. Her stomach growled. She should have had some breakfast. Too late now.

This wasn't part of the plantation. The trees were spread haphazardly around, with large spaces between them. Hoping that the soldiers didn't get a sudden urge to patrol, they ran from tree to tree to the north-eastern corner of the site.

One of the prisoners was working close to the fence. He had his head low, a cap covering it. Zhou was further away, over a slight rise. She wouldn't be able to get his attention without also alerting this prisoner. She bit her lip, wondering if she dared trust him.

She'd come this far – she wasn't leaving without talking to

Zhou. She crawled to the fence, followed by Luke, and whistled. The prisoner jerked his head up, looking straight at her. His mouth dropped open in a wide O.

Bec nodded her head at Zhou.

'I need to talk to him.'

The prisoner straightened, looked at Zhou, and back at them. He took his cap off and rubbed his bald head. For a moment, Bec wondered if she'd made a big mistake, but he nodded and walked over to murmur in Zhou's ear.

Zhou swung around and met Bec's eyes. He dropped his shovel, and scrambled to pick it up, squeezing it with both hands, so tight that the veins in his hands popped out. He checked behind him, his eyes darting around the site, then hurried over to the fence. He knelt down as though he was weeding. The other prisoner joined him.

'Bec?' Zhou muttered out of the side of his mouth, without looking at her. 'What the hell are you doing here?'

Bec gave the other prisoner a suspicious look.

'This is Rob,' Zhou said. 'You can talk in front of him.'

Bec shrugged. 'Rescue mission, of course. Sorry it took a while – it's been a busy few months. Plus I didn't know where you were.'

'You came to rescue me?' Zhou straightened and ran his hands through his hair. Remembering that he was supposed to be weeding, he dropped back down. 'I can't leave. None of us can.'

'He's right,' Rob said.

'What are you talking about? There's like a handful of useless soldiers, some poorly positioned cameras and this fence,' she flicked a finger at the fence, 'Which I could blow up in two minutes. We've got some logistics to figure out, but my team can handle it.'

Zhou shook his head. 'It's not the soldiers and fence that are keeping us here. It's these.' He held out his hands, showing her two flat pieces of metal around his wrists, and matching ones around his ankles.

'What the hell are those?'

'Restraints,' Rob said.

Bec frowned. 'They don't look like they're restraining you.'

'They don't work like cuffs, they get into your head,' Zhou said. 'If we even try to think about escaping, we get the most piercing headache you've ever felt. And if we leave – they'll kill us.'

'Some of the younger guys tried to escape not long after we got here.' An exhausted sadness filled Rob's voice. 'We watched them die – writhing on the ground in pain. We couldn't do anything for them.'

Bec stared at the bits of metal, her brow furrowed. How could they do what Zhou and Rob were describing?

'First the THONGs, now these – restraints,' Luke said. 'How much weird ass technology does the PM have?'

Bec looked from Zhou to Rob. 'This is crazy. There must be some way we can get those things off you.'

Rob wasn't looking at her. 'Soldiers,' he hissed.

Zhou lifted his head. 'Shit. Get out of here, Bec.' He gave her a sad smile. 'Thanks for trying. I – didn't think you would.'

'Zhou -'

'Go!'

Bec felt her chest tighten. 'This isn't over. The Resistance is full of smart people. I'll get them to figure out how to deal with those things.' She nodded at his wrists.

Bec and Luke scrambled back into the trees as two of the soldiers appeared, but they weren't quick enough. One of the soldiers shouted, and a moment later bullets hit the trees around them.

'Run!' Bec shrieked.

They ran, their feet pounding on the ground, gasping for breath. The soldiers stopped firing, impeded by the demountables. The firing started again as they flew across the road. The bullets hit their THONGs.

Her phone vibrated as she bounded into the treeline. Nathan was calling her into a group chat. She swiped at it without slowing.

'Are you okay?' Nathan demanded. 'Are they firing at you?'

'Yes and yes,' Bec gasped. 'Start running – we'll meet you back at the bitumen road. Ash?'

'On my way,' Ash said.

Bec shoved the phone in her pocket and forced her legs to keep pumping through the pines. They exploded out of the other end of the plantation onto the bitumen. Nathan crashed out a second later. Bec's throat felt raw from gulping in air. No sign of a pursuit – yet. She scanned the road for Ash.

She heard a car engine, and swung around, but it was a white sedan. A moment later Ash came careening down the road and swerved around the sedan, screeching to a halt next to them. Bec, Luke and Nathan flung themselves into the tray. Ash slammed her foot on the accelerator and roared away.

Bec clung to the edge of the tray. The wind whipped her face. She felt her breathing and heart rate slow after their mad dash. Luke scanned the sky, his brow furrowed.

He saw Bec looking at him. 'Chopper!'

Bec lifted her head. Now that Luke had pointed it out, she could make out the throb of a helicopter over the sound of the ute.

She pulled her phone out of her pocket. 'Ash – helicopter.'

'Shit,' Ash said. 'Dan?'

'Property on your left – two hundred metres,' Dan said. 'Have you turned that vehicle THONG on?'

'Bec?'

'On it.'

Ash jerked on the steering wheel, pulling into a rural property. The wheels spun on the dirt road. Bec pushed her phone back in her pocket, scrambled in her pack and yanked out one of the THONGs that Josie had described as 'extra strength'.

A locked farm gate appeared in front of the ute.

'Hold on!' Ash yelled.

Bec grabbed at the edge of the tray with the hand that wasn't holding the THONG. Ash didn't try to crash through the thick metal gate, but swung the ute off the road onto the grass and smashed through the fence on the side. Bec was flung backwards against the edge of the tray.

Distracted, Bec didn't see the helicopter overhead until it reared up in front of the ute. Ash swerved to the right and headed across a paddock towards a line of straight, thin trees – another pine plantation. The ute bumped over the dirt.

There was the sound of gunfire and lumps of dirt flew up behind the ute. Ash zigzagged across the paddock. 'Bec!' she yelled.

Bec bent her knees and pushed her feet into the floor of the tray, using them to wedge herself against the tray. She let go of the edge. There was a loud bang and a jolt as one of the bullets hit the side of the ute. Bec gritted her teeth and ran her fingers over the THONG. The rotating balls set into the THONG lit up as her fingers touched it. She focused on recreating the pattern Adam had taught her, ignoring the bumps and sways of the ute. There was a click, and the helicopter noise was muffled. Bullets from the helicopter hit the ground around the ute, but none hit the ute itself. Three bullets in rapid succession seemed to bounce off the air above the ute.

'It works!' Bec grinned at Luke and Nathan.

'We've got another problem,' Luke said, nodding behind the ute.

An armoured vehicle approached from behind, gaining fast.

'Ash – go!' Bec yelled. She pushed the THONG into her pocket and clung to the side of the tray.

Ash stopped zigzagging and accelerated towards the pine trees. The armoured vehicle overtook on their left side, forcing Ash to the right. A soldier shot at them from the vehicle, aiming for the ute's tyres. The bullets bounced off the air near the ute. Nathan returned fire. The soldier ducked down into the vehicle.

Ash smashed through another fence. A second vehicle appeared on their right – one of the black four-wheel drives favoured by the Boneheads.

The ute was almost at the treeline. The armoured vehicle changed direction, heading straight for the ute. Nathan fired at it.

Bec's eyes widened. 'It's going to hit us!'

She grabbed the side of the tray with both hands. There was a loud bang. A metallic screech filled her ears and the ute tipped.

Nine

Bec's body was flung free of the tray. She clung on with her hands. Her forearms screamed in pain. Her eyes were squeezed shut. One of the packs bumped against her right elbow on its way to the ground, almost forcing her to lose her grip. Her rifle sling bit into her neck as her rifle swung away from her body.

The ute landed upside down. It bounced side to side on its roof, the metal crumpling, then silence fell. Everything was still. Bec opened her eyes. She was hanging almost upright above the ground. She let go, and landed on top of Luke. She rolled off. Her hands were burning. She pressed them against her thighs.

The silence was broken by the sound of gunfire, but nothing hit the ute. The vehicle THONG was still holding up.

'Luke? Nathan?'

Luke groaned. Nathan let out a string of expletives.

Bec peered through the rear window. She could just make out Ash, hanging in her seatbelt. She wasn't moving.

Bec pulled her phone out of her pocket. 'Dan?'

'Still here. What happened?'

'They knocked over the ute.'

'Fuck.'

'I'm putting you on silent.' Bec switched the phone to silent and pushed it into her pocket.

The gunfire continued. Luke peered out of a gap between the tray and the ground.

'What the hell? Aren't they on the same side?'

Bec crawled over to see what he was looking at. The armoured vehicle had stopped within touching distance of the ute. Four soldiers had climbed out of it, but they weren't paying attention to the ute or Bec's team. All four had their rifles trained on something in front of the ute and were firing rounds of bullets.

Craning her neck, Bec could make out the black four-wheel drive. It was parked a few hundred metres in front of the ute. A Bonehead was walking towards the armoured vehicle, ignoring the bullets hitting its shield and landing on the ground around it.

'Out the other side – quick.'

They squeezed out the gap on the right side of the ute. Bec scrambled to the door of the cab and yanked on it, but it was stuck. Luke pushed her out of the way, planting his feet and pulling, his muscles straining, but he couldn't free the door.

The gunfire ceased. Bec took that as an ominous sign, and tugged at the door again.

A gasp escaped Luke's lips. A long arm, encased in black, reached over Bec's head, and took hold of the door. Bec lunged backwards. The Bonehead they had seen on the other side of the ute pulled the door off its hinges. It released Ash from the seatbelt and lifted her out. Bec clutched her rifle with her burning hands.

The Bonehead placed Ash on the ground. Blood dribbled from a gash in her forehead. Luke approached with caution. The Bonehead didn't move. He dropped to his knees next to Ash, and put his cheek next to her mouth.

'She's unconscious, but breathing.'

The Bonehead lifted its sunglasses. Dark red rings encircled its eyes. Bec squeezed her rifle, ignoring the pain from her hands.

'Are you -'

'Yorilla,' the Bonehead said, a small smile playing around its mouth. 'Like I said the last time we met – humans think all of us look the same.' To Bec's relief, it dropped its sunglasses back over its eyes.

'You killed all the soldiers.' Nathan came around the back of the ute and spoke in an accusing tone.

Yorilla sneered at him. 'Just saving your unimportant lives.' It looked at the helicopter, still hovering overhead. 'If you want to continue to keep those lives, I suggest you come with me. They,' it nodded at the helicopter, 'Have called for backup, and several more vehicles are on their way.'

Bec lifted her rifle higher, her hands shaking. 'We're not going anywhere with you. Last time I was in a car with you, you killed Captain Waters without even blinking. And you made me out to be a cold-blooded murderer.'

'That was all your Prime Minister and his pet reporters. He doesn't want anyone to know his 'Law Enforcers' are not as tame as he's led everyone to believe. And I won't kill you. I told you – I want to negotiate.'

'Sure,' Bec said, 'But you don't need all four of us to negotiate with, do you?'

The smile played around Yorilla's mouth again. 'You're learning. But killing you doesn't serve me any purpose. Whereas they,' it nodded at the helicopter again, 'Are very keen to see you dead.'

Bec's body went cold. She suppressed a shiver. Every part of her was screaming to stay as far from Yorilla as possible, but the ute wasn't going anywhere, and they wouldn't get far on foot with Ash unconscious.

Luke looked up. His back and neck were tense. 'We need to get her to a doctor.'

'You are all wanted by your own government,' Yorilla said. 'How will you get medical help without getting arrested? What's your plan?'

Bec shrugged. 'Who said we need a plan? We prefer to wing it,' she said, in her most airy tone.

'Ah. Which explains why my family keeps having to save you.'

'The soldiers' vehicle -' Bec said.

Nathan gave a quick shake of his head.

'It's not going anywhere,' Yorilla said.

Bec squeezed her hands on the rifle, but released as the burning sensation increased. Her mind raced. What options did they have?

'Come with us,' Yorilla said. 'We have a house in the suburbs – a real safe house, not one of those ridiculous places that you consider 'safe'. We can get medical help for your friend there.'

Bec exchanged a glance with Nathan. His eyes were wide and damp and his forehead had beads of sweat on it. He clutched his hands together and shrugged. Bec looked at Luke, but his eyes were on his sister.

She turned back to Yorilla. 'Deal.'

Yorilla's smile widened. Before Luke could stop it, it scooped up Ash and strode back to the four-wheel drive. Luke jumped up, his eyes on Ash.

'Go,' Bec said. 'We'll get the packs.'

Luke jogged after Yorilla. Nathan slid back to the ute and retrieved his rifle, his shoulders relaxing once it was in his hands.

Bec crawled under the ute and pushed the four packs out to Nathan. She bit her lip. The hidden compartment was full of the explosives that Christine had given them the day before. She was loath to leave them behind, but she didn't trust the Boneheads enough to put them in their vehicle.

'Sam's going to kill me,' she muttered, leaving them and crawling out. The sun hit her eyes, and she felt dizzy. She closed her eyes and waited for her head to stop spinning.

'Should have had breakfast.' There was no time to eat now. Nathan was carrying his and her packs to the four-wheel drive. She shouldered Luke and Ash's packs and followed.

A second Bonehead, wearing sunglasses, had climbed out of the driver's seat and was standing in front of the four-wheel drive, blocking their access to it. Bec wondered if it was the same driver as the last time she'd run into Yorilla. Yorilla was right – apart from the two variations in bone colour, all Boneheads did look the same to her.

The driver was speaking to Yorilla in a language Bec had never heard before. The words had the same lack of inflection that she'd noticed when the Boneheads spoke English – a flat, even tone. Yorilla, still holding Ash in its arms, replied in the same language. The driver snarled a reply. Yorilla barked a string of words back.

'Is there a problem?' Bec asked.

Yorilla turned its sunglasses-clad eyes on her. 'Kalliga is less inclined than me to make allowances for differences in our cultures. It is not our way to put the lives of the injured ahead of those of the healthy. I pointed out that you were unlikely to cooperate if we left your injured friend behind.'

Bec wrinkled her brow. 'You'd leave an injured friend to die?' They really were monsters.

Kalliga snarled something else in the strange language, then switched to English. 'Are you judging us, ustiga? It is preferable for an individual to die to strengthen the family, than to stay alive and weaken it.'

'Even if you are the individual?' Bec's tone was sceptical.

Kalliga's face twisted in a sneer. 'I do not fear death. You humans – you reek of fear at the very idea of death. Each of you is like a cornered animal – doing whatever it takes to keep yourself alive, regardless of the outcome for anyone else. You don't need a life purpose; you think being alive is a purpose in itself.'

Bec's mouth dropped open. Kalliga tossed its head and strode back to its seat at the wheel of the vehicle. Yorilla laid Ash in the back. Luke scrambled in after her and sat cross-legged, his legs around her head. Nathan put the two packs he was carrying in with them.

Yorilla closed the door and climbed into the passenger seat. Bec tossed the remaining packs onto the seat and floor behind Yorilla. She and Nathan squeezed together in the middle seat and the seat behind Kalliga. There was no way she was going to sit behind Yorilla, after what the Bonehead had done to Captain Waters.

Kalliga accelerated across the paddock to the dirt road. The helicopter fired at the vehicle, but the bullets bounced away. The helicopter circled overhead, keeping pace with the vehicle.

Yorilla turned to Bec, any expression hidden by the sunglasses. 'That's interesting technology you're carrying. The THONGs your PM gave us shield us, but not an entire vehicle.'

Bec stiffened. Now the enemy knew about the extra strength THONGs. Should she have turned it off? She relaxed her shoulders, dismissing the thought. Yorilla and the helicopter pilot must have already noticed that the helicopter couldn't fire at the ute.

Yorilla spoke to Kalliga in the strange language. Kalliga pulled to a stop and got out. It shut the door, leaving the engine running, and opened the rear door. It gestured at Luke to pass it a large, metal box. Lifting the box onto the ground, it slammed the door shut and knelt down below the back of the car. A few minutes later it stood, wearing earmuffs, with the headband low around its neck, since it wouldn't fit over the bone on its head. It lifted a long weapon onto its shoulder, pushed a spear-shaped object into the front and screwed it in.

Yorilla bared her teeth. 'We might not have your shield technology, but we have other ways of dealing with helicopters.'

'RPG,' Bec said. She'd been taught how to fire a rocket-propelled grenade by the same man who had taught her how to fire a gun. He was one of the leaders of her first resistance group, an ex-soldier who had fought in Afghanistan. The Boneheads had killed him on the same day the resistance group blew up Governor Macquarie Tower. Her eyes filled with tears. She blinked them away before Nathan or Yorilla noticed.

Kalliga moved away from the vehicle, angled the weapon upwards and fired. There was a bright flash of light and a loud whooshing sound. Bec slapped her hands over her ears. Blue-grey smoke surrounded Kalliga. Bec peered at the sky through the car windows. The helicopter had vanished. Bec didn't know if it had been hit or had fled.

Kalliga replaced the weapon in the back of the four-wheel drive – with Luke and Ash. Bec narrowed her eyes. Maybe it would come in handy if they needed to escape the Boneheads' clutches. Kalliga slid back into its seat and drove towards the highway. Bec shook her head. Somehow she didn't think the two Boneheads made many mistakes. If they were confident enough to leave a serious weapon within reach of their enemy, there must be a reason for their confidence.

She looked at the backs of Yorilla and Kalliga's heads, their horns almost touching the roof. As far as she knew, no one else in the Resistance had spoken with any of the Boneheads. She should make use of the opportunity.

She asked the first question that came into her mind. 'What does ustiga mean?'

Yorilla glanced back at her, any expression hidden by the dark glasses. 'Mammal. Or any animal that doesn't lay eggs, really. Which is mostly mammals. For humans – I guess it's a derogatory term. Like you calling us Boneheads, or monsters.'

Kalliga swung the steering wheel and pulled out onto the highway in front of a hot pink convertible, forcing it to brake. The convertible driver slammed the palm of her hand on the horn.

'What do you prefer, then?' Nathan asked. 'Law enforcers?'

Kalliga made a scoffing noise. It allowed the four-wheel drive to cross the white lines in the middle of the highway, and pulled the vehicle back a moment before it hit a car coming in the opposite direction. 'Our family does not enforce your Prime Minister's law – we would not lower ourselves to work for an ustiga.'

'We call ourselves the Anaia,' Yorilla said. 'Loosely translated – the Southern People.'

'An – eye – a,' Bec repeated, fixing it in her memory. She looked out the window. Flat, grassy fields lined both sides of the road, with the odd clump of pine trees or eucalypts.

'Are you male or female?' she asked Yorilla.

'I am an egg-layer,' Yorilla said, 'So I guess in your language that makes me female. Kalliga cannot lay eggs, so you would consider it – him – male.'

So the people who had speculated that the Red Bones and Grey Bones were different genders were wrong. Bec suspected those who had suggested that the Grey Bones were immature Boneheads were wrong, too. Yorilla seemed far too confident to be a child.

Kalliga pulled off the main road and zig-zagged through quiet suburban streets lined with introduced deciduous trees. He pulled into the driveway of a sprawling mansion. It covered three levels, with rendered grey walls and decorative arches facing the street on all three levels. Large floor to ceiling windows covered three sides of each level.

'Where are we?' Bec asked.

Yorilla didn't answer. She pressed a button on a remote and a door to a large garage slid open. Kalliga drove in and parked next to two identical black four-wheel drives. Yorilla swung out and went around the back.

'Where are we?' Bec's tone shifted up an octave.

Kalliga bared his teeth in a mocking smile. 'Our family's nest in this world.' He opened the car door, slid out and spoke over his shoulder. 'None of them will be pleased to meet you.'

 Bec looked at Nathan. 'This is not good.'

Ten

Yorilla lifted Ash out of the back of the vehicle. Luke scrambled after them. Yorilla looked back at Bec and Nathan. 'Come.'

Nathan opened the door and climbed out. Bec felt a strong urge to stay where she was. Taking a deep breath, she forced herself to follow. Her legs felt shaky.

Kalliga had left the garage through a side door. Yorilla strode in the same direction. Luke stopped near the door to look back at Bec and Nathan. His eyes were wide, and his face pale.

The door opened into a huge living area, with sloping wooden ceilings, white walls and tiles and grey carpet and furniture. Living and eating areas and a kitchen with white cupboards merged together. Large, leafy plants in pots were dotted throughout, giving the house the feel of a jungle. There seemed to be Boneheads everywhere – eating, cooking and talking in the same, flat language that Yorilla and Kalliga had spoken. Bec's stomach rumbled when she smelt the food, reminding her that she still hadn't eaten. The Boneheads had to duck their heads at the lower ends of the ceilings, which were not designed for their height. Bec stared at them. None of them had mahogany bony plates – they were all Grey Bones.

Those near the door fell silent as Yorilla entered with the humans, the silence spreading, until all eyes were on them. Bec picked out a couple of Boneheads with the same red ring around their eyes as Yorilla and Kalliga, but most of them had the more common black eyes.

A Bonehead seated at the dining table stood, and strode over to them. The other Boneheads parted to let it through. It was tall – about a head taller than Yorilla. It barked at her in their language.

Yorilla replied, and they engaged in what seemed to be an argument. Kalliga joined a group of Boneheads seated in lounge chairs not far from the door. He leant back against one of the chairs, crossed his arms against his chest and watched, his body language indicating that he wasn't supporting Yorilla.

Luke kept his eyes on Ash, watching for any change in the rising and falling of her chest. Yorilla didn't seem to notice Ash's weight in her arms.

After a few minutes, the tall Bonehead beckoned to the Boneheads in the lounge chairs, and barked a word at them. Two of them stood and strode out the door.

'They'll fetch a human doctor,' Yorilla told Luke.

The tall Bonehead ran its eyes over the humans. Bec forced herself to meet its black eyes, not blinking. It bared its teeth at her and strode away, returning to the kitchen table.

'Come,' Yorilla said again, weaving her way through the clumps of silent Boneheads. None of them moved out of her way to make it easier.

Bec's eyes flickered over them as she followed. She clenched her hands around her rifle, then released as pain flared from the burns on her hands. She could feel her heart racing in her chest. She tried to swallow, but it felt like something was blocking her throat.

Yorilla jerked her head at one of the Boneheads with red rings around its eyes. It fell in behind them. Nathan gave it a wide-eyed look.

Yorilla led them up a carpeted stairway hidden in an alcove at the back of the living area. Behind them, Bec could hear the Boneheads pick up their conversation, their voices rising in a babble.

Upstairs there were several bathrooms and a large number of bedrooms. Yorilla led them past the bedrooms and through a door into a small, paved courtyard. At the opposite end of the courtyard was a small building with a glass sliding door. A low wall ran from either side of the house to the building. The wall and building were both in the same grey render as the house. A bench seat ran along one side of the wall, with grey bricks, a grey cement top and large grey outdoor cushions. Each corner of the courtyard held a large terracotta pot with a small citrus tree in it.

Her hands full with Ash, Yorilla waved at Luke to open the sliding door into the small building. 'Guest wing,' she said. 'You'll be safer here than in the main house.'

The door led into a small living room, with two white couches, a wooden table with four matching chairs, and a small television hanging on the wall. Beyond the living room Bec could see a white tiled bathroom and a bedroom with a double bed covered in a white waffle doona.

Yorilla deposited Ash on the bed. Luke hurried after her and leant over the bed, checking Ash's breathing. Yorilla beckoned Bec and Nathan to come inside. The other Bonehead stayed outside the door.

'Lock the door,' Yorilla said. 'Darmiqua will make sure no-one comes in. I'll bring the doctor.' She disappeared out the door.

Nathan turned the door lock. He leant against the door, his hands pressed against it, as though he needed help to stay standing. 'She called this a safe house? That did not feel safe.'

'Safe from the PM, maybe. Not from her own family.' Bec turned to Luke. 'How's Ash?'

Luke clenched and released his fists. 'The same. Still breathing; still unconscious.'

'I hope the 'human doctor' gets here soon.'

Luke glared at her. 'This is your fault!' he said, his voice rising an octave. 'You always do this! You always dive right in – never mind if someone else gets hurt! We were supposed to be collecting intel.'

Bec's eyes widened. She'd never heard Luke raise his voice to anyone before. Her face reddened. 'You're usually there right behind me!'

'Because you never give me a choice!'

'Hey!' Nathan's voice was so high pitched it was almost a scream. He closed his eyes and took a deep breath in. He opened them again and spoke in his usual tone. 'Enough. We're in enough trouble without fighting.'

Luke pressed his lips together and turned his back on them. Bec sank onto one of the wooden chairs. She trembled. Her hands ached. She checked her phone. 'No service. Dan will be losing his mind.'

Nathan stumbled away from the door and flopped on one of the couches. Bec opened her mouth to tell him not to sit on the white couch in dirty clothes, then closed it again. If the Boneheads killed them, it wouldn't be because they messed up the room.

Nathan switched the television on with a small remote and flicked between channels, with the sound muted. Bec jumped up and paced up and down the small space.

'Can you stop already?' Luke snapped. 'You won't make the doctor any quicker.'

Bec frowned and sat on the edge of the wooden chair. Her leg jiggled up and down. Her stomach ached from lack of food. She watched Nathan flick through all the channels for a second time. He flicked so fast to the next show that Bec doubted he had taken in what show was playing.

She sprung up and peered out the glass sliding door. Darmiqua stood with its feet planted, back to the door. The midday sun was pouring down on its head. The door from the main house opened and Yorilla entered the courtyard with a young Asian man carrying a large bag. He was very thin – too thin, Bec thought – with short hair and a thin patch on top. He seemed very young to be going bald.

'Finally!' Bec unlocked the door and slid it open.

Nathan sat up and switched off the television. Yorilla waved at the Asian man to go in. He scuttled past Darmiqua with a wide-eyed look. There were sweat beads on his forehead.

'This is Doctor Soo,' Yorilla announced. She slid the door closed behind him and stood outside, speaking with Darmiqua.

'She's in the bedroom,' Bec said.

Doctor Soo flicked his eyes towards her, then hurried through to Ash. Luke stood and gave him space.

'Thank you for coming,' he said.

Doctor Soo gave a quick snort. 'I wasn't given a choice.' He put down his bag and began examining Ash. 'What's her name?'

'Ashleigh Callan,' Luke said.

He sat on the edge of the bed and checked her breathing.

'What happened to her?'

'We were in a car crash.'

'Hit her head?'

Luke shrugged. 'I guess so. The car rolled.'

He shone a torch into her eyes, then checked her blood pressure. He gave Luke a sidelong glance.

'Are you prisoners here?'

Luke paused. 'Not – exactly.'

Doctor Soo finished his examination and sat back. 'I can't tell what she needs without a CT scan. You'll have to take her to hospital.'

Bec sighed. 'Easier said than done.'

Doctor Soo flicked his eyes towards her again. 'I recognise you – from the wanted ads.'

Bec opened the sliding door. Yorilla and Darmiqua paused their conversation and looked at her. 'He says we need to take her to hospital – for a CT scan.'

Yorilla frowned and strode past Bec into the room. She loomed over the doctor. More sweat beaded on his forehead and he shifted his feet. 'You will take her to hospital.'

'Me? I -' he stopped speaking as Yorilla's frown deepened. 'Uh, of course.'

'Darmiqua will carry her to your car. You will not tell anyone about this place, or anyone or anything you have seen here. We will know if you do.'

'Of course.' Doctor Soo sounded breathless. He glanced at Luke. 'I'll take her to Emergency at Canberra Hospital. You can call them to find out how she is.'

Luke nodded. 'Thank you.'

'You shouldn't use her real name,' Bec said.

Doctor Soo gave her another quick glance. 'It might confuse her if she wakes and gets called a different name.'

'Better that she's confused than arrested.'

He shrugged. 'I'll say I don't know her name. You can sort it out later.'

Yorilla spoke to Darmiqua in their language. Darmiqua entered, picked up Ash and strode away, with the doctor hurrying behind. Luke sank back onto the bed. His skin looked grey and clammy.

Yorilla turned to Bec. 'It is time we talked business.'

'Can we eat first?' Bec asked.

Yorilla frowned and strode out of the room without a word, but remained in the courtyard until Darmiqua slid back through the door and took up position in front of the building.

'She really doesn't trust her family,' Nathan said, watching Yorilla stride through the door into the house.

'If they're all as deadly as she is, no wonder,' Bec said.

'What do Boneheads eat, anyway?'

'Dunno.' Bec shrugged. 'I'm hungry enough to eat it, whatever it is.'

'What if it's like – raw bugs – or something?'

Bec pulled a face. 'Maybe not.'

They waited a few minutes, but Yorilla didn't return. Nathan turned the television back on, still muted. Mike Davies' face appeared on the screen. He held up two swords. The camera zoomed in. The handle of one sword was wrapped in the black leather preferred by the Boneheads, while the second was wrapped in the brown leather of a sword made by the Resistance.

'Turn the volume up, Nath,' Bec said.

Nathan unmuted the television, but they had missed whatever Mike was saying about the swords. The camera moved away from the swords and the view widened to show a square, brown brick building – the kind of utilitarian architecture that Bec most despised. A woman with red curls was kneeling on the ground in front of it.

Bec started and sat forward. 'Isn't that Elise?'

Nathan jumped up and moved closer to the television. 'Yeah, I think it is.'

Luke frowned and moved to the bedroom door to watch.

The camera zoomed in on the woman. She looked into it, her eyes wide and damp. There was no mistaking – it was Elise Taylor.

Sunlight flashed off something metal on her wrists. Bec narrowed her eyes. 'Look,' she moved closer to Nathan and batted his arm with her hand. 'She's wearing those restraints, the same as Zhou.'

A Bonehead came into view. He was holding what looked like a long rope. Bec drew in a breath. It wasn't just a rope, but an electrified whip. She'd watched the Boneheads beat Amber with one almost three months ago. Amber's back still carried the scars.

'I thought she was working for them,' Nathan said.

'She must have pissed them off.'

The Bonehead lifted the rope and swung it through the air. It landed on Elise's back and flicked back up into the air.

Elise screamed. Bec turned her face away.

'Ugh,' Nathan said.

There were shouts off-screen. The camera swung around, away from Elise, but before it could refocus the screen went blank. A moment later Charlotte Lee's face appeared. 'In sports news, Australian swimming legend -' she began, without acknowledging that the previous feed had been cut.

'I want to know what Elise did,' Bec complained.

'You won't find out watching that. They'll just spin some bullshit about terrorists or something,' Luke said. 'And anyway,' he nodded towards the sliding door, 'Yorilla's back with food.'

'Is it bugs?'

'Looks like pizza.'

Nathan switched the television off. Yorilla slid open the door. The smell of pizza filled the small room. Bec breathed it in. Yorilla dumped seven large pizza boxes and three bottles of soft drink on the table. Bec and Nathan exchanged glances. How much pizza did Yorilla think they could eat?

Yorilla sat on one of the white couches while they ate, standing around the small table. Bec checked the boxes: three margarita, three vegetarian and one garlic pizza. No meat. She devoured several slices. It was delicious – oily and salty.

When she couldn't manage another bite, she wiped her hands and mouth on a napkin and narrowed her eyes at Yorilla.

'Ask,' Yorilla said.

'Why do you want to negotiate with Amber?'

'She has the lechiko. She can close the gate.'

'The gate?'

'The gate that your Prime Minister – the Walker – has opened, to bring our people into your world.'

'I don't understand.'

Yorilla was silent for a moment. 'One with the lechiko can open a gate between worlds, but it requires power – huge amounts of power. They could keep it open for a minute, maybe - long enough for a couple of people to slip through, but no more. But the Walker has found a way to keep the gate open.' Her face darkened and she bared her teeth. 'It is koiakoi - an abomination. It must be closed.'

Bec frowned. 'If Walker's opened this gate, he's not going to want it closed. I'm not sure the Resistance will want to risk Amber. She's one of our best assets against – well, you know.'

'Against us.' Yorilla gave her a mocking smile. 'Yes, I know. That's why I didn't want to discuss our offer with you last time we met – because you didn't know that you needed it. You do, now.'

Bec wrinkled her brow. What did she know now that she hadn't known before? 'What do you have to offer?'

Yorilla bared her teeth. 'I can teach Amber how to remove the restraints that are keeping your friend Zhou in his prison. And several other people the Resistance would like to free.'

Eleven

'Amber.' The floor under her knees and hands was covered in rubber tiles, like in a gym. She pushed her hands into it. It felt soft. She couldn't remember moving from the front of the apartment, but she must have. Her sword and helmet were gone, but she was dressed in the same clothes.

'Amber.' The voices were insistent. She begged them to leave her alone, but she didn't know if she spoke the words out loud or just in her mind. Every time they dragged her out of the fog – every time they forced her to pay attention to what was happening, to think – her head exploded in pain. She wanted to stay lost in the fog.

'What have they done to her?' Kim. That voice was Kim's. For some reason she had thought Kim was dead.

'I don't know.' That was Ren's voice, but he sounded different. Tired. Less confident.

In her head, she heard Ren's voice say something different: If you'd stayed in the truck, we wouldn't be in this situation. Tears dribbled down her face.

Lean. This voice was also inside her head, but it wasn't one she recognised.

Leave me alone! Amber pushed at the voice, forcing it out of her head. She gasped for breath, as though she'd pushed a heavy weight – something physical – not just an imaginary voice. She slid back into the fog.

'Wake up, Amber. I want you to watch this.' This was a different voice. She hated this voice.

She opened her eyes. Her vision was filled with blue eyes, so pale they were almost grey. Red eyelashes surrounded them. The eyes moved back, revealing a smug smile above a short, red beard. Lieutenant Colonel Nichols. He moved to her left side.

She was outside again. She blinked, trying to focus. She was standing in an empty car park in front of a square building of ugly brown bricks, the top stained with black mould. A large metal drainpipe ran from the roof to the ground. Tall eucalypts surrounded and shaded the car park, their straight, white trunks and twisted branches emphasising the ugliness of the building. A black four-wheel drive and three army vehicles were parked on the street.

Two Boneheads with deep mahogany bony plates were rolling out a long rope from the door of the building into the car park – an electric whip. Amber squeezed her hands, remembering the time she'd been beaten by one. Her body shook.

Further to her left, Ren, Josie, Kim and Elise were lined up in a straight line. A soldier stood behind each, rifles ready. There was a large bruise on the side of Josie's face, but otherwise she looked back to normal. Kim's face was swollen and marred by bruises, and she held her right arm close to her body, as though it was broken. Ren, Josie and Kim were handcuffed with their wrists in front of them.

Three soldiers stood apart from the group. One of them had Jaws on a lead. As Amber watched, Jaws got his mouth around the lead and tore at it with his teeth. The soldier wrenched it out of his mouth and kicked him in the side.

To her right, Mike Davies spoke into a camera, held by the same young cameraman who had been with him the last time she'd seen him, in Parramatta. They each wore a THONG on a long leather strap around their necks.

The last time she'd seen him, the cameraman had his hair in a topknot. He now wore his hair short, but he still had his neat beard. As though he felt her eyes on him, he gave Amber a sideways glance.

One of the soldiers forced Elise forward and ordered her to kneel. She did what she was told, a blank look on her face. Her face was pale, which emphasised her bloodshot eyes and the dark bags under them. Amber stared at her. She still wore the metal bracelets – she'd called them restraints – on her wrists and ankles. If she'd told the truth, and she hadn't betrayed Amber, how had she resisted the things in her head long enough to contact the Resistance? Could the restraints be resisted?

The roots in Amber's head tightened, not enough to drown her in pain, but enough to make her abandon the thought.

Lean. She'd thought she'd gotten rid of the voice in her head, but it was back. Could she? She tried to reach for the power, but as soon as she thought about it, the pain screamed through her head. She couldn't think. She pulled back.

Tears ran from her eyes. Maybe Elise was strong enough to resist the restraints. She wasn't.

Mike Davies had stepped aside. The cameraman was focused on Elise. One of the Boneheads lifted the rope, ready to swing.

Amber couldn't watch. She knew what the whip felt like. She closed her eyes.

'Watch,' Nichols said into her ear.

She kept her eyes closed. The roots convulsed, sending waves of pain into her temples. The pain forced her to her knees. She snapped her eyes open. More tears ran down her face.

The whip landed on Elise's back. Elise screamed.

Ren's voice echoed in her mind, accusing her. If you'd stayed in the truck, we wouldn't be in this situation.

Somebody shouted. Jaws had managed to bite his way through the leash. He ran to Amber, his stubby legs pounding across the concrete. She felt another sharp pain, this one like a knife stabbing her hand.

Jaws had sunk his teeth into her hand. The pain of his bite

distracted her from the pain in her head for a second, just long enough for her to think.

Lean!

She reached out with her mind, and felt the power fill her. The pain in her head and her hand dulled. Time slowed.

Leaning, the restraints on her wrists and ankles glowed with a red light. Could she remove them? Elise had seemed to think so. She focused her attention on the ones of her wrists, directing the power towards them, pouring it into them. They heated up. Amber felt the heat as a mild itch, but she knew that when she let go of the lean it would hurt. She ignored it, and continued to pour the power into the restraints. There was a snap, and the restraints broke open, the edges melted and twisted. The roots in her head seemed to melt away, the pain vanishing with them. The red light faded from the restraints on her ankles. Amber focused, directing the power at them. They snapped open, falling to the ground. She was free.

She pulled Jaws off her hand, holding him with her hands outstretched. Blood dripped from her hand onto the concrete.

Lieutenant Colonel Nichols shouted at the soldiers.

Amber put Jaws on the ground. His collar, with its THONG, was gone. She felt a sudden chill and patted her jacket pocket. Her own THONG was gone, too. The soldiers would be able to shoot her.

The soldiers were slow to react to Nichols' orders. They fumbled with their rifles. Amber leant harder on the power, making time slow further. Two of the soldiers lifted their rifles and prepared to fire.

Amber dived at Nichols, wrapping her right arm around his neck. She pulled in tight and wrapped the fingers of her left hand round her right hand, choking him. The soldiers froze, their rifles pointed at her.

Nichols fought her grip, trying to step forward and kick back, or to step on her instep.

She didn't know what to do next. She hadn't realised how difficult it would be to hold him, even with the extra strength and speed that leaning gave her. All her attention was focused on keeping her feet and body out of his reach. Some of the soldiers were moving closer, preparing to pull her off him.

Over Nichols' shoulder, she could see Ren wrestling with the soldier that had been standing behind him. He was impeded by the handcuffs. Josie kicked backwards, catching the soldier behind her in the groin. He hunched over in pain.

The Bonehead holding the rope dropped it and drew its sword. The other Bonehead followed its lead. They approached Amber together.

She was in trouble. She was struggling to hold Nichols. She wouldn't be able to fight off the soldiers or the Boneheads. If she let go of Nichols, the soldiers would be able to shoot her.

Nichols knew it, too. He had pulled her arm away from his throat with both hands. 'Give – it – up,' he gasped.

'Amber Yu!'

Mike Davies sounded very close to her. No doubt he wanted his cameraman to get a great shot of her grappling with Nichols. She ignored him and tried to tighten her grip around Nichols' throat.

With a bellow, Nichols threw his body weight forward and kicked his left leg behind him. She jumped out of the way of the kick and lost her grip on him. He flung himself forward, away from her and towards the Boneheads. As soon as he was out of range, two of the soldiers fired.

Twelve

Mike Davies leapt to Amber's side. The bullets hit his shield and fell to the ground.

'Here!' He thrust something black towards her. It was the black leather-wrapped hilt of her sword. Her mouth dropped open. She met his gaze, her eyes wide, and wrapped her fingers around the sword.

He released the sword and lifted the leather band holding his THONG over his head. He dropped it over her neck. She felt the weight of the THONG against her chest.

'Won't you need it?'

His mouth twisted and he met her eyes. 'I think if you lose this fight, I'll be dead anyway.'

As she turned to face the Boneheads, he knelt to scoop something up from the ground. He moved back to where his cameraman was standing, still filming.

The Boneheads approached together, one on either side of her, with their swords in a defensive position, protecting their bodies and faces. She held her sword in the same position and relaxed into a fighting stance, on her toes, her left leg forward and knees bent.

They attacked at the same time, one striking toward her head and the other towards her legs. She caught the high blow on her sword and leapt to the side to avoid the low blow. The Bonehead that had struck at her legs swung the sword upwards towards her chin, while the other again struck towards her head. She jumped backwards, out of reach. The Boneheads struck again, one towards her torso and the other at her legs. Leaning, she had enough time to see and avoid the blows, but the coordinated attacks left her off balance and on the defensive.

The blows kept coming. She countered attack after attack, her sword dancing through the air. The power kept her from feeling tired, but she couldn't find a break in which to attack. It was taking too long. What if the Boneheads sent backup?

She saw movement on the street to her left, near the vehicles, and caught a glimpse of a blue and yellow beanie with a pom pom. Distracted, she almost let one of the Boneheads' swords catch her on the side. She pivoted out of the way at the last minute.

The Boneheads both struck towards her neck at the same time. She caught one sword on hers, but she was too slow to counter the second. She needed to duck out of the way, but she was off balance and likely to go sprawling. Before she could work out what to do, another sword caught the blow. Kim, holding her brown leather-wrapped sword in her left hand. She still wore the cuffs on her wrists, but someone had cut the linking chain between them.

'I thought your arm was broken,' Amber said.

'Only one arm.' Kim blocked a second blow from the same Bonehead. She turned so that her back was to Amber's.

Now that she only had one Bonehead to worry about, Amber went on the attack. She struck blow after blow, using every move that Kim had taught her in a dizzying mix. She was careful to avoid falling into any kind of rhythm or pattern. Now it was the Bonehead's turn to be off balance. It caught each move, but started moving backwards. Amber kept up the attack, trying to find an opening. She pushed the Bonehead back, away from the building, towards the trees. The Bonehead stumbled on the gutter at the edge of the concrete. Amber swung her sword towards its neck. The Bonehead lifted its sword to catch the blow, but in a quick move Amber dropped the weight of the sword down and swung it up, catching the Bonehead under its chin. The Bonehead fell to its knees. She swung the sword from left to right, straining with both arms to drag it through the Bonehead's throat, and wincing at the feel of the sword catching on skin and muscle. The Bonehead landed at her feet with a thud, blood spraying onto the concrete.

Kim was backing away from the other Bonehead, struggling to hold the sword and block its blows one-handed. It swung its sword towards Kim's neck. With a yell, Amber flung herself towards them. The Bonehead swung around. It lifted its sword, but it was too slow. She sliced her sword into its abdomen, and forced it up. She tugged it out and lurched backwards. The Bonehead dropped to the ground.

She met Kim's eyes. They were wide and damp. Sweat dripped from her forehead.

'Thanks.' Kim's words came out in a gasp.

'Back at you.'

Bullets hit her shield with a metallic ping and bounced away. Lieutenant Colonel Nichols and some of the other soldiers had retreated to the side of the building and were firing at them. Josie and Ren's cuffs had been cut like Kim's, so they were no longer impeded by them. Josie had wrestled a gun from the soldier she'd kicked, and was returning fire. Ren was on the ground, still wrestling with the soldier that had been behind him. As Amber watched, he rolled the soldier over so that he was on top of him, and Josie smashed the butt of her rifle into the soldier's head.

Mike and his cameraman had retreated to the trees. The cameraman continued to film the scene. The soldiers directed occasional bullets at them, but they hit the cameraman's shield.

Elise was curled in a ball over her knees where she'd been left.

There was the roar of an engine and the delivery truck rounded the corner. The soldiers turned their guns on the truck, firing.

The bullets hit a shield and fell to the ground. The soldiers shouted, sounding shocked. Amber's chest expanded, proud of Adam's work in helping to develop the new, extra-strength THONGs.

'Time to go,' Ren roared across the car park. Josie waved at Mike and the cameraman to run to the vehicle and ran to lift Elise.

'Amber!' she shouted.

Jaws launched himself at the Bonehead lying on the ground, tearing at its flesh with his teeth. 'Jaws, no!' Amber grabbed his body with both hands and pulled, but he hung on.

'Yew,' Kim said, forcing his mouth open so that Amber could pull him away.

'Amber!' Josie yelled again.

Amber pushed Jaws at Kim. 'Take him.' She ran to Josie, ignoring Kim's protests.

'Can you get the restraints off?' Josie sounded out of breath.

Amber focused on the restraints, directing the power towards them. Elise screamed.

'Stop! Stop! You're burning me.'

Amber pulled the power back.

Elise sobbed, holding both wrists with the opposite hand.

Josie lifted Amber's wrists. There were white welts all the way around both. 'Is that how you got them off? By burning your skin?'

Amber blinked. 'I didn't notice.' When she stopped leaning, that was going to hurt.

'We need to go,' Josie said, trying to lift Elise.

'I can't,' Elise wailed.

Josie looked at Amber. Amber shook her head. 'She can't, not with those things on. Trust me. Should I try again?'

'No, no, no.' Tears streamed down Elise's face.

'Go,' Josie said, standing. When Amber didn't move, she

yanked her to her feet.

A hand grabbed her ankle.

'Amber.' Elise's voice was hoarse. 'My girls.' She winced and closed her eyes, clutching her head. The rest of her words came out in a rush. 'The PM wants to use them – he thinks they're like you. Please – save them.'

Josie tugged at Amber's arm. Amber didn't know what to say to Elise. Nobody knew where Alice and Lucy were.

Elise forced her eyes open and met Amber's. 'Please.'

If Bec were here, she wouldn't hesitate to lie. It was a kindness. Amber channelled Bec – making her voice firm and confident. 'Don't worry, I'll get them out.'

Elise closed her eyes and fell forward over her knees. Josie tugged Amber's arm again, and they ran to the vehicle.

Ren opened the door at the back of the truck. Their packs were still there. 'You'll have to go in the back.'

Josie pulled back. 'No way.'

Ren pushed her towards the dark space. 'Just for a few minutes until we can change vehicles. We don't have time to argue – the soldiers will be getting backup.'

Swearing under her breath, Josie climbed in. Amber followed. Ren slammed the door shut, plunging them into darkness. The last thing Amber saw was Lieutenant Colonel Nichols drag Elise to her feet.

Amber couldn't see a thing. She could feel the packs behind her and hear Josie fumbling among them.

The truck swerved, and she was flung sideways. One of the packs landed against her side.

'Fuck!' Josie said.

'Why did Tev bring this stupid truck? How can he outrun the enemy in this?'

Josie swore again as the truck swerved in the opposite direction.

'There's so few cars on the roads at the moment, any other vehicle sticks out like a sore thumb. Delivery trucks are about the only things that are inconspicuous.'

'Except that they'll be looking for one, now.'

'Ren said we'll be changing vehicles in a few minutes. I'll kill him if he was bloody lying about that. Ah – found it.' Josie switched on a torch, casting a yellow light over the space. 'That's better. I knew it was in my pack somewhere.' She shivered. 'It's fucking cold.' She flashed the torch towards Amber. 'Aren't you cold?'

'I'm still leaning.'

'Shouldn't you let it go?'

'I don't think this trip will be improved by vomit flying around the truck.'

Josie pulled a face. 'Ew. I see your point.'

Amber looked at the smooth walls. 'Does this thing have ventilation?'

Josie snorted. 'No. The truck's refrigerated. That's why it's so bloody cold. Don't worry, we'll be fine for a few hours.'

'Okay.'

Josie gave her a sidelong look. 'I expected you to freak out.'

'I think I used up my quota of freaking out for today.' She curled her legs and rested her head on her knees. Tears dribbled down her face. 'We left Elise.'

Josie tilted her head. 'I thought you had a massive grudge against her.'

'Yeah, well.' Amber buried her face in her knees for a moment. 'Those restraints – I had no idea such a thing existed. I couldn't bear it – the pain. I don't know how Elise stands it.'

Josie considered her for a moment. 'We can't save everyone.'

'Yeah. I know.' But if she ever did see Alice and Lucy again, how would she explain to them that she'd left their mum behind?

The truck swerved again, sending several packs flying, then crunched to a halt. A few moments later Ren opened the back door.

Josie gave him a punch as she climbed out. 'Don't ever make me travel in there again.'

'Not a problem. We're dumping the truck.'

Amber jumped down onto concrete. They were in an underground car park. It reminded her of the car park under her apartment in Epping – full of individual garages with roller doors, plus a couple of spare car spaces with 'Visitors car park' above them. Someone had stuck a piece of A4 paper to the first one with sticky tape, with the words 'Visitors only!!!' written in black marker and underlined three times. Most of the garage doors were closed and locked, but she could see two that were open. One was empty, and the other had a dark blue four-wheel drive parked in it. 'Where are we?'

Ren turned his gaze on her. His eyes were icy cold. He spoke in a clipped voice. 'Random apartment car park. Erin directed us here.' He nodded at a tall woman with short, silver hair, large tortoiseshell glasses and a wide smile who was hovering nearby. She was dressed in a grey suit with a light grey scarf. Amber guessed she was one of Marissa's people, although she didn't look anything like Amber would expect an intelligence agent to look.

'Did the soldiers follow us?'

A slight smile played around Ren's lips. 'They tried. But all their tyres had been slashed.'

'Those kids!' Amber said. 'That's what they were doing.'

'Tev convinced them it would be a more useful contribution to the war effort than flinging petrol bombs at army vehicles.'

'Amazing, Tev,' Josie said, as Tev swung out of the vehicle. 'Can't believe those kids listened to you.'

Tev grinned. 'It may have helped that I took them several cases of beer. I would have done it myself, but I didn't want to leave the truck.'

Kim climbed out and made a beeline to Amber, holding Jaws in front of her body with her left arm. 'You can have this monster.' Amber took him. 'Look what he did!' Kim held out her arm, which had deep scratches on it. Spots of blood bubbled out of the scratches.

Amber winced. 'Sorry.' Jaws struggled in her arms. She dumped him on the floor, and he trotted off to sniff the garage, making snuffling noises.

Mike and his cameraman climbed out of the truck. They hung back from the group. Amber looked at Mike. 'Thank you. I would have been screwed if you hadn't given me the sword.'

Mike rubbed the back of his neck. 'Thank Will,' he said, nudging his cameraman. 'He talked me into it. Said you were the only hope any of us have of getting out of this mess, and we'd better keep you alive.'

Amber frowned and looked at her feet. She didn't want anyone relying on her. Especially after what had happened at the apartment. Why hadn't she stayed in the truck?

She looked at Kim. 'Are you still leaning?'

Kim gave her a blank look. 'Oh, yeah.'

'We need to let it go.'

Ren turned to Erin. 'Don't suppose you've got any buckets?' Amber scowled. The smile returned to Ren's lips. He seemed quite pleased that she was about to suffer.

'I'll see.' Erin bustled away, through a door at the back of the garage. Amber rummaged in her pack and pulled out two small bowls. She scraped some cat food into one, and poured some water from her water bottle into the other. She tipped her head back and drank the rest of the water in one long gulp. Jaws raced over and buried his face in the cat food.

Erin returned with a couple of metal basins. 'Will these do?'

Ren passed them to Amber and Kim.

Amber sighed. She put the basin on the ground and knelt next to it. Mike and Will were watching her with curious looks on their faces. She turned inward and let go of the power. A burning pain from her wrists ran up her arms. Her eyes filled with tears. Her stomach churned, and she vomited. Her wrists felt white hot. The pain made her head spin. She vomited again. She gasped for air, and vomited a third time. The basin wasn't big enough, and the vomit slopped over the sides. A few tears dribbled down her face.

She lifted her head. Mike and Will were no longer watching her. They were kneeling next to Kim, who was lying on her back on the ground, with Erin and Ren kneeling over her. Josie and Tev stood nearby, watching.

Ren was counting out loud to a fast, even beat, and pushing Kim's chest with his hands. Amber realised, horrified, that he was doing CPR.

Water. She needed water. There was a tap just outside the entry to the car park. Amber stumbled to it and wrenched the handle around. She plunged her wrists under the water, gasping as the water reduced the pain.

Ren reached the number thirty, and paused. Erin pinched Kim's nose and pushed her head back, placing her mouth over Kim's. She breathed into Kim's mouth, turned her head to the side, and breathed into her mouth again. She nodded to Ren. He started counting and pumping Kim's chest again.

Tev nudged Josie and muttered something in her ear. She turned around, her eyes widening when she saw Amber. She strode to the entrance to the car park, staying just underneath the concrete ceiling.

'Amber! You need to stay undercover.' She searched the sky.

Amber didn't move. She didn't care if there was a helicopter full of Boneheads hovering right above her head. She wasn't taking her wrists out from under the water.

'What happened to Kim?'

Josie shook her head. 'She just did what you did – knelt on the ground in front of the basin and closed her eyes – and collapsed. Ren said something like that happened to her before? At Base?'

'Yeah, she fainted, but she was fine afterwards. Reena thought it might have been the shock from letting go of the lean. But she was only leaning for a short time – not like today.' Amber felt her body shaking. Apart from her wrists, which sent burning pain up her arms, she was icy cold. Her chest felt tight. Why hadn't she thought that the fainting episode might have been a warning of bigger problems? Kim had said that Reena told her to be careful leaning.

'Marissa's people have called for medical help. We just need to keep her alive until it gets here.' Josie sounded like she was trying to convince herself as much as Amber. She flung her head back, listening. 'Car! Amber, get inside.'

Amber pulled her wrists out of the water, tightened the tap and ducked undercover, clenching her teeth against the burning pain from her wrists. She could hear the car slow at the top of the driveway. It felt strange to worry about one car. In normal times, the roar of cars would be heard day and night.

Josie spoke into a headset, her words tumbling out in a rush. She paused for a moment, then called across the garage, 'It's ours.'

Ren nodded and continued to pump Kim's chest. Amber let out a breath of air, her shoulders relaxing. A budget, Chinese-made sedan pulled into the garage. Two women leapt out.

Amber ducked back outside and stuck her wrists back under the tap, closing her eyes in relief as the water numbed the pain again.

Josie frowned. 'At least keep your eyes open. And your ears.'

Amber snapped her eyes open.

'Come inside as soon as you see or hear anything,' Josie ordered, before hurrying back to the group around Kim. Amber watched between their legs as the two women tried to revive Kim with a defibrillator. Surely it shouldn't take this long? She felt her stomach clench. She watched the water splashing over her wrists and washing over the concrete and prayed – the same words over and over. Please don't let Kim die.

The older of the two women sat back on her heels. 'I'm sorry.'

Ren stood, clenching his fists. 'Thank you,' he said to the two women. He pulled a headset on and spoke into it.

Josie wrapped her arms around herself and walked away to the far end of the garage, where Jaws was sniffing at a wall.

Amber squeezed her eyes shut. She opened them again and looked at the sky. How? She demanded, not sure whether she was asking God, or whatever the power was that she tapped into when she was leaning. Kim had survived! They'd beaten the Boneheads together! How was this possible?

If you'd stayed in the truck, we wouldn't be in this situation.

'Mike Davies said I should look at your wrists.'

Amber looked into brown eyes, a lighter colour than her own. It was one of the women who had tried to save Kim.

The woman knelt and held out her hands. 'May I?' Amber shrugged. The woman reached into the water and took Amber's hands, turning her wrists to look at the burns. 'They hurt?'

'Like hell.'

'Good. I'd be more worried if they didn't. They don't seem too deep.' She sat back on her heels. 'You need to keep them clean. I'll put a dressing on them, but make sure you get a doctor to look at them when you get back to Base. I'll give you something for the pain, too.'

'Thanks,' Amber muttered. The woman strode to the sedan. Keeping her wrists in the water, Amber wiped her face and nose on her sleeve. The woman returned with a bag. She turned the tap off and drew Amber under the cover of the garage. She handed Amber some white tablets and a plastic water bottle. Amber swallowed the tablets and looked away, clenching her jaw, as the woman wrapped her wrists with a gauze dressing.

Erin had disappeared into the apartment building. She returned with several blankets. Ren, Tev and Erin wrapped Kim's body in the blankets and placed it in the back of the blue four-wheel drive. A few more tears dribbled down Amber's face.

Ren strode over and watched the woman bandage Amber's wrists. 'The soldiers are putting up roadblocks. Marissa's people are going to direct us, but we need to leave now.'

'Okay.' Amber looked at the woman. 'Thank you.'

The woman nodded and handed her some more of the white tablets. 'You can take a couple every four hours. Good luck.'

Amber's mouth twisted. 'Thanks.' She hurried to the far end of the garage and scooped up Jaws, dodging a swipe of his claws. She squeezed into the back of the blue four-wheel drive next to Josie, Mike and Will. Ren was in the front passenger seat, where he could relay directions from Marissa's people to Tev. They waved goodbye to Erin and the two medical women. Amber hadn't learnt their names – not even the one who had dressed her burns.

Amber kept her wrists in front of her, with her elbows balanced on her knees. Her wrists burned. The painkillers hadn't done much to ease the pain. Jaws stretched out on her lap and attempted to take bites out of Josie's arm.

'I'm going to make a wombat stew for dinner,' Josie told him.

'Hey, he saved us back there.' Amber shifted him next to the car door.

'Him?'

'Yeah. I couldn't lean with those restraints on, until he bit me.'

Josie glared at Jaws. 'Maybe we won't have wombat stew tonight. But I'm making no guarantees about tomorrow night.'

Amber stared out the window. The sun was pouring in, warming the vehicle, but she felt cold. She thought about Kim's body, wrapped in blankets just behind her seat. Kim would never be warm again.

If you'd stayed in the truck, we wouldn't be in this situation, Ren's voice told her.

For the second time that day, Amber channelled Bec. Get the fuck out of my head, she said to the voice. Arrogant ass.

But her stomach clenched with guilt.

Thirteen

Bec rubbed her eyes. The morning's excitement and the constant underlying worry of being in Yorilla's 'safe' house was wearing on her. The stomach full of pizza wasn't helping, either.

Yorilla watched through her sunglasses, the dark lenses hiding any expression.

'I'll have to put your proposal to the Resistance,' Bec said. 'I don't know what they'll say.'

Yorilla opened her mouth, but Nathan interrupted. 'Bec,' he said, his voice squeaking. Bec swung around. Her eyes widened. Six Boneheads with grey bony plates swarmed over the stone wall with drawn swords: three on either side of the courtyard.

Yorilla pushed past Nathan and slid open the door with one hand, drawing her sword with the other. 'Stay here,' she said, her voice even more clipped than usual. 'Lock the door.' She leapt to Darmiqua's side.

Nathan slammed the door shut and turned the lock. He glanced at Bec, his face white. Yorilla and Darmiqua stood side by side, swords drawn, waiting. The six interlopers approached, taking slow, cautious steps. At some unseen signal, they flung themselves forward in an explosive surge.

The courtyard rang with the clang of swords. Apart from the noise from the swords, the Boneheads fought in silence.

Bec had never seen sword fighting like this before. The attacking Boneheads delivered each blow with complete precision – every move pounding Yorilla and Darmiqua with the maximum amount of force possible. Not an ounce of energy was wasted. Yet Yorilla and Darmiqua held their ground, catching each strike on their swords in a dazzling dance.

Bec felt a shiver run down her spine. She couldn't imagine any of the Resistance fighters being able to stand against these Boneheads without leaning. The Resistance needed Amber – and a million more like her.

Nathan was thinking along the same lines. 'Remember all those Boneheads we saw at Corella Creek Farm? What chance does the Resistance have?'

A defeated look crossed Luke's face.

Bec stared at them. The Resistance was made up of amateurs like her team. If they gave up, the Resistance would fizzle out.

She lifted her chin and squared her shoulders. 'What are you talking about? We've all stood against the Boneheads at least once – and won. So have many others in the Resistance.' She waved a hand at the Boneheads. 'All the style and technique in the world won't help them defeat us, because they don't care enough. Kalliga can sneer that we're like cornered animals, but our fear of death makes us survivors.'

Nathan nodded and squared his shoulders. Luke gave Bec a sidelong look and twisted his mouth. 'You've got a future on the inspirational speaker circuit.'

One of the attackers brought its sword down towards Darmiqua's head. Darmiqua lifted its sword to catch the strike. At that moment, another of the attackers slid its sword into Darmiqua's side. Blood spurted out of the wound, and Darmiqua collapsed.

The six attackers moved back as Darmiqua's body landed with a thud on the pavers. Yorilla hefted her sword.

'She can't fight six at once,' Bec said. 'We have to help her.'

'What can we do against them?' Nathan's voice rose in a squeal.

'Anything!' Bec snapped. 'Distract them, so Yorilla can kill them. If they get her – we're next.'

Luke drew his hunting knife. He nodded at Bec, his blue eyes narrowed. 'Go.'

Bec drew her sword and slid open the door. She rushed at the nearest Bonehead with her sword raised. It swung around with a snarl, holding her off with its blade.

Luke let out a holler as he threw himself at the attackers. His short knife should have been useless against their longer swords, but they seemed shocked by the attack. He managed to nick one Bonehead's arm before it swung its sword up to protect itself.

Another Bonehead lifted its sword over Luke's head. Nathan called out a warning. The Bonehead swung its sword down in a lethal blow.

Just before the blow landed, Yorilla lunged forward. In one smooth move she sliced the Bonehead open from its pelvis to its chest, then drew the sword up and out and swung it in a curve to the left, slicing open the throat of the Bonehead that Luke had nicked. Luke stepped back, gasping, his eyes wide.

The Bonehead that Bec had engaged pushed forward, forcing her backwards. Her legs hit something hard – one of the terracotta pots holding a lemon tree. The Bonehead swung its sword, catching hers and forcing it out of her hand. It clattered to the ground. The Bonehead swung its sword towards her face. Nathan attacked it from behind. It kicked backwards and connected with his groin. He curled forward and dropped his knife, his hands wrapped around his penis. Without pausing, the Bonehead brought its leg forward and kicked backwards again, its foot hitting his face and sending him flying backwards.

The Bonehead faced Bec once more.

The door to the house flew open and more Boneheads streamed into the courtyard. A Bonehead with red rings around its eyes stabbed the one that had been about to kill Bec from behind. Swords clanged on all sides. There seemed to be Boneheads everywhere. Bec couldn't make sense of which Bonehead was an attacker and which was on Yorilla's side. After a few short moments, silence fell. Bec scanned the courtyard. The six attackers were dead on the ground, along with Darmiqua and one other Bonehead. The remaining Boneheads were smiling and clasping each other's shoulders.

Bec was starting to recognise differences in the facial features of the Boneheads. She recognised Kalliga among those celebrating, and the tall Bonehead that Yorilla had argued with downstairs.

Luke helped Nathan to stand. Nathan's face was covered in blood.

'Are you okay?' Bec asked.

He screwed up his face. 'I think my nose is broken.'

Bec winced.

Yorilla appeared behind Nathan. She frowned at Bec. 'I told you to stay inside.'

She'd lost her sunglasses. Bec looked into her eyes, with their disconcerting red rings. 'You're welcome,' she said, her tone heavy with sarcasm.

Yorilla snorted.

'Who were they?'

Yorilla scowled. 'Another family – Tanusta. I don't know how they found our nest - the location is a secret. Someone will be in trouble.'

Bec looked at Darmiqua's body. 'I'm sorry about Darmiqua.'

Yorilla looked surprised. 'Why?'

Bec drew her brows in. 'Kalliga was telling the truth? You don't care if people die?'

'No. Mourning is a waste of energy.'

'Is it because you believe in an afterlife?'

Yorilla laughed. 'Heaven? Or coming back as an ant? No. But in a sense our people live on – through their families. We are all part of the same line, extending back into history.'

The tall Bonehead called something across the courtyard. The other Boneheads turned to look at the humans. The smile left Yorilla's face.

'Come,' she said. 'We have a problem.'

The tall Bonehead stalked through the door to the house. Yorilla and the other Boneheads followed it down the corridor and stairs. Casting wary glances at the other Boneheads, the humans stuck close to Yorilla. Bec wrapped her arms around her. It said something about their situation that she felt the safest place was with the Bonehead who had slashed Captain Waters' throat open.

Once again, the open-plan living area was full of Boneheads – those who had fought on the roof, and many who hadn't. The tall Bonehead picked certain people out of those present and snapped at them in the Bonehead language.

'What's he saying?' Bec asked Yorilla.

'He's giving out tasks to prepare for another attack. That was just an advance, stealth attack. Now that the Tanusta know where we are, they will try again with a larger force.'

The tall Bonehead stepped in front of Yorilla and spoke to her in a loud voice. Yorilla drew herself up and snarled something in reply. Several Boneheads crowded around, all speaking at once. Bec hunched her shoulders, looking up at the towering Boneheads. They were surrounded. Her heart pounded and she felt out of breath, as though she was running.

Yorilla held up a $50 note and pitched her voice to carry over the clamour. 'J'kiro. J'kiro.'

The tall Bonehead nodded. It beckoned a Bonehead at the far end of the room. This Bonehead was shorter than most of the others. Its grey skin was even more wrinkled. Bec assumed it was elderly, although she didn't know if Boneheads' skin wrinkled with age like humans' did. It approached with two large plastic cups, one with bright yellow sunflowers on it and the other with a picture of a cartoon cat. It placed the cups on a nearby table and held out its hand. Yorilla placed the $50 note in its hand and stepped back. The tall Bonehead placed a second $50 note on top of hers. The elderly Bonehead spoke a few sentences.

Bec found herself standing with Yorilla on one side and Kalliga on the other. Kalliga had his arms crossed across his body. Bec looked at Yorilla. 'What's going on?'

'J'kiro. A vote,' Yorilla said. 'It is how we maintain peace in the family – disagreements are resolved by j'kiro.'

One by one, Boneheads came forward and tossed a coin in one cup or the other. Yorilla stepped forward to toss one into the sunflower cup. Kalliga didn't move.

Bec's stomach churned. 'What are they voting on?' she asked Kalliga in a quiet voice.

He cast a dismissive glance at her. 'What to do with you. Yorilla thinks we should stick to the plan – continue the negotiations. Toracka thinks we need all our fighters to focus on defending ourselves from the Tanusta.'

Bec's muscles tensed. 'And if Toracka wins the vote?'

He bared his teeth at her. 'They won't need you anymore.'

'But – we helped you.' Bec cringed as the words came out in a whine. 'We helped you fight the Tanusta.'

'And two days ago members of our family allowed you to escape Corella Creek unharmed. I think that makes us even.'

Bec felt heat rise up in her face. 'That's not the same thing at all! We risked our lives to help you. You – ungrateful -'

Yorilla returned in time to hear this. She tilted her head and eyed Bec. 'And yet you are not so different from us, Rebecca Williams. Your friend Zhou risked his life to help you, too – and how hard did you try to help him? We didn't think we'd have a problem explaining our offer to you, because you'd find out about the restraints trying to rescue him. But I had to feed you his location before you even bothered.'

Bec's mouth dropped open. She took a step back, almost stepping on Nathan's foot. He moved out of the way. Yorilla gave a slight smile and turned her back on Bec to watch the voting.

The stream of Boneheads tossing coins dried up. Kalliga hadn't moved.

'Aren't you going to vote?' Luke asked.

He snorted. 'No. I don't care what happens to you.'

Yorilla snarled at him, and said something in their language. Scowling, Kalliga pulled a coin from his pocket and stepped forward to toss it into the sunflower cup.

When no more Boneheads approached the cups, the elderly Bonehead tipped the cups upside down. Bec looked at the two piles of coins. They seemed fairly even. She felt lightheaded. They were surrounded by Boneheads. If they tried to escape, she doubted they would get more than a few steps before one of the Boneheads took them down.

The elderly Bonehead counted the coins. Bec's body shook. Was her fate going to be decided in such a clinical manner, by monsters who didn't know her, and didn't care to?

The count seemed to be taking forever – like time had slowed, the way Amber said that it did when she leaned. She was shaking so much now that it was noticeable. Yorilla frowned at her.

The elderly Bonehead spoke in a voice loud enough to carry across the room. Yorilla and Toracka exchanged a glance. Both were expressionless – neither showing any sign of pleasure or disappointment. Bec looked from one to the other. She felt desperate. Which way had the vote gone?

'You can stop.' Kalliga rolled his eyes at her. 'You won.'

Yorilla turned to them. 'Come. They prepare for war – it would be better if we were not here.' She jerked her head at Kalliga and strode towards the door to the garage, forcing any Boneheads in her way to jump aside. The humans followed in her wake.

Bec let out a breath of air as the door slammed shut behind them. Kalliga unlocked the four-wheel drive.

Bec pulled back. 'Where are we going?'

Yorilla looked at her. 'Another safe house.'

Bec shook her head. 'No. No way.'

'Where do you want to go? Back to the school?' Bec shot a wary glance at her. A small smile crossed her face. 'I did tell you your 'safe' houses are not safe.'

'Your safe house was not safe, either,' Luke said.

'He has a point,' Kalliga said.

Yorilla narrowed her eyes. 'The Red Bones do not know about the school. If they did, you would be dead already. And that school would be a smoking ruin.' She gave a nod. 'We will take you there.'

'That's not necessary,' Bec said. 'We can take a bus or something.'

'No. We will drive you.'

Bec decided to let it go. 'Can you at least drop us a few blocks away? Monique will have kittens if we turn up with Bone- I mean, if we turn up with you.'

'Deal,' Yorilla said. 'Come.'

She took the passenger seat. The humans climbed into the back. This time, Bec sat behind Yorilla. If Yorilla wanted to kill them, she would have done it by now.

Yorilla pressed the remote to open the garage door. Kalliga drove out and turned left onto the street.

Bec took slow breaths in and out, trying to calm her racing heart. Her body wouldn't stop shaking. She watched the houses speed by, thinking that she had never felt more relieved to leave a house before.

She looked at the others. Nathan was white as a ghost. Blood still covered his face, and his nose was at an odd angle. Luke stared out the window with a grim look.

She needed to take her mind off how close they had come to death.

'That j'kiro thing – you do that all the time? The money – and the cups?'

Yorilla glanced at her. 'It is the way we make decisions when two or more members of the family disagree. Each family member can vote once, by throwing a coin into the cup. In our world we use other items – food, precious stones, q'wakay. I have to say, your money makes it simpler. Either way - to vote, you must sacrifice something. The sacrifice ensures that only those who care about the issue vote.'

'So the Bone – I mean, the people – who didn't throw a coin into one of the cups, didn't care enough about the issue to pay?'

'That's right.'

'You paid more, though,' Luke said. 'You and that other Bonehead – you both paid $50.'

Yorilla nodded. 'Those bringing a matter to j'kiro must pay a larger amount. Otherwise people might bring any minor matter to j'kiro. We would spend all our time voting. Nothing would ever get done.'

Kalliga flew through a roundabout without pausing. There was a screeching of brakes and cars already in the roundabout were forced to stop. Nathan grabbed the edge of his seat and dug his fingers into the leather.

'You will contact the Resistance?' Yorilla said. 'And put our proposal to them?'

Bec nodded. 'How can I contact you to let you know their decision?'

'You can't. I will call you – in a few hours.'

Bec frowned. Her phone was brand new – Dan had only given it to her the day before. She didn't know the number herself. Was

Yorilla that omniscient?

Kalliga stopped in the middle of the road, forcing several other cars to the wrong side of the road to drive around him.

'We're three blocks away. As promised.'

Yorilla fixed Bec with her red-ringed eyes. 'Our family's nest – you must not disclose its location. If you do, my family will hunt you and kill you.'

Kalliga said something in his language, then switched to English. 'And us. They will kill us, too, for taking you there, and for letting you go.'

'Your own family will kill you?'

Yorilla leant back in her seat. 'Of course.' She flicked her eyes to Bec. 'We have been watching you for a while. You prioritise your Resistance ahead of individuals, in the same way we prioritise our families. I respect that. Most humans are too ruled by their emotions.'

Bec squirmed. Yorilla made her sound heartless.

Yorilla gave a sharp nod. 'Some of your decisions are not wise, but I do not think you will disclose the location of the house.'

Luke and Nathan slid out of the car. Bec tossed Luke and Ash's packs onto the ground and followed, while Luke pulled the other packs out of the back. As soon as he shut the door, Kalliga sped away.

Luke watched the vehicle scream around the corner. He turned to Bec and shook his head. 'She knows everything about you. She knows you better than you know yourself.'

Bec scowled. 'I don't think so.'

'I think she likes you,' Nathan said.

Luke snorted. 'Great. Maybe she'll be less likely to slice your throat open.'

'What the fuck happened to you?' Dan had lost his hair tie, and clumps of hair stood out from his scalp, as though he'd been running his hands through it. He probably had.

Bec looked around the long classroom. She couldn't see the Chief Minister. Several refugees sitting on mattresses near the door turned to stare at them. Two children, a boy and girl aged around eight, stopped still in the middle of a game of Tip.

'You swore,' the boy said. 'You said the F-word.' Satisfied that he'd done his duty, he took off again, pushing the girl in the back and yelling, 'You're it!'

'No fair!' yelled the girl, running after him.

Bec put a hand on Dan's arm. 'Keep your voice down, hey? I don't want to give Monique an excuse to kick us out.'

'Speak of the devil,' said Nathan. Monique tapped over to them in her high heels, winding her way around the mattresses and sleeping bags strewn over the floor.

'Perhaps we can talk outside?' she said in a bright voice.

Bec dropped her pack against a wall. 'Bring the laptop,' she said to Dan. 'We need to call Sam.'

They followed Monique into the corridor outside. Monique stopped in front of a bright poster with pictures of fruits and vegetables with smiling faces.

'Where's Ash?' Dan demanded, before Monique could speak.

'Hospital,' Bec said. 'She was injured when the car crashed.'

'Is she okay?'

Luke scowled. 'We don't know yet.'

'How did you go at the site?' Monique asked.

Bec jerked her head at Nathan. 'Show her the photos.'

Nathan took his camera out of its bag and scrolled through the photos he'd taken of the prisoners.

'Are your friends among them?'

Monique pointed at the New South Wales Premier and three other prisoners Bec didn't recognise. 'They are.' She gave Bec an expectant look. 'Do you have a plan to get them out?'

Bec pulled a face. 'We've run into a problem. Have you heard anything about the enemy using restraints?'

Monique frowned. 'No. What kind of restraints?'

Bec hesitated. Zhou's claims about the restraints getting into the prisoners' heads seemed too crazy to share with Monique. Monique lifted one groomed eyebrow.

Bec shrugged. 'All the prisoners were wearing these things that looked like metal bracelets. My friend Zhou said if they tried to escape, the restraints would kill them. So, unless we can figure out a way to remove the restraints, we can't get any of the prisoners out.'

Monique drew her brows in. 'I'm disappointed to hear that.'

Bec was afraid that Monique's next words might be to kick them out of the school. She picked her words. 'We made a – contact – that is willing to tell us how to remove the restraints. But only in return for a favour from the Resistance. We need to call Sam to discuss.'

Monique considered Bec for a moment, then gave a brisk nod. The action reminded Bec of Yorilla. She couldn't help thinking that Monique and Yorilla had a bit in common. Both would be dangerous if you were on their bad side.

'Let us know how you go,' Monique said. She looked at Nathan. 'Come and see me when you're done. I'll see if I can do something for your nose.' She strode back into the classroom.

As soon as the door swung shut behind her, Dan exploded. 'I've been trying to call you for hours. I thought Yorilla must have killed you all.'

'Sorry,' Bec said, sounding anything but apologetic. 'I would have called, but there wasn't any mobile service at Yorilla's house.'

'She took you to her house?'

'Well – her family's house, anyway.'

'They called it their nest,' Luke said. 'I didn't see any eggs though, or any young Boneheads.'

'Anaia,' Nathan said. 'They call themselves Anaia.'

'How did you get away?'

Bec shrugged. 'She brought us back.'

Dan swore again. Bec glanced at the door. 'Let's go back to the basketball court. I need to call Sam and the MG.'

'Anything happen while we were away?' Luke asked, as Bec led the way to the basketball court.

Dan gritted his teeth and made an obvious effort to relax his shoulders. 'You'll want to check out the news,' he said. 'Amber was on it.'

Bec swung around. 'Amber? Is she okay?'

Dan shrugged. 'I don't know details, but from the news it looked like she was kicking butt. Mike Davies helped her.'

'The Mike Davies? That complete dickhead? What was in it for him?'

'Nothing, as far as I can tell. Making amends, maybe? Couldn't stomach collaborating with the enemy any longer?'

Bec plonked down on the asphalt in the middle of the basketball court. The sun was low over the rounded hills and the air was already cooling, but the asphalt felt warm. The sun must have been heating it all day. 'Let's have a look. Then we'll call Sam.'

Dan opened the laptop and pulled up a video. It showed Elise Taylor kneeling in front of the square, brown brick building.

'We saw this!' Bec said. 'On television. But it cut out.'

Dan nodded. 'Yeah, the TV news only showed the first part, but the full video was streamed to social media. The government is trying to block it, but people keep uploading it faster than they can take it down.'

They watched in silence. The video showed Amber grappling with Lieutenant Colonel Nichols – Mike Davies giving her a sword and THONG – Amber and Kim fighting and killing the Boneheads - Amber and Josie talking to Elise - the truck driving away, leaving Elise behind.

'Those restraints,' Bec said. 'Elise was wearing them. Is that why they left her?'

'Or because Elise is a lying, traitorous, b-' Nathan stopped mid-word, aware of Bec's eyes on him. Bec was very clear about her feelings on gendered insults.

Dan shrugged. 'You'll have to ask Amber.' He tapped some keys on the laptop. 'I'll call Sam.'

Sam answered the call from the MG's tent. 'Rebecca. Unless you're calling from beyond the grave, I take it that Dan's worst fears have not been realised.'

Bec gave Dan a sideways glance. Dan ran his hand through his hair.

Sam stepped back from the screen. The MG and Marissa came into view.

'You have some information for us?' the MG asked.

Bec took a breath in. She briefed them on everything that had happened at the prison site, during their escape and at Yorilla's house. Luke and Nathan chimed in with occasional clarifications. Dan added some choice swear words, particularly when she talked about the j'kiro.

Dan uploaded the photos that Nathan had taken. The MG, Sam and Marissa were silent as Sam scrolled through them. He looked up at the screen. 'It does look like the Premier.'

The MG scratched the back of his neck. 'You realise this could be a setup.'

'It seems a bit – elaborate – for the Boneheads, if it is,' Bec said. 'They usually just go in all guns blazing.'

'Governor Macquarie Tower was a setup,' Luke pointed out.

Bec squeezed her hands together. She didn't want to think about Governor Macquarie Tower. 'It wasn't anything complicated, though. They just circulated misinformation about the PM's location, and then used normal intelligence to catch those involved.'

'If Amber closes this gate,' the MG said, 'What's to stop Walker from opening another one?'

'According to Yorilla, the massive amounts of energy required.'

'And she says the gate is in Canberra?'

Bec nodded.

'That matches other intelligence we've received,' Marissa said.

'If the enemy ramps up using these – restraints – it would be helpful to know how to remove them,' Sam said. He looked at the MG. 'It could be useful to free the Premier, too.'

'More importantly,' Marissa said, 'In less than a day, Rebecca has learnt more about the Boneheads than any of our operatives have managed to – even the ones at Parliament. If we can maintain this relationship between us and this Yorilla -' She shook her head.

The MG tapped his fingers against the desk, his brow furrowed.

'If what Yorilla says is true, if Amber closes the gate, the PM won't be able to bring any more Boneheads in,' Bec said.

'We'll be stuck with the ones that are already here, though,' Sam said. 'Permanently. Do we want that?'

The MG continued to tap his fingers against the desk. He shook his head. 'We need more information before we make a decision on the gate.' He looked at Bec. 'I'll send Amber to you – with some of our other operatives – but on an intelligence gathering mission only. Find out what you can, about the gate, the Boneheads, the restraints - but I don't want the gate closed at this stage.'

Bec nodded. 'Got it.'

The MG glanced at Sam. 'It won't be straight away. Amber's not at Base at the moment.'

'We saw,' Bec said. 'She's okay?'

'She's on her way back,' Sam said. Bec noted that this didn't answer her question. 'I'll send you the meeting location and time, when I can arrange it.' He looked over her shoulder at

Luke. 'I'll also send some people to Canberra Hospital, to keep an eye on Ashleigh.'

Behind her, Bec felt Luke's body slump as some of the tension drained from it. He let out a breath. 'Thank you,' he said.

The MG met Bec's eyes, his gaze sharp. 'One more thing. I'm relying on you to ensure our directions are carried out, particularly in relation to the gate. Amber can be – erratic.'

Bec bit back a laugh. She schooled her expression into something serious. 'No problem.'

She ended the call and turned to Dan with a triumphant smile. 'See? I'm the reliable one – Amber is the erratic one.'

Luke snorted. 'Yeah, you reliably dive into danger with no planning, and reliably ensure we get chased by a helicopter.'

Fourteen

It was dark when Tev pulled the blue four-wheel drive over on the edge of a dirt road in Barrington National Park. It had been a long, slow drive avoiding roadblocks and main roads. Sam wasn't willing to send the helicopter to pick them up with the soldiers and Boneheads on high alert.

The car's headlights lit up the roadside, showing Christine and a teenage boy sitting on an embankment on the side of the road, wearing head torches. Two packs and a stretcher lay on the ground below them.

Christine bounced up and gave Amber a one-armed hug. Amber held her arms behind her back to avoid her wrists being bumped. 'I'm sorry about Kim,' Christine said.

Amber buried her face in Christine's arm. Christine smelt of lavender-scented washing powder mixed with a slight musty odour from the tannins in the creek. Amber filled her nose with it, replacing the smell of stale sweat and dry blood from her own clothes, then pulled away.

'Oh, and Bec says hi,' Christine added.

'You've spoken to her?'

'Yeah – dropped some supplies off to her a couple of days ago.'

'Was she okay?'

'Same as always. Except for her hair – it's short and blonde – bleached within an inch of its life.'

'I can't picture that.'

Tev and the teenager lifted Kim's body, still wrapped in blankets, onto the stretcher. Josie climbed in the back of the four-wheel drive and tossed the packs out. Amber and the Resistance fighters dug around in them for their head torches.

'We brought some camo netting to hide the vehicle,' Christine told Tev.

Tev raised his eyebrows. 'I thought I was just dropping off.'

'Sam wants you to come to Base, too. They need you for some new operation.'

Tev shrugged. 'Alright.'

Amber gave Jaws some more food and water. She sank onto the soft, black dirt on the edge of the embankment and watched the others carry the stretcher and packs to the edge of the road. Her eyes ached and her wrists burned. She thought of the painkillers in her pack, but it had only been two hours since she'd last taken some.

Tev drove the four-wheel drive into the trees on the edge of the road and turned off the engine, plunging the road into darkness, apart from the small lights from head torches. Christine and the teenager pulled armloads of multi-spectral camouflage netting out of their packs, and helped Tev to cover the vehicle. Amber's eyes drifted closed.

'Time to go,' Ren said. Amber blinked her eyes open. Standing on the road, he was lower than her. His head was tilted upwards to meet her eyes, the light from his head torch hitting the leaves of a eucalypt above her. Small moths swarmed around the light. 'You okay?'

'Yeah.' She slid off the embankment.

'Here.' He handed her a muesli bar and walked away. Amber didn't feel hungry, but she opened the wrapper and took a bite. It tasted like cardboard, but she felt more awake when she'd finished it. The others were shouldering packs. She put Jaws' dirty bowls into a plastic bag and squeezed it into her pack.

Ren returned with Mike. 'Mike said he'll carry your pack for you. Will is going to carry Kim's.'

'Thank you.' Amber zipped up her pack and sat back on her heels. Mike lifted her pack onto his shoulders.

Jaws yawned, showing his pointed teeth. Mike shuddered. 'I'm not carrying that thing. Those carnivorous wombats are creepy.'

Amber yawned in turn. 'He can carry himself.'

Christine and Liam lifted the stretcher. Their packs looked almost empty without the camouflage netting.

Ren plunged into the bush, holding a compass. The others followed, with Josie taking up the rear. It was the second time Amber had walked into the camp, but they had taken a different route the last time. The Resistance fighters were determined not to create a path that would lead the enemy to their base, so they used a variety of routes and starting points. They were taking one of the shortest routes this time. Ren was concerned about how tired they were, and they had the stretcher to manage.

Amber's world shrunk to the small circle of bush lit by her head torch. She walked behind the teenager, the light illuminating his legs and boots as he stepped over fallen logs and trailing vines, his hands clutching one end of the stretcher. Thick tree ferns, taller than Amber's head, surrounded her, their soft leaves stroking her. Jaws circled, rubbing against her legs. Somewhere outside the circle of light she heard the loud thumps of wallabies fleeing. The low, vibrating call of a tawny frogmouth filled the air. Moths darted in and out of the light.

'Stinging tree,' Ren called. Christine and the teenager took a wide berth to avoid the large plant with the heart-shaped leaves. Amber stumbled after them.

'What's a stinging tree?' Mike asked Josie.

'Giant stinging tree. Incredibly painful if you touch the leaves – it burns and stings, and the hairs stay in your skin, so the burning can keep recurring for about six months.'

'There's ticks and leeches, too,' Tev told him, his voice bright and cheerful. 'So make sure you check yourselves when we get to camp.'

'Sounds delightful,' Mike said.

Amber's legs felt heavy. Lifting them to step over vines and tree roots required more energy than she had left. She stumbled every few seconds. Her right foot caught on a large tree root, and she fell hard on her knees. She put her hands out to catch herself, and cried out in pain as her weight fell on her wrists. Tev helped her to her feet and stayed next to her, steadying her with a hand on her elbow when she tripped. She would have felt embarrassed, but she didn't have the energy. It took everything she had to keep putting one foot in front of the other.

At last, the thick bush opened up. Amber recognised the saddle above the camp. Ren stopped to speak to the two fighters on guard duty. Amber stumbled to a halt, Tev next to her. She stared at the view with glazed eyes. There were no clouds, and the entire sky glowed with stars, but she was too tired to enjoy the view.

Mike nudged Tev from behind. 'Don't stop. The leeches will get us.' He cast a nervous glance at the nearby trees.

A malicious grin spread over Tev's face. 'Come on,' he said to Amber. 'Just down the hill.'

All Amber wanted to do was sleep for a week, but Tev led them to the kitchen tent. Usually by this time most of the camp residents would be in bed, but tonight the area under the gazebo was packed with people, all sitting in the dark, drinking coffee.

Sam stood and made his way towards them. Christine and the teenager placed the stretcher just outside the tent. The people in the tent fell silent.

Megan appeared out of the darkness, pushed past Sam and threw herself onto the dirt next to the stretcher. Christine removed the blankets covering Kim's head, switched her head torch to red and directed the light towards Kim's face. Megan moaned. She wrapped her arms around Kim and put her forehead against Kim's chest, still moaning.

Amber couldn't drag her gaze away from Kim's blank eyes, eerie in the red torch light. She knew she should sit, but finding a log felt beyond her. If she sat on the ground she didn't know if she'd ever get up.

Megan lifted her head and met Amber's gaze. Her face twisted. 'This is your fault. You taught her how to lean, and it killed her.'

Amber swayed back on her heels, feeling Megan's words like a shock to her chest. It was true – she had taught Kim to lean, but she hadn't known that leaning could kill. How could she? She knew almost nothing about the power – she didn't know where it came from, what its purpose was, or even the full extent of what it could do. And now Kim was dead.

And Megan didn't know that Ren had told her to stay in the truck, and she hadn't. If that story got out, everyone in the camp would blame her.

She stared at Megan, unable to defend herself. Her lack of response riled Megan. She leapt to her feet and drew her right hand back in a fist. She drove her fist towards Amber's face. In her fury, she forgot everything they'd learnt in training to avoid telegraphing their moves. Amber saw that Megan intended to hit her – saw the punch coming – but didn't try to block or avoid it.

Amber felt the punch connect with her face, just below her left eye. She staggered backwards, hearing a ringing in both ears. A sharp pain spread across her forehead. Tev caught her under her armpits before she fell.

Christine pulled Megan away. Megan sobbed – loud, choking sobs that echoed around the camp.

Amber squeezed both eyes shut. Tears filled her eyes. A man seated on a folding chair inside the tent leapt up. Tev helped Amber to sit on the chair. She opened her eyes, blinking in the dim light, holding her cheek with her hand. Her head throbbed. Jaws wound a figure-of-eight shape around her ankles.

Ben appeared out of the darkness and handed her some ice wrapped in a tea towel. She pressed it against her cheek.

The ice numbed the pain in her cheek. It matched how she felt inside – numb.

She closed her eyes again. She could hear people talking on all sides of her, but it was like they were speaking from far away. The words washed over her. Jaws plonked himself down on her feet and chewed her shoelace.

'Amber,' Ren said.

She blinked her eyes open.

He was frowning, his eyes on the tea towel she was holding to her cheek. Amber stared at him through glazed eyes.

'Can you walk? The MG wants to see us.'

Amber wanted to say that she couldn't walk – couldn't move ever again. But she wouldn't put it past Ren to get someone to carry her. She nodded and forced herself to stand, the ice still pressed to her cheek. Jaws pulled himself up and trotted next to her.

Sam, Josie, Tev, Mike and Will were waiting for them outside the kitchen tent. Amber's eyes were drawn to the place where Kim's body had been, but somebody had taken it away. Christine and Megan had disappeared.

Sam scowled. He jerked his head at Ren. 'Go ahead – I need to talk to Amber.'

'Come on.' Ren led the way downstream.

Sam followed until they were out of earshot of the tent, then stopped and turned to Amber, still scowling. He waved at her face. 'Kim's dead, which leaves you as the only one who can fight the Boneheads. Now is not the time to be indulging yourself.'

Amber's mouth dropped open. 'How is being punched in the

face indulging myself?'

Sam gritted his teeth. 'You let her hit you to indulge whatever guilt you're feeling over Kim's death.'

Amber felt heat rise into her cheeks. She clenched her fists and bared her own teeth at Sam. 'Did you expect me to knock out the grieving girlfriend?'

'No – I expected you to duck. Are you telling me that after three months of training you haven't learnt how to dodge a punch?' He shook his head and strode ahead, forcing her to walk faster to keep up. Her head throbbed.

She ground her teeth. Sam was a jerk.

Three teenagers were sitting outside the MG's tent, chatting and laughing. She recognised the one who had told her that the MG wanted her – two days ago? Three? She couldn't remember.

She followed Sam into the tent. The rest of the group were standing near the door, all talking to the MG and Marissa at once. Ren glanced at her as she entered. He shook his head.

'Whatever happened to 'It's not all on you, Amber',' she muttered. She slid around the group and sank into the nearest folding chair. Jaws flopped on the floor next to her, his head on her feet. She pressed the ice against her cheek and closed her eyes.

She could hear Ren's voice rise above the others, until they stopped talking. He described what had happened at the apartment in Pennant Hills. Josie added a detail he'd missed. Amber drifted to sleep.

She heard a baby crying. She blinked her eyes open. The ice had melted, leaving her with a damp tea towel. She dropped it on the floor of the tent.

There was a tray of finger food on the floor in front of her, two-thirds empty. Empty plates and coffee cups were scattered around the food. Josie was sitting on the chair next to her, leaving a respectful gap between herself and Jaws. The others were spread over the other folding chairs or on the tent floor.

Sam held open the tent flap to allow Adam, Dom and Zac to duck into the tent. Adam was holding a wailing Oliver over one shoulder.

'Adam.' Amber's voice was a croak.

Adam swung around. He hurried to her side and ran his eyes over her, frowning. She tried to guess what he was unhappy about. Her injuries? The blood splatters on her clothes?

Oliver let out a louder wail.

She held out her hands and Adam deposited Oliver in them. She buried her head in his hair. He snuggled into her chest and stopped crying.

Adam took one of her hands, squeezing it.

'Thank you for coming,' the MG said. 'I realise it's late. But I'd like your opinion on something.'

He nodded at Mike Davies, who pulled four semi-circles of metal out of his pocket and placed them on a small, folding table.

Amber narrowed her eyes. The edges of the metal were warped and twisted, as though they'd been melted – which they had. They were the restraints that Amber had burnt off her wrists and ankles with the power. The burning in her wrists seemed to flare up at the reminder.

Adam squeezed her hand again and let go. He picked the restraints up, one at a time, and ran his fingers over them. 'They look like plain metal bands.'

'They aren't,' Ren said. 'The soldiers use them to control people, somehow.' His eyes flicked towards Amber. Adam didn't notice.

'We've heard about them from another source, which indicated that they can be used to kill, too,' Marissa added.

Amber blinked. She remembered the tree roots digging into her brain and the way they'd flooded her head with pain. Why hadn't she guessed they could kill? Of course they could.

Josie nudged Amber, careful to keep away from Jaws, who was fast asleep. 'Want some food? Coffee?'

'I'd kill for a coffee.'

Josie ducked outside and sent one of the teenagers to the kitchen tent for more coffee.

Dom and Zac checked out each piece of metal in turn. Dom shrugged. 'Can't see anything. Want us to take them back to the lab to check them out?'

The MG nodded. 'Please.'

Adam looked at Amber. 'Should I take Ollie?'

Amber shook her head and tightened her grip on Oliver. Adam gave her a quick kiss. 'We missed you,' he whispered.

Dom scooped up the pieces of metal and the three of them left the tent. Amber rested her chin on Oliver's head.

Chelsea and Claire slipped into the tent with two trays of coffee cups. They placed them on the ground near the food tray. Josie thanked them.

Amber passed Oliver to Josie and picked up a coffee. She wrapped her hands around her cup and breathed in the scent, then took a large sip. She could feel her spirits lift at the taste.

Sam threw himself onto one of the folding chairs, almost upending it, and looked at Amber. 'While you were asleep, Ren and Josie told us what happened, but we're keen to hear it from your perspective. In particular, what did you mean about the gate calling you? And what happened when the Lieutenant Colonel put the restraints on.'

Amber felt her eyes fill with tears. She kept her gaze on her coffee cup, and began to speak.

Amber woke to Oliver crying and Jaws hissing. Her head throbbed. Her cheek and the bottom of left eye ached.

Her mouth twisted. Sam wouldn't be impressed. She prodded her cheek with a finger. It was swollen. Her wrists burned and itched, reminding her that the woman who had treated them had said she should get them checked by a doctor.

Adam's sleeping bag was empty. She hadn't heard him come in or leave. She suspected he'd spent the night in his lab.

Jaws let out a loud grunt and Amber heard the sound of nylon tearing. She sprang upright. He'd torn the tent flap away from the zip. Cursing, she unzipped the rest of the flap to let him out. 'That's going to leak next time it rains, you bloody marsupial.' He'd left a trail of poo on her sleeping bag. She scooped up handfuls of it and flung them out of the tent.

Oliver yelled. She picked him up and bobbed from side to side while she mixed a bottle of formula for him. He clamped his mouth around it and sucked, making loud slurping noises. She closed her eyes and let out a loud sigh.

It was sunny outside, which made a nice change, although she could still hear the odd drip of water falling from the trees onto the tent roof. She had better do something about repairing the tent sooner rather than later. Knowing Barrington Tops, the sunshine wouldn't last long.

She wrinkled her nose. She'd changed out of her bloody clothes the night before and left them screwed up in a ball at the bottom of her sleeping mat, but she still stunk. Oliver let the bottle teat slip out of his mouth and yawned. She dressed him, gathered her bucket and toiletries and slid out of the tent with him in her arms. There was no sign of Jaws.

'Good riddance,' she muttered, casting a dark glance at the ripped tent flap. She set off uphill to the kitchen tent. Jaws appeared out of the undergrowth, covered in burrs. He rubbed against her legs, spreading the burrs onto her pants. 'Thanks a lot.' She tried not to trip over him.

Sarah was lying in a patch of sunlight outside the kitchen tent, soaking up the sun while she watched the kids. She sat up when she saw Amber.

'Wow, that's a serious black eye you've got there,' she said, reaching out to take Oliver.

Ben walked over, wiping his hands on a tea towel. He winced when he saw her face. 'Coffee?'

'I'll come back for one. I need a wash.'

It was a relief to wash the sweat and dirt off in the icy water. The water soaked through the gauze around her wrists, stinging at first but then easing the pain. She closed her eyes and put her face into the water, letting the cold numb the pain in her cheek and eye.

Jaws eased into the water and doggy-paddled towards her.

She lifted her head. 'I didn't know you could swim!' He looked like an ordinary wombat, with his head poking out of the water and his mouth closed, hiding his sharp teeth. He climbed back onto the rocks and shook the water out of his fur like a dog. Amber smiled. 'Don't think just because you're cute I'm going to forgive you for wrecking the tent.'

She finished washing, dried and dressed herself and returned to the kitchen tent. She waved to Sarah, who had moved, following the sun.

Ren and Josie were sitting at a log table, nursing large cups of coffee and looking half asleep.

'Oh good, you're awake.' Josie yawned. 'Sam and the MG want to see us once we've had some breakfast.' She waved for Amber to sit. Ben brought her a large cup of coffee.

Ren pointed at Amber's eye. 'How do you plan to fight with that?'

'It's not affecting my vision. And I assumed we were done with fighting for a while.'

Josie twisted her mouth. 'I think Sam has other ideas.'

'What?'

Ren gave Josie an annoyed look. 'Ignore her – she doesn't know anything. She's just guessing.'

After breakfast, they walked to the MG's tent. Tev was standing outside, gazing up at the slope behind the camp. He turned and gave them a wide grin.

'Sunshine,' he said. The sun poured through the trees. Steam rose from the damp leaf litter.

The MG was seated at his desk, tapping at a laptop. Sam and Marissa were sitting on the folding chairs, talking. Sam looked up as they entered and waved them over. He took in Amber's swollen eye with a scowl.

He didn't waste any time on civilities. 'I'm sending you four to Canberra,' he said.

Amber felt her stomach drop. Already? When they'd just got back?

Josie frowned. 'Amber's injured.'

Sam gave Amber a cool look. 'Amber should have ducked.'

Amber glared at him.

'Not just her eye,' Josie said, 'Her wrists, too.'

'Have you had a doctor look at them?' Sam asked.

'Not yet.'

'Do that,' he said, dismissing the concern. 'It's an information gathering exercise only. I'm hoping you won't need to fight at all. I need you to meet Rebecca Williams and a Bonehead she's – befriended.'

Josie's eyes widened.

Ren let out a bark of laughter. 'If anyone was going to befriend one of the monsters, it's her.'

'I'm not sure befriended is the right word.' The MG joined them and sat down. 'More like an alliance for mutual convenience.'

Amber squeezed her hands together. It would be good to see Bec again. But – a Bonehead?

'So – what does this Bonehead want?' Josie asked.

'She wants Amber to close the gate that Walker is using to bring the Boneheads into Australia,' the MG said. 'Which you are not to do – at least not yet.'

'Why does she want it closed?'

'We don't know,' Marissa said. 'I'm hoping you'll find out.'

Amber felt a shiver run down her spine. She squeezed her hands so tight that it hurt. 'Will it be anything like the gate at Elise's apartment?'

'We don't know,' the MG said.

Josie gave Amber a concerned look. 'If the one in Canberra is open, the effect on Amber might be worse.'

'Or less – who knows?' Ren said.

'If it's like the one at Elise's apartment, I won't be able to lean near it,' Amber said. She shot a sidelong glance at Ren. 'Or stay away from it.'

Sam leant over his knees and rubbed his temples with his fingers. 'We need to learn more about leaning.'

'I wonder what Yorilla knows?' Marissa said. 'Rebecca said she had her own word for leaning, so she must know something.'

'Yorilla?' Josie asked.

'Rebecca's Bonehead friend.'

Sam sat upright and looked from Amber to Ren. 'At any rate, you'll be prepared this time. You know the gate might affect Amber, so you can factor that into your planning.'

Ren bobbed his head in a slow nod.

'You might not need to go near it,' the MG said. 'As I said, we're not asking you to close it at this stage. We just want to hear what this Bonehead has to say, and collect as much intelligence as possible.'

Sam nodded. 'I've arranged for you to meet Rebecca and Yorilla tomorrow morning at a quarry outside Canberra. Christine can give you more details – she did a supply drop there the other day.'

Amber picked at a loose thread on her pants. Her stomach knotted in fear. What if the Boneheads captured her and put the restraints on again? She could almost feel the roots slithering through her head again, the intrusion in her mind, drowning her in pain. She had almost been lost to them the last time – it was only because Jaws had bitten her at the right time that she'd managed to break free. And what were the chances of that happening again? Jaws didn't take orders from anyone.

As if on cue, Jaws jumped onto a spare folding chair and started sharpening his claws on the material, shredding it. He looked up, met her gaze, and returned to sharpening.

And what about the dangers of leaning? It had killed Kim. And this gate – what if she needed to fight Boneheads near it, but couldn't lean? They would destroy her.

An information gathering exercise only, Sam called it, as though he was asking nothing of them. She felt a rush of anger. Her stomach twisted again and her hands shook.

The sound of voices outside the tent interrupted her dark thoughts. Marissa walked to the tent flap and opened it. Adam, Dom and Zac entered.

Adam looked at Amber, his eyes lighting up, then turning to a frown when he saw her black eye. He held out one of the warped metal restraints. 'We've been over these with a fine-toothed comb.'

'And?' Sam asked.

'Nothing.'

Sam raised his eyebrows.

'There's no chips, no electronic circuits, nothing to indicate they've been tampered with. As far as we can tell – they're just bits of metal.'

'That doesn't make sense,' Amber said, her voice rising in pitch. 'They got into my head.'

Zach shrugged. 'Maybe there was something in the bits that melted? There's nothing in these that could have affected you – at least not that we could find.'

The MG and Sam exchanged glances. 'Thank you for your efforts,' the MG said, 'And for staying up overnight. We appreciate it.'

'Sure.'

They handed the restraints to Sam. Adam stopped next to Amber's chair. 'Sorry about last night – I got caught at the lab. Everything okay?' he asked in an undertone, pointing at her eye.

'It's nothing,' Amber said. 'I'm fine.'

'Ollie's okay?'

'He's with Sarah.'

'Come and find me when you're done here?'

She nodded. He squeezed her shoulder and left the tent.

Sam turned back to her. 'Regardless of what Yorilla offers, you are not to close the gate unless advised by us – understand?'

Amber shrugged. 'It's not like I know how to close it anyway.'

Sam drew his brows in. She rolled her eyes. 'Yes. I understand.'

Fifteen

Bec paced back and forth, her feet kicking up clay dust from the old quarry. The dust swirled up, catching the early morning sunlight and highlighting the rays. Yorilla squatted on the ground, watching her through the dark sunglasses.

'You're wasting energy.'

Bec sighed. 'I wish they'd hurry up.'

'Why? It doesn't matter what time they get here.'

'I'm bored.'

'You should gather strength for the challenges ahead.' She shook her head. 'Humans.'

'You shouldn't judge us all by Bec,' Luke said. He was perched on the bull bar of the four-wheel drive. Nathan leant against the bull bar next to him. Kalliga was inside, sitting at the wheel. 'She's a special case.'

Bec held up her middle finger in Luke's direction.

Nathan lifted his head. His nose was covered with a dressing and there were dark bruises under his eyes. 'That'll be them now.'

Bec focused. She could just hear the roar of a car engine. The roar grew, echoing around the quarry.

A blue four-wheel drive appeared on the road. It slowed and pulled over. Bec danced over to it. Josie and Ren climbed out, their rifles in their hands. Bec gave them a wide grin, but their attention was on the Boneheads. Josie gave her a grim nod. Ren's eyes roved over the site, resting on Yorilla and Kalliga.

'Only the two of them?' he asked Bec.

'Yeah.'

'Two of your team, in addition to you?'

'Yeah.' She held up her phone. 'Dan's our backup. And Ash is – well, you know.'

Ren gave Yorilla a long, dark look.

Bec cleared her throat. 'I think Yorilla genuinely wants to negotiate.'

Ren gave her a sideways glance. He didn't look reassured, but he leant on the door of the four-wheel drive and jerked his head at Amber. 'There's two Boneheads, one on the ground and one in the vehicle.'

Amber climbed out, holding her sword with one hand and wrestling Jaws with the other. He was expressing his displeasure about something by sinking his teeth into her forearm.

'Get off!' Amber shook her arm. Josie forced Jaws' mouth open and pulled him off. She dumped him on the ground. He shook himself and stalked away, sniffing the car tyres.

Amber lifted her head to meet Bec's gaze. 'Hey. Nice haircut.'

Bec stared at Amber's black eye and swollen cheek. Her eyes widened.

'What?' Amber asked.

'Your eyes are red.'

Amber raised a hand to her cheek. 'That's what happens when you let someone punch you in the face.'

'But – both eyes?'

Amber wasn't listening. Her eyes were on Yorilla. Bec drew her brows in, looking at Yorilla's sunglasses. She felt unsettled. The red in Amber's eyes reminded her of the rings around Yorilla's sclera.

Amber stalked towards Yorilla. Jaws barrelled after her and got under her feet. Ren and Josie exchanged glances and followed, one on either side.

Yorilla watched them approach. 'Amber. Nice to meet you at last.'

Amber glared at her. 'What do you want with me?'

'I want you to close the gate that Walker has opened between the worlds. In return, I'll teach you how to remove the restraints.' Yorilla's eyes flicked to the bandages on Amber's wrists. 'Without having to burn your skin off.'

Amber placed the tip of her sword on Yorilla's chest. 'How about you just tell me in return for me not killing you and your friend?' She nodded at Kalliga.

'Amber!' Bec was shocked.

Yorilla sniffed the air and tilted her head. 'You threaten me with death, yet you stink of anger. How will you access the lechiko if you're so angry?'

'The – what?'

'She's talking about leaning,' Bec said.

Ignoring the sword, Yorilla uncurled and stood, towering over Amber. Amber kept the sword pointed at her chest. Yorilla gave her a disdainful look and turned to Bec. 'Is this how your people negotiate?'

'No.' Bec glared at Amber. Then she twisted her mouth. 'Sometimes.'

Yorilla let out a bark of laughter. 'And mine too, for that matter.' She looked at Amber. 'But I did not travel to your world to fight you, Amber Yu. I was sent here to ensure the gate is closed.'

Amber removed her sword from Yorilla's chest, but kept it in her hand. 'What's to stop Walker opening another gate?'

'As I explained to Rebecca, the amount of power required. A person could only do it once without dying.'

'Bullshit,' Amber said.

Bec's mouth dropped open.

Yorilla drew herself up. 'Are you accusing me of lying?'

'Walker has opened one before. In Sydney.'

Yorilla frowned. 'Impossible.'

'There is a gate in Sydney,' Ren said. 'We saw it. We were told Walker opened it and later shut it down, but I can't vouch for the accuracy of our source.'

Yorilla stared at him for a moment. She gave a slow nod. 'The Walker has managed a number of impossible things. You will give me the address. My family will investigate this.'

Ren narrowed his eyes at the order, then shrugged. 'I guess we can do that.'

She turned back to Amber and bared her teeth. 'If we need to stop the Walker from opening another gate, we will do so.'

'Why do you want the gate closed? Seems like you guys have got a pretty sweet deal – swanning through the gate and terrorising the natives.'

Yorilla's face darkened. 'The price to keep the gate open is higher than you know.'

'What price?'

Yorilla stared at her through her dark glasses. 'This is not relevant. I offer you a deal. What is your response?'

Amber met her gaze with a glare of her own. 'Is this how your people negotiate? I'm not going to deal if I don't know what I'm getting.'

Yorilla stared at Amber for a moment, the blank sunglasses giving nothing away. Then she gave a brisk nod. 'I will show you. But I suggest you do something about your anger – you might need the lechiko.' She bared her teeth again. 'Where we need to go, everyone will want to kill you.'

Ren narrowed his eyes. 'Where's that?'

'A farm outside Canberra. Hold.' Yorilla walked to the four-wheel drive and leant in window to speak to Kalliga. Ren watched her, drumming his hand on his rifle. She returned with a tourist map of Canberra – the type that you could pick up for free at hotels or holiday parks. She squatted on the ground and spread it out. Ren squatted next to her. Amber joined them, sheathing her sword but resting her hand on the hilt.

Jaws strolled past Amber and settled himself on top of the map.

Yorilla pushed him away. He snapped at her fingers. She pulled them back and gave Amber a stern look. 'Why haven't you trained this animal? It will be a nightmare when it's full grown.'

'It's already a nightmare,' Josie muttered.

Amber pulled Jaws off the map, holding him away from her to avoid his claws and teeth, and dumped him behind them.

Yorilla pointed at the map. 'Here.'

Bec peered over Amber's shoulders. Her stomach clenched. 'We can't go there! There's Boneheads everywhere.' Yorilla bared her teeth at Bec. Bec felt her cheeks warm. 'I mean – Anaia.'

Ren looked up at her. 'You know it?'

'Corella Creek Farm.'

Ren frowned. 'The farm where you saw the PM?'

'And at least a thousand Bone – Anaia.'

'We won't be going into the main part of the farm, where the troops are stationed,' Yorilla said. 'What I want to show you is in another part of the farm. There are members of my family stationed there who will ensure we aren't disturbed.' She looked at Bec. 'They saved Rebecca and her friends the other day.'

Bec raised her eyebrows. 'Saved? All they did was generously resist the urge to kill us.'

Ren considered the map. 'I want to check it out before we take Amber.'

Yorilla glanced at the sun. 'There's no time. It's Friday. If we're going to do this, we need to do it soon. The Walker spends his weekends at the farm. You don't want to be there when he is.'

Amber clenched the hand on the sword so tight that her knuckles went white. 'I agree with her. I don't want to meet Walker.'

Ren looked unhappy. 'Can we have a moment to discuss this?'

Yorilla stood, scooping up her map. 'Of course.' She walked back to the four-wheel drive.

Ren stood and met Josie's eyes. 'What do you think?'

174

'Risky as hell,' Josie said.

Ren looked at Bec. 'Can we trust her? Yorilla?'

Bec screwed up her face. 'I think so. She's the only Bonehead I've known, so she could be playing with me and I don't realise. But I don't think she's that subtle.'

Ren stared at Yorilla, who was speaking to Kalliga. He clenched his jaw. 'Our primary objective is to keep Amber alive.'

Amber jerked her head up. 'Since when?'

'We're here to collect intelligence, though,' Josie said. 'Are we ever going to get a better chance than this?'

Ren let out a sigh. 'I guess not. I hope we don't regret this.' He looked at Bec. 'Are you happy to stay with them? We could squeeze the three of you into our car, but it will be a crush.'

'We're fine. It gives us a chance to ask Yorilla questions – that's why I accepted her offer of a lift in the first place.' Dan and Nathan had disagreed with her decision, but they'd given in without too much arguing. She must be wearing them down.

'Good thinking,' Ren said, his thoughts somewhere else. He strolled over to Yorilla. 'We'll see you there.'

Yorilla bared her teeth. 'Good.'

Bec joined Nathan at the front of the four-wheel drive. 'Did you notice Amber's eyes?'

'Yeah.'

'What?' asked Dan, over the phone.

'There's red rings forming in them. She said it's because she got punched, but they look like Yorilla and Kalliga's eyes.'

Luke slid down from the bull bar. 'I can see why you two are friends,' he said. 'She's just as arrogant and reckless as you are.'

Bec stuck her middle finger up at him again. Then she shook her head. 'She didn't use to be. I don't know what's gotten into her.' She walked back to Amber, who was staring into the distance. 'I'll see you there.'

Amber nodded. Her fingers tightened around the hilt of her

sword. She made an effort to relax them. 'It's good to see you.'
Bec gave a wide smile and flung an arm around her shoulders.
'Definitely.'

Kalliga drove away first, kicking up dust with his usual
disregard for sensible speed limits. Bec looked out the back
windscreen. Tev was following close behind.
Bec turned around. 'Why do you have red rings around your
eyes?' she asked.
Yorilla and Kalliga exchanged glances. 'You noticed that
Amber's eyes have similar rings? They're the mark of the
lechiko.'
Luke leant forward. 'You have it too? You can lean, like
Amber?'
Bec drew her brows in. 'Why don't you just close the gate
yourself, then?'
Yorilla shook her head. 'Not like Amber. We have a small ability
– not enough to close the gate.' She looked at Kalliga. 'In the
past some of our family were as strong as Amber - stronger - but
the curse fell out of favour and our family tried to breed it out.
Now only our Nalyrd remains of those who were strong with
lechiko, but we have some throwbacks like Kalliga and I who
can access the power in a limited way.'
'Nalyrd?' asked Bec.
'Our ancestor? Matriarch? I don't think there's a word for it in
English. Our Nalyrd was strong with the curse once, but it has
faded with old age.'
'Why did it fall out of favour?'
'Why? I think it's because the Red Bones don't have it - it has
always run in Grey Bones families.' Yorilla smirked and waved
a hand. 'Enough politics.'
Bec looked out the window at a paddock dotted with lichen-
covered rocks. They passed a road sign with the words Drink

Drive/Die in a Ditch painted on it. She averted her gaze, determined that none of them would die in a ditch that day.

One more question swirled around her mind. If the lechiko was some Bonehead power – or curse – that they'd pretty much bred out, why did Amber have it?

Kalliga drove over a small culvert and pulled onto the grass verge. Three horses grazed in a paddock opposite. They lifted their heads as the humans and Boneheads slid out of the four-wheel drive, their ears twitching, then returned to grazing. Tev pulled up behind them.

Bec put her phone against her ear and lowered her voice. 'Dan? Anything I need to know?'

'Nothing that I can see, but like last time, I'm pretty much blind.'

'Okay, thanks.'

Tev stayed in the blue four-wheel drive, but Kalliga joined the group. Bec glanced at him. 'You're coming with us?'

He ran his eyes over the group, looking unimpressed. 'Yorilla insists that we keep you alive.'

They shouldered their packs. From the way Ren and Josie balanced their packs on one knee before they swung them over their shoulders, Bec thought theirs must be heavier than they looked.

Amber wrapped her arms around her shoulders. She stared towards the south-east, her eyes blank, and shifted from foot to foot. Jaws sat back on his haunches, his eyes watching her as though he was trying to decide where to bite her.

Bec aimed a pretend kick at him. He bared his teeth at her. She shook her head. 'Didn't even flinch.' She looked at Amber. 'What's wrong?'

Amber pulled an uncomfortable face and squirmed as though she was trying to dislodge a spider that had slithered down the back of her shirt. 'The gate is here. I can feel it – calling.'

'You can feel it?' Yorilla considered her. 'You are remarkably strong with the lechiko.' She looked at Kalliga. 'I wonder if she could match the Walker?'

Kalliga gave Amber a dismissive look. 'Too emotional. I can smell that one's anger and fear from here.'

Amber scowled and wrapped her hand around the hilt of her sword.

Kalliga snorted. 'See?'

Yorilla frowned. 'The gate is in the main part of the farm, where the troops are stationed – not where we're going. Come.'

She strode to the culvert. On either side, a dry gully ran between two hills, a barbed wire fence separating it from the road. Eucalypts and the odd willow grew along both sides of the gully. Yorilla pushed the wire down and stepped over it, then held it down for the humans to climb over.

Amber didn't move. She stared at Yorilla, her brow wrinkled.

Kalliga waited for her. 'We don't have time to waste,' he said.

Amber took a deep breath in and followed the others over the wire.

Yorilla strode along the side of the gully, setting a fast pace that didn't allow for the humans' shorter legs. Bec sucked in air as she tried to keep up. She stopped, panting. Amber stopped next to her. She wasn't even breathing hard. Bec gave her a resentful glare, but Amber didn't seem to notice. She was frowning.

'What's that noise?'

Bec hadn't heard anything over her own breathing. She tilted her head and heard a faint ringing. She gritted her teeth. 'Swords. Lots and lots of swords – wielded by Boneheads.'

Amber's eyes widened. 'Like in that video?'

'Exactly.'

The noise grew louder as they continued down the gully. Amber was taking long, slow breaths, as though she was trying to keep herself calm. She still had one hand wrapped around the hilt of her sword. The knuckles on her hand were white.

Yorilla left the gully and climbed a hill. As they neared the top, she squatted down. The others followed her lead, keeping low. Bec rounded the top of the hill and felt the breath catch in her throat. They were looking down at the cluster of buildings that she had seen from the other side. Lines of Boneheads were once again drilling with swords.

The main building was a lot larger than Bec had realised. From the front, it looked like a medium-sized, rendered brick farmhouse, but a long extension had been built at the back of the building with prefabricated concrete sheets and a tin roof. There were no windows. Bec screwed up her nose. The builder hadn't made any effort to integrate the extension with the original building. The effect was jarring.

Behind the main building, taking up all the flat ground between the building and the hill, were ten demountable buildings. They were almost identical to the ones that Bec had seen at the old paintball site where Zhou was imprisoned. To the east, more demountables mingled with farm sheds. Bec guessed they needed somewhere to house all the Boneheads. She counted twelve Boneheads standing in the shadows of the buildings.

'Fair sized operation, isn't it?' Luke said.

'Whatever's down there, they're not taking any risks,' Josie said. 'That's a lot of guards. And none of them are humans.'

'It's the gate,' Amber said. Her voice sounded strained. Josie shot her a concerned look and moved within arm's length of her.

Looking around, Bec could see the hill that she, Luke and Nathan had climbed the last time. It was the same hill that she was on now, which curved around behind the buildings.

Ren studied the site and the Boneheads through a pair of binoculars. 'I thought you said we weren't going where the troops were stationed?'

'We're not,' Yorilla said. 'We're staying on this side of the hill.'

Amber stared at the Boneheads, squeezing the hilt of her sword. She narrowed her eyes. 'Can I borrow the binocs?'

Ren passed them to her. She squinted through them and turned the focusing wheel. 'Look!' She clutched Bec's arm, her grip so tight that it hurt.

Bec tried to wrench her arm away. 'What?'

Amber let go and pointed close to the buildings. It was the same place Bec, Luke and Nathan had seen the PM training. Bec narrowed her eyes. 'What?' she asked again.

Amber pushed the binoculars into her hands and pointed again. Bec focused the binoculars in the direction she'd indicated and scanned the area. In front of the lines of Boneheads were three figures. One seemed about as tall as the Boneheads. The other two were much shorter. She fiddled with the focus wheel and the figures became clearer. The tall one was a Grey Bone, but the other two were humans – children, she thought. The shortest one had bright red curls. Bec's mouth dropped open.

'Is that Alice and Lucy?'

'Maybe? I can't be sure from this distance.'

Bec stared through the binoculars. The two shorter figures were also drilling with swords, but at a slower pace than the Boneheads. The more she watched, the more convinced she was that it was Alice and Lucy she was watching. She'd spent almost three months hunting the girls. Were they in Canberra all along? Why hadn't the Resistance's intelligence networks heard any word of them?

She returned the binoculars to Ren, a grim look on her face. The girls – if it was them – were surrounded by Boneheads, and out of reach.

'Come,' Yorilla said. She led the way a short distance down the hill, then traversed across the hill until they reached a rough track. It led to a large shed next to a dam. Bec smelt it long before they reached it – the smell the same as sheds used to house livestock everywhere.

Yorilla strode towards the shed, not bothering to hide their approach. Two Grey Bones, armed with rifles and swords, stepped out of the shadows surrounding the shed. Bec froze. She heard a slight scrape as Amber drew her sword.

Yorilla waved a hand. 'You can put that away.'

Amber ignored her.

The Grey Bones approached. One had a twisted horn on the far left of its bony plate. Bec's shoulders relaxed a little. 'They're Yorilla's relatives,' she breathed.

Twisty addressed Yorilla in their language. Yorilla replied. Twisty gave a sharp response. Kalliga removed two small, coloured packages from one of his pockets, and held them out, one on each hand. Bec eyed them. They were each about three centimetres square and wrapped in bright Christmas paper, with pictures of smiling Santa's and reindeer. Twisty and the other Bonehead exchanged glances. They each took one of the packages and stepped back out of the way. Yorilla swept forward without another glance at them.

Bec hurried to keep up. 'What did Kalliga give them?'

'Q'wakay.'

'What's -' Bec started, but the words died on her lips. She heard a sharp intake of breath from Amber. The entrance to the shed was open, and it didn't contain livestock. It contained Boneheads. At least a hundred of them.

Sixteen

Amber shifted into a fighting stance, her sword in front of her. Yorilla gave her an impatient look. 'I said you can put that away. They won't bother you.' She stared at the shed, a grim look on her face. 'They aren't able to.'

She strode forwards.

'What's wrong with them?' Josie asked in a hushed voice.

Bec looked at the motionless Boneheads. She frowned. The Boneheads' eyes followed Yorilla as she approached, but there was no expression on their faces. Their arms hung at their sides. They didn't move or fidget.

Amber lowered her sword. Bec looked at her and raised her eyebrows. 'No swords,' Amber said, nodding towards the Boneheads.

She was right. It was the first time Bec had seen a Bonehead without a weapon – no swords, no guns, not even a knife. Amber sheathed her sword and walked forward to join Yorilla. Bec and the other humans followed. Kalliga stayed with Twisty.

Yorilla stopped about a metre from the entrance to the shed. Jaws strolled past her, sniffing, then froze. He returned to Amber and wound around her ankles. Even he seemed to sense there was something wrong with the Boneheads.

Yorilla bared her teeth. 'This is it – the price we're paying for the Walker's gate.'

'I don't understand,' Amber said.

'The Walker keeps the gate open by draining the energy that is inside people – my people – and leaves them like this. They do not talk. They have less brains than a mosquito. They are like – like one of your robot vacuum cleaners. They do what they are told, sometimes, if what they are told is so simple that even a nestling could do it, but they do not think.'

'Like zombies,' Bec said.

'They are not dead, yet they do not increase the family's resources. They eat and drink and shit and contribute nothing.'

Bec stared at the motionless Boneheads. 'I'm surprised you care,' she said, without thinking. 'You didn't care about Darmiqua.'

Yorilla's face darkened and she put her hand on her sword hilt. With a visible effort, she removed her hand from her sword and spoke through her teeth. 'You understand nothing, human – less than the youngest nestling on our mound. It is only because you are ustiga, and therefore stupid, that I do not kill you for that insult.'

Bec's heart raced. Her mind threw up an image of Yorilla slashing Captain Waters' throat. She had allowed herself to get comfortable with Yorilla. It was a mistake she couldn't afford to make.

'I'm sorry,' she said. 'I didn't mean to offend you.'

Yorilla relaxed and turned back to stare at the Boneheads. 'There is honour in death,' she said, 'Especially death that strengthens the family, whether by achieving a victory, like Darmiqua, or by enabling limited resources to be shared, like a nestling that doesn't survive.' She waved a hand at the Boneheads. 'But this is not death. It weakens, not strengthens. There is no honour in this.'

Bec looked at Amber. She was staring at the zombie Boneheads, but her eyes were unfocused. She didn't seem to have noticed the exchange between Bec and Yorilla.

'Show me the gate,' she said.

Ren shifted behind them. 'Amber -'

Yorilla looked at her. 'You will help?'

Amber lifted her chin, meeting her gaze. 'Your people are no friends of mine. You are the first Boneheads -'

'Anaia,' Bec said.

'You are the first Anaia I've met who haven't tried to kill me. But this -' she waved at the lines of listless Boneheads, 'This is wrong. I will help you stop it, if I can.'

Yorilla gave a sharp nod of her head. 'Come.' She started back up the hill.

Bec grabbed Amber's arm before she could follow. Amber raised her eyebrows.

'Have you forgotten the MG's orders?'

Amber glared at her. 'Have you forgotten that Alice and Lucy might be on the other side of the hill?'

Bec's eyes widened. 'Amber, there's like a thousand Boneheads over there. We're not going to be able to get Alice and Lucy out.'

'I thought you were serious about rescuing them.'

'I am!'

Amber snorted. 'Sure. As long as you can do it without impacting on whatever your current mission is. You haven't changed – always putting the cause ahead of people.'

Bec felt a rush of heat through her body. Luke was wrong – Amber wasn't as reckless as Bec – she was more reckless. Bec squeezed Amber's arm hard enough to hurt. 'You want to risk the lives of everyone here to rescue the girls, yet you talk about me putting the cause ahead of people? I have to look after my team. You only have to look after yourself. Even that you don't have to do on your own - you've got Ren and Josie to pick up the pieces if you screw it up.'

Jaws snarled and snapped at Bec's feet. She snarled back.

Yorilla turned around. 'Is there a problem?'

Amber shook Bec's hand from her arm, her face flushed. 'No.' She gave Bec another glare and flounced after Yorilla, with Jaws loping behind her.

Bec turned and looked at Ren. He was muttering to Josie. Josie hurried to catch up to Amber.

Bec stomped over to Ren. 'Amber's impossible,' she spat. 'She won't listen to me.'

'No,' he said, narrowing his eyes. 'It's something about the gate – it seems to confuse her.'

Bec ground her teeth. 'She didn't seem confused to me. Just her usual stubborn self.'

They dropped to the ground as they neared the top of the hill, and crawled to peer down onto the cluster of buildings. The Boneheads were still drilling with their swords, but the small figures that might have been Alice and Lucy were gone.

Ren looked at Yorilla and Amber. 'I'm sorry, but this -' he waved a hand at the buildings and guards, 'Is too much for us to tackle alone.'

Yorilla gave a small smile. 'I thought you might say that. I'm afraid I have to disagree.'

Bec felt a sudden chill. 'What -'

She didn't finish her sentence. Two Boneheads appeared behind them – one of them with a twisted horn. Other Boneheads sprung up around them, in silence. They were surrounded.

Amber leapt to her feet. 'What are you doing?'

Yorilla shrugged. 'I hoped you'd help voluntarily, but I was never going to rely on it.'

Amber tugged at her sword. Kalliga grabbed her from behind and wrenched both arms back by her wrists. Amber gasped as he put pressure on the burns. Jaws put his ears back and readied his body to leap at Kalliga, but another Bonehead tossed a wire net over the top of him and pulled it in. He struggled to break free, making low grunting noises.

With the same small smile on her face, Yorilla drew Amber's sword from her sword belt and moved out of Amber's reach.

All around her, the Resistance fighters were engaged in small scuffles with the Boneheads. Luke had a knife in each hand. He feinted, dancing in and out, to hold off two Boneheads.

Bec drew her sword. The smile slid from Yorilla's face. Her eyes met Bec's. 'Put it away.'

Out of the corner of her eyes, Bec saw a third Bonehead attack Luke from behind. Luke fell to the ground.

Bec felt her hand shaking. She was no match for Yorilla, who had killed a man with one stroke. 'No.' Her voice shook.

Yorilla gestured at one of the Boneheads, and it moved forward and slammed Bec's hand with the flat of its sword. Bec bent over in pain, dropping her sword. Tears filled her eyes. The Bonehead pressed its sword against her throat.

In a few minutes, the Resistance fighters had succumbed to the Boneheads. One Bonehead held a sword to Nathan's throat. Several surrounded Ren and Josie, who were kneeling on the ground.

Bec felt light-headed. Her vision blurred. She stumbled backwards, ignoring the Bonehead holding the sword to her throat. She had known that Yorilla was brutal – alien – but she had felt sure they could trust her.

Amber was still fighting, like a cornered animal – kicking, clawing and punching Kalliga. Unlike the Boneheads that had subdued Bec and the other Resistance fighters, Kalliga wasn't using his sword against Amber. Bec narrowed her eyes. The Boneheads didn't want to risk killing Amber by accident. That could be helpful.

'Should we put restraints on that one?' a Bonehead asked.

'They don't work on her,' Yorilla said. 'She'll just burn them off.' She stepped in front of Amber. 'Stop fighting, or I'll tell Achina to slit Rebecca's throat.' She stepped back so that Amber could see that the Bonehead had its sword pressed against Bec's throat. Amber sagged in Kalliga's grip.

Twisty opened Ren's pack. 'There's some serious explosives in here.'

Ren scowled.

'Bring it,' Yorilla said. 'And the others.'

Twisty picked up Ren and Josie's packs, swinging one over each shoulder as though they weighed nothing. Another Bonehead removed Nathan and Luke's packs from their backs. Achina and Kalliga didn't move to remove Bec or Amber's packs. Bec suspected they didn't dare; they were worried Amber would use any momentary distraction to free herself and Bec.

One of the Boneheads looked at Jaws, who was writhing in the dirt, wrestling with the net. It wrinkled its nose. 'There's something wrong with this nyth.'

'It's fine,' Kalliga said. 'She just hasn't bothered to train it.'

The Bonehead lifted the net and held it at arm's length. Jaws continued to roll around, trying to get his claws through the net.

Achina moved its sword back, so that it rested against Bec's shoulder, and pushed her forward. She could feel the cold metal against her neck. From the edge of her eyes, she could see the other humans being marched down the hill, towards the cluster of buildings. Yorilla strode ahead of them. The Boneheads moved in silence. She could hear soft intakes of breath from the other humans, the raucous cries of a flock of white cockatoos wheeling overhead and the clang of swords from the long lines of Boneheads drilling in the fields.

Yorilla stalked through the rows of demountables. Two Boneheads stepped out from the shadows and barked a challenge to Yorilla in their language. She snapped something back without slowing her pace, forcing them to move out of the way. Bec saw their eyes widen as they saw Amber. The Bonehead said something else, still in its language, but this time she picked out the words 'Amber Yu'.

Amber didn't seem to notice. Her eyes were unfocused and sweat beaded her forehead. Kalliga held her in a firm grip.

Yorilla barked an order. The Boneheads forced Ren, Josie, Luke and Nathan up the steps towards one of the demountables. Bec turned to follow. 'Stay,' Achina said. She felt the sword bite into her neck, not enough to draw blood, but enough to make it clear Achina was serious. Bec froze.

Yorilla swept forward again. Kalliga and Achina forced Amber and Bec to follow, surrounded by a guard of Boneheads. Twisty fell in alongside Bec, still carrying the two packs.

They entered the farmhouse through the verandah. A wide doorway with a flimsy fly screen opened into a hallway, with rooms on either side. Bec caught a glimpse of a living room that looked like it hadn't been updated since the 1940s, with four brown upholstered armchairs, floral curtains and a wooden sideboard.

Four Grey Bones lounged on the armchairs. They sat up as the Boneheads pushed Bec and Amber past the room. Six human soldiers appeared in the doorway of another room, watching them pass with their mouths open. They were the first humans Bec had seen at the site apart from Walker and the children they had thought were Alice and Lucy.

'That's Amber Yu and Rebecca Williams!'

Bec pressed her lips together. Great – we're famous.

Yorilla ignored the original farmhouse rooms and opened a heavy door into a corridor that was part of the extension, with cement floors and plain white walls. Kalliga and Achina forced Amber and Bec into the corridor. Yorilla let go of the door. It slammed shut behind her. She opened another heavy door on the right into a windowless room. There was no furniture in the room – not even a bucket to use as a toilet. Downlights lit the room with a blue light. Kalliga and Achina pushed Amber and Bec into it and Yorilla slammed the door shut on them without a word.

Bec stood still for a moment, blinking. She wrapped her hand around the door handle and tried to turn it, but it was locked. She turned to Amber. 'Well, this is comfy.'

Amber was trembling. Her eyes were still unfocused. She walked to one of the walls and pressed her hands and head against it.

'Amber?'

Amber blinked and lifted her head. 'The gate. There's people trapped in it. They're calling me.'

'People trapped in the gate?' Bec shook her head. 'We've got other problems – like us being trapped in this room.'

'Yeah – sure – it's just -' Amber seemed to lose her train of thought. She leant her head against the wall again.

Bec wanted to shake her. 'I can't do this on my own!' she said, but Amber didn't seem to hear. She looked around the room. Cement walls, heavy door, Boneheads and soldiers outside. Maybe it was a mercy Amber was unaware of their situation.

She heard a low murmuring. The Boneheads hadn't taken her phone. She pulled it out of her pocket. The murmuring she'd heard was Dan, speaking very fast.

'Dan?'

The murmuring stopped. Dan spoke into the phone. 'Bec?'

Bec's lip trembled. 'We're in trouble.'

'I know – I've been listening. I couldn't quite follow what was going on, but I got the general gist. I'm speaking to Base, but -' he trailed off.

'What?'

'They're considering their options – but that's a lot of Boneheads. I think they're worried they'll just be sending more people to the same fate.'

Bec swallowed. It felt like there was a hard ball blocking her throat. If she was the MG, would she want to risk more people on a doomed rescue? The logical decision would be for them to cut their losses. But one of those losses was her. Bec decided she didn't want them to be logical.

'What about Monique and Gordon?'

Dan snorted. 'It's not likely they'll help, is it?'

Bec wanted to shake him, too. Didn't he know Walker could be here any minute? She took a deep breath in. 'Just – ask them? Please?'

Dan was silent for a moment. 'Of course.'

She bit her lip. Of course Dan knew. It was amazing that he wasn't having a complete meltdown. She drew in another breath. 'Thanks, Dan.'

'I told Tev to get out of there, in case Yorilla sent someone back for him, but he's staying in the area. Let me know if you need him.'

Bec rubbed her forehead. 'Just – ask him to keep hanging nearby. I don't think there's much he can do right now.'

Seventeen

Bec sat on the floor with her pack pressed against the wall. The concrete felt cold and hard against her backside. Her right hand ached from when the Bonehead had smashed it with its sword. She pressed her hand against the cold concrete, hoping it would be like putting ice on it.

Amber didn't move from her position against the wall.

'Do you want to take your pack off?' Bec asked her. She didn't reply.

Bec tapped her phone against her leg.

'Well, this is boring,' she said out loud. 'But I guess Walker will be along soon to liven things up.'

'Seriously?' Dan replied.

'Oh, you're back. What did Gordon and Monique say?'

'Monique's eyes bulged when I suggested they help. I thought her head was going to explode. But Gordon said he'll speak to some of his contacts and see what they can figure out.'

'It might be too late by then.'

Dan was silent.

'Dan?'

'I'm doing everything I can.'

Bec sighed. 'I know.' She heard the sound of a key in the door. Her muscles tensed. 'Something's happening.' She pushed the phone into her pocket and stood, suppressing a shiver.

The door swung open to reveal Yorilla and Kalliga. Kalliga dumped Jaws on the ground. Jaws swung around to bite him, but he kicked out with his foot, and Jaws ran to Amber instead.

'I've bought us some time, but we need to move,' Yorilla said. She was holding Bec and Amber's swords. She frowned at

Amber. 'What's wrong with her?'

Bec gaped at her. 'What?'

Jaws wove around Amber's legs. 'What's wrong with her?' Yorilla said again.

'She said there's people trapped in the gate – calling to her.'

Yorilla let out an impatient sigh. 'Hopeless. Here.' Yorilla thrust the hilt of Bec's sword into Bec's hand, pushed her sunglasses into her pocket and handed Amber's sword to Kalliga. She placed her hands on Amber's shoulders, pulled Amber around to face her and shook her.

Jaws snarled and opened his mouth to bite Yorilla's leg.

Yorilla focused her red-rimmed eyes on him. 'Nyon,' she said, in the Bonehead language. Jaws froze, then retreated behind Amber's legs and snarled at her.

Bec looked at her in awe. 'How did you do that?'

Yorilla ignored Bec and shook Amber again.

Amber cracked her eyes open. Her face was screwed up as though in pain.

'Amber. Figure out which thoughts are yours, and which aren't, and build a shield around yours. Use the lechiko.'

'I can't,' Amber gasped.

'You can.' Yorilla shook her again. 'Focus.'

Kalliga leant against the doorway and crossed his arms. 'You'll have to help her.'

Yorilla thinned her lips. She placed her hands on either side of Amber's head and stared into Amber's eyes.

Bec hesitated. Was Yorilla hurting Amber? She looked at the sword. She could stab Yorilla with it – but Yorilla had just given it to her. What the hell was going on?

Amber blinked, her eyes focusing on Yorilla.

Yorilla released her head. 'How's that?'

'Better.' She wriggled her shoulders. 'It's like an itch at the back of my mind, but I can think again.'

'You'll have to keep renewing the shield, which will sap your strength.' Yorilla thinned her lips again. 'If you had half-decent control over your thoughts and emotions, you wouldn't need it.' Kalliga handed Amber her sword.

Amber stared at the sword, frowning. 'Didn't you just attack us?'

Yorilla shrugged. 'It was the easiest way to get you past the guards. And make sure those bodyguards of yours didn't get in the way.'

'They're not my bodyguards.'

'Come.' Yorilla strode out the door.

Bec and Amber followed. Kalliga fell in behind. Achina and Twisty were standing guard at the heavy door into the original farmhouse. Yorilla headed in the opposite direction, towards the end of the corridor. Jaws wove around Amber's legs and continued to snarl at Yorilla.

Bec caught up to Yorilla. 'You could have warned us.'

Yorilla didn't slow her pace. 'If I'd done that, you wouldn't have smelt of fear. The guards would have known it was a setup.'

'You think I wouldn't have smelt of fear walking into a place chock full of Bone- Anaia?' Bec shook her head. She squeezed her sore hand. 'You didn't have to get your friend to smash my hand.'

Yorilla shrugged. 'I told you to drop the sword.'

Achina called something in the Bonehead language.

'Soldiers,' Yorilla said. 'Quick.' She opened the nearest door, pushed Amber and Bec into the room and slammed the door behind them.

It was another windowless room, but this one was furnished. Two small single beds took up most of the space. There was a hanger with black clothing on it – children's sizes. A large, clear plastic container stood underneath it. At first glance she thought it was a toy box, but then she realised it held swords and hand weights. Another door at the back opened onto a small bathroom.

'Amber!' a voice shrieked. A child with wild red curls flew out of the bathroom and threw herself onto Amber.

'Lucy!' Amber's voice shook. She wrapped her arms around Lucy. 'Where's Alice?'

'Here.' A pre-teen with long, blonde hair pulled back into a ponytail sidled out of the bathroom, her eyes narrowed with suspicion. Both children were dressed in black, long-sleeved shirts and black tracksuit pants. The metal restraints encircled their wrists. Their hair was wet, as though they'd just washed. Their faces were red from too much sun, and the skin on their noses was peeling. 'What happened to your eye?' Alice asked.

'Somebody punched me.'

Yorilla opened the door.

Lucy shrieked and buried her head in Amber's stomach. Alice crossed her arms across her chest. 'You're not allowed to come in here. If you're caught, you won't get paid.'

Yorilla snorted. 'I don't need your PM's stinking q'wakay.'

Amber pulled back from Lucy, checking her over.

'Are you hurt? Did they hurt you?'

'They didn't hurt us,' Alice said.

'They make us do sword fighting, even if we're really tired,' Lucy said. 'And when I fell over and hurt my knee, they made me keep going, even though the blood was running down my leg.' She pulled up the left leg of her pants and pointed at a large scab on her knee. There was another restraint wrapped around her ankle.

'It wasn't bad.' Alice rolled her eyes. 'Walker doesn't let them hurt us.'

Lucy glared at her. 'He makes us train with the Boneheads. They're scary. And they don't want us there. They don't want us to learn sword fighting.'

'They're scared of us,' Alice said. 'When I realised that, I wasn't scared of them anymore.'

'You are, too,' Lucy said. 'You just pretend you're not.'

'They're scared of you?' Bec asked. 'Why would they be scared of you?'

Alice shrugged.

'Only the Red Bones,' Yorilla said, her tone dismissive. She pointed at Lucy. 'She has the lechiko. The Red Bones fear the lechiko, because no matter how strong and tall they are, or how hard they train, one with the lechiko can overcome them.'

Amber ran her fingers over the flat pieces of metal around Lucy's wrist. She shuddered. 'Do these hurt? Do they wrap around your brain?'

'At first they did. They were really bad. But I got used to them. Mostly I don't notice them now. They hurt Alice more.'

'Only if I think about escaping,' Alice said. 'Or if I get angry and think about fighting someone for real – not just in training.'

'We need to go,' Yorilla said. 'The Walker will be here soon.'

Amber sat on one of the beds, pulling Lucy down with her. 'I'm not going anywhere without Alice and Lucy.' Jaws sniffed Lucy's legs, then plonked himself on the ground next to Amber's feet.

'We can't take them. The restraints will kill them.'

'So take the restraints off.'

Yorilla's red-rimmed eyes bulged. 'No. Not until you close the gate.'

'You don't have to show us what you're doing. Bec and I can leave the room. Alice and Lucy can shut their eyes. That way you'll still have your bargaining chip.'

Yorilla frowned.

'Consider it a demonstration that you can deliver what you're promising,' Amber added.

'I can deliver,' Yorilla snapped. 'But I was told not to deliver until you start to close the gate.'

'Then I guess none of us will get what we want.' Amber crossed her arms.

'Are you serious?' Yorilla's voice was full of disbelief. 'Your Prime Minister will be here soon. Do you know what he will do to you?'

Amber just stared at her, lips pressed together.

Yorilla looked at Bec. Bec shrugged. 'I'd just do it. She's as stubborn as a hangry three-year-old.'

Yorilla looked from Amber to Bec and back again. She spoke through gritted teeth. 'Alright, mammal. But if you ask me for anything else, I will not be so patient. And I'm blindfolding them.'

'If you hurt them, I'll kill you,' Amber said, her voice ice cold. Bec stared at her.

Yorilla gave her a cold look. 'Maybe, maybe not. Kalliga is right – you are too emotional.' Amber glared at her. She didn't move from the bed. Yorilla let out a loud sigh. 'I will not hurt the nestlings. Why would I?'

'I wouldn't put anything past you Boneheads.'

Yorilla bared her teeth.

Bec stepped between them. 'Stop it with the racist bullshit,' she said to Amber. She turned to Yorilla. 'I thought you were in a hurry?'

Amber stood, pulling Lucy upright with her. 'Racist,' she muttered. 'Since when is 'Bonehead' a race?'

'It's nothing. We are the Anaia.'

Bec dragged Amber from the room. Jaws trotted behind them.

Bec closed the door behind them and leant against it. Achina and Twisty were still in position near the door. There was no sign of any soldiers.

Kalliga looked at Bec.

'She'll just be a minute,' Bec told him.

Jaws sniffed at her feet. She aimed a pretend kick at him. He sneered and walked away to sniff at the floor.

Amber paced back and forwards, her fingers wrapped around her sword hilt as though she was preparing to make good on her threat to Yorilla.

Bec let her head fall back against the door. Her mind threw up an image: the freight train that she, Amber and the girls had escaped on almost three months ago. She felt like she was on a train again, speeding towards a destination that she had no control over. Yorilla and Kalliga expected Amber to close the gate. If she didn't, Yorilla and Kalliga would probably kill them all. Ren and Josie were out of the picture. Amber felt like a stranger – for the first time since they'd met, Bec had no idea what she was thinking.

The door handle moved. Bec jumped out of the way. Yorilla opened the door and held it for Alice and Lucy to exit.

'Did you take the restraints off?' Amber asked.

'Of course,' Yorilla said.

Amber checked Alice's arms and legs. Yorilla scowled.

'You're sunburnt,' Amber said, noting the difference between the bands of white skin around Alice's wrists and the reddened skin on the rest of her arms.

'The Boneheads don't understand about sunscreen,' Alice said. 'They've got elephant skin.'

Yorilla's scowl deepened.

Lucy ignored them and started walking down the corridor.

'Lucy!' Amber hurried to catch up to her. 'Lucy, stop!' Amber grabbed her by the arms and held her. She swung around to Yorilla. 'What did you do to her?'

Yorilla glared at her. 'Exactly what you insisted I do – took the restraints off.'

'Then what's wrong with her?'

Bec looked from Amber to Yorilla. They were baring their teeth at each other. Yorilla fingered her sword. Bec ran to Lucy and dropped to her knees in front of her. Lucy was rigid. She looked past Bec as though she wasn't there, her eyes glazed. Bec was sure that she would keep walking as soon as Amber let go.

'It must be the gate.' The words tumbled out of Bec's mouth. 'It's calling to her, like it did to Amber.'

Amber narrowed her eyes and gave Bec a quick glance.

'Come on, Amber,' Bec said. 'She's got the same power you have. Why wouldn't she react to the gate in the same way?'

'She didn't before,' Amber said.

'Yes, she did.' Alice had joined them. 'She never looked like that before, but she always wanted to go down that corridor to the room at the end, even though we weren't allowed to.'

'The restraints would have dampened the call,' Yorilla said. 'That's one of the things they do – block the lechiko.' She looked at Amber. 'That's why Lieutenant Colonel Nichols was unprepared when you burnt them off. You shouldn't have been able to do that.'

'Can you help Lucy, like you did Amber?' Bec asked.

Yorilla glared at Amber. 'If I'm allowed to.'

Amber glared back at Yorilla.

'Stop being an idiot,' Bec said to Amber. 'Let her help.'

Amber gritted her teeth. 'Fine.'

Yorilla swept forward and knelt in front of Lucy. Amber let go of Lucy and crossed her arms. Yorilla placed her hands on either side of Lucy's face and stared into her eyes. Lucy blinked. Her eyes focused on Yorilla. She jumped backwards and turned around, burying her head in Amber's stomach again.

'She should be fine for a while,' Yorilla said.

'Thank you,' Bec said. She raised her eyebrows at Amber.

'Thanks,' Amber said. It sounded like she was forcing the word out.

Yorilla curled her lip, and strode down the corridor without a word. Kalliga jerked his head in the direction she'd taken. 'Go.'

Bec took a deep breath and followed Yorilla.

Amber caught up to her and took her arm. 'I don't know what to do,' she said in a low voice.

Bec met her eyes. 'Neither do I.'

Amber bit her lip, her eyes wide with fear. She kept her arm wrapped around Bec's arm. Bec felt some of the tension release from her shoulders. She didn't know what was going to happen, but at least Amber wasn't as much of a stranger as she'd thought.

Yorilla knocked at the end door. It opened a crack. A soldier stuck his head out. Bec recognised the soldier at the same moment that Amber's hand tightened around her arm. His eyes fell on them and widened in recognition.

'You.' It was Private Jerome.

He jerked the door to slam it closed, but Yorilla grabbed the side of it with her left hand and gave him a hard shove with her right, knocking him backwards. The room was larger than the other rooms they'd seen in the extension, but otherwise the same – white walls, cement floor, no windows. The far end was dominated by an arch. It was different to the gate that Amber had described seeing in Sydney. The bricks that had been used to build it were a matching, dark grey colour, and fitted together perfectly.

Four Red Bones were sitting on plastic chairs in front of the gate. Jerome landed on the floor in front of them. They leapt to their feet and drew their swords. Jerome babbled into a hand-held radio, asking for backup.

Yorilla wrenched the door off its hinges and tossed it aside. Kalliga signalled Achina and Twisty. They left their position at the door and trotted down the corridor, drawing their swords.

'Stay out of the way,' Kalliga ordered the humans, motioning for them to stand to the side of the doorway. Bec, Lucy and Alice did what he said, but Amber tossed her pack next to the door and drew her sword. He gave her a dismissive look and swept past her into the room, with Achina and Twisty right behind him.

Amber stayed where she was, watching, her sword clenched in her hand. Jaws crouched at her feet, looking ready to pounce.

The Red and Grey Bones leapt at each other, their swords ringing as they met. They whirled in and out, circling each other as though in a wild dance. At first, Bec was overwhelmed by the spectacle, but after a few minutes she started to pick out differences in the fighting styles. The Red Bones were taller and more muscled and their strikes landed with more force. Kalliga and Yorilla were faster, more precise. Not as fast as Amber, Bec thought, whose speed always seemed unnatural, but faster than the other Boneheads. She wondered if they were leaning – or drawing on the lechiko, as Yorilla would call it. Achina and Twisty's style was solid, defensive. They caught each blow from the Red Bones and deflected it, giving the impression that they'd be happy to continue to do so forever.

Private Jerome had backed away to the wall, staying out of the way of the fighting Boneheads. The door at the end of the corridor slammed open. Jerome smiled as five Grey Bones streamed in, followed by the soldiers that she'd seen in the farmhouse.

Jerome's relief was short-lived. Three of the Grey Bones attacked the other two. Bec still had trouble distinguishing between different Boneheads, but she thought she recognised at least one of the Grey Bones that had joined Yorilla and Kalliga at the top of the hill. How many of the thousand or so Boneheads at the site were on Yorilla and Kalliga's side rather than the PM's?

The soldiers lifted their rifles and fired down the corridor, seeming unconcerned whether the bullets hit friend or foe. Chips of plaster and concrete flew from walls that were hit, but the bullets that flew towards humans or Boneheads hit shields and dropped to the ground.

The soldiers drew knives and swords instead. Ignoring the five Grey Bones battling near the door, they approached Bec, Amber and the girls in a half-circle. Bec and Amber stepped in front of the girls, who pressed themselves against the wall. Bec pointed her sword at the soldiers. She glanced at Amber. Amber had closed her eyes. She took deep breaths in and out.

The soldiers drew closer. Bec's palm felt sweaty. She switched the sword to her left hand, wiped her right on her clothes and switched it back. She gave Amber a nervous look. 'Hurry!'

Amber opened her eyes and hefted her sword. Bec breathed out. Leaning, Amber should be able to handle six soldiers with ease.

The soldiers seemed to think so, too. They shortened their strides and slowed their pace. A couple of the younger soldiers glanced back at the door, as though they wanted to flee.

The door flung open again. More soldiers had arrived – many more, along with a red-haired man who Bec would have preferred to have never seen again – Lieutenant Colonel Nichols. The six soldiers approaching them seemed more afraid of Nichols than they were of Amber. They increased their pace and stride again until they were trotting towards Amber and Bec.

Amber stepped in front of Bec and swung her sword. She moved so fast she was a blur, disarming and knocking down one soldier after another, sending knives, swords and soldiers flying. Bec noticed that she didn't kill any of the soldiers, but some of them would have a nasty concussion. The soldiers kept coming, directed by Nichols. He was taking his usual approach of leading from behind.

'Coward,' Bec muttered.

There was a roar that made the entire world shake. Bec clapped her hands over her ears, but it made no difference – the noise seemed to be inside her body as well as out. An unnatural wind buffeted her body, almost knocking her over. She curled on the ground and squeezed her eyes shut. Then the noise was gone. She opened her eyes. Amber was still standing, her feet planted and her sword in her hand, but she was one of the only ones. Most of the soldiers were picking themselves up, uncurling from the ground. Bec blinked. Behind Amber, she could see the sky. She lowered her gaze. A chunk of the left side of the extension was gone. She looked out onto demountables. Behind them, she could see the hill.

Josie, Luke and Nathan were picking their way through the rubble, along with a couple of the Grey Bones who had been on the top of the hill. Josie had a broad grin on her face.

The fighting started again. More and more Boneheads and soldiers joined the fray. Bec could no longer make any sense of what was going on – of who was a friend or enemy. She drew back until she was right in front of Alice and Lucy, close enough to touch them, and focused on stabbing anyone who tried to get near. She saw Josie backing away from two soldiers, and jumped forward to stab one of them. Josie gave her a grin and took out the other.

'Where's Ren?' Bec yelled over the noise of the fighting.

'Figuring out what to blow up next!' Josie yelled back. 'No doubt he's loving it!'

Bec jumped back to protect Alice and Lucy again. Josie disappeared into the maelstrom. A young soldier with frightened brown eyes swung his sword at Bec. She caught the strike on her sword, but he wrenched the sword from her grasp, sending it spinning across the floor. He swung his sword towards her neck. Amber appeared and slammed his sword with hers. He backed away from her into the crowd.

Bec's sword had disappeared. Alice thrust a long knife into her hands. Bec didn't know where she'd got it from.

Kalliga and Yorilla emerged from the room with the gate. 'Come!' Yorilla yelled, herding Bec, Amber and the girls into the room. The left wall had partly collapsed, but the room and the gate remained standing. There were bodies on the floor, including those of the Red Bones that Kalliga and Yorilla had been fighting. Achina and Twisty were fighting the other two Red Bones in the rubble from the left wall. The Red Bones seemed to be losing steam. Achina and Twisty looked as fresh as when they'd started. Yorilla and Kalliga pushed the humans around the right side of the room. Bec saw Jerome crawling out from under a section of the wall.

Yorilla clutched Amber's arm. 'The gate!' She pointed at the gate with her other hand. 'Close it now, before the Walker gets here! We can keep them occupied.' She waved at the Boneheads, soldiers and Resistance fighters.

'I don't know how!' Amber shouted.

'Use the lechiko! Let it guide you!'

Amber looked at Bec, her eyes wide with fear. The red rings in her eyes seemed even more pronounced than before.

'Do it!' Yorilla said, giving Amber a shake.

Soldiers and Boneheads were flooding the room, pushed back by the mass of fighters in the corridor. A Bonehead swung its sword at Yorilla's head. She dropped Amber's arm and caught the strike on her blade. She slid back a step then lunged forward, surprising the Bonehead. Her blade pierced one of its eyeballs and it let out a shriek that filled the room.

A soldier with an extra long knife ducked around behind them and lunged at Amber, her knife positioned to slice into Amber's abdomen. Amber stepped sideways and brought the flat of her blade down on the soldier's wrist. She cursed, but held onto the knife.

Jerome had freed himself from the rubble and picked up a sword from one of the dead Red Bones. Bec turned in time to see him hurtling towards them with the sword in both hands. Bec lifted her knife, but she knew it was too short to stop Jerome's sword. She felt a rush of fear.

Jaws leapt forward and clamped his teeth around Jerome's leg. Jerome stumbled and fell to the ground, the sword clattering in front of him. He kicked his leg, trying to shake Jaws off.

'Enough.'

The man's voice cut through the clanging of swords, yells, grunts and insults. The force of the command wrapped around Bec's heart. She tried to move, but she was frozen in place. Her insides felt ice cold, like she was actually frozen.

Jerome didn't seem in any better condition. Fear filled his eyes as he realised he couldn't move. All around her, people were frozen. Even Jaws was frozen.

There was movement to her left. She used every ounce of her willpower to force her eyes to look sideways. The man who had uttered the command pushed aside a piece of hanging plaster and moved towards them through the rubble. Bec felt her breath catch in her throat. Prime Minister Walker. The one who had brought all this down on them.

The training she'd had in combat fled her mind. All she wanted was to charge at him – to leap and tear him apart like a wild animal destroying its prey. But she couldn't move. All she could do was watch as he drew a sword.

Eighteen

'Enough.'

Amber felt the word run through her body. It tried to force her to stop, to bend to its will. Without her even reaching for it, the power flamed in her mind, forcing the alien power to retreat.

The sudden silence was shocking. For a second she thought she'd been deafened by another one of Ren's explosions. But then she saw the soldier she'd been fighting – frozen.

Her eyes darted around the room. Nothing moved. Bec was frozen with her knife pointed towards Jerome. Josie was standing over an unconscious soldier on the ground, her rifle lifted as though she'd just hit him in the head with it.

Amber's eyes drifted back to the soldier she'd been fighting. It would be so easy to slice her throat. One less enemy to fight. She shook her head, plucked the knife from the soldier's hand and tucked it into her sword belt.

Her back pricked. She swung around. A man was standing in the gap in the wall – Walker – the Prime Minister. He caught her gaze and a smile appeared on his face. He drew his sword.

Her legs felt unsteady. Her heart pounded so hard her chest hurt. She should have kept still, pretended to be frozen – maybe he wouldn't have noticed her. It was too late. He was striding straight towards her.

She dodged behind the soldier she'd been fighting. The smile still on his face, he slammed the sword against the soldier, knocking her to the floor as though she was just a statue, or a mannequin.

If he treated his own soldier that way, what would he do to her? Amber backed away, towards the gate. He kept coming.

She looked at Bec – still frozen. They were all frozen.

She stopped and planted her feet, lifting her sword into a defensive position.

Walker stopped just out of reach, his eyes narrowed, assessing her. He walked in a wide circle around her, forcing her to turn to follow him.

'Amber Yu,' he said, lengthening the words in a long drawl. 'What an unexpected pleasure. I've been wanting to speak to you for a long time.'

'Funny,' Amber said, filling her voice with defiance. 'I've been wanting to kill you for a long time.'

Walker threw back his head and laughed, a roaring laugh that filled the silent room. 'You're arrogant,' he said, a wide smile on his face. 'I like arrogance. But -' he dropped the smile and bared his teeth, 'You are not ready to defeat me.'

Amber swallowed. She prayed a desperate prayer. Please protect me!

Walker attacked, bringing his sword up from the ground towards her throat. Amber jumped back and caught his sword on hers just in time. He swung it back to the right and then in an instant reversed direction and slammed it towards the right side of her head. She ducked under it. Before she could stand it was swinging towards her legs.

Was this how the Boneheads felt when they fought her? None of the previous fights she'd had had prepared her to fight someone so fast. Every time she dodged or caught the sword there it was again, flying towards a different part of her body. There was no time for her to do anything other than counter the next attack.

Walker swung his sword towards her throat from the right side. She blocked it with her sword and pivoted to the left. She kept her eyes on the sword as it slid off hers, preparing for the next strike, but it didn't come. Instead, Walker sprang forward, so close to her that she could feel his breath on her cheek. A long knife appeared in his left hand. He stabbed it towards her eyes. She ducked down and right, but it stabbed into her left shoulder. Walker yanked it upwards, tearing the skin and muscles. She swung her sword towards him, but he leapt out of range, and swung his sword at her legs.

She dodged. Blood flowed down her arm. He swung his sword towards her side and kicked out with his foot, a side kick that caught her in the ribs. She stumbled and her foot twisted. There was a flash of pain in her right ankle, dulled because she was leaning.

Walker lurched forward, losing his balance. Amber's mouth dropped open and she felt an icy hand squeeze her heart. Lucy had freed herself from the command that had frozen everyone and launched herself onto Walker's back, wrapping her arms around his neck.

He would kill her. Amber dived forward, swinging her sword up in an arc and driving it down towards Walker's head. He straightened, flinging Lucy off his back, and blocked her blade, sliding his sword out and slamming the sword handle into her injured shoulder. Lucy rolled under the arch.

Something changed. Small, coloured lights flashed and danced in the air inside the gate. There was a hum, almost imperceptible at first, but increasing in volume.

'Lucy!'

Walker's sword flew towards Amber's head. She blocked and pivoted. He forced her back, away from the gate. The lights inside the gate flashed faster and faster.

From the corner of her eye, she saw someone else move. Alice forced her way through the air, her face screwed up with effort, teeth bared, as though she was walking through thick mud.

Walker swung his sword again and again, so fast that Amber didn't have time to pivot. She backed up, further and further, towards the right wall.

Alice broke free of Walker's power and sprinted towards Lucy. She wrapped her hand around Lucy's wrist and hauled her away from the gate. The lights and the hum disappeared.

Walker let his sword drop to the ground then swung it up, catching Amber's sword and giving a quick twist. It was the same move Amber had used to disarm Reuben almost a week earlier. Amber clutched at her sword with all her strength, but it was forced out of her hands. It clattered to the ground. Walker sprang forward, swinging his sword in an arc, forcing her backwards. She drew the knife that she'd taken from the frozen soldier. It was a long, nasty-looking blade, double sided, with a slight curve and sharpened point. It reminded her of a knife from a pirate movie.

It was too short to help her against Walker's sword. He sliced his sword through the air, forcing her to keep moving back, until she hit the wall. She felt the prefabricated concrete against her back. There was nowhere else to go. His sword sliced the air too fast for her to pivot away, and the knife was too short to block it.

A victorious smile lit Walker's face. He raised his sword above his head – a killing blow. Amber flung the knife up across her face and head in a useless gesture. She prayed – a desperate cry for help.

An enormous boom sounded from outside the building, even louder than the one that had blasted a hole in the wall. Her ears throbbed and her eyes watered.

The roof caved in, dropping plaster onto her head. A supporting beam fell towards the frozen soldier she'd been fighting when Walker arrived, who was lying on the floor where Walker had knocked her. The soldier seemed unable to move, or even cry out.

The soldier disappeared under the weight of the beam. Amber reminded herself that the soldier had tried to kill her. But she'd seen the terror in the soldier's eyes before the beam landed. She was a scared human, just like Amber.

A second explosion made the ground shake. It broke Walker's spell. There was movement all around her as humans and Boneheads regained control of their bodies. Too late. Walker had hesitated when the explosion sounded, but now his sword swung towards her. It was over.

Someone roared, so loud that she could hear it through her ringing ears. Out of nowhere, Yorilla threw herself at Walker, wrestling him to the ground.

'The gate,' she shrieked at Amber. 'Go through the gate.'

Amber scrambled to her feet. Her heart leapt at the thought of going through the gate. Yorilla had numbed the voices from the people trapped in it, but they were still there, their desperate need pounding at the shield Yorilla had built in her mind. It was all she could do to stop herself from diving through the gate. But she couldn't abandon the others.

Yorilla was wrestling Walker for his sword. For a moment, Amber thought Yorilla had the upper hand. There was the flash of a knife. She called a warning, but it was too late. Walker had stabbed Yorilla in the back. Yorilla collapsed on top of him. Walker pushed her away, towards the gate.

Bec appeared at Amber's side. 'Do what she said,' Bec screamed in Amber's ear, and pushed her in the back. 'Take Alice and Lucy. I'll be right behind you.'

Walker was on his feet. He raised his sword. There was no more time. Alice and Lucy were standing near the gate, arms wrapped around each other. Amber ran straight at them, bowling them over. They tumbled under the gate.

A hum filled Amber's ears, and lights danced over her face. She glanced back. Bec had grasped Yorilla under her armpits and was dragging her in Amber's wake. Kalliga vaulted over the collapsed beam and ran towards them. Jaws released Jerome and bolted towards her, his ears down and teeth bared.

The world disappeared in a cacophony of noise and colour. The voices that Yorilla's shield had held at bay flooded her mind – hundreds of them. They wanted something from her. She could give them what they needed, they told her, but she didn't know what that was.

What do you want?

Her mind was overwhelmed. She fell into unconsciousness.

Nineteen

The ground was soft. Bec's right hand was curled around the knife. She pushed her left hand into the ground. Damp, moist leaf litter. She opened her eyes and stared up, feeling too lethargic to move. Trees towered above her – eucalypts, the tallest ones Bec had ever seen. The canopy was so dense that she couldn't see the sky. It was impossible to tell the colour of the tree trunks, because every inch was covered with other lifeforms. Vines slithered up trunks and draped over branches. Every trunk hosted several epiphytes - large, luxurious growths with smaller plants living within their leaves. Fungi of all colours and shapes clustered around the tree roots and exploded from the trunks. Mosses and lichens fought for any remaining space.

Strange grey birds with red lumps on their heads flittered above her. She squinted at them. They looked more like dinosaurs than the feathered birds she was used to. Insects buzzed around and landed on her hands, sucking blood. She couldn't seem to find the energy to care.

The gate was on her left, so close that if she reached out a hand she could touch it. She stared at the nearest grey brick. It had a logo stamped into it that indicated it was made from recycled plastic. The gate – into which Walker had fed the lives of the Anaia – was environmentally friendly. She would have laughed, but she didn't have the energy for that, either.

Voices swirled around her, in a strange language. Boneheads. Some part of her felt a sense of urgency. Danger. She tried to will some energy into her muscles, but they seemed to have melted into the leaf litter. She felt like she was becoming part of the forest.

Something dug into her back – hard, with sharp corners – not soft like the ground. Her pack, she thought. She was still wearing it.

She rolled over, off the pack. There was a body lying next to her. Yorilla. Yorilla had been hurt, she remembered.

She forced herself to sit up, shaking leaves from her hair. Her clothes were damp with sweat. The air was cool, but heavy with humidity. No breeze reached the forest floor.

She pushed the knife into a pocket on her jacket and crawled the couple of steps to Yorilla. 'Are you okay?' The words came out in a rasp.

Yorilla looked at her, her strange, red-rimmed eyes moist. 'Dying,' she whispered.

'Where are you injured?' Bec tugged at Yorilla's clothing.

'No.' Yorilla batted her hands away. 'The wound cannot be repaired.' She met Bec's gaze. 'I thought –' she whispered.

Bec put her head close to Yorilla's mouth, so she could hear.

'I thought it didn't matter if death came early or late. But now I find – I am afraid. I don't want to die. It is shameful.'

Tears pricked Bec's eyes. She forced them to stay there. 'There's no shame in enjoying being alive and wanting it to continue,' she whispered.

'Maybe I didn't enjoy it as much as I could have.'

'None of us do.'

Yorilla closed her eyes. 'You will make sure Amber closes the gate, won't you?'

'I promise.'

She held Yorilla's hand as her chest stopped rising and falling.

'Bec.'

Amber was on her feet. Bec stared at her, wondering how she had found the energy to stand.

'She's dead.' Bec swallowed. Her throat felt thick. Tears pricked her eyes. She hadn't expected to care that the Bonehead was dead. 'Yorilla's dead. And I just lied to her – while she was dying.' The tears leaked out of her eyes and ran down her face.

'I'm sorry,' Amber said. 'But you need to get up.'

She held out her right hand. Bec took it. Amber was shaking, as though she was struggling to stand herself. She staggered as she pulled Bec up.

Bec's eyes were drawn to Amber's left shoulder. Her jacket was soaked in blood. She was pressing her left arm into her stomach and clutching her side with her left hand. Bec remembered – Walker had stabbed Amber, while Bec had watched, frozen. She felt like she was remembering something from a long time ago.

She looked around. They were surrounded by the tall eucalypts. Each tree was a few metres from the next one in all directions, creating a patchwork of trees surrounded by a sea of thick, rotting leaf litter. The fruiting bodies of fungi poked up through the leaf litter.

The gate stood in the space between two trees. In every other space surrounding them stood a Bonehead with a drawn sword – both Red and Grey Bones. Unlike the Boneheads she'd seen in her world, these ones wore clothes that fitted their bodies tightly, and seemed to change from light green to dark green as they moved. Long hoods in the same material hung down their backs.

Alice was kneeling on the ground. She tried to stand, but the energy required was too much, and she sank back on her knees. Tears ran in two lines down her face. Bec stared at her, shocked. Alice didn't cry – she was the toughest kid that Bec had ever met.

Lucy sat cross-legged next to her. Her eyes were on the gate. There was a dead look in them. A long, leafy twig was stuck in her hair. It fell across her face, into her eyes, but she didn't move to brush it away.

Jaws was lying near the children. Bec thought for a moment that he was dead, too, but then she saw his sides moving as he breathed in and out.

Kalliga seemed less affected by the journey through the gate than the humans. He had drawn his sword and was arguing with the other Boneheads in snarls and abrupt sentences, his teeth bared. One word he repeated several times – Nalyrd. Bec remembered Yorilla using the same word for someone she'd described as her ancestor or matriarch.

One of the Red Bones lowered its head, showing its coloured plate and horns. Kalliga returned the nod and sheathed his sword. The other Boneheads sheathed their swords too, and several of them flung their hoods over their heads and melted back into the forest.

'What happened?' Bec asked.

'They have agreed to let you live to meet with my Nalyrd. Beyond that – they have not made any commitments. Come. It is a long walk and we must arrive before dusk.'

'Where to?'

'My family's nest.'

'I can't go on some long walk to your – nest.' Amber's voice rose into a squeal. 'I need to get back to my son. And my husband.'

Bec crossed her arms across her body. 'I'm not going, either. The last time I went to one of your nests they almost voted to kill me, remember?'

Kalliga gave a frustrated sigh. He stabbed a finger at the gate. 'Go through that and your PM will kill you before you recover enough to stand. Stay here, and those guards, the ones that I just wasted energy negotiating with for your lives? They won't waste time voting whether to kill you. They'll just kill you.'

'So we're trapped?' Amber said in a small voice.

Kalliga didn't bother replying. Bec sank down next to Yorilla's body, looking into her blank eyes. Kalliga knelt opposite her, removed Yorilla's sword belt with one swift movement, and stood.

'Come.'

Bec looked at him. 'What about her body?'

'Leave it. The beasts will eat it.'

'What? Can't we bury it, or -' Bec was about to suggest burning it, but she couldn't see any wood in the forest that was dry enough to burn. 'Or something?'

'Why? Then the small beasts will eat it – the beetles and insects and fungi. It makes no difference.'

'It makes a difference to me,' Bec said in a small voice. Tears dribbled out of the corner of her eyes.

'Why do you waste energy like this?' Kalliga demanded. 'You will need it for the walk.'

More tears ran down Bec's face. 'I just want to do something for her. Don't you do anything? Speak a few words about her life, or something?'

He snorted. 'Do you speak to your dead to assuage your guilt at not celebrating them enough when they were alive?'

Bec stared at him for a moment. 'I don't know. Maybe.'

'We celebrate people when they are alive, so we have no need to say words to them when it is too late.'

Bec dipped her head. 'That makes sense.'

His eyes smouldered. 'I don't need you to affirm my people's culture, mammal. Can we go now?'

'Wait.' Bec swung her pack off her back, and pulled out her first aid kit. She looked at Amber. 'Let me look at your shoulder.'

Amber's eyes were on the gate. She blinked at Bec, then shrugged her jacket off and pulled her shirt back from the wound. Blood dribbled down her arm. Bec pressed some thick padding against it, and used several pieces of fabric tape to hold it onto Amber's shoulder. It was a blessing Amber's pack had been left on the other side of the gate – Amber wouldn't have been able to carry it.

'It's not perfect, but it will have to do for now. Did you need anything for your ankle?'

Amber shook her head and pulled her jacket back on. 'It's just a sprain.'

Bec wiped her hands and zipped up the first aid kit. She dropped it into the pack and lowered her voice. 'If we leave here, we'll never be able to find the gate again on our own.'

'That won't be a problem,' Amber said, her voice sounding strained. 'I'll know where it is.'

'It's still calling to you?'

'It's worse than before. Now they know me – the voices. They want something, but I don't know what.'

'What happened to Yorilla's shield?'

'It's still there. I keep feeding it, but it's taking a lot of energy to keep it in place.' She squinted at Kalliga. 'We'd better go. I think he's getting impatient.'

She bent to pick Jaws up, gritting her teeth in pain. Bec considered offering to carry him, but Jaws opened bleary eyes and snapped at her. She jumped back as his teeth clicked together. She helped Alice to her feet instead. She held out her hand to Lucy, but Lucy didn't move.

'We have to go,' Bec said, her tone more gentle than normal.

Lucy gave her a blank look. 'I'm not going.'

'They'll kill us if we stay here.'

Lucy dropped her gaze, staring at the gate. 'I know – I heard what that Bonehead said. I'm still not going.'

Bec stifled a frustrated sigh. She squatted down and met Lucy's gaze. 'What's going on?'

'I heard voices in there. They were trapped.' She lifted her eyes and met Bec's again. 'It's no use. We can't free anyone – those voices, or my mum. Walker traps everyone.' She spoke without emotion, her tone matter-of-fact.

Bec gave Amber a helpless look, but Amber was staring at the gate again, not listening. Bec thought of something. She rummaged in her pack, underneath the first aid kit, and pulled out the blue teddy. She pushed it into Lucy's hands.

Lucy's mouth fell open in a wide O. She wrapped her arms around the teddy and buried her head in its fur. 'I thought I'd lost him forever.'

'See? You never know what the future will hold. You don't give up hope – not ever.' Bec's voice was fierce.

Lucy dipped her head in a nod, and allowed Bec to lift her to her feet, clutching the teddy.

Bec swung the pack onto her back and looked at Kalliga. 'We're ready.'

'About time.' He strode between two trees, his shoes kicking up leaf litter.

Amber hefted Jaws as though his weight was difficult to manage, and followed, limping. Bec frowned. How was she going to manage a long walk?

Lucy took one step and stumbled. Bec caught her and held out her arm. 'You can lean on me.' She looked at Alice. Tears still ran down Alice's face, in complete silence. Bec thought it was unnatural. 'Do you need help, too?'

'No,' Alice said, with force. She flounced after Amber and Jaws. With a sigh, Bec fell in behind.

Kalliga was waiting for them to catch up. Three of the other Boneheads pulled their hoods over their heads and fell in behind them. Amber looked at them with wide eyes. 'Are they coming with us?'

'They make sure we go to my family's nest – and nowhere else,' Kalliga replied.

'What happens if we go somewhere else?'

Kalliga cast a look at her that was full of disdain. He plunged into the forest without answering.

Bec wondered how Kalliga knew which way to go. There was no path, or any landmarks that she could make out, and the sun didn't penetrate the canopy. She didn't see him checking a compass or any other kind of device.

For all she knew, he didn't know where he was going.

It was slow going. Their feet sank into the deep leaf litter, making it feel like they were walking through sand. Vines trailed over every surface and hid among the leaf litter, waiting to trip them. Rotten branches and logs collapsed when they stepped onto them, pitching them into the leaf litter. They scrambled over larger logs, covered in moss and fungi. Strange insects settled on any uncovered skin, leaving itchy welts behind. They discovered a type of bracken that left painful stings if they brushed against it. It was indistinguishable from the other, harmless bracken.

Alien sounds filled their ears – strange bird and frog calls, not like the ones they'd heard in the bush at home. Bec saw enormous holes dug into the sides of embankments and under the roots of the trees. She hoped she never met the creatures that lived in them.

The three guards kept pace with them, their green clothes seeming to merge with the colours of the forest. Bec thought they would be able to make themselves almost invisible if they wanted to.

Amber kept falling behind Kalliga. Her face was white. After he had waited for her to catch up for the third time, he stopped.

'You need to move faster. The forest is not safe after dusk.'

Amber looked close to tears. 'I'm trying.'

Kalliga nodded at Jaws. 'Why are you carrying the nyth? If it can't keep up, leave it behind.'

'What?' Amber's mouth dropped open. 'No!'

Kalliga gave her an impatient look. 'We have hundreds at home.

I can give you another – one that has been trained.'

'I'm not leaving Jaws to die!'

Kalliga snarled. 'You would waste energy and risk all our lives for an insignificant beast?'

Amber glared at him. 'He's not insignificant. He's saved my life.'

'Maybe,' Bec said, 'You could carry Jaws for her.'

Again, Bec was grateful that looks couldn't kill, or she was sure that the one Kalliga gave her would have been lethal. He stomped over to Amber and took Jaws out of her arms. Jaws snapped at him. He grasped Jaws' muzzle and snarled something in his own language.

He bared his teeth at Amber. 'Keep up. My patience is at an end.' He strode into the forest.

'I'm not sure he had any patience to begin with,' Bec muttered. Lucy laughed. Alice lifted her head and gave Lucy a shocked look, as though she'd forgotten what laughter sounded like.

It was a long time before Kalliga stopped again. The humans struggled in his wake. Amber limped, clutching her arm. The bandages on her wrists were grey with dirt. Alice had long ago stopped crying, but her and Lucy's eyes grew large with tiredness. They stared at the passing scenery without taking it in.

Kalliga pointed at a small creek bubbling over grey stones. 'The water is safe to drink.' He dropped Jaws next to the water, knelt and scooped handfuls into his mouth.

Alice and Lucy threw themselves onto the muddy ground next to the creek and gulped water. Bec wondered whether safe for the Boneheads equalled safe for humans, but she was too thirsty to care. She knelt in the mud and drank, then splashed water on her face to remove some of the sweat.

The water seemed to revive Jaws. He wandered away to sniff at the plants growing near the creek.

Amber had her arms wrapped around her chest, squeezing. Kalliga looked at her.

'This is the last safe water before my family's nest.'

Amber blinked at him, then knelt and had a drink.

'Are you okay?' Bec asked.

Amber wiped her mouth and sank back onto the ground, ignoring the mud seeping into her pants. 'It's just my ankle and shoulder. And I can still feel the call.'

'Me too,' Lucy said.

Bec splashed some more water onto her face. 'Ugh, it's so muggy.'

Amber pulled a face. 'Just like home. It never seems to stop raining in Barrington.'

The three guards hadn't joined them in drinking from the creek. Bec cast sideways glances at them. Two of them were taking sips from small bottles. None of the Boneheads seemed bothered by the humidity. Did Boneheads sweat? They weren't, from what she could tell.

'Time to go,' Kalliga said.

Bec felt more energetic after the short break. The water seemed to have cleared away the ill effects of the trip through the gate. Lucy and Alice's eyes had brightened. Lucy stopped clinging to her, although she stayed close, eyeing the guards. Jaws had recovered his usual energy. He trotted next to Amber, his head held high.

Amber continued to struggle. Her eyes were glazed and she winced when a small branch whipped her injured shoulder as she passed. Her limp had worsened. Bec frowned, but there wasn't anything they could do. They had to press on.

The route started to climb. Kalliga didn't reduce the pace to match the change in terrain. Bec was soon gasping for breath. The forest changed. The ferns and bracken were replaced with shrubs. Some, like the twisted banksias and grevilleas, looked identical to ones that Bec had seen in her world. Others, like several different species of shrubs with peeling, purple bark, were completely foreign. As they climbed higher, the trailing vines disappeared. Bec breathed a sigh of relief. She wouldn't miss them.

After two hours of solid climbing, the eucalypts had thinned out. They were shorter, and allowed more sunlight to reach the ground. Small flowers popped up out of the leaf litter. Kalliga led them onto a clear plateau. For the first time, Bec got a feel for the place where they'd found themselves. In all directions, the forest stretched as far as she could see, but there were pockets of cleared land: high points like the one they were on; rocky outcrops; the odd patch of grassland.

Clouds drifted across the sky. The sun was low. Bec wondered how long they had until it disappeared below the horizon. Kalliga had been clear that they needed to arrive before dusk. She shivered. What came out in the forest at night?

'What is that?' Lucy pointed at a rocky outcrop a few hundred metres away, separated from them by a deep canyon. Something was moving on it – something huge.

'Turek,' Kalliga said. 'Keep away from them. They're venomous, and they eat nestlings, even the older ones.' He eyed Lucy. 'You are not much larger than our older nestlings.'

Bec didn't think they needed the warning to keep away from the turek. It was eight metres long, with a pointed head, thick body covered in dark grey scales and long, thick tail. It was walking on four short, muscled legs, each ending in five long, sharp claws. The scales on top of its head were bright orange.

'It's a giant goanna,' Amber breathed.

It was a goanna, Bec thought, in the same way that a lion was a house cat.

'It's a dinosaur,' Alice said.

'There's no dinosaurs on the southern continent – only on the northern,' Kalliga said.

The humans stared at him.

'Did you just say there are dinosaurs on the northern continent?' Amber asked. 'Live ones?'

'They're not extinct in our world. That's why we live on the southern continent.' He turned away. 'Come.'

Amber watched him stalk to the end of the plateau. 'Do you think he's having us on?'

Bec shrugged. 'He's never shown any sign of having a sense of humour before.'

'Maybe Bonehead humour is different to ours.'

'Or maybe they do have dinosaurs. Why not?'

'I'd like to see real live dinosaurs,' Alice said.

'Definitely not,' Amber said. 'I'm drawing the line at dinosaur-watching tours.'

'Me, too,' Lucy said in a quiet voice. She was staring at the turek, her arms wrapped around the teddy. Her whole body was trembling.

Bec took her arm and led her after Kalliga. 'We'd better keep moving.'

From the plateau, they started to descend. The forest closed in around them. Kalliga picked up the pace. He bounded down the hill, his long legs seeming to skim over any obstructions. The girls were almost running to keep up. Bec struggled through the leaf litter. She kept tripping on invisible obstacles – vines, tree roots, rocks – and landing with her hands on the ground. Amber had fallen behind.

The ground flattened out again. Kalliga paused next to a patch of the purple-barked shrubs and waited for them to catch up. Bec bent over her knees, sucking in breaths of air.

'Look out!' Kalliga's voice rang out.

Bec jerked upright and followed his gaze. Amber had stopped a short distance up the hill to catch her breath. The three guards waited nearby, watching. Bec let out a gasp. A turek was stalking Amber through the vines. This one was even larger than the one they'd seen on the rocky outcrop. Amber swung around at Kalliga's warning. Her eyes widened. She backed away and fled down the hill. Her right foot caught on a vine. She tripped and sprawled on the ground.

Kalliga drew his sword and bounded back up the hill towards Amber. Bec glanced at the three guards. They didn't move. It was clear they had no intention of intervening.

The turek leapt, opening its jaw wide. Lucy let out a whimper. Kalliga wasn't going to reach Amber in time.

Twenty

Jaws leapt forward to meet the turek. He locked his jaw on the beast's throat and scratched it with his claws. The turek thrashed around, trying to dislodge him. Amber scrambled upright and drew her knife. The turek flung Jaws away. He landed against the base of a eucalypt and didn't move.

Amber lunged forward and stabbed at the turek with her knife. It let out a deep hiss and backed away. Kalliga reached Amber and pointed his sword at the beast. It hissed again and turned, its enormous tail flailing in the dirt. It disappeared into the undergrowth. Amber was surprised that the huge creature could move so fast.

She ran to Jaws and placed a hand against his body. His side was moving up and down. He was alive.

Kalliga sheathed his sword. 'That nyth is not normal,' he said, looking at Jaws through narrowed eyes. 'No nyth should stand up to a turek, not even a fully grown adult. How did you train it to do that?'

Amber gave him a blank look. 'I didn't.'

Kalliga shook his head. 'Here.' He held out Yorilla's sword.

Amber stood and pulled the sword belt around her waist. Kalliga strode back down the hill. Amber lifted Jaws and cradled him against her body. She caught sight of the three Bonehead guards, hidden within the trees.

'Thanks for the help,' she said, her voice heavy with sarcasm.

One of the guards looked down its nose at her. 'We agreed that we wouldn't kill you – yet. If the forest kills you, that is its business. Kalliga may be willing to waste energy protecting ustiga; we are not.'

Amber scowled. She hugged Jaws against her chest and limped after Kalliga.

Kalliga increased his pace. Amber struggled to keep up. Her ankle sent sharp pains up her leg with every step.

Ahead of them, Amber caught glimpses through the trees of a wide, shallow stream. As they approached, Kalliga froze. He put a hand up and dropped to the ground, behind a fallen log. Amber dropped too, her heart racing. What now?

She slid through the leaf litter to the log. The stream curved its way through the forest, gushing over and around smooth, grey stones. An enormous kangaroo with a shaggy red coat stood on the opposite bank, its head down, drinking water. Its legs were like tree trunks, with huge, defined muscles. It lifted its head and stood upright, staring in their direction, even though they were hidden behind the log. Amber held her breath. It was the largest kangaroo she had ever seen – at least three and a half metres tall. A joey's legs and head hung out of its pouch.

The magnificent animal shook its head, spraying water from its snout, then stared in their direction again. With a final shake of its head, it bounded away, each leap covering more than ten metres.

Amber let out the breath she had been holding in a gasp. Kalliga stared after it. 'You are fortunate to see an ang'kala. They are rare, and sacred to my people.'

'I can see why,' Amber said.

'In ancient times, when the ang'kala were not so rare, the nalyrd would be selected by the ang'kala: if a person could get close enough to touch one, they would be considered favoured by the ang'kala and worthy to be a nalyrd. There was some sense to it. It requires considerable patience and bravery to approach an ang'kala, which you also need to be nalyrd. These days we vote for the nalyrd, but the favour of the ang'kala is still a potent symbol.'

Amber gave Kalliga a sideways look. The ang'kala seemed to have cast a spell over him. It was the first time she'd heard him speak without sneering.

Kalliga stood and shook himself. He stepped over the log. 'Come.'

A howl rang out over the hills – a mix between a donkey braying and a dingo howling. Amber froze. She had heard that call before, when the Boneheads had been hunting them. Another voice joined the first, then another, and another, until the air was full of the cries.

Amber squeezed the unconscious Jaws. 'Giant wombats.'

'Nyth,' Kalliga said.

'There's so many of them,' Alice said, her eyes wide.

Kalliga bared his teeth. 'My family's nest. We are almost there.'

Amber's heart beat faster. She glanced at Bec. Bec's face was pale and she was pressing her elbows into her sides. She saw Amber looking at her and gave a shaky smile.

Kalliga followed the stream. The stones along its banks grew larger, and the stream became narrower and deeper. Amber began to notice signs of habitation: tree stumps that were so smooth the tree must have been cut by a blade; rocks with figures carved into them. The route Kalliga was taking turned into a rough path, worn into the ground by the passing of many feet, the vegetation on its edges trimmed.

The trees cast long shadows on the ground. Kalliga kept glancing at the sun, which was low in the sky. Amber noticed their guards doing the same. What came out in the forest after night? Something worse than the turek? She opened her mouth to ask Kalliga, then closed it again. Better not to know.

She heard the sound of running water. The stream curved around, and ahead of them was a flat rock platform, several metres above their heads. The stream bubbled over the rock and fell in a waterfall to the ground below.

Five Boneheads appeared on the rock platform, armed with wicked-looking knives and dressed in the same tight, green clothes as the guards. One of them threw its knife. It landed within a centimetre of Amber's foot. She leapt back, landing hard on her ankle again, and gasped in pain.

Kalliga picked the knife up and called out to the Boneheads in his language. One of the Boneheads called back. Kalliga scowled and responded. After a moment, a different Bonehead called something to him. He relaxed.

'We can go up.' He glanced at the guards. 'They need to leave their weapons.'

The guards didn't seem surprised. They were already stripping themselves of swords and knives, and piling them on a flat rock.

'Won't they get damaged?' Bec asked.

'One of my family will collect them and bring them into the nest, and return them tomorrow when they leave.'

'You don't want us to leave our weapons?'

'No. You are guests.'

'We are?'

'My Nalyrd wants to meet you.'

'Do you usually try to kill your guests?' Amber asked, rubbing her injured ankle.

Kalliga gave her a dismissive look. 'If they'd been trying to kill you, we wouldn't be talking. I'd be arguing with Rebecca about what to do with your body.'

Amber stared at him. Was that a joke?

One of the Boneheads on the rock platform lifted a coiled rope in one hand. He flung it over the right side of the rock platform, where the rough path led up a steep, muddy slope. It hit the side of the platform with a slap and slithered to the ground.

'Come,' Kalliga said. He grasped the rope and walked up the slope, using the rope to steady himself.

'You go,' Amber said to Bec.

Bec climbed up, placing her feet with care. Amber gestured for Alice and Lucy to follow her. Alice slithered up, her feet slipping in the mud. Lucy followed. Once she was at the top, Amber held Jaws against her body with her right arm and took hold of the rope with her hands. She placed her left foot against the path and then placed her right foot above it. Her ankle gave way, and she slid down the slope to the ground, covering her clothes in mud. Clenching her teeth, she clutched the rope again and put her left foot back on the path. She took a deep breath, and focused on climbing, one step after another.

She scrambled on all fours onto the rock platform. The three guards followed behind her, stepping easily onto the platform and around her, making her feel clumsy.

The platform was made of two separate, weathered pieces of granite. She was standing on the smaller piece, which was about five metres wide. The large piece stretched for about fifteen metres along the edge of the cliff. The stream flowed between the two pieces. Small ferns clung to the side of the platform, buffeted by the water, and on the edge of the platform a twisted eucalypt grasped both pieces of granite with its roots and grew over the top of the waterfall.

A tall, stone wall crossed the platform, constructed from many grey granite rocks of different sizes and shapes. In each direction it curved away and ran to the edge of a granite escarpment that towered above them about a kilometre behind the rock platform. The wall created a protected half-circle underneath the escarpment. There was a small gap in the wall where the stream flowed out.

Kalliga was speaking to one of the guards. Bec, Alice and Lucy knelt on the large piece of rock, using cupped hands to scoop water out of the stream into their mouths.

Amber jumped across the stream to join them. 'Is the water safe?'

'Kalliga says so,' Bec said.

Amber sank to her own knees and drank. She sat back on her heels and shifted Jaws in her arms, looking over the valley below. The sun was hovering just above the tops of the trees. It would be dark soon.

The thrum of voices trying to break through the shield in her mind was gone. The day's walk must have put enough distance between her and the gate. She let the shield fade away, relieved to have one less thing sapping her energy.

Bec was staring at the gap in the wall and shifting from one foot to the other. She wrapped her arms around herself and rubbed them with her hands.

Amber stood. 'Are you okay?'

Bec tightened her arms and spoke in a low voice. 'The last time I was in a Bonehead nest, they wanted to kill me, and my team. At least that time we had Yorilla with us. She did her best to convince them to let us go. Now we've only got him.' She gave Kalliga a sidelong look. 'No way he's sticking his neck out for us.'

As though he could feel her eyes on him, Kalliga turned towards them. He jerked his head towards the gap in the wall. 'Come.'

He placed one foot on each side of the rock platform, straddling the stream, and walked through the gap.

Amber glanced at Bec. Bec gave herself a shake and filled her voice with airy confidence. 'What's the worst that can happen?' She bounded after Kalliga.

'You had to say that?' Amber asked.

Lucy made a move towards the gap, but Alice pulled her back and looked at Amber.

Amber took a breath in. 'We'd better go,' she said to Alice.

She sent Alice and Lucy through the gap first. Lucy led the way, with Alice keeping a hand on one of her shoulders. Amber didn't know whether Alice was comforting Lucy or herself.

She followed them through the gap, taking care to step on the rocks. Four Grey Bones stood on the other side of the gap, two on either side of the stream, their hands hovering over their sheathed swords. They didn't step back as she came through, forcing her to continue to straddle the stream as she passed between them. The last rays of sunlight cast odd shadows across their faces. Their pure black eyes watched her in silence. She hid a shiver.

She blew out a breath of air as she joined Kalliga, Bec and the girls on the left side of the stream, and turned to look at the Boneheads' nest. She didn't know what she'd expected, but this wasn't it. Every inch of ground within the semi-circle of the wall was covered with plants – most of them about ankle height. Some she recognised from her own world, or from the forest, but many she'd never seen before. There was no order or pattern to where they grew – all mixed together in a riot of leaves and colour.

The ground between the wall and the escarpment was strange. It sloped upwards, but at regular intervals small, rounded hillocks rose out of the ground, covered with the same plants as the rest of the ground. Large, weathered granite rocks, like the ones they were standing on, were scattered across the ground. Wide, low circular pots had been placed on the rocks. Plants spewed out of them in a tangled mess.

The three guards who had followed them from the gate slid through the gap. One of the Boneheads standing on the edge of the stream directed them along the wall.

'Where are they going?' Amber asked.

'We have accommodation for uninvited outsiders near the wall. Most families have something similar. We don't welcome outsiders as guests often, but no-one would ever refuse another Anaia shelter from the forest after dusk.'

Amber looked back at the wall – protecting them from whatever was in the forest.

The air filled with high-pitched shrieks, mixed with the howls that she'd come to recognise as the call of the giant wombats – the nyth. She held the unconscious Jaws close to her body, protecting him with both arms, in case the local nyth objected to the interloper.

The source of the shrieks appeared: a group of the smallest Boneheads she'd ever seen. The bony plates on their heads were missing the six sharp horns Amber was used to seeing, although some had small lumps where the horns would be. Unlike the adults, who all wore the same tight, green clothes, the children wore clothes in bright, primary colours that hung loose on them. Amber wondered if, like human parents, Bonehead parents dressed their children in clothes large enough 'to grow into'.

The small Boneheads were surrounded by small nyth. They ran through the plants, squashing some. The nyth stopped a metre or so from Kalliga and the humans, but the small Boneheads surrounded them on all sides.

Lucy drew back and clutched Amber.

'Nestlings,' Kalliga said. 'They are harmless.' He spoke to them in his language. With more high-pitched shrieks they reformed their group and tumbled away, the nyth following them.

Kalliga turned his gaze on Amber and waved a hand at the nyth. 'See those nyth? They know what is expected, and they are younger than yours.'

Without waiting for her reply, he strode forward through the plants, stepping on them as though they were unimportant. The humans followed.

The sun had disappeared. The sky was a dark pink; the clouds like orange and pink paint strokes across it. Kalliga led them past several of the odd, round hillocks. Amber saw a group of Boneheads leaning over the plants on top of one of the hillocks, their silhouettes black against the coloured sky. She couldn't tell what they were doing.

They rounded yet another of the hillocks, and Amber stumbled. The ground was broken by several of the large, flat granite rocks like the platform at the entrance. These ones were clear of plants, and many, many Boneheads – all Grey Bones – sat or stood on them, or sat on small granite boulders that were dotted around them. Huge adult nyth lay or sniffed among the plants surrounding the rocks. Wide square poles, each about two metres high, were stuck in the ground around the rocks. A warm, yellow light emanated from each pole. The light made it easy to see, without feeling too bright or artificial.

A low murmur came from the Boneheads, but they fell silent as Kalliga and the humans approached. Those that were sitting stood.

Amber cringed. Every single one of the Boneheads wore a sword, and all of them placed their hands on their sword hilts.

Kalliga swept past them, his eyes on the one Bonehead that had remained seated, on a worn granite boulder, with several Boneheads hovering around. Something about the scene reminded Amber of a king on a throne, even if the 'throne' was a rock.

Kalliga came to a stop in front of the seated Bonehead. 'This is my Nalyrd.' The contempt that Amber was used to hearing when Kalliga spoke had disappeared – his voice filled with reverence. He pointed at each of the humans in turn. 'Amber Yu, Rebecca Williams, Alice Taylor, Lucy Taylor.'

The Bonehead was shorter than any she'd met before, its skin more wrinkled and folded. Amber met its gaze and stared. Apart from a small black hole where its pupil was, the Bonehead's eyes were completely red. Her eyes, Amber corrected herself. Yorilla had said that nalyrd meant matriarch, so presumably the Bonehead was female.

'I am Rayeta,' the Bonehead said in a deep, gravelly voice, 'I must ask for your indulgence if I make a mistake – I have not had the opportunity to speak your language before now.'

'What you just said was perfect,' Bec said, wrinkling her brow. 'How can you speak so well, if you haven't spoken it before?'

'Because others in my family have,' Rayeta said. 'Through q'wakay, what one knows, all know.'

'Q'wakay?'

'What your PM calls Quake,' Kalliga said.

Amber wrinkled her brow. 'That's the drug that Elise gave me.'

There was a rasp of metal. The Boneheads surrounding Rayeta drew their swords in one swift movement and pointed them towards Amber.

Amber stumbled backwards. Balancing Jaws in the crook of her left arm, she drew Yorilla's sword with her right and reached out to the power. It rushed into her body, filling her.

Twenty-one

'Nyon!' Rayeta roared. 'Enough!' Amber felt the power behind the command. It felt different to when Walker had given the same order and frozen everyone in the farmhouse extension. That had felt like a sledgehammer, forcing Walker's will on everyone. This felt less intrusive. It almost convinced her that the urge to lower the sword was her own. She waited for the power to burn it away, but it didn't respond. She found herself lowering the sword. The guards did the same.

One of the guards let out a low growl. He rattled off a string of words in the Bonehead language.

'What did he say?' Bec asked.

Kalliga sounded bored. 'He said it is denarr – forbidden - for an outsider to take q'wakay. Her life should be forfeit.'

'What?' Bec's eyes widened.

The same command that had made her lower her sword had left Amber too lethargic to feel afraid, but she shot Kalliga a glare. He couldn't feign interest in her life?

'She didn't drink it,' Kalliga added, with a sigh. 'One of the Walker's pets injected her with it. It just knocked her out.'

'So, she didn't use q'wakay to commune.' Rayeta waved a hand, and Amber felt the power disappear. She was free. Rayeta gave the Boneheads who had drawn their swords a stern look. 'It is to be expected that there will be misunderstandings when species from different worlds meet. We should hear each other out first, and draw swords as a last resort.'

The Boneheads sheathed their swords and stepped back next to Rayeta. They glowered at Amber.

Amber bit her lip. Two minutes in their nest and she had

already made enemies.

Rayeta beckoned them closer. Amber didn't want to move closer to the Boneheads with the swords, but she didn't think it would be a good idea to upset Rayeta. She stepped forward, followed by Bec, Lucy and Alice.

Rayeta looked at Bec. 'Rebecca,' she said. 'Yorilla spoke of you.'

Bec's eyes filled with tears. 'Walker killed her. I'm sorry.'

'Do not be sorry. To be killed by so powerful an enemy, in pursuit of the family's interest, is an honour. We should celebrate, not mourn.'

Bec clenched her hands into fists, but said nothing.

Rayeta's lip curved. 'You do not agree.'

'I'm sad that she's dead. And I spoke to her when she was dying – she wanted to live, too.'

Kalliga's gaze hardened. 'You shame her,' he snarled.

Bec brushed tears away. 'I don't mean to.'

Rayeta turned her stern look on Kalliga. 'No-one can shame Yorilla. Her place of honour in our family is assured. And a friendship between our two species should be celebrated.' She nodded. 'You are welcome to our nest, humans.'

She raised her voice and called out to a Bonehead standing on the other side of the platform. 'Kimissa.'

The Bonehead strode over. Ignoring the humans, it looked straight at Jaws, and held out its arms to take him.

Amber stepped back, pulling Jaws close into her body.

Kimissa lifted its gaze, as though seeing Amber for the first time. 'Your nyth is hurt.'

'A turek flung it against a tree.'

'After,' Kalliga said, 'The nyth attacked the turek.'

Kimissa stared at Kalliga. 'The nyth attacked a turek?'

Kalliga nodded. Kimissa stared at Jaws. 'This is – unusual.' It held out its arms again.

'Kimissa won't hurt your nyth,' Kalliga said, sounding bored again. 'He'll help him.'

Amber kept hold of Jaws. 'I want him back.'

Bec raised her eyebrows at Amber. 'You do? Why?'

Kalliga snorted. 'Believe me, nobody here wants to keep your untrained nyth.'

Amber looked at Jaws. He hadn't moved since she'd picked him up. She would have to trust the Boneheads to help him. She held him out to Kimissa. Kimissa took him in his arms and strode away.

Rayeta turned her gaze on Amber and closed her eyes. Minutes passed. Amber shifted from foot to foot. Had Rayeta gone to sleep? If her skin was anything to go by, she was old. Perhaps meeting with them had tired her out. She glanced at Kalliga, but he didn't move, his eyes fixed on Rayeta.

Rayeta opened her eyes again. She turned to Kalliga. 'She is not powerful enough to close the gate,' she said, nodding at Amber.

Kalliga jerked his head back. 'Yorilla thought she was. Yorilla thought she might be as powerful as the Walker.'

'Perhaps,' Rayeta said. 'It is hard to get a strong reading.' She shook her head. 'She is too emotional; the lechiko comes and goes, like a skittish nyth joey.'

Amber felt a flash of anger. 'I'm sorry that I'm not as unfeeling as you all are.'

Rayeta gave her a calm look. 'You mistake control for lack of feeling, Amber Yu. And you misunderstand my concern. When you use the lechiko, you feel unwell afterwards?'

Amber shrugged. 'Yeah. It makes me throw up.'

'We call it rynsard – the backlash. It can kill the lechiko user.'

Amber sagged. 'It killed Kim – my friend.'

Rayeta nodded. 'I feel that closing the gate is beyond you. The rynsard would kill you before you completed the task.' She looked at Kalliga. 'And you forget: the Walker did not open the gate on his own. He uses our people's energy to make up for what he lacks in himself.'

'So there's nothing we can do?'

Rayeta narrowed her eyes. 'There is always something we can do, Kalliga. Kill the Walker, for one. Block his access to our people. But there is something simpler than that.' She nodded at Lucy. 'The nestling is more powerful than Amber. She should be strong enough to close the gate.'

Amber frowned. 'You want Lucy to close the gate?'

'Yes.'

'And you think she can withstand this backlash?'

'Long enough to close the gate, yes.'

Amber drew her brows in. 'What does that mean? Will she survive afterwards?'

Rayeta tilted her head. 'Possibly.'

Amber gave a firm shake of her head. 'No. I'm not risking Lucy's life.'

'No?' Kalliga sounded incredulous. He moved in close to Amber, towering over her and forcing her to look up to meet his gaze. 'Do you think this is a game? The Walker's thirst for power won't be sated by your country. He will continue to bring in soldiers from my world to take over country after country, killing your people as he goes, until your whole world is controlled by him and his army. He will do it by sucking the energy out of more and more of my people, until both our worlds are shadows of what they once were. Stopping him is more important than one nestling's life!'

Amber crossed her arms. 'I'm not risking Lucy's life,' she repeated.

Kalliga bared his teeth.

Lucy stepped forward and took Amber's hand with her right hand. Her left was still wrapped around the teddy. 'Maybe we could do it together.'

Amber looked at Lucy. 'It's too risky.'

Lucy met her gaze. 'Yorilla said she'd tell us how to take those restraints off if you closed the gate.'

Amber wrinkled her brow. 'Yeah -'

Lucy shrank back against Amber, but lifted her chin and faced Kalliga. 'Now that Yorilla's dead - will you tell us how to take the restraints off?'

Kalliga ran his eyes up and down Lucy, sizing her up. 'If you close the gate - yes.'

Lucy tilted her head to meet Amber's eyes again. 'They put the restraints on my mum, too. Maybe if we know how to take them off, we can rescue her.'

Amber paled. 'Lucy - your mum -' She hesitated. The girls would hate her if they knew she'd left Elise behind in the car park. 'We don't know where she is,' she said.

Lucy glared at her. 'Bec says you don't give up hope. You never know what the future holds.'

Bec turned to Rayeta. 'Could Amber and Lucy close the gate together?'

Rayeta closed her eyes for a moment, then snapped them open. 'Yes. I would have to teach Amber how to share Lucy's power, but that is possible. The power would be shared, so the backlash would be shared.'

'Enough that both of them would survive?'

'Yes.'

Kalliga bared his teeth at Amber. 'Is that good enough for you, mammal?'

Amber looked from him to Rayeta. 'I guess so. Yes.'

Kalliga stepped back and looked at Rayeta.

'This will take some thought,' Rayeta said. 'It will not be easy to teach Amber what she needs to know.' She ran her eyes over them. 'It is late. You are tired. We should rest now, and eat, and consider this in the morning.'

She waved a small Bonehead over. Like the ones that had

surrounded them earlier, this one had small lumps in place of horns, but it was much more composed than the nestlings they had seen earlier. There was a look in its eyes that made Amber think it was older than it looked.

'This is Dansera.'

Kalliga bestowed a smile on Dansera. 'I heard you completed your first q'wakay commune. Congratulations.'

Dansera gave him a nod.

'Dansera will take you to the guesthouse,' Rayeta said. 'You may go anywhere in our nest, but I ask that you take Dansera with you, and do as she asks. She will ensure that you do not break any of our rules through lack of knowledge or understanding.'

Bec nodded. 'Thank you.'

Amber opened her mouth, then hesitated.

'Is there something else I can do for you, Amber Yu?' Rayeta asked.

'I need to get home. My son needs me.'

Rayeta gave Kalliga a quizzical look.

'Human nestlings require intensive care for many years,' Kalliga said. 'Their parents are often devoted to them.' Kalliga wrinkled his nose as though the idea was distasteful.

'Ah, of course, they are mammals.' Rayeta turned to Amber. 'I am afraid we must detain you, at least for tonight. We do not venture into the forest at night – there are dangers here that you do not have in your world. Perhaps you can return tomorrow, but there is much we must discuss first. For now, go with Dansera.'

The Boneheads either side of Rayeta were fingering the hilts of their swords as though itching to draw them, despite Rayeta's admonishment. Even if the forest was safe, Amber knew she didn't have the energy to walk back to the gate, let alone take on Walker and his minions on the other side. Her ankle and shoulder were aching. She nodded to Rayeta, and limped after Dansera.

Oliver would be fine with Adam and Sarah to look after him. She swallowed, feeling a lump in her throat, and blinked back tears.

Dansera strode through the ubiquitous plant life, lighting the way with a small, hand-held version of the large poles. The last of the light had disappeared while they were talking to Rayeta, and the sky was now lit by stars that appeared and disappeared as the clouds passed under them. Amber stared up at them, trying to pick out the Southern Cross, or any other familiar constellations. There was nothing she recognised. They might be hidden behind the clouds, but she suspected they weren't there.

A breeze had sprung up, cooling the sweat on Amber's skin and clothes. She wondered where the guesthouse could be. Apart from the gate, the wall was the only construction she'd seen since they'd arrived in the Boneheads' world. The Boneheads described their home as a nest – were they going to be expected to sleep in some kind of bird's nest?

Dansera stopped next to one of the hillocks. She reached forward and pulled aside an armful of plant tendrils and vines, revealing a hole that stretched from the ground almost to the full height of the hillock, about as tall as Amber. An adult Bonehead would need to duck to enter it. The light from Dansera's torch hit the floor just inside the entrance, showing a sloping dirt tunnel. Beyond, the tunnel was black. Dansera gestured for them to climb through the hole.

Amber shrank back. 'What is this place?'

'Our guesthouse.'

Dansera waved at the hole again, looking confused that Amber didn't move.

'You might need to go through first,' Kalliga said in a bored tone. Amber jumped. She hadn't realised that he'd followed them.

'Hold this, then,' Dansera said. Kalliga took hold of the armful of vines. Dansera stepped into the hole and started down the tunnel, disappearing into the shadows. 'Come,' she called back to them.

Amber hesitated and squinted into the tunnel. She couldn't see anything.

'You do realise that you're in the middle of our nest?' Kalliga said. 'If we wanted to kill you, we could do it just as easily up here as down there.'

Amber scowled at him. 'Thanks, I feel so much better now.'

She took a deep breath and stepped into the hole. Bec and the girls followed.

The tunnel was steeper and shorter than she'd expected. After a few paces, it opened out into a circular room, taller than the largest Bonehead she'd seen, and so wide that she thought it must take up the entire hillock. It was lit with the same warm, yellow light as the platforms above, but here the light came from three strips, each about fifteen centimetres wide, that circled the room: one just below the ceiling; one at Amber's shoulder height; and one at her waist height. In the centre of the room was a round pool of water. A low platform, about knee height, circled one side of the room. It was made from packed dirt and covered in layers of material, in the same bright colours as the clothes worn by the nestlings. Amber guessed it was for sleeping on.

On the other side of the room, a trench ran from one end to the other, with water running down it. Opposite the tunnel entrance, a pipe ran out of the wall. It divided into two, with one end extending over the edge of the pool, and the other over the trench. Water fell from the pipe into each. Amber couldn't see any outflow in either the pool or trench, but there must have been one, because the water level in both stayed the same.

'You can drink the running water. Don't drink from the pool – it's for washing.' Dansera pointed at the trench. 'That is for your waste – what you call a toilet.'

Bec nodded.

She ran her eyes over the four humans. 'I'll bring you something clean to wear.' She pointed at some squares of material, the same as on the platform, folded on the side of the pool. 'You can use those to wash and dry yourselves.'

'Thanks,' Bec said.

'Don't take too long,' Dansera said. 'The meal will be served soon.'

Bec dropped her pack near the door. Amber lay on the sleeping platform while the two girls bathed. The material was thin and soft. She stared at the strips of yellow light above her. She was so tired, she thought she could have slept even if they had been sleeping in a bird's nest. Her eyes closed.

Bec nudged her awake. Bec's hair was wet, and she was dressed in the green clothes with long green hood favoured by the Boneheads, although they hung loose on her.

'Your turn,' Bec said. 'Dansera says we need to hurry or we'll miss the meal.'

Amber struggled up. She looked for the girls. They were lying on the sleeping platform, dressed in bright red clothes. Lucy was smoothing the fur on her teddy. Alice watched her with a disapproving look, but didn't say anything.

Amber removed her sweaty, mud- and blood-stained clothes, peeling the jacket and shirt over her injured shoulder. She clenched her teeth in preparation for the cold as she stepped into the water, but it was lukewarm. She slid down until her head was submerged. The water stung the wound on her shoulder and the burns on her wrists, but eased the pain in her ankle and eye.

She sat up and used one of the squares of material to scrub herself, washing off layers of dirt, and rinsed her hair. She removed the dirty bandages from her wrists and the padding from her shoulder, and patted the wounds with a clean square of material. While she washed, Bec prowled around the room, picking up the material on the sleeping platform and putting it down again, checking out the strips of lighting, kicking her shoes against the dirt floor. Amber shook her head. She doubted Bec would find any clues in the basic room that would help the Resistance fight the Boneheads.

She dried herself on another piece of material and wrapped it around her. Bec replaced the bandages on her wrists and padding on her shoulder, and then handed her a folded piece of green material. 'Dansera dropped off the clothes while you were sleeping.'

Amber unfolded the material. It was a single piece, like a jumpsuit, with a long hood. Dansera hadn't provided any underwear, so she put her own undies and bra back on, still damp with sweat. She stepped into the jumpsuit. There were no zips or buttons – the material stretchy enough that she could pull it up over her waist and shoulders and it sprang back around her body. There were large pockets on the inside where you could keep small items, like knives. Like Bec, it hung loose on her rather than tight like the Boneheads – their bodies the wrong shape.

She twisted back and forth, admiring the way the material changed from light to dark green as it moved. 'We should keep these. Great camouflage.'

'Not ours,' Alice said. She looked down at the bright red jumpsuit and screwed up her nose.

'Maybe it's so they don't lose their kids,' Amber said. 'Those nestlings seem pretty energetic.'

'Check out the hood.' Bec pulled her hood over her head. It fell over her face and down to her neck.

Amber laughed. 'You need a bone on your head.'

'Yup.' She pushed the hood back off her face. 'We'd better go – Dansera's waiting.'

The laughter left Amber's face. She pulled the sword belt back on and settled it against her hips. Time to face the Boneheads again.

Twenty-two

Kalliga had disappeared. Dansera was pacing outside the tunnel. 'Oh good, you're ready. I'm hungry.'

The nestlings and nyth they'd seen earlier were tumbling down a nearby hillock, crushing plants with their passage. They bounded over to the humans, surrounding them and babbling in the Bonehead language.

'Hi,' Amber said.

'They can't speak your language,' Dansera said. 'They haven't communed with q'wakay yet.'

She raised her voice and spoke in a harsh tone. With a last babble of voices, the nestlings and nyth bounded away again. Amber could hear them long after she lost sight of them among the mounds.

Dansera led them back to the rock platform where they'd met Rayeta. There were many more Boneheads at the rock platform now, standing around in small circles, talking, or kneeling next to large, wooden platters spread across the rock. They stared at the humans; some with curiosity, and others with distaste.

Dansera waved at the platters. 'Eat.'

Amber approached the platters with some trepidation. They seemed to be full of the same plants that grew over every spare piece of land within the nest.

Rayeta approached from behind her. 'Is this food suitable for you? I understand that humans eat meat. We cannot digest it.'

'It's fine,' Bec said. 'We can survive without meat. Some people never eat it.'

Rayeta knelt next to the platter. Amber gave her a sideways look. She seemed very flexible for someone as old as Amber had assumed she was. She wondered if Rayeta was younger than she'd thought, or if the Boneheads didn't lose as much flexibility as they aged as humans did.

Rayeta scooped up a small amount of vegetables in her fingers and put them into her mouth. Amber copied her. She chewed the vegetables. They were limp, and very salty, as though they'd been boiled for a long time in salt. It wasn't a bad flavour, but a bit bland. She helped herself to some berries. These were uncooked and had a tart flavour.

Kalliga approached. Rayeta stood to talk to him. Bec knelt next to Amber. She whispered in Amber's ear. 'I never imagined that if monsters took over the world, they'd be vegetarian.'

'Thank goodness they are,' Amber whispered back. 'I was worried we'd be eating eyeballs or raw meat or something.'

Alice and Lucy sat cross-legged next to Bec. Alice screwed up her nose. 'The Boneheads eat this stuff in our world, too, but they always gave us human food.'

Rayeta and Kalliga sank down next to Amber. Amber cast nervous glances at them, but they were focused on the food. Amber forced herself to keep eating.

Rayeta turned to her. 'There are things I must teach you if you are to close the gate together with the nestling.' She nodded at Lucy, who frowned at being called a nestling. 'The easiest way to teach you would be for us to commune with q'wakay.'

'I don't understand,' Amber said, lifting a handful of berries towards her mouth. 'How will taking some drug teach me what I need to know?'

'Q'wakay allows us to see into each other's minds.'

Amber dropped her hand and stared at Rayeta. 'I don't believe you.'

Kalliga let out a low growl. 'Watch what you say, mammal.'

Rayeta held up a hand and said something to Kalliga in their language. He clenched his teeth. Rayeta looked at Amber. 'I assure you it is true.'

'You'll be able to see into my mind?'

'We'll be able to see into each other's minds,' Rayeta said. 'You will gain the combined knowledge of my family.'

Bec's eyes widened. 'She'll know all about the Boneheads?'

Kalliga growled again. 'Anaia.'

Bec gave Amber a wide-eyed look. Amber scowled. She knew Bec was thinking about the MG's order to collect intelligence about the Boneheads. 'What if I don't want to take your drug? When Elise gave it to me -' she glanced behind her, at the other Boneheads, in case they attacked her again, 'it knocked me out. I couldn't move for ages.'

'Because Elise injected you with it,' Kalliga said. 'We don't take it that way – we drink it.'

Amber waved a hand. 'Whatever. What if I don't want my head full of your combined knowledge?'

'Communing can't be forced,' Rayeta said. 'It must be your choice.'

Kalliga gave her a mocking smile. 'I'm sure we can convince you it's worth your while. How about this – you'll learn everything we know about sword fighting. Maybe enough to defeat the Walker.'

Amber stared at him. 'You can't just learn that stuff in your mind. You have to practise – train.'

'You need to train to build muscles and fitness, true. But communing will teach you every move you could ever need.'

Amber stared at the berries, bright red against the green jumpsuit. Could she really learn how to fight, just like that? It seemed too easy.

Rayeta waved at the food. 'Eat, rest. We will discuss this again tomorrow.'

She rose to her feet and joined another group of Boneheads, talking in a soothing voice in their language.

Kalliga gave Amber a cold look. 'The combined knowledge of my family is not given lightly, mammal. Very few outside of our family have ever been given the chance you are being given.' He strode away.

Bec spoke in an awed voice. 'You can't say no.'

Amber scowled. 'How would you like to let Rayeta see into your mind?'

Bec screwed up her face, then shrugged. 'It's worth it.'

Amber wiped her hands on the green jumpsuit. 'I think I've had all the salty vegetables I can stand.'

'Me too,' Bec said. She stood.

Amber winced as she put weight on her ankle. Sharp pains ran up her leg.

'Where's Dansera?'

'Here,' Dansera said, behind them. 'Do you want to return to the guesthouse?'

'Can we look around the – nest?' Bec asked.

'Of course.' Dansera looked pleased that they wanted a tour. She puffed out her chest and led them away from the platform, producing her small torch from the folds of her jumpsuit.

Amber limped after the others. All she wanted was to return to the guesthouse and collapse. But Bec wouldn't miss any chance to collect intelligence.

Dansera led them through the hillocks, pointing out different ones. 'Sayera lives there.' 'Iralda used to live there.' It didn't mean much to Amber, who hadn't heard of any of the names mentioned, and there wasn't much to see. In the dark, all the hillocks looked the same. Amber wondered if they were the same on the inside as the guesthouse.

She interrupted Dansera, who was pointing out the home of someone else they hadn't heard of. 'Can you tell us about q'wakay?'

Dansera pointed towards the dark escarpment. 'The q'wakeen is grown over there – that's what q'wakay is made from. I can show you, but not until morning.'

The sleeping platform in the guesthouse was comfortable, with the strange material serving as mattress, sheets and blankets. Amber lay down with her head near Bec's head.

'You are going to do this communing thing, aren't you?' Bec said.

Amber stared at the strip lights above her. There didn't seem to be any way to turn them off, although they hadn't tried very hard to find one. None of them liked the idea of being in the pitch dark underground. 'I haven't decided yet.'

'If they offered it to me, I would, like a shot.'

'I know.' Amber turned to the wall and closed her eyes. She pretended to sleep, but her mind was racing. If Kalliga was telling the truth, she could be an expert sword fighter – tomorrow. She wouldn't have to let Reuben pound her into the mud for months, with no guarantee that she would ever learn enough to fight Walker. She would just know it all. All she had to do was let Rayeta see into her mind. The thought made her cringe, but did it matter? Once she went back to her own world, she'd never see Rayeta again.

None of them slept well that night. There was no door apart from the vines, and Bec kept sitting up, thinking someone was coming down the tunnel, but there was never anyone there. The salty vegetables had left them thirsty, and each of them got up more than once to gulp water from the pipe.

Amber gave up on sleeping before the sun had even risen. She slipped off the sleeping platform, testing her weight on her ankle. It felt much better than the day before, so at least the bad night's sleep had done something. Her shoulder and wrists were stiff and aching, and her eye felt tender. She washed herself in the pool and pulled her dirty underwear and the jumpsuit back on.

Bec sat up, ran her hands through her hair, and let out a groan. 'I need coffee.'

'Maybe the Boneheads have something like coffee. They grow all those plants – maybe one of them is similar to a coffee plant.'

'I wish.'

Amber walked out of the tunnel and watched the sky lighten. The escarpment blocked the sun to the east, so she thought it would stay cool and dim in the half-circle nest for a long time. Dansera arrived. 'Are you ready to go?'

'I am. I'll just see if the others are.'

Amber ducked into the tunnel and returned with Bec and the girls in tow. Bec had had a wash, and looked fresh, but the girls' hair was tangled and stuck out at odd angles.

Dansera led the way between the hillocks towards the escarpment. They weren't the only ones awake early. Amber saw Boneheads working among the plants.

It took longer than Amber would have expected to reach the escarpment. Dansera took a convoluted route through the hillocks. Amber noticed that she never went near any of the Boneheads that were out and about. Amber's ankle started aching again. She gritted her teeth and ignored it.

Near the escarpment, the number of rocks and large boulders increased. The plants petered out and they found themselves jumping from rock to rock. The escarpment towered over them, like a giant wave about to come crashing down on their heads. Amber thought that even when the sun was in the west the sunlight would never reach the ground near the escarpment. They clambered onto one large boulder, and Dansera pointed down. About a metre below where they were standing, a stream ran along the edge of the escarpment. The rocks on either side were covered with what looked like rotting logs. The bases of the logs were straight, as though they had been cut with a blade, and no trees grew under the escarpment. Amber assumed the Boneheads had placed the logs there.

The logs were covered in a strange, purple growth. Small, white fruits grew on top. Dansera squatted and pointed at them. 'That's the q'wakeen.'

A lone figure moved along the stream, checking the logs.

'That's the q'wakeen yarli,' Dansera said, pointing at the figure. 'Roughly translated – q'wakeen nurse. It's a very important job; only the most trusted family members are allowed to do it. They take care of the q'wakeen, keep it healthy, make sure it has enough logs for food.'

Amber stood and prepared to climb down to the stream.

'Wait!' Dansera said. 'Only the yarli are allowed to go down there.'

Her movement had drawn the attention of the figure, who left the logs and hurried to where they were sitting.

The figure called something in the Bonehead language.

'She's telling us to keep back.'

'Sorry,' Amber said, squatting down again.

The yarli came closer, breathing heavily. She squinted at them, and said something else in the Bonehead language. Dansera replied in the same language. The yarli turned to them.

'You must not come any closer,' she said, switching to English. 'You might be carrying the kinrodo.'

'What's kinrodo?' Amber asked.

The yarli's face turned dark. 'A disease. If it gets into a q'wakeen crop it can destroy it within days.'

'The q'wakeen yarli have to decontaminate all their clothes and every part of their bodies before they approach the crop,' Dansera said. 'That's why they're the only ones allowed near it.'

Bec squinted at the q'wakeen. 'Is q'wakeen a type of fungi? The fruit looks like mushrooms.'

'No, it's a different evolutionary branch,' the yarli said. 'But some fungi have a similar effect on the brain to q'wakeen, just less intense.'

Dansera was looking at the sky. 'We should get back. They will be serving the morning meal soon. They'll ask questions if you're not there.'

Fresh platters of food had been placed on the rocks, but the food looked much the same as what they'd had the night before. Amber didn't think she could stomach any more salty vegetables. The girls picked at some fruit.

Bec surveyed the food platters and screwed up her nose. 'I'd face Walker's army right now if it would get me a coffee.'

Kalliga appeared behind them. 'Dansera said that you went to see the q'wakeen this morning.' Amber nodded. 'And?' he demanded.

Amber knew what he was asking – was she going to commune with Rayeta? The thought scared her, but it was also tempting. She couldn't kid herself. When they'd fought, she'd been no match for Walker. What if she had to face him again? This could save her life. She almost didn't dare think it, but maybe she could even – defeat him.

She looked at Kalliga, and then Bec. Both of them were watching her with narrowed eyes. She let out her breath in a sigh. 'I guess so. Yes.'

Kalliga gave a sharp nod with his head, and strode away. Rayeta had returned to what Amber thought of as her throne, and a group of Boneheads had formed around her. Kalliga pushed his way through to the front.

A babble of voices rose from the Boneheads around her. They seemed to be arguing about something.

Rayeta turned towards them and beckoned. 'As the matter involves the humans, they should be involved in the discussion,' she said, in English.

Bec and Amber exchanged glances. 'Somehow, I don't think they want to offer us coffee,' Bec muttered.

Amber wrapped her arms around herself. She and Bec walked towards the rock throne. Alice, Lucy and Dansera left the food platters and followed.

One of Rayeta's guards spoke in the Bonehead language.

Rayeta held up a hand. 'Speak in the human language, Sayera, so our guests can understand.'

'It is forbidden for outsiders to commune with q'wakay,' Sayera said. 'Our family agreed to the ban.'

'No agreements are set in stone,' Kalliga said. 'No-one can see what is to come.'

Rayeta nodded. 'We agreed at the time because we could see no reason not to. We did not know any outsiders other than the Walker.'

Sayera cast a glare at Amber and Bec. 'You must teach the humans in the human way.'

Kalliga laughed. 'The human way is glacial. Their children go to school for thirteen years to learn to be adults.'

Dansera looked at Alice with wide eyes. 'You have to spend thirteen years learning?'

Alice shrugged. 'Or more, if you go to uni, or TAFE. Why, what do you do?'

'Nestlings don't learn, they play,' Rayeta said. 'When they decide they are ready to put play behind them, they take q'wakay and commune with the nest. They learn all they need to know by communing.'

Dansera puffed her chest out. 'I had my first q'wakay commune last week. Now I am an adult.'

Lucy's mouth dropped open. 'You don't have to go to school at all?'

'Wish we didn't,' Alice said.

'We don't have time to teach Amber in the human way,' Rayeta said. 'We need to act now, before more lives are fed to the Walker's gate.'

'Are you forgetting why giving outsiders q'wakay was banned in the first place?' Sayera spat.

Kalliga snarled. Rayeta frowned and snapped something at Sayera in the Bonehead language.

Sayera glowered and spoke in a sullen voice. 'It is forbidden.'

'This must be decided by j'kiro,' a quiet voice said. It was a Bonehead with skin as wrinkled and folded as Rayeta's. Two of its horns had been sheared off.

'What's j'kiro?' Amber asked.

'A vote,' Bec said.

The new Bonehead dipped its head. 'She is correct.' It nodded to Amber. 'I am Enqua.'

'Nice to meet you.'

Enqua dipped its head again, and turned back to Rayeta. 'I will call the family together.'

Rayeta nodded. 'Do that.'

Amber picked at the food while Boneheads dribbled in from all directions. Rayeta and Kalliga's family was larger than she had realised.

Bec put an arm around Amber's shoulders and squeezed. 'Are you okay?'

Amber shrugged. 'I'm scared.' She looked at the Boneheads. 'But they might not let me do it, anyway.'

'They will,' Bec said. 'This is Yorilla and Kalliga's family. They're not going to worry about some rule.'

Enqua had placed two large buckets on the ground. The Boneheads lined up and walked past the buckets, tossing small items into them as though they were playing a child's game.

'What are they throwing in there?' Amber asked Dansera.

Dansera shrugged. 'Whatever they want. There is no rule,

except that it has to be something of value.'

Sayera stalked forward. Dansera nudged Amber. 'Be careful of him. He is not your friend.'

Amber and Bec exchanged glances.

'Thanks for the warning,' Amber said.

She chewed on a berry, screwing up her nose at its tart flavour. It was obvious that the Boneheads were favouring one bucket over the other. If Bec was right, they would agree to allow her to commune with q'wakay. Her stomach clenched. She put the berries down.

The line of Boneheads petered out. A few more Boneheads slipped over and threw something in one of the buckets. Enqua waited a moment, and when it was clear that no more were coming, tipped out the contents of the two buckets. It was obvious to Amber that one bucket contained far more than the other, but Enqua counted each object anyway.

Enqua stood. Amber took a deep breath. She twisted her fingers in front of her.

Enqua spoke in a loud, carrying voice in the Bonehead language, then switched to English. 'The family has decided in favour of allowing our Nalyrd and the human named Amber to commune with q'wakay.'

Most of the Boneheads turned to look at Amber. She ducked her head. Her heart was racing.

Sayera scowled and spat something in the Bonehead language. Enqua responded in a calm voice. Sayera bared his teeth and stormed away from the platform.

Rayeta's remaining guards laid a large piece of the same soft material that the Boneheads used for clothing, blankets and towels on the rock. This one was a sky blue colour. Rayeta sat cross-legged on one side of it. She gestured for Amber to sit opposite her.

Amber looked for Bec. She saw Alice and Lucy, standing near

Dansera, but she couldn't see Bec. She turned and sat, crossing her own legs. Goosebumps sprang up on her skin. Her legs and arms felt shaky, and she had a sudden need to go to the toilet, but she didn't want to say anything. She clenched her teeth.

Enqua poured a brown liquid into two wooden bowls and handed one to Rayeta and one to Amber.

'Drink all of it,' Rayeta said. She lifted the bowl to her mouth and poured the liquid down her throat.

Swallowing a lump that had formed in her throat, Amber copied her. The liquid had an earthy, bitter taste. The flavour reminded Amber of the kava she had drunk once on a holiday in Vanuatu.

'Close your eyes,' Rayeta said.

They were already closing of their own accord. The bowl dropped from Amber's hands. She didn't notice Enqua pick it up. It felt as though her mind was expanding. She could feel Rayeta, her mind calm, in control. Behind her, she could sense many minds, pressing in on her. Alice – a bundle of resentment, towards her mother, the Boneheads, the soldiers, Walker – and underlying it all, to Amber's surprise, the strongest bitterness towards herself, because she hadn't kept her family together. Amber wanted to wrap her in reassurance, but her mind had moved on to Lucy. Lucy's fear of the Boneheads was so strong that it was almost overwhelming, but she held it back by clinging to her belief that Amber would protect her. Amber felt her stomach twist. She'd let Lucy down, leaving her mother in the hands of the Boneheads.

She felt birds flying overhead, dragging her away from the girls – birds of prey, riding the winds, their eyes searching for small mammals to eat. The clouds, being blown across the sky. And then a force gathering, like a tsunami, behind her, around her, through her, until it came crashing down on her and lifted her up at the same time, and she found her mind joining with

Rayeta's mind. But it was not just Rayeta's mind, but all the minds that Rayeta had communed with, and the minds of those they had communed with, thousands of lives filling her until she thought her head would burst. The q'wakay tore down all her walls and defences, so she could do nothing to stop the onslaught.

She saw the Boneheads on the treacherous northern continent, hunting small mammals and fleeing dinosaurs – real monsters. She saw them take to the seas and make their way to the southern continent, where there were new dangers – giant marsupials, and animals like the turek that had a common ancestor with the dinosaurs.

She saw how q'wakeen was discovered in their earliest days on the southern continent, and brewed into q'wakay, and understood that their society had evolved in tandem with their use of q'wakay – that it was an integral part of their community, their identity.

Words filled her mind, and she knew how to speak the Bonehead language. No, she corrected herself, not Bonehead – Anaia.

She saw hunters and warriors, perfecting their sword fighting techniques, and knew, now, how to move her body to block and strike, how each move should feel.

She learned the paths the Anaia took through the southern continent, and knew she would never be lost in the forest.

She saw Anaia appear with the ability to access a strange power – the lechiko. It was found in both Red and Grey Bone families, but some Grey Bone families nurtured it, selecting for it, until it became known as a Grey Bone trait. She learned that the lechiko could give the user many abilities, more than the strength and speed she had used it for, or the power and control Walker used it for. She learnt how to wield it, to shape and control it, but she also learnt that it came at a cost. Kim was far from the only user to have been killed by it. She saw the Anaia grow to fear it, calling it a curse, rather than a gift.

She saw the kinrodo parasite appear, destroying not just q'wakeen, but the foundations of Anaian society. She saw how fear of the parasite had ripped through delicate treaties and alliances that had kept Anaian families safe for decades. And she saw how Walker had taken advantage of their fear, how he encouraged the division between the families, and between Red and Grey Bones, how he manipulated them, and offered himself, and her world, as the solution.

Twenty-three

Bec's eyes followed Sayera as he stormed away from the platform. She felt unsettled. Dansera's warning ran through her mind. She glanced at Amber. Amber was watching the guards spread out some kind of rug. She would be fine without Bec for the moment. Bec slunk backwards, towards the edge of the platform. Alice turned and stared straight at her. Bec made a subtle gesture with her hand to tell Alice to look away, not to draw attention to her. Frowning, Alice turned back to watch Amber.

Sayera strode through the plants to the gap in the wall. Bec followed at a distance. It was easy for her to stay out of sight. Sayera was tall even by Bonehead standards, and he wasn't trying to hide.

Like when they arrived, there were four guards near the gap in the wall. Bec watched as Sayera approached them. He spoke to them, then straddled the rocks and slipped through the gap in the wall. Bec squatted on the ground and watched, chewing on her lip. She couldn't follow him through the gap and stay out of sight. She didn't know if the other Boneheads would even let her follow; she was supposed to stay with Dansera. It was probably unnecessary, anyway. None of the other Boneheads were worried about Sayera.

She stood, her eyes still on the gap. Without a sound, all four of the wall guards collapsed on the ground. Bec's mouth dropped open. One of the guards landed with its head in the stream. Without thinking, Bec sprinted towards the guards, leaping over plants that threatened to trip her.

The guards lay where they'd landed, motionless. Bec

concentrated on the one whose head was in the water. She didn't know if it was alive, but if it was, she had to move it before it drowned. She tried to pull the guard up, but it was too heavy for her. She slid into the water. At this point the stream was deep and narrow, hemmed in by thick rock. Standing on the rock stream bed, she had to lift her chin to keep her face out of the water. She pushed the guard's head up, out of the water. The water streamed off its face.

The current dragged at her. She tried to push the guard back onto the rock platform, but it didn't budge. She felt her feet slipping. She was trapped, unable to move the weight of the guard. She didn't know how long she'd be able to keep her footing against the current. She tried again to lift the Bonehead, her arms screaming in protest. It didn't move. She closed her eyes and took deep breaths, focusing on staying upright and holding the Bonehead's head above water.

The Bonehead's weight was dragged from her grasp. Hands clasped her wrists, and she was pulled from the water and dumped on the rock platform. The rock scraped her knees. She blinked water from her eyes. Kalliga rolled the guard onto its side and checked its breathing.

'Alive,' he said. He searched the guard and removed a flat, circular disk, about the width of his palm, from its jumpsuit. He rose in one smooth movement, straddled the platforms and ducked through the gap in the wall.

Bec wiped water from her face and hurried after him. She was shaking. Cold water dripped from her clothes and ran down her body.

Sayera stood over several more unconscious guards on the platform outside. When he saw Kalliga, he drew his sword, but he backed away rather than attacking. Kalliga ignored him and searched the valley below, a grim look on his face. About a hundred Boneheads appeared from the forest and surrounded the stream and the path to the rock platform.

Kalliga squeezed the disk that he'd taken from the guard. A loud, shrieking noise sounded across the nest. Bec clapped her hands over her ears.

Kalliga drew his sword and stalked towards Sayera. Sayera snarled and spoke to him in the Bonehead language. Kalliga answered in the same language.

Boneheads were swarming up the cliff. Bec reached into her wet jumpsuit and pulled out her knife. She felt faint. 'Who are they?'

Kalliga didn't take his eyes off Sayera. 'Go back inside the wall.'

Sayera bared his teeth at her. 'The Tanusta.'

Kalliga leapt at Sayera. Their swords met with a clang. Kalliga drew back, ready to strike again, but three Tanusta pulled themselves onto the rock platform, swords drawn, forcing him to turn to ward off their attack.

Sayera raised his weapon to hit Kalliga from behind. Bec jumped between them, pointing her knife at Sayera. He sneered. 'Pitiful.'

She just needed to distract him so Kalliga could deal with the Tanusta. 'Why would you betray your own family?'

Sayera sniffed. 'You're worrying about the wrong things, human. You should be asking why communing with outsiders was banned in the first place. It was as much to protect the outsiders as us.' He swung his sword from the side, sent her knife flying over the rock platform and then swung back in the other direction. Bec knew in an instant that it would slice her open. She couldn't move out of the way fast enough.

The back of a sword slammed into Sayera's forehead, below the bony plate. He collapsed.

Boneheads streamed through the gap in the wall, swords drawn. More Tanusta swarmed onto the rock platform. She was surrounded by Boneheads fighting.

Kalliga spoke in Bec's ear. 'Go back inside the wall.'

Bec looked into his red-ringed eyes. 'Why was communing with outsiders banned?' she demanded.

Kalliga grasped her shoulder and pushed her towards the gap so hard that she almost fell. 'Go!' He swung around and engaged another Tanusta.

Amber. An icy fear gripped Bec's heart. She turned and ran back through the wall. A Bonehead was checking the unconscious guards. It looked up as she ran past. More Boneheads were running towards the wall, ready to defend the nest against the Tanusta. They stared at her as she flew in the opposite direction.

'Bec!' Alice called to her. She, Dansera and Lucy were standing at the top of a hillock, surrounded by nestlings and nyth. Bec swung around and leapt up the hill.

'Why are you all wet?' Alice asked.

Bec ignored her and looked straight at Dansera. 'Why was communing with outsiders banned?'

Dansera looked away. 'I'm not supposed to tell you.'

Bec wanted to shake her. She stepped into her line of vision. 'My best friend is communing with Rayeta right now! I encouraged her to. I -' Bec's voice cracked. 'I told her she couldn't say no! If there's some risk to what she's doing -'

Dansera's eyes were wide. She stepped back from Bec. Alice stepped forward and took her arm. She glared at Bec. 'Whatever's wrong, it's not her fault.'

'It's alright,' a voice said behind them. Bec swung around. It was Enqua. 'I will tell you what you want to know.' Enqua limped up the hillock, narrowing its eyes. 'You stink of anger and impatience. There is no need. Rayeta and Amber have started communing. There's no way to bring them back now.'

Bec clenched her fists and took a deep breath. 'Tell me.'

Enqua leant against a boulder. 'Long before the gate was built, the Walker used to come to our world. He was a traveller. We called him The Walker Between Worlds.'

Bec wrinkled her brow. 'We thought Walker was just his name.'

'I believe he has many different names in many different worlds,' Enqua said. 'One of the Red Bone families invited the Walker to join them when they communed with q'wakay. That is how we learnt to speak your language – the Red Bones learnt it from the Walker, and relatives of ours, the Tanusta -'

'The Tanusta are your relatives?' Bec's voice rose in disbelief. 'They're attacking you!'

'Ah, well, relatives -' Enqua shrugged and continued. 'Some members of the Tanusta communed with the Red Bones, and we communed with them.'

Bec shook her head. 'I wish it was that easy to learn languages in my world.'

'After the Red Bones communed with the Walker, they said that he changed. He became violent. He started gathering Anaia to him, building an army. He killed any Anaia who tried to stop him, or turned them into – into animals. No – less than animals, creatures without thought.'

'Zombies.'

'Even the Red Bones who communed with him -' Enqua shook its head. 'It is unthinkable to us. Your mind becomes one with the minds of those you commune with; to take away those minds -' It shook its head again. 'It is like taking a part of yourself. After that, the families agreed to forbid anyone to give q'wakay to outsiders, in case it changed them, too.'

Bec's heart raced. She clutched her head. 'Are you saying that Amber might turn into a – a megalomaniac?'

She heard Lucy gasp.

'No,' Enqua said, its voice firm. 'I am saying that the Red Bones said the Walker changed after they communed with him. I never believed it. It was his nature to seek power. Communing gave him the information he needed to gather his army, that is all.'

'We have to stop them,' Bec said. Her voice sounded like it was coming from far away.

'You cannot,' Enqua said. 'Once they have started communing, they cannot be brought back, until the commune is complete.'

Bec ignored Enqua's words. She leapt off the hillock and raced to the platform. It was a lot emptier than the previous times she'd been there, with so many of the Boneheads fighting the Tanusta. Amber was sitting cross-legged on the rug opposite Rayeta. They were as still as statues, their eyes closed. Sweat dripped down Amber's face, but she didn't move to wipe it away.

Three Boneheads stood guard over them. Bec dived past them and threw herself onto the ground in front of Amber, taking them by surprise. She grasped Amber's shoulders and shook hard. 'Amber! Wake up!' Amber's body rocked in response, but she didn't open her eyes.

One of the guards grabbed Bec's arms from behind and pulled her backwards, away from Amber. It spun her around and threw her onto the rock. Bec felt the rock smack into her bum and left hip. Tears sprung in her eyes.

'What are you doing?' the guard demanded.

Bec looked up at the three guards, now standing between her and Amber. 'Wake her up!'

'She's not asleep, mammal,' the guard who had thrown her said, its voice full of contempt. 'No-one can wake her.'

'I did not lie to you.' Enqua's voice came from behind her. 'There is no way to wake her. She will come back when the commune is complete.'

Bec stood, clenching her fists. Enqua limped closer, followed by Dansera, Alice and Lucy. 'And when will that be?'

Enqua glanced at the sun. 'It is hard to say. Communes vary.'

Bec glanced at the guards. They had their eyes on her. She doubted they'd let her near Amber again. Her throat felt bone dry. Pressing her lips together, she flounced to the water pipe, and gulped handfuls of water. Her stomach rumbled, reminding her that she hadn't eaten much at breakfast. The large food platters had been cleared, but they'd been replaced with smaller ones piled with fruit. She helped herself to a round fruit, about the size of an apple, that had been cut in half. The skin reminded her of watermelon. The fruit was watery, like watermelon, but not as sweet.

A small Bonehead, about Dansera's size, jogged to the platform and spoke to Enqua in their language. Bec picked out the words Tanusta and Rayeta. Enqua replied, frowning. The Bonehead ducked its head and jogged away.

'What did it say?' Bec asked.

'Our warriors have fought back the Tanusta, but they have dug into the valley. They demand the deaths of Rayeta and all the humans. They said they will lay siege to our nest until their demands are met. They will not let anyone in or out.'

Lucy's face paled. She moved closer to Alice. Bec drew her brows in. 'But – won't that mean they have to stay out overnight? I thought the forest wasn't safe?'

'No doubt they will build temporary walls and moats to keep the beasts at bay,' Enqua said.

Bec shivered. Would the Boneheads give them up? Surely they wouldn't give up Rayeta – even Kalliga seemed to revere her. But the Boneheads had a very different attitude to death than humans: they spoke as though dying was an honour, especially if it somehow strengthened the family.

It was better to know what was going to happen than to imagine the worst. She lifted her chin and looked straight at Enqua. 'So – what now?'

Enqua considered her with its black eyes. 'We will seek guidance from our Nalyrd when they finish communing. No decisions will be made until then.'

The sun rose high in the sky. It beat down on the rock platform. Bec's jumpsuit and hair had dried. She wiped sweat from her face and chewed on a nail. Amber had been sitting, motionless, for hours. At intervals Enqua poured water into both Rayeta and Amber's mouths, and they swallowed, but showed no sign that they could feel it.

Lucy and Alice had gone to sleep, lying on their backs, their arms covering their faces. Bec was surprised that they could sleep on the hard rock. She felt tense and unsettled. She couldn't relax until she knew that Amber was okay.

The guard that had thrown her to the ground spoke to Enqua in their language. Enqua turned to Bec. 'They're coming back.'

Bec jumped to her feet and hurried over. The guard kept its eyes on her as she approached, so she stopped out of reach. She squinted at Amber and Rayeta, frowning. She couldn't see any change in them.

Rayeta opened her eyes. She swayed, looking disorientated for a moment, and Enqua and the guard hurried to steady her. They helped her to her feet. Amber's eyes opened a moment later. Bec rushed towards her. This time the guards didn't try to stop her. Bec threw herself down on the rock in front of Amber.

'Amber? Are you okay?'

Amber put a hand on her forehead. 'Yeah.' She blinked several times. 'A bit dizzy. I've got all these memories in my head, but they're not my own.'

Bec swallowed hard. 'But you're – still you – right?'

Amber lowered her hand and focused on Bec. She gave a crooked smile. 'Yeah, still me.'

Bec swallowed again. 'Good,' she said. Her voice sounded too high-pitched.

Enqua and the guard had led Rayeta to her rock seat. Kalliga jogged back from the gate. Someone must have told him Rayeta and Amber had woken.

Rayeta, Enqua and Kalliga spoke in animated voices in their own language. Amber tilted her head as though she was listening. After a moment, she stood, and said something in the same language.

Bec scrambled up off the ground. 'You can speak their language?'

Amber turned to look at her. 'I have their memories, and their ancestors' memories.'

Bec shook her head in disbelief. 'So what are they saying?'

'They're concerned about this siege. They can hold out indefinitely here – there's plenty of food and water – but as long as we're trapped here we can't close the gate.'

'And we can't stay here – you need to get home to Adam and Oliver,' Bec said.

'Mmm,' Amber said, but she sounded as though she wasn't listening.

Bec felt her chest tighten. Amber's just distracted, she told herself.

Amber closed her eyes and kept them closed for a moment.

'Are you okay? Do you need to sit down?'

Amber opened her eyes. 'I'm fine, I was just sorting through the memories. I've got an idea.' She walked closer to Rayeta and spoke in a low voice so that only Rayeta, Kalliga and Enqua could hear. Rayeta narrowed her eyes, and replied in an equally low voice.

Bec shifted from foot to foot, wishing she knew what they were talking about. She shook her head. Did Amber really have the Boneheads' ancestors' memories? How could she walk around with all that in her head?

Amber and Kalliga turned to Bec.

'Come,' Kalliga said. He strode towards the wall. Amber followed with a slight limp.

Bec ran to catch up with them. 'Come where?'

'To the valley floor,' Amber said. 'We need to have a chat with the Tanusta.'

'What?' Bec stopped. 'The Tanusta want to kill us!'

'We're going to convince them not to,' Amber said, without stopping.

Bec ground her teeth. If Amber wanted Bec to risk her life, the least she could do was explain the plan. Bec considered refusing to follow Amber and Kalliga, but then she'd miss the action. Cursing them both under her breath, she ran after them.

The four guards that Sayera had knocked out were gone. Two new Boneheads stood on either side of the gap. They watched in silence as Kalliga straddled the platforms and slipped through the gap, followed by Amber. Bec hesitated on the threshold, her eyes darting around the scene in front of her.

The Tanusta had retreated to the valley floor. About two thirds of them hovered in two lines, evenly spaced, stretching in a curve either side of the platform. They stood far enough from the platform to avoid any knives thrown from above. The remaining third were digging a long, wide hole that curved behind them and ended a short distance from the stream. Bec guessed that once the digging was complete they would dig through to the stream and fill it with water, creating a moat to keep the animals out, like Enqua had said they would.

The Boneheads on the platform stood in silence, backs straight and weapons drawn, watching every move the Tanusta made. Bec's eyes were drawn to the one figure that wasn't standing. Sayera was slouched against the wall, his eyes glazed. His wrists and ankles were encircled with metal restraints like the ones that had stopped Zhou escaping, and that Amber had insisted Yorilla remove from Alice and Lucy.

So the restraints worked on Boneheads, too. Bec filed that piece of information away to tell Sam and the MG.

Amber stalked past Sayera without a glance. Kalliga spoke to some of the Boneheads on the platform, then called out to the Tanusta. The Tanusta stirred. One of them called something back.

Kalliga and Amber jumped across the stream and walked to the end of the platform, where the muddy path led to the valley floor. The path was even muddier now: the soil churned into clumps by the Tanusta's attempts to get to the top of the platform.

The rope that they'd used to climb to the platform when they arrived was coiled near the wall, one end secured to a metal ring that jutted out of the wall. One of the Boneheads picked most of the coils up and carried them to the edge of the platform. The rope stretched taut. The Bonehead flung the coils over the side of the platform. It fell to the ground. The Tanusta nearby stirred, but didn't move. Amber took the rope in both hands and looked back at Bec. 'Come on.'

Bec glanced at the lines of Tanusta waiting on the valley floor, then back at Amber. Her heart pounded in her chest. 'You can't be serious.' Her voice squeaked.

Amber's expression reminded Bec of Kalliga at his most impatient. 'You'll be safe. This will work better if we both go.'

Without waiting for Bec's agreement, she placed her feet on the path, straddling the rope, and stepped down the slope.

Bec's face felt like it was burning, but her body was icy cold. She didn't want to follow Amber, but she didn't want her to face the Tanusta alone. Was this how Luke, Ash and Nathan felt when Bec leapt into danger and forced them to follow? Gritting her teeth, she walked to the end of the platform. Amber reached the ground and dropped the rope. Bec picked it up and slid after her.

She let the rope fall to the ground. All the nearby Tanusta had their eyes on her and Amber. Their sword blades glinted in the late afternoon sun. Bec was shivering even more now. Amber strode towards the line of Tanusta, the slight limp almost invisible, her body calm and confident. She hadn't even drawn her sword. Bec stumbled after her. Amber stopped just out of sword range, settling into a comfortable position, her feet just wider than hip width and her arms relaxed. Bec glanced back at Kalliga and the other Boneheads on the platform. The ones closest to the edge of the platform balanced knives in their hands, their muscles taught, prepared to throw at any Tanusta who moved closer.

'What now?' Bec muttered.

A small smile flitted across Amber's face. 'This,' she said.

There was a rumble in the distance. Was it thunder? Some of the Tanusta in the back lines called out, an unusual note in their voices. Bec saw movement far down the valley. Something enormous was heading towards them – fast. A new kind of monster?

Twenty-four

Bec realised, with a jolt, that it wasn't a large monster that was racing towards them. It was a huge mob of ang'kala.

There were close to a hundred of them. Their massive leg and tail muscles ate up the distance between them and the Tanusta. They bounded over the Tanusta's moat without slowing. The Tanusta were shrieking, their careful lines breaking up as they attempted to flee, but the lead ranks of the ang'kala leapt over them, too, and came straight towards Amber and Bec. Bec was frozen to the spot, her eyes wide with fear. One of the massive beasts leapt straight at her. She closed her eyes and waited for it to hit her.

A musty scent filled her nose. It reminded her of the pet mice her sister had kept when they were kids. Warm breath blew on top of her head. She opened her eyes. The giant kangaroo had landed right in front of her. Dead leaves and twigs had billowed out from where its long feet had hit the ground. It towered over her, its stomach at her head height, its flank moving as it breathed in and out. She looked into its peaceful brown eyes. More ang'kala surrounded her and Amber. Amber reached out and stroked the flank of one. The ang'kala closest to them moved away, to be replaced by more. She pressed her arms into her body, trying not to move. Still more ang'kala swarmed around the two humans, their bodies bumping against them. Bec breathed in their strong scent.

At some invisible signal, the mob flowed away from them and bounded back down the valley, leaping over the moat. The Tanusta were scattered across the area, their straight lines gone. After a moment, three Tanusta separated from the others and approached. Bec glanced at Amber. She stood firm as they halted, still just outside of the reach of any knives above. One of them spoke in a loud voice, its eyes on Amber, but speaking loudly enough that the Boneheads on the platform could hear.

'What's it saying?' Bec asked.

'The sacred ang'kala have given their favour to the humans. We withdraw our complaint and demands. We will depart.'

As Amber translated, the three Tanusta met her and Bec's eyes in turn, nodded their heads and turned and walked away. Other Tanusta fell in behind them.

A voice shrieked. It was Sayera. He ran to the front of the platform and shouted after the Tanusta.

Kalliga growled something at him, and he sank to his knees, clutching his head.

The Tanusta didn't turn around.

'What did he say?' Bec asked.

'He told them that it was a trick.'

'Was it?'

'Of course. I used the lechiko to attract the ang'kala.'

Kalliga grabbed Sayera by the back of his jumpsuit and dragged him through the gap in the wall.

'What are they going to do to him?'

'Kill him, I imagine.' Amber's voice was calm and disinterested.

Bec stared at her. 'Come on,' she said. She grabbed the rope and struggled back up to the rock platform as fast as she could. With a shrug, Amber followed.

'Quick,' Bec said, once Amber reached the platform. She ran to the gap in the wall, dodging the Boneheads on the rock platform. They stared, but didn't try to stop her. She bounced through the gap, past the guards, and towards the rock platform. Amber followed at a walking pace, protecting her injured ankle. As Bec arrived at the rock platform, Kalliga dragged Sayera to where Rayeta was seated and threw him on the stone in front of her.

Bec leant over her knees, gasping for breath. She had a stitch in her side.

Kalliga drew his sword.

Bec rushed forward. 'What are you doing?'

Kalliga tilted his head. 'He betrayed the family. He must die, without honour.'

Amber limped towards them. 'Are you just going to let them kill him?' Bec demanded.

Amber shrugged. 'Thousands die every day. Why are you worried about this one?'

'Because -' Bec hesitated, unsure herself. Why not let them kill him? It would mean one less Bonehead enemy to worry about. She'd never worried about killing Boneheads before. But Amber had – Amber always worried. 'Because you would be!'

Amber frowned. 'I thought you wanted me to become a warrior. To fight for the Resistance.'

'Maybe – yes -' Bec squirmed. 'But I want you to be you.'

Amber stared at her for a long moment. She turned to Rayeta and Kalliga. 'Why not banish him instead? There's precedent for that.'

Kalliga's face twisted. 'Do not presume to recite our own history back to us, human. He is a traitor. He deserves death.'

Rayeta raised a hand. 'It is not you who have been wronged here, Kalliga,' she said, her voice mild. 'The Tanusta demanded my death, and those of the humans.' She eyed Bec. 'You should be aware, Rebecca Williams, that in our world banishment and death are intertwined. Few can survive the forest at night. Sometimes another family will offer sanctuary, but it is unlikely anyone will do that for a traitor.'

Bec swallowed. At least he would have a chance. It was more than Kalliga would give him. 'I understand.'

Rayeta nodded her head. 'I will relinquish my claim on his life in return for banishment, if that is what you want.'

Bec bit her lip. 'Thank you.'

Rayeta turned to Kalliga and spoke to him in their language. Kalliga scowled, but pulled Sayera to his feet and prodded him back the way they'd come. Sayera stumbled on the rock. Bec followed.

'You don't have to go,' Amber said.

'I'm making sure Kalliga doesn't kill him.'

'He won't disobey the Nalyrd's orders.'

Bec shrugged and followed Kalliga anyway. Kalliga marched Sayera back to the gap in the wall and onto the rock platform. He snarled something to the Boneheads remaining on the platform. They looked at Bec. She shrank back against the wall.

The rope was once again coiled on the platform. One of the Boneheads flung it to the valley floor. Kalliga took Sayera's wrists in his hands and closed his eyes. Nothing happened for a moment, and then the restraints on Sayera's wrists and ankles sprung open and fell to the ground. Bec frowned. How had Kalliga done that?

Kalliga snarled at Sayera in their language. Sayera bared his teeth and responded, then looked at Bec, venom in his eyes. He picked up the rope and slid down the slope. Once he was at the bottom, the Bonehead that had thrown the rope down pulled it back up. Another Bonehead handed Kalliga a sword and a knife. Kalliga flung them over the cliff. Sayera jumped back as they landed in the dirt at his feet. He picked them up and looked up at the rock platform again. Kalliga turned his back on Sayera and, with a dark glance at Bec, strode back through the gap. Bec bit her lip. The other Boneheads on the platform were watching her. She shivered, wrapped her arms around herself and ducked back through the gap in the wall.

The evening meal had been served when she returned to the

rock platform. The sun was setting, turning the sky orange and pink again.

Amber was talking to Rayeta. Alice and Lucy were picking at the food without enthusiasm. Bec sank down next to them. Her whole body ached with tiredness.

Alice pointed to a round, brown vegetable about the size of a cherry tomato. 'Those are okay. They taste a bit like potatoes.'

Bec took one and bit into it. 'Mmm, not bad.' Like the other vegetables, it had been cooked in salt. It had a more floury texture than a potato, but the flavour was similar. Bec and the girls ate their way through them.

Amber joined them. Jaws wound between her feet.

'Try these,' Bec said through a mouthful. 'They're good.'

'Thanks.' Amber finished the last few. Alice picked at the other vegetables, looking for something else that suited their tastes. Bec ate more of the fruit that reminded her of watermelon.

'Kalliga wants to take us back to the gate tomorrow,' Amber said.

Alice's head shot up. 'We're going home?'

Amber nodded.

'Yay!' Alice grinned at Lucy. 'Though I'm sorry we didn't get to see a dinosaur.'

Lucy screwed up her nose. 'I'm not.'

Bec frowned. 'The gate will bring us out in that room in the middle of the enemy's stronghold. And if it's anything like last time, we'll be flattened. We won't be in any shape to fight anyone.'

'It won't be like last time.' Amber's tone was confident. 'I can protect us from the gate, so it doesn't sap our energy.

Lucy's brow furrowed. 'What if they take us prisoner again?' she said in a small voice.

'They won't.' A smile played around Amber's lips. 'I've got some tricks up my sleeve, now.'

'Like with the Tanusta?'

'Exactly.'

Amber turned back to the food platters. Bec watched her. She had never heard Amber sound so self-assured before. Amber chewed some berries, staring at the food platters without seeing them.

'Rayeta and Kalliga expect me and Lucy to close the gate.'

Bec sat back on the rock. 'The MG and Sam don't want us to – at least not yet.'

'I know.'

'What are you going to do?'

Amber shrugged. She looked at Rayeta. 'She saw into my mind. She knows that I might not do it, but she hasn't said anything.'

'What about the restraints? They were going to tell us how to remove them.'

'I already know.' The last rays of sunlight had disappeared. Amber stared out into the darkness, her eyes unfocused. 'You don't know what it was like – Rayeta could see everything. Everything I've ever done, every thought I've ever had, in my life. I couldn't hide any of it. But neither could she.'

Bec opened her mouth to reply. A small nyth barrelled over the rock platform towards them. Bec leapt to her feet, and Alice and Lucy scrambled away. Amber let it bump her with its head, knocking her backwards onto the rock. 'Jaws!'

Kimissa followed Jaws. Amber looked at him. 'Thank you for healing him.'

'I didn't do much. It takes a lot to kill a nyth.'

'Cos they're built like tanks,' Alice said, screwing up her nose.

Kimissa's eyes were on Jaws. 'There may be some benefit in being less prescriptive in nyth training. Your nyth is more courageous and resourceful than ours – none of ours would attack a turek. I recommend you give it some basic training, though, or it will cause havoc in your nest.'

Amber gave Kimissa a vague nod.

'I tried to teach it some commands while it was with me, but the only one I could get it to pay attention to was Yarun.'

'What does that mean?' Bec asked.

Kimissa looked around. A small lizard was sunning itself on the edge of the rock platform. He looked at Jaws and raised his voice. 'Yarun!' he said in a loud voice, pointing at the lizard.

Jaws flung himself forward. The lizard attempted to flee, but Jaws pounced and bit it in half. He returned and dropped its head on the rock in front of Kimissa.

'Well done,' Kimissa said, holding out his hand with something in it. Jaws licked it up.

'Ew,' Lucy said, eyeing the lizard's head.

'Yarun means attack, or bite,' Kimissa said.

Bec laughed. 'He probably only follows that command because he wants to bite anyway.'

'You should have better luck with more time – training doesn't happen overnight.'

'How do you train them?' Bec asked.

'The same way you train any animal – give them food when they do what you want. I understand in your world you train – wolves?'

Bec smiled. 'Dogs. Very, very distant relatives to wolves.'

'The same approach should work with the nyth.' Kimissa nodded to them and disappeared.

Bec looked at Amber. 'It's good advice.'

Irritation flashed in Amber's eyes. 'I heard, thanks.' She stroked Jaws' fur.

Lucy yawned, which made Alice yawn.

'If we're going to do that hike again, we should try to get a better night's sleep tonight,' Bec said. She looked at Jaws and screwed up her nose. 'I'm not sharing a bed with that monster,' she told Amber.

Bec and the girls made Amber and Jaws sleep on the far end of the platform, near the tap, while they spread out at the end near the tunnel. They were so exhausted that they slept well, despite the lighting, salty food and their own fears.

They got up at first light. Bec pulled her pack on, watching as Amber slid off the sleeping platform. 'How's your ankle?'

'Good,' she said, testing her weight on it. 'Much better. It should be okay for the walk.'

'That's good.' Bec grimaced. 'I'm not looking forward to doing that hike again. Particularly with Kalliga – I think he's pissed at me for not letting him kill Sayera.'

Amber snorted. 'I think Kalliga is pissed at everyone, all the time.'

Bec grinned at her. Perhaps she didn't need to worry; that sounded like the normal Amber.

Kalliga was in a hurry to leave, so that he could get there and back before dark. They gobbled some more of the small, potato-like vegetables and fruit, and then said goodbye to Dansera, Enqua and Rayeta.

Rayeta looked at Amber. 'Our minds have been one, Amber Yu, and the knowledge we hold of the other cannot now be taken from us. This is a sacred bond, even if the gate is closed and the pathway between our worlds is severed.'

Amber nodded, her face serious.

'But don't come back,' Kalliga said, scowling at them.

Rayeta sent a couple of her guards to accompany them to the gate. Walking in the cool, early morning air was easier, and they were refreshed after a good night's sleep. Jaws trotted at Amber's feet. They made good time along the stream and up to the plateau. The trees were full of birds of all sizes, screeching and twittering, and they were swarmed by biting insects, but there were no signs of turek or other large beasts.

On the plateau, Lucy lifted her head. 'I can feel the gate calling again.'

'Stop a minute,' Amber said to Kalliga. She knelt and put her hands on either side of Lucy's head, and stared into her eyes, the same way that Yorilla had. After a moment, she let go. Lucy relaxed.

'It's gone,' she said, a brilliant smile lighting her face.

Kalliga strode on, forcing them to hurry. Bec's eyes were on Amber's back. What else had Amber learnt while she was communing? Bec clenched her teeth.

The humidity increased as they struggled down the hill. Sweat dripped down Bec's back, where the pack sat. The bird calls declined, until she could only hear the odd twitter. The humidity didn't bother the insects; they were worse than ever.

Amber sometimes took the lead, and Kalliga let her. Bec couldn't fathom how Amber knew the way. Every direction in the forest looked the same to her.

Kalliga stopped at the same creek they'd had a drink at on the way. The girls, Amber, Bec and Jaws flung themselves down and gulped handfuls of water. Bec finished drinking first and stood to let Kalliga and the two guards access the water. She gazed around the bush. Frog calls filled the air. There was a rustling in the bracken behind her, and she approached warily, in case it was a turek or some other terrifying beast. She caught a glimpse of a grey horn and wrinkled skin through the trees, but when she moved closer there was nobody there.

Kalliga stood, wiping water from his mouth.

'Are there other guards following us, like last time?' Bec asked him.

'No. They went home yesterday.' He narrowed his eyes. 'Why?'

'I thought I saw someone, through there.' Bec pointed at the patch of bracken.

'I doubt it. This is neutral territory – there's no nests nearby. That's why the Walker built his gate out here.' He looked at the others. They had finished drinking. 'Let's keep moving.'

The humidity became more and more oppressive. It weighed down on them. Kalliga and Amber took it in turns to lead the way. Bec heard occasional rustlings in the scrub, and thought she caught a glimpse of a Bonehead. She shivered and tried to tell herself she was imagining it. She felt like they had been walking through the same patch of bush for hours. For all she knew, Kalliga and Amber were leading them in circles. Her leg muscles ached, and she was thirsty again, but there was nowhere to get a drink.

They walked through a grove of trees that looked identical to every other grove of trees, and the gate was in front of them. Its recycled plastic brick structure felt odd surrounded by nature. Bec looked at the place where they'd left Yorilla's body, but it was gone. She imagined wild animals – monsters like the turek – dragging the body away. She shuddered and averted her eyes.

As they approached the gate, guards appeared from the trees. They blocked the way, but didn't draw their weapons, which Bec hoped was a good sign. Kalliga spoke to them in his language. Bec shifted from foot to foot.

A Red Bone looked at Amber and Bec, its eyes smouldering. 'We will allow you to return to your world, mammals, but do not come again. If you do, we will kill you.'

Amber gave him a sweet smile. 'Same back at you, if you come to ours.' Bec's eyes widened. The Red Bone glowered at her.

Amber knelt and picked up Jaws, resting him on her left arm. She held out her right hand. 'We need to hold hands. As long as we're touching, I can protect you from the gate.' Lucy took her hand. Alice joined hands with Lucy and Bec.

Bec glanced at Kalliga, wondering if he was going to say goodbye, but he scowled at them. 'Get on with it.'

They stepped into the gate. Alice's hand in Bec's was slippery with sweat. A hum filled Bec's ears. Alice was clenching her jaw. Lucy had her eyes closed. Amber eyes were unfocused. Small, coloured lights danced over their faces and bodies. The hum increased in volume, but it seemed to be muted compared to when they'd come through the gate the last time. Bec wondered if it had something to do with what Amber was doing.

There was a shout from behind them. Bec turned her head. Sayera appeared from the trees, running towards the gate. Kalliga tried to grab him, but he dodged past and threw himself through the gate. There was a loud crack, and Bec's eyes were blinded, as though someone had taken her photo with the flash on.

The hum had gone. Bec blinked her eyes. She felt disorientated. She had expected to return to where they'd left from, but this room was different. It was smaller, and its walls and roof were intact. It had the same white walls and cement floors as the other rooms in the extension to the farmhouse, though, so she guessed they were in the same place, just a different room. Her gaze was drawn to two Red Bones, standing at the back of the room, their hands on the hilts of their swords.

Sayera was crumpled on the ground. She could see his side rising and falling, so he was still breathing. Probably knocked out by the gate, like they had been the last time they'd gone through it.

Alice let go of her hand. The girls, Bec and Amber were all standing, so whatever Amber had done to protect them from the gate must have worked.

Private Jerome stood in front of the gate, holding a rifle. The sword that he'd taken from the dead Red Bone was in a sheath against his right leg. His eyes were on Jaws, in Amber's arms. He scowled. The right leg of his pants was rolled up, revealing a bandage around his ankle. Bec gave a small smile.

'Welcome home,' a sneering voice said. Lieutenant Colonel Nichols stepped into their view, a smile on his lips. 'The Prime Minister is on his way. He would have waited to greet you himself, but we didn't know when you'd be back, and he had important business at Parliament.'

Amber let Jaws slip to the ground and drew her sword in one swift move. She stepped one foot back, moving into a fighting stance.

Nichols held up a hand. 'I suggest you drop that sword, Ms Yu, and do exactly what I say. Unless you want your friends to die, of course.'

Twenty-five

Nichols waved the same hand to the right with a flourish. Six people were kneeling on the floor, restraints wrapped around their wrists and ankles. A soldier stood behind each person, pressing a rifle into the back of their head.

'In case you're wondering, we took all their THONGs away. So nothing will save them if my men fire.'

Bec ran her eyes along the line of prisoners. Ren, Josie, Luke, Nathan and – Bec's mouth dropped open. 'Dan? What are you doing here?' She glanced at the sixth person – it was an Asian woman she didn't recognise.

Dan's head lolled on his neck, his eyes glazed.

Nichols kicked Dan in the stomach. He fell forward, gagging. 'Oh, your lapdog here was very worried when he couldn't find anyone to rescue you, so he decided to come himself. He even managed to convince this young woman here to abscond with a police helicopter, but the only thing they achieved was to get themselves captured.'

Bec felt her stomach turn over, as though the kick had been directed at her. Dan had risked his life to rescue her? She glanced at Amber. To her surprise, Amber had a small smile on her face. Despite Nichols' threat, she hadn't moved to drop her sword.

'If Dan is Bec's lapdog, what does that make you?' Amber jerked her head around at the soldiers. 'Walker's lemmings?'

Bec frowned. She had never heard Amber speak with this tone before – her voice filled with the same icy confidence as Nichols'.

Nichols raised his eyebrows and his tone turned menacing. 'Drop the sword now, or I will select one of your friends to kill first. Which one, do you think? Perhaps Ren Tanaka? We could do without him, with his penchant for blowing things up.' Amber didn't move. Nichols drew his brows in. 'I know you're fast, Ms Yu, but not as fast as bullets. My men will kill them. All of them, if necessary.'

The smile didn't leave Amber's face. 'You always underestimate me, Lieutenant Colonel,' she said. Then she moved – so fast that Bec's eyes couldn't focus on her.

'Shoot them!' Nichols shrieked, but by the time the words were out of his mouth, it was too late. Every one of the soldiers that had been holding a rifle to a prisoner's head was slumped on the ground, dead.

Bec covered her mouth with her hand. The last time Amber had fought the soldiers – only two days ago – she had knocked them unconscious, not killed them. What had happened to her friend?

The Red Bones drew their swords and threw themselves at Amber. Amber was a blur. The sound of swords clashing rang across the room.

Nichols ran past them to a door at the back of the room. He flung it open, screaming for back up. Jerome backed away, holding his rifle high, his eyes wide and glistening.

Jaws stalked towards Jerome. Alice grabbed him from behind and held him. He growled and snapped at her hand. She growled back at him. 'He's got a sword, you stupid animal. Your THONG won't protect you from that.'

Lucy tugged at Bec's hand and pointed at Ren.

'Bec,' Ren said, his voice strained, so she only just heard him above the ringing of swords. Bec ran to him. 'Pocket,' he gasped, his eyes screwed up as though in pain.

Bec threw herself down in front of him and felt in his pockets. She pulled out a small explosive device. She searched his other pockets and found a detonator.

'Door frame,' he said, jerking his shoulder towards the door that Nichols had exited through.

Bec stood and clenched her teeth. Amber and the two Boneheads were between her and the door. Jerome was to her left, his finger on the trigger of his rifle. She ran to the right-hand wall and slid along it, past the fighters.

As she reached the corner of the room, the fighters barrelled towards her. They were so fast that they were almost on top of her before she had a chance to move. At the last minute, Amber swung around and led them in the opposite direction. Bec let out her breath in a gasp and ran to the door.

She could hear Nichols screaming orders down the corridor. She knelt and set the explosive, then backed away. Amber and the Boneheads had moved towards the right wall, so she scurried down the middle of the room, to where the prisoners were kneeling. She crouched on the ground and covered her ears with her arms. Alice and Lucy saw what she was doing, and flung themselves down, covering their ears with their hands and closing their eyes. She closed her own eyes and pressed the detonator.

The sound and pressure of the explosion hit her. Once it had passed, Bec lifted her head and opened her eyes. The back wall had collapsed into the door frame, bringing part of the roof with it and blocking the exit so that Nichols and his backup would have to break through the rubble to get in.

There was a loud ringing in her ears, even though she'd blocked them. The prisoners were in a worse state than her. Ren had expected the explosion, but none of the others had. Dan covered his ears and moaned.

The explosion had knocked Amber and the Red Bones, too, but they straightened as soon as the pressure passed and re-engaged. Bec eyed them. Kalliga hadn't lied when he'd said Amber could learn to fight by communing. Before, Amber had used a few different strikes and relied on her speed to win. Now there seemed no end to the different combinations of strikes and blocks that she used.

As Bec watched, Amber blocked a high strike from one of the Boneheads, then in a surprise move tossed her sword to her left hand and swung it in a curve, slicing the Bonehead's throat. As that Bonehead crumpled to the floor, she spun the sword so it pointed backwards and flung her weight back, skewering the other Bonehead behind her. Both bodies landed on the ground.

Amber slid her sword into her sword belt and threw herself down in front of Ren. She put her hands around the restraints on his wrists and closed her eyes. The restraints on his wrists and ankles swung open and fell to the ground. He lifted his head and breathed a sigh of relief. Amber moved along the line of prisoners, doing the same thing, until they were all free.

Ren jumped to his feet and eyed Jerome. Jerome was still standing in the corner, his rifle pointing at them. His hands were shaking.

'Drop the weapon,' Ren said, his voice like steel.

Jerome's finger twitched on the trigger.

'Drop it, and kick it over here. Or I'll get Amber to take it from you.'

Jerome cast a terrified glance at Amber. He released the trigger and placed the rifle onto the ground, then kicked it towards Ren.

'And the sword.'

Jerome drew the sword and threw it. It landed on top of the rifle with a clatter.

Ren scooped up the weapons.

Bec looked at Amber, feeling a rush of envy. What must it be like to have an enemy soldier surrender at the mention of your name?

Dan and Nathan struggled to their feet. Dan clutched his stomach.

The strange woman flung herself at him, pummelling him with her fists. 'You – complete – arsehole!'

Dan covered his face with his hands. Bec started laughing.

'Bit of help?' Dan asked her.

'I hate to interrupt you using Dan as a punching bag, but can you at least tell us what he's done so we can cheer you on?' Bec asked the woman.

She dropped her fists and stepped back, giving Dan a disgusted look. 'He kidnapped me – at gunpoint.'

'Dan!' Bec stared at him in disbelief.

Dan raised his hands, as though trying to ward off her anger. 'I needed the chopper, and someone to fly it. I tried to recruit her the usual way, but she wouldn't be recruited.'

Bec shook her head. 'I can't believe you.'

He dropped his hands and glared at her. 'You would have done the same.'

Bec grimaced. 'True.' She gave the woman an apologetic look. 'Sorry. Do you have a name?'

'Thahn.' Her eyes still flashed with anger.

Bec gave Dan a crooked smile. 'Thank you, for coming. That was brave.'

Thahn snorted. ''Stupid' is the word I'd use.'

Dan winced. 'I almost didn't. I tried to convince myself you wouldn't rescue me if our positions were reversed – that you'd prioritise the Resistance, and I should too. But – I knew the real reason I didn't want to come was because I was scared, and you've never let fear stop you from anything.'

'Oh.' Bec blinked at him.

Amber interrupted. 'What are we doing about the gate?' she asked Bec.

'The gate?'

'Do you want me to close it? Yes or no?'

Ren swung around. 'Leave it,' he said. 'A decision will be made about it later.'

Amber was still looking at Bec. 'Yorilla wanted it closed.'

An image of Yorilla flashed into Bec's mind, her body broken.

'You will make sure Amber closes the gate, won't you?' She thought of all the Boneheads she'd met at Kalliga's nest – Rayeta, Dansera, Enqua, Kimissa, the q'wakeen yarli, the guard that she'd saved from the stream – and imagined them turned into mindless zombies, like the Boneheads Yorilla had shown her in the shed. They were all at risk as long as Walker's gate stayed open.

Ren frowned at Bec. The MG's words echoed in her head: 'I'm relying on you to ensure our directions are carried out, particularly in relation to the gate.'

If their roles were reversed – if her family wanted the gate to stay open – Yorilla wouldn't close it.

'Yeah,' Bec sighed. 'Just leave it.'

'Okay.'

Ren relaxed. He looked at Josie. 'How are we getting out of here?'

Bec knew she'd made the right decision. Yorilla would have done the same.

But – did she really want to be like the Boneheads? 'Wait -' she said.

Amber looked at her.

'I changed my mind.'

'Bec -' Ren said.

'Quiet,' Amber said, with a wave of her hand.

Ren opened and closed his mouth, but no sound came out. Bec looked from Amber to him, her mouth dropping open.

'What?' Amber's voice was full of impatience.

'Yes.' Bec looked straight at Amber. 'Close it.'

'Bec, what are you doing?' Josie said.

'Close it,' Bec said again, louder.

Sayera stirred and sat up, blinking. He looked around in confusion.

Amber turned to Lucy. She held out her hand. Lucy bit her lip, her arms wrapped around her teddy.

'I'll need your help,' Amber said, in a soft voice.

Lucy released one hand from the teddy and thrust it into Amber's. Amber closed her eyes. For a long moment nothing happened. Then the gate started humming again. This time there was a crackling sound as well. It filled the air. Bec wriggled. The sound made her feel uncomfortable, itchy, as though she had a bug inside her clothes. The pitch and volume increased. She clapped her hands over her ears, but it didn't reduce the sound, which seemed to be vibrating through her body.

Amber's face was screwed up, her teeth clenched. Lucy was gasping for breath. The sound grew louder and louder. Jaws had stopped fighting Alice. He sat back in her lap and howled, adding to the noise.

A wind blew around the room, though there was nowhere it could have come from. It, too, grew stronger and stronger. Bec crouched on the floor, trying to escape it.

There was a shimmer in the air. The small lights that had appeared in the air inside the gate when they'd travelled through it reappeared, but this time they weren't just inside the gate, but all around it, stretching from one side of the room to the other.

Lucy wailed. 'It hurts, it hurts.' Amber fell to her knees, moaning, her eyes still closed. Lucy tried to wrench her hand free from Amber's, but Amber held it in a vice-like grip.

The wind grew stronger and stronger, pressing down. Bec was pushed flat on the ground. She struggled to lift her head.

There was a pop, and some of the pressure was released. Bec scrambled to her knees and stared.

The lights continued to flicker in the air surrounding the gate, but the back wall of the room had vanished, replaced by tall trees stretching into the distance. There was no mistaking it. It was the same forest that they'd just left. The wind that whipped around her was also whipping the trees. The branches swung to and fro. Leaves, twigs and small gumnuts cascaded onto the ground. Three Boneheads pushed their way into view of the gate, their backs bent as they struggled against the force of the wind. One of them straightened, and Bec recognised Kalliga.

He met Bec's eyes. 'She's lost control of it,' he yelled, over the noise of the wind and the crackling in the air. 'If she can't bring it back under control, she'll kill us all.'

'What can we do?' Bec shouted back.

He shook his head. 'I'll see if I can do something. Make sure nobody interrupts her. If she loses concentration -'

'What?'

His face looked grim. 'End of the world. Both worlds.'

He sat on the ground, cross-legged, and closed his eyes.

Lucy wailed and tried again to pull her hand free. Alice let go of Jaws and tried to crawl to Lucy, but the wind pushed her back.

Jaws howled again and started moving towards Amber, his short, stocky body pushing through the wind. Sayera sprung sideways and grabbed him by the back legs, holding him in place. He struggled, snapping at Sayera's hands.

The wind formed a cone around Amber and Lucy, keeping everyone back. Amber curled over her knees, her head almost hitting the ground.

Lucy's wail turned into a scream that seemed to go on and on. Bec felt dizzy. She tried to suck in air, but couldn't seem to breathe properly.

Alice tried again to crawl to Lucy, but again the wind pushed her back. She looked at Bec with feverish eyes. 'She's killing her!'

Bec shook her head – Amber wouldn't kill Lucy. But at that moment Lucy's scream was cut off, and she slumped on the ground. Her face turned grey. Her free hand fell open, and the teddy rolled onto the floor. Still Amber held her hand tight.

Bec's heart raced. If Alice was right, she had to stop Amber. The real Amber, the one Bec desperately hoped was still inside, would never forgive herself if she killed Lucy. But – what if by interrupting her, Bec destroyed the world?

'Kalliga!' Bec yelled. Kalliga didn't move, lost in whatever he was trying to do.

Bec tried to crawl to Amber and Lucy, but the wind was too strong. She couldn't get near them. Part of her felt a sense of relief. If she couldn't get to them, it was out of her hands.

Her eyes fell on Sayera. He was clinging to Jaws. Jaws clawed at his hands, trying to get Sayera to release him.

She didn't allow herself to think. Didn't let herself consider what forces her decision might release. She just did what Luke and the others always accused her of doing – and leapt. She dived on top of Sayera, startling him, so that he let go of Jaws. She rolled off him.

'Yarun,' she yelled at Jaws, pointing at Amber's wrist.

Jaws really was built like a tank. He set his feet on the floor and pushed through the wind, each step slow and steady, but making more progress towards Amber and Lucy than Bec or Alice had been able to.

Sayera tried to reach for him, but the wind pushed him back, too. 'What did you do?' He shook his head over and over, as though by refusing to believe she'd set Jaws free he could undo it. 'If he interrupts them – you've doomed us.'

Lucy didn't move. Bec couldn't see her chest rising and falling. Go on, she thought, keep breathing. For a moment she envied Amber her religious beliefs – she wished there was a god she could pray to. Amber was curled over her legs, gasping. Her hand was stretched out, still clinging to Lucy's hand.

The wind swirled around them. Jaws pushed closer and closer. He opened his mouth, revealing his predator's teeth, and sank them into Amber's wrist, through the bandage that covered her burn.

Twenty-six

Amber knew that Lucy was weakening – dying – but she didn't dare release her. Lucy's power was the only thing anchoring Amber to the world. Rayeta had underestimated how much power – how many lives – Walker had fed into the gate. The desperate call that she and Lucy had both felt from the gate had come from those Anaia - their spirits desperate to escape the prison they were trapped in. In trying to close the gate, Amber had released them. Separated from their bodies and trapped for so long, they had become a pure destructive force. The force swirled around her like a cyclone, tearing down the wall between her world and the Anaian world. She could feel both worlds as though they were living, breathing beings.

Amber tried to grip the force, to bring it under her control, but as fast as she gripped one strand of power another sprung free, and another. She was losing.

'Help me!' Her prayer was a wail.

A sharp pain hit her, from her wrist. Her hand spasmed, and released Lucy's hand. Lucy's strength was ripped away from her. The strands that she had gathered escaped. She was cast adrift. She felt as though she was somersaulting over and over in a maelstrom of power. She screamed.

The force slammed towards the earth; her earth, and the Anaian earth. It uprooted trees, tearing away the grass and soil, killing any life in its path – animals, people, Anaia. As each life was snuffed out she felt it, like a body blow. The force surged towards Kalliga and the other Anaia at the gate, and towards Bec and the Resistance fighters.

'No,' she whispered. She pictured a shield, and flung it in front of the force. The force slammed into it, and roared around the edges, like a wave hitting a rock. It roared in her mind, pulled back, gathering itself to slam into her shield again. She knew her shield wouldn't withstand it. She sobbed. It was hopeless. There was nothing she could do.

We are here. Rayeta's voice spoke into her mind. The roar of the force quietened. Power fed into her, anchoring her to the world again. The power was different to what she'd taken from Lucy. That had been strong, hot, full of fire and lava. This power came from a hundred different threads, each weak and cool, some so weak that they were like the silk from a spiders' web, but they wrapped around each other to form a strong rope. Rayeta had gathered power from every member of her family with the slightest trace of the lechiko. She could recognise some of the threads. A thin, wispy one was Enqua. A thick rope was Kalliga. The threads came from both worlds – those of Rayeta's family living in Amber's world, as well as those living in the Anaian world.

Hurry, Rayeta prompted her.

Amber reached out to the destructive force again, gathering the strands of power, dragging them together. One strand escaped her grip. It circled her shield, then tore into the earth again, racing towards the room where her friends were. A helicopter stood in its path. Something urged Amber to save the helicopter. She threw another shield out, blocking the strand, then grasped it and pulled it in.

The force fought her, trying to free itself. Tears streamed down her face. She wouldn't be able to hold it for long. 'What now?' she screamed to Rayeta.

Mine. A different voice spoke into her mind. She felt a flash of recognition – it was the same voice that had kept telling her to lean while she was wearing the restraints. She felt the lechiko flare in her mind, growing, larger and larger, until it was a ball of fire, then flaming out of her hands and consuming the strands of power. The flames were snuffed out, and a thin wisp of smoke drifted into the sky. The force was gone.

She felt the wall between her world and the Anaian world hardening again, reforming.

Well done, Rayeta said into Amber's mind, and then she and her family were gone.

Amber vomited over and over, until there was only pale liquid coming up. She wiped her mouth and pulled herself into a sitting position. Jaws butted his head against her knee. She placed her hand on his head.

She struggled to take in the scene in front of her. She felt like she'd been torn into tiny pieces, flung apart, then smashed back together, so that all the pieces bruised, and some shattered. Part of her still seemed to be connected to the world. She could sense things that she shouldn't be able to.

The roof was gone. The gate was a twisted pile of rubble – the lives that had fed it freed at last. The wall that had stood behind the gate, opposite the exit door, was gone too, and other rooms that had stood behind it had been flattened. Outside, for as far as she could see, the grass had been ripped from the ground, the trees and bushes uprooted, leaving bare soil and rocks. Anaia bodies, and those of a few human soldiers, were strewn around the site, twisted at odd angles. A zigzagging line of torn ground headed towards the helicopter, and stopped. The helicopter was one of the few remaining things still standing.

In the opposite direction, from the exit door forward, the building still stood, including the original farmhouse. Through the strange connection to the universe, she could sense people and Anaia, moving and breathing. Not everyone had died. She hadn't killed them all.

She searched over the hill for the shed where they'd seen the zombie Anaia. It had been destroyed. There were no survivors.

A violent shake shook her body.

She looked for Lucy. She had her face buried in the fur of her teddy. Alice had wrapped both arms around her.

Something sharp nicked her throat. Sayera stood over her, his sword touching her. 'I knew it was a mistake for Rayeta to commune with you, but I never imagined that you might destroy both our worlds. I should kill you before you do more damage.'

Amber felt the cold metal against her neck. She didn't have the energy to move, or to argue, even for her life. Maybe Sayera was right; maybe it would be safer for the world if he killed her.

'Don't.' Bec's voice was a croak. Tears dribbled down her face. 'Please.'

'Oh, I haven't gotten to you,' Sayera said, a dangerous note in his voice. 'What you did? That was the most reckless thing I have ever seen. I should kill both of you.'

Amber stared at him, feeling numb. She wished he'd stop talking, and just do it.

Sayera's mouth twisted, and he removed the sword from her throat. 'I should, but my family has already banished me; I have no honour. I think I'll let you live – for my own amusement. Should be fun to see what you do next.'

He sheathed the sword and strode past the remains of the gate, stepping over the rubble and into the fields. Amber collapsed over her knees. Another violent shake shook her.

'Amber? Are you okay?' Bec sounded wary.

Amber wrapped her arms around herself, trying to stop her body shaking. 'I just need a minute.' She felt liquid trickling down her arm. The bandage around her wrist was red with blood. 'Did Jaws bite me?'

She lifted her head to meet Bec's eyes. Bec swallowed hard. 'Your eyes -'

'What?'

'They're completely red. Like Rayeta's.'

'Are they?' Amber ran a hand over her eyes. 'I might have to start wearing sunglasses, like Yorilla and Kalliga.'

Bec was staring at her as though she'd grown a second head.

'It's okay. I'm still me,' Amber said, although she wasn't sure if that was true.

Bec gave her a tight smile. 'Yeah. Of course. Of course you are.'

Ren joined them. 'I'm surprised that Bonehead didn't kill you.' He sounded as though he wouldn't have minded if Sayera had. He surveyed the twisted gate with a clenched jaw. 'So,' he said, drawing the word out, 'We're stuck with them – the Boneheads that are already here.'

'Only the ones Amber didn't kill,' Bec said, looking at the bodies on the ground outside.

'The MG will not be pleased.'

Bec winced. Amber gave him a blank look.

Ren pressed his lips together, as though trying to stop himself from saying anything else. 'Do either of you have a phone? Nichols took ours.'

'Yeah.' Bec fumbled in her pocket and switched her phone on. It took a while to connect, then started beeping as several messages downloaded. Amber looked over Bec's shoulder. They all seemed to be from Dan. Bec thrust the phone at Ren. He pressed some buttons and put it to his ear, walking out of earshot.

Dan, Nathan and Thahn picked themselves up off the floor for the second time. Bec looked at Thahn. 'Do you think we can use the chopper to get out of here?'

Thahn took a deep breath in. 'Sure.'

Dan stared at the line of torn ground heading for the helicopter. 'I can't believe it survived the – well, you know.'

'I saved it,' Amber said. 'At the last minute. I shielded it.'

'Oh.' Dan looked at her as though she was a wild beast. 'Good thinking.'

Amber looked around the room. Jerome was sobbing in a ball in the corner. Ren had hung up the mobile and was speaking to Josie, but his eyes were on Amber. She wanted to know what he was saying. She hesitated. She didn't have enough energy to lean, but it would only take a thread. She reached out and gripped the thinnest thread of power, and flung it towards Ren and Josie. She could hear them as though she was standing next to them.

'I'm not worried about Nichols' protege,' Ren said. 'I'm worried about her. We couldn't control her even before this latest – development.'

'Is anyone in this bloody Resistance controllable? Bec's just as bad.' Josie's eyes danced. 'Instead of recruiting sword fighters, we should recruit people who know how to take orders.'

'Bec's not as dangerous as she is.'

Josie turned serious. 'But if Sam isn't worried -'

Ren shrugged. 'Apparently not. Anyway, the MG said to bring them. I can't exactly complain about others not following orders if we don't.' He shook his head. 'We need to get out of here.' He turned and bellowed across the room. 'Time to go! Helicopter – now!'

His words broke through the lethargy of the group, and one by one they started running. Josie pulled Jerome to his feet and forced him towards the helicopter. He stumbled ahead of her. There didn't seem to be any fight left in him.

Amber dropped the thread of power and stared at them, shivering.

'Amber?' Bec was waiting for her. 'We need to go.'

Amber scooped up Jaws, and followed Bec to the helicopter.

Thahn didn't keep the helicopter in the air for long before setting it down again. Amber followed the others out, her arms wrapped around her. She was shivering with a bone-deep cold.

They were in a cleared paddock surrounded by bush. Amber had no idea where they were. There were no landmarks. The bush was a scrubby eucalypt forest that might be recognisable to a botanist, but to her looked the same as any other scrubby eucalypt forest.

She moved away from the helicopter and squatted on the ground, putting her head in her hands. She felt lost; her head so full of the Anaias' memories she couldn't tell where she finished and they began. At least the strange connection to the world had faded away.

She didn't need to use the lechiko to eavesdrop on the others – she could see the way they looked at her. Bec stared at her as though she was a stranger. Anger rolled off Ren; she didn't think he'd forgive her in a hurry for silencing him. The other Resistance fighters cast wary looks at her when they thought she wasn't looking. Jerome turned white with terror if she glanced at him. And Lucy and Alice looked at her as though she was a monster: more monstrous than the Anaia.

Adam had been shocked when he'd seen her using the power at Dubbo. What would he think of her now?

Jaws butted his head against her leg. She ran her hand over his head. Of course he didn't care – he was a monster himself. Tears filled her eyes and dribbled down her cheeks.

Someone squatted next to her. Amber lifted her head. Bec.

'Ren said it'll take us a while to get to Resistance Headquarters. We're taking a convoluted route – Sam and the MG are worried about us leading the enemy to them.'

Amber gave her a blank look. She was so tired she didn't think she could move, let alone travel some convoluted route back to Base.

Bec placed a hand on Amber's shoulder, her touch light, lacking her usual confidence. 'You'll see Ollie soon.'

Ollie. His big brown eyes filled her mind. She saw him smiling, and her chest tightened with love. The Anaias' memories seemed to fade into the background. She buried her head in Bec's shoulder. 'I miss him so much,' she whispered.

She felt Bec relax and hug her tighter.

'We need to move,' Ren said. 'We've got a long walk ahead of us.'

She looked up at him. 'I'm so tired.'

He pressed his lips together. 'I'm sure you are. But it's not safe here.'

Amber wished Sam would send a vehicle to collect them. She felt a sudden chill. 'What happened to Tev?'

'He's fine. He was far enough away when – when the site was destroyed.'

'Oh. Good.' Amber felt her chest ease a little. At least she hadn't killed Tev.

Ren looked at Bec. 'Sam said Ash is out of hospital, too. You'll see her when we get to Base.'

A look of relief flashed across Bec's face. 'Thank you,' she said.

Ren jerked his head. 'On your feet. Let's go.'

Bec stood and held out a hand to Amber. She allowed Bec to pull her to her feet.

'Just put one foot in front of the other,' Bec said. 'Think about why you want to get to Base: because you can't wait to see Ollie.'

Amber nodded. 'Yeah.' She was silent for a moment, then the corners of her mouth turned up in a sly grin. 'And also, I can't wait to beat Reuben at sword fighting – without leaning. I hope he likes mud in his hair.'